EQUINOX

PATRICK NAKASKA

EQUINOX

This book is written to provide information and motivation to readers. Its purpose is not to render any type of psychological, legal, or professional advice of any kind. The content is the sole opinion and expression of the author, and not necessarily that of the publisher.

Printed in the United States of America.

ISBN   978-1-64552-119-8   (Paperback)
ISBN   978-1-64552-120-4   (Digital)

Lettra Press books may be ordered through booksellers or by contacting:

Lettra Press LLC
30 N Gould St. Ste N
Sheridan, WY 82801, USA
3035861431 | info@lettrapress.com
www.lettrapress.com

EQUINOX

Contents

PROLOGUE

Tumbling down an unlit highway on a windy desert night; a convoy of vehicles makes their way deeper into the sand. The convoy charges purposely and fiercely into nowhere, transporting a very specific group of individuals, among other things.

"You think them stars got planets round'em, Pete?" Churned Ernest Mackenbee, a wily, bearded man, chewing a toothpick and wearing sunglasses. Ernest never went anywhere without his sunglasses. Even at night, he wore them unapologetically.

"I don't know, Ern."

Pete wasn't in the mood for talking. He couldn't shake the feeling of something peculiar about the situation he found himself in. He had done lots of big digs before, but none like this.

"Man. . .outside the city without all the lights in the way you can really get a grip on these stars witcher' eyes. . . it's beautiful. Dontcha' think so Pete?" Ernest said, exhaling a subtle breath of stale tobacco and coffee.

"I guess so Ern." Replied Pete. He wasn't like Ernest. He couldn't simply accept the simplicity of life like Ernest could. A well-paying job, a wife, a nice cottage in the country somewhere, retirement . . .

He was a thinker. Given his circumstances, he couldn't help it. His uncle and grandfather worked in the upper tiers of the military and air force. In his teens he would occasionally listen in on their conversations with his father from the top of the stairs, kept awake only by the subtle vibrations of two deep voices reverberating through the paper-thin walls of their modest saltbox home. Sometimes he could only record bits and pieces, other times he would fall asleep on the top step only to have his father find him there. Weeks before his grandfather's passing, the conversations were loud, abrasive, and he heard everything whether he wanted to or not. At a very young age, he knew exactly what it meant to let his 'curiosity get the best of him', as his mother often begged him not to.

One night, Pete returned to his old habit of peering into his father's secretive conversations. Normally he would be asleep already, having nearly grown out of it. This time, the circumstances were unusual. It was later than normal, and on a Tuesday rather than the normal Sunday. His grandfather showed up drunk, barging into the house well after midnight, carrying with him a belligerent disregard for the home's occupants, and Pete swore he was loud enough to wake up half of the neighborhood.

Although peaked, Pete's curious nature was chased away by his unwillingness to listen to his panicking, skittish grandfather tell stories that frightened him more than he cared to experience. It wasn't because he didn't believe his grandfather's ramblings that he chose not to listen, but because he was genuinely terrified of the possibility that some of his grandfathers' stories may be true. He remembered the feeling he had that night while failing to sleep; one of denial, guilt and sheer terror – an almost unexplainable and certainly unwelcome, uneasy feeling. What little sleep he got was riddled with nightmares and he awoke in a cold sweat. He decided that morning that he could not dwell on that night or he would go crazy, perplexed by impossible questions with equally impossible answers.

Pete was beginning to feel something in the pit of his stomach, maybe from the unpleasant bumps caused by rocks being kicked up by the thick rubber tires, or something else. Whatever it was, it felt *just like* the feeling he had that night when he was 18. He looked at Ernest, whose head was out the window, his shaggy brown hair catching the wind while he gazed in awe at the black night sky. Pete's attention quickly focused to the front of the vehicle, where two of their armed escorts sat, each bearing

32 round fully automatic submachine guns and covered head to waste in Kevlar. They didn't talk to any of the digging crew much, nor did the crew talk to them, adding to their eerie aura of professionalism. Beyond the hulking nose of the military truck red lights flashed as the massive vehicle in front of them began to slow.

"What's goin' on here guys?"

The guard in the passenger seat turned his head slowly as the vehicle came to a halt.

"Both of you stay put."

Both guards popped open their doors and leapt out of their chairs onto the barren freeway, weapons trained intently into the endless desert on either side. Giant floodlights shattered the darkness, scanning dozens of meters into the sand. Pete's stomach began to tie up as he gripped the shoulder of the seat in front of him and waved his head around frantically. A scratching message eeked over the driver's headset.

"ComVee 2 is out. Fifteen minutes. Give those civvies a chance to stretch their legs out, over."

Pete hopped out of the vehicle after the guard gave him permission. His weapon corralled firmly against his chest, he finally communicated.

"One of the vehicles up front blew a tire, Mr. Schlesinger. Repairs should take no longer than ten minutes. Feel free to take a walk, but stay in range of the spotlights." The guards handed them both a sandwich wrapped in crinkly foil, a dusty bottle of water, and turned to walk toward the front of the convoy.

"Ern, let's take a walk."

The two convened at the back of the truck and began marching down the boulevard of steel hulks illuminated in bright indigo light. Pete hadn't eaten in hours and made quick work of the sandwich. He entered the vehicle he had been trapped inside for the last nine hours before the convoy assembled, so he didn't have much time to see the entirety of it before they left. The first three vehicles he passed were much like the one he was in, only much more heavily armed – a mounted machine gun on the top to go along with a full firing squad's worth of pistols, assault rifles and shotguns mounted on metal racks inside the flatbed. Metal containers lining the sides of the truck contained grenades, ammunition and plastic explosives. Some trucks were lined only with seats to transport troops. A significantly larger, multi-axle truck near the middle boasted a five-meter high antenna and a large parabola dish which rotated and gyrated on a metal platform. As they passed, the guards remained alert, silent and focused.

"Got a cigarette Pete?"

"Yeah, you got my lighter though." Pete fumbled into his breast pocket and retrieved his cigarettes.

"What do you think is really goin' on here?" I mean, these guys are packin' heat. You think we're safe?"

"Yeah Ern, I do."

"But this is strange. When's the last time you had this kind of security detail on a dig? And wasn't the site supposed to be just after we crossed the border? Seems like it's been an awful long time since we-"

"I'm sure, Ern. You heard what the director said. What was that word he used? Extenuating circumstances requiring uhh utmost umm security? Hell Ern', they ain't payin' us to ask questions. We're just out here to dig, that's it."

Ernest shot a glance at Pete, caught off guard by his interruption, but it was the reassurance he was looking for to help put his mind at ease.

"Besides, if they were gon' kill us then why the hell would they feed us first?" The pair chuckled as they inhaled second long drags of smoke into their lungs. Pete had questions of his own but decided it was a good idea to ignore his urge to ask.

After five minutes at a slow pace, a row of massive flatbed trucks dozens of feet in length came into view, spread across the highway, completely covered in camouflage tarps. The tarps flapped in the inconsistent wind revealing little as to their hidden contents. *It could be anything*, thought Pete. Because of an unhinged latch one of the tarps flew up high enough to reveal landing gear and a smooth, metallic egg-shape.

"Choppers." Pete muttered to himself.

After they had passed the mysterious flatbeds, the last few vehicles in the line were all-white vans covered in chrome plating, mounted grates on the front. Pete walked up to one of the windows, cupped his hands over his eyes with the burning cigarette in hand and looked inside. Crates of foodstuffs lined the interior – bags of rice, fresh vegetables, and what seemed to be a deep freeze on the bottom.

Pete and Ernest reached the very last vehicle in the line and looked back into the distant road and darkness, just barely visible beyond the bright indigo.

"Hell of a job we got, eh Pete?"

"Pays the bills." Pete took a moment to sympathize with Ernest. He hadn't quite realized how long they had been on the road, nor had he yet taken the time to really converse with him. He remembered all at once that this was just a job, and that life would go on after they were finished, although it felt as if that day would never come.

"How's your daughter doin' Ernest, she still in school?" Pete asked.

"Yeah, she is. Why I'm out here breakin' my back. Education is expensive ya' know?"

"Oh I know!" Pete exclaimed, momentarily remembering his life outside this endless desert he was in, and the fruitful moments he held cherished in memory. It was a momentary reprieve from the situation.

The light on top of the supply van began to flicker on and off, eventually shutting off completely.

"What the hell?"

"Must be a burnt fuse. Guess they forgot to bring mechanics!"

Neither of them said anything for half a minute, as their heads slowly tilted back, eyes fixated on the bright beacons of light in the sky that had suddenly become entirely visible again.

"Hell of a view".

"You got that right, Pete."

"You guys better get back to the front, we'll be leaving soon."

Pete was surprised that the soldier could see them leaned up against the van in the darkness, but then again they were professionals. They were probably being watched the entire time. Pete and Ernest complied, flicking their cigarettes into the air, their dimming embers barely visible from a few feet.

On their way back to the vehicle, Pete noticed a difference in the soldiers, who were now patrolling in greater numbers. Nearly all of them were armed. The vehicles they had passed earlier strapped with weaponry were now all but bare, the metal cases flung open and depleted of their holdings. On the other side of the convoy, groups of 10-12 soldiers huddled together, seemingly coordinating something.

"Figures." Said Ernest.

"Whaddya mean, figures?

"Well they wouldn't come out all this way, wit' all them guns, for nothing, ya know?"

"I suppose." Replied Pete. Both he and Ernest were filled with mixed emotion, unsure whether to feel absolutely safe, or the opposite.

The last few meters back to their vehicle were filled with the clinging and clanging of machine guns being cocked and readied; magazines being thrust into their rightful spot. The swashbuckling of gear and clamoring of boots on the ground drowned out the constant electric hum emanating from the line of vehicles. The guard from before, now fitted with the latest GEN III MCP night-vision goggles, emerged from the other side of the convoy. Not a sliver of skin was visible on his body.

"Mr. Schlesinger, Mr. Mackenbee, please re-enter the vehicle. We're Oscar Mike in 2."

"Just in time Pete!" said Ernest, seemingly oblivious to the tension apparent in the air. He hopped in jovially, shimmying his rear across the seat to the other side of the wide truck.

"How long to our destination, sir?" Pete asked. The Guard did not reply, but simply motioned his hand towards the door. Pete hesitated, but entered.

"Why so sour, Pete? We gotta' be there soon!?" Ernest said, half-asking. Within a minute the vehicle was on the move. The floodlights turned off in unison, immersing the convoy in utter darkness once again.

The feeling within the cab was entirely different. Although the guards were still calm, mute and devoid of emotion, there was something that could not be seen, touched or heard. The quick stop may have had other purposes than to repair a downed vehicle.

"I guess they did bring mechanics after all, Pete! That was a quick touch up!" Said Ernest, a wide grin stuck to his face.

"Awful quick."

The irony in their friendship was that it only existed because of Pete's acceptance of Eugene's inferior intellect, and Eugene's childish reverence of Pete's superior brain. From an analytical perspective, they were completely different people bound together by their employment. Pete wished he could think as little as Ernest. He wished he was perhaps slightly dumber, maybe less perceptive, or perhaps had less of an ability to sniff out a lie. Trying to explain his sentiment to Ernest, he knew, would be like explaining algebra to a monkey. Conversely, it was a relief to him that he didn't have to. He leaned his head back, thoughts racing, hoping he wasn't right this time. He slowly dozed off, his thoughts washed away by the droning vibration of rolling tires.

"Air leak my ass" He mumbled to himself.

Morning came over the horizon, illuminating the scorched desert for miles. Nothing but rocky mesas, the occasional tumbleweed and scores of sandy dunes met the eye. Pete woke up to the drumming, chest-thumping sound of choppers, at least half a dozen of them maneuvering in all directions above the convoy. Ernest was still curled up into an unconscious ball. They must be close to the site, which was beginning to seem more like a military base. Pete rolled down his window, clutching a pair of binoculars and bringing them to his face. At the absolute edge of his enhanced vision, he could see what looked like a chain link fence encasing a depressed area. The sun created a slight glint giving it away – otherwise the way the landscape was shaped rendered it completely invisible from the road. Pete had to strain his eyes to make out the fence.

"I think we're finally here, Ernest. Time to earn our pay" Pete said as he jostled Ernest with his left hand. It was all he would need to move Ernest, whose sinewy frame barely amounted to 150 pounds. He awoke abruptly, making sure his signature Aviator sunglasses were covering his eyes.

The convoy began to slow. In front of him, Pete could see the convoy breaking right, following an invisible road randomly into the desert. Only the tops of the vehicles were visible. The rest was engulfed in plumes of dust being churned into the air by the bulky tires traversing the plain.

"Please roll up your window Mr. Schlesinger. You too Mr. Mackenbee."

It was the first words they had heard from the guard since the midnight stop. They complied, and for good reason – the sand was coarse and irritating, some of it barely sneaking in the last sliver of his window as he rolled it up.

As they came upon the compound, the vehicles began to drift into a slow halt. As they inched closer, the chain link fence entered view. It extended farther than Pete could see. A patchy voice shouted from the guard's radio. He abruptly clicked a button on his headset, making it silent, attempting to hide the message from the civilians. He fumbled the press a few times, apparently nervous, allowing a few snippets to leak through.

"Insertion . . . .inside . . . . . . .teen minut-"

Insertion? Thought Pete, perplexed by the lingo. The only time Pete ever heard *insertion* was from young, academic-type contractors referring to drilling into the ground – inserting long lengths of steel to increase the depth of the hole. The *insertion* from the soldier's message sounded cold and tactical.

"Copy that." The guard replied.

The vehicle finally pulled up to the edge of the fence, where a single guard stood, asking for a specific piece of paper.

As Pete quickly realized, there was no shortage of space in the compound. Plumes of dust revealed what looked like fifteen vehicles moving. They plowed into the desert, nearly escaping vision entirely. A faint glimmer of light rode the horizon, which by now was scorching hot and glimmered in a way that could trick the eye. Phil reached for his binoculars once more and aimed them towards the glimmer, revealing the expanse of the fence, which carved a line miles wide into the desert at a perfectly right angle.

"It's a big fuckin' square Ern." Pete blurted out, momentarily forgetting the presence of the guards. Ernest propped up on Pete's shoulder like an excited child, peering out his window. Upon further examination, he noticed divots in the sand where sandbag supply posts held piles of goods. Soldiers traversed the fence up and down. At each corner stood towers covered in a sandy-colored tarp, revealed only by the movement of snipers manning their perch.

The vehicle in front of theirs peeled off and followed the other vehicles revealing the rest of the base. On top of a hill two-hundred meters to their left, a half-cylinder shaped metallic building stood on top of a slightly raised plateau.

"Copy that sir, en route now." Said the guard, responding to a message only he could hear.

Inside of the metallic bunker were dozens of people and their equipment. Booths and cubicles lined the interior, along with giant, man-sized computers. An array of workers pushed buttons, held clipboards and conversed. Men in hardhats and white trench coats marched up and down the corridor, writing things down and listening to anecdotes of data from an army of subordinates. They carried on with purpose, seemingly oblivious to Pete, Ernest and their escorts as if they were used to having armed men in their proximity.

"Mr. Black is waiting in the back for you Mr. Schlesinger." Said the guard as he turned to face Pete and motioned his hand towards a corridor that lay between the outside wall of the bunker and a superficial wall on the inside.

"Thanks." Pete thrust his hands into his pockets and entered the narrow passage. Lining the outside of the wall was a grid of pocket-sized boxes - some of them with big, clunky boots in them, charred by sand and grit. It was a familiar and soothing sight to Pete, who assumed the boots belonged to low-level drill-hands, the kind of folk he was used to seeing all the time during regular jobs. For a brief moment, it pierced the shroud of mystery and disillusionment he felt.

He entered a door with "Black" inscribed on it.

"Hello Mr. Schlesinger. You're late." Said Black, wearing glasses and peering over his desk at an array of papers. He was a massive man, broad in the shoulder with clean cut dark hair and a few straggling strands of gray. His leathery face was carved with ridges like a worn baseball glove. Pete did not quite know how to respond.

"Mr. Black, I assume?"

Pete adjusted his belt nervously as he spoke.

"Have a seat, Peter. I'm going to be straightforward with you. We have encountered a slight problem on this site. Things have . . . hit a standstill, so to speak, which of course is why you are now sitting in front of me. Your superiors speak very highly of you, which is something I am happy about. Before we get into the logistics, I'm going need to ask you one question." Black spoke with precise clarity and focus. Also, referring to him as Peter, his full name, instantly denoted an impressing feeling of authority.

"And uhh, what's that sir?"

Black removed his reading glasses and rubbed his eyes for a moment, revealing a subtle twinkle in his eye hidden before. He postured up and locked his mits together on the table, staring into Pete's hazel eyes.

"Can I trust you, Peter?"

"I don't quite understand what you mean s-"

"It's a pretty simple question Peter. Can I trust you? Can I trust you not to ask questions, and to do your job? You are here to make sure that hole gets drilled. Whatever happens between now and the completion of that task, as well as what comes after . . . Well those things are not of your concern. . . . They need not be spoken of. Do I make myself clear?"

As Black said his piece Pete noticed a peculiar set of tattoos on his fingers, as well as a black ring on his pinky finger. Both men engaged in a ten second stare, seeming to come to an understanding. It was clear to him that the influence of the soldiers guided Mr. Black's tone. More likely than not, someone higher in the food chain was breathing down his neck.

"This is some awfully cloak and dagger shit, Black."

Black did not respond with words, but the intensity of his flat-eyed stare said enough. Pete stared into the desk for a moment, weighing his options, of which there were very few.

"I guess I read ya' loud and clear. As long as me and Ern' are here that hole will get as deep as heavenly possible."

"That's what I like to hear."

Pete had dealt with arrogant managers before, but Black was a special case. After the brief conversation, he didn't want to know what was really happening out in the desert. As Black made painfully obvious, it was way above his pay grade. He was content with finishing the job, getting paid and getting home. Black rose from his chair towering half a foot over Pete, who was not a short man himself. They shook hands and something very strange happened.

As Pete grasped the burly hand extended towards him, thoughts of joy, of his family, of being back in Idaho in the summer time rushed into his mind and body instantaneously. He left the office abruptly, bringing a wave of euphoria with him. By the time he saw Ernest again, the feeling had worn off.

"That was quick! What'd he say Pete? What's goin' on?" barked Ernest like an excited child.

"There a mess hall around here boys?" asked Pete. The soldiers responded in kind.

"This way Mr. Schlesinger."

"Pete! Who was in there?"

"Black."

"Black? Whaddya' mean Black? Who's Black?" pestered Ernest.

"An asshole."

"Ha ha ha! You never get along with SMs Pete! What's the game plan?"

As they reached the entrance, Pete noticed a stairway tucked into the corner, invisible to his eye when they first entered. It led down into a basement.

"Right down here guys. You got until 0900. That gives you just under an hour. We'll be outside to take you to your quarters." The guards filed out of the building, slinging their weapons around their backs and removing their sweat-filled helmets, for the first time acknowledging the intense heat, and the fact that they too were irrevocably human, and most likely just cogs in the wheel of this shadowy operation.

"Looks like they're human after all, Pete!" said Ernest, giggling.

"Come on Ern, let's get some breakfast. We got a long day of work ahead."

* * * *

Dusk rolled through the compound atop a gentle wind, folding the last band of daylight onto the horizon. Pete, Ernest and about twenty other labourers scurried around a two-story high drilling platform. They had been working all day since noon managing to destroy two drill heads and increase the depth by only fourteen feet.

"Something's gotta's give, Ern. We keep on hittin' this weird rock, can't seem to break through."

Standing on top of a metal grated platform directly above the hole, Pete and Ernest struggled to keep the group of diggers on task.

"I don't know Pete, I ain't seen readings' like this before. Waves are goin' down double-length, comin' back up cut in quarters. Not to mention we're losin' drill heads faster than we can replace em' Whatever that shit is, it don't wanna' be drilled."

Pete had done military contracts before, but only for well-known air-force and army bases near metropolitan areas. Usually they would drill four separate holes and hollow out in between, creating a network of tunnels in which they could put men, digging machines and explosives to speed up the process. Pete only knew of this single hole in the ground at this site, which didn't make very much sense to him. But as he had decided in Black's office, he didn't care to know more than he needed to.

"Well, they seem pretty determined to get through this stuff. I think we're gonna' have to bring it in."

"Bring what in?" asked Ernest, confused.

"Member that bit I was workin' on at Texas Tech back in 68?" said Pete, with a grin on his face. He was pleased with himself for finally being able to reveal his prized possession.

"Kind of?" replied Ernest.

"Boss saw fit to invest in a prototype last year. Wasn't supposed to tell anyone, but now's as good a time as any. Go tell Jack over there."

"Whaddya' mean Pe-"

"Just do it Ern, he'll know what you're talkin' about." Said Pete sternly, assertive in his role as the man who would see this hole dug or his reputation lessened. Despite the encroaching soldiers observing his every move and the risk of failure, Pete was in his element. He had been digging for decades and wasn't about to let some 'strange readings', as Ernest put it, stand in his way.

The giant bit was brought to the site from one of the flatbed trucks by way of a mobile, miniature operating crane which placed it on top of the platform, ready to be buckled into the 12 foot pipe that would carry it into the depths.

"Thicker armor means better spearheads, Ern." Said Pete, smirking at his proclaimed achievement. It had taken them almost an hour to raise the full length of the drill shaft, remove the mangled drill bit and fasten the new one on. It was nearly twice the size and bore six-inch titanium plated teeth formed in spiral patterns.

"She's beautiful ain't she?" Ernest asked.

The drill began to grind once more.

As it began to penetrate the entrenched rock inch by inch, the ground beneath Pete began to vibrate. The vibrations rose to a rumbling that nearly displaced his footing.

"Holy shit!" Pete heard, as an alarmed man in a hard-hat sprinted from the base of the hole, along with two others in different directions.

Oh no, thought Pete. Not now, not on his watch. But it was inevitable.

The mighty bit caught fiercely into the rock, collapsing a roof of debris and revealing an antechamber. A huge reverberation shot up the shaft, snapping the metal rod implements in half like twigs. Bulkheads exploded bits of shrapnel out of the hole, into the platform and into some of the workers surrounding. A thick plume of black, ashy air trailed the shockwave, breaching the top of the orifice and spraying hundreds of feet into the air. It covered almost everyone and everything. It looked like oil, but it was clearly not – it was accompanied by a putrid odor and taste that made Pete want to vomit.

Before Pete could come to his senses, an explosion rocked the holding device at the top of the platform, crippling the entire structure and sending both he and Ernest over the rail. He managed to grab a hold of the railing and secure himself from falling, but Ernest was not so lucky. A splinter of metal from one of the mangled steel implements shot through his torso and carried him clear from the platform. Phil watched as his friends' lifeless body plummeted and smacked into the desert floor.

In his desperation, he clung to a nearby ladder and began to peddle his way down. His arms gave way, unable to bear the intense pain caused by multiple shattered ribs. He fell ten feet onto the sand and had the wind knocked out of him. Pete tightly gripped his midsection, revealing tattered ribbons of wet, sticky cloth. For a moment he looked up and saw blood. Several soldiers rushed over to him before he passed out, dragging him to safety.

Pete woke up on a stretcher hours later surrounded by soldiers and nurses. The split-second events of his last conscious moments shot through his mind at lightning speed – the explosion, his ribs, the workers . . . Ernest.

He popped up from the stretcher, but didn't make it far. The intense pain in his midsection curbed his spastic jolt, forcing him back to where he laid. Nurses rushed to him with a large syringe while soldiers held down his arms. The drugs took effect quickly.

"He'll be out for a while, Lieutenant. What did the commander have to say?"

"The drill made breach. These poor bastards never had a chance. No one even told them."

"Well of course they didn't Lieutenant. Had they known what they were getting themselves into, none of em' would have come here. Mr. Mackenbee?"

"Dead."

Both soldiers took a moment to honor the dead civilian, although they were forbidden to show that kind of compassion.

"Commander said we're goin' in. I want five platoons and a six-man firing squad ready by 1100. Full ST gear."

"Roger that Lieutenant."

The soldier left the room barking orders into his headset.

Once again, Pete awoke on a stretcher. He had missed what seemed like a full day in his induced coma. The drugs were still coursing through his veins, keeping his head foggy and his body inoperable. He could barely muster words for the nurse, who took every wobbly hand gesture as a request for cold water and more morphine.

Within a few hours he regained full consciousness, and full memory. And of course the debilitative sharp pain in his abdomen. The drugs only dulled it slightly. Mr. Black would have some serious explaining to do. He attempted to leave the confines of the makeshift hospital tent he found himself in, but was greeted instantly by two soldiers carrying m16s. The sight of the weapons, and the feeling of confinement boiled his blood. He was ferociously angry and had the image of Mr. Black's rigid face on his mind.

"Come with us Mr. Schlesinger. Mr. Black wishes to speak with you."

Pete hadn't the physical or mental strength to say otherwise. He followed them out of the tent, each breath more painful than the last. The soldiers guided him past a row of tents with injured soldiers and workers alike. He felt very lucky to be alive.

They came upon the dig site, visible from a distance as a smoldering ruin engulfed in blue and red flames. Men clad in the confines of space-age looking HAZMAT suits sprayed water and extinguisher fluid from reservoirs fastened to their back onto the inferno, attempting to contain it. Some carried long hoses attached directly to trucks.

Mr. Black stood eerily close to the fire, multiple guards by his side with his hands firmly knotted behind his back.

"Mr. Schlesinger. I am sorry for your loss. Did the nurses patch you up proper-"

"FUCK you Black, FUCK ALL OF YOU!! It's about time you told me why the hell I'm here! And where is Ernest!?" shouted Pete, with an energetic burst of rage. The soldiers did not hold him back. Perhaps some of them were becoming just as fed up as he was. They did however train their guns on Pete, which was enough to silence his cries.

"Like I said Peter, I am deeply sorry for your loss. Ernest is not the only one who suffered. I am surprised at your resilience, broken ribs and all. Most men in your position would not be so ready to leave a warm bed. There is still, however, the task at hand."

Pete was taken aback by Black's utter lack of compassion evident in his manner of speech.

"What the fuck are you talking about?" Shouted Pete with utmost disgust. Black turned around and faced him.

"We're going down there Peter."

"What? Like hell we are! Wait till' the Director hears of what you done here, Black, he'll have your ass!" Pete shouted, collapsing to his knees as he bellowed threats. He spit a stringy mixture of saliva and blood at the ground near Black's feet as he advanced, stopping him in his tracks.

The rumbling of mechanized vehicles which had disappeared earlier materialized from within the belly of the compound, getting closer and closer to the all but vanquished flames. Several troop-transports boxed the area in as Black and Pete spoke.

"You're gonna' have to fuckin' kill me Black, because I'm not takin' one more god-damn order from you." Shouted Pete, panting heavily, barely able to keep his head above his shoulders.

Pete felt a cumbersome army boot plunge into his back, forcing his face into the ground. The unmistakable barrel of an m16 assault rifle prodded his skull.

"Perhaps, Mr. Schlesinger, that will be your fate. But I still have use for you." Said Black, as the soldier pointed his gun away from Pete's head.

"He could be of some help down there, but not much sir. Maybe we should just leave him up here." said a young Sergeant from one of the firing squads.

Although in a weakened physical and emotional state, Pete remained perceptive as he always was. It seemed peculiar to him that one of the soldiers would question Black's judgment.

"I want him in my sight from this point until we leave. Leaving him up here with the nurses could prove . . . Disruptive. Make sure his wounds are properly adhered to. He will help us identify what we find down there. There are not many able-bodied geologists with his base of knowledge left to pick from. Carry on soldier."

The truth was, Black could not risk Pete getting out of the compound on his own – not with the incriminating information he was now burdened with. He felt his once firm control of the soldiers slipping through his hands. They may have been susceptible to a convincing plea from a desperate civilian.

"Copy that sir." Replied the soldier, albeit reluctantly.

Maybe, Pete thought, the chain of command here wasn't as concrete as he thought. It seemed peculiar to him that a lowly sergeant deserved such a thorough explanation.

"Come, Mr. Schlesinger. We need to get you into an ST suit." Two soldiers grabbed Pete's arms and helped him to his feet. They marched over to the trucks, which opened their hatches, revealing rows of suits. A large group of soldiers were already beginning to outfit themselves.

Pete noticed the telltale insignia of Lieutenant on the shoulder of one of the soldiers guiding him.

"Why are you doing this?" He whimpered desperately, each muttered word taxing his crippled torso. The pain was extreme.

"Believe me, Mr. Schlesinger. I don't like it any more than you do. But we have our orders." Replied the Lieutenant, sternly.

"I can get you some morphine if it helps. But I can't give you too much."

"Fuck your orders." Grumbled Pete as he jerked his arms free and headed towards the line of trucks. The soldiers let him go and he lit a cigarette, falling against one of the trucks for support.

"Tough son of a bitch." Said the Lieutenant as he looked on, both admiring and feeling sorry for Pete as he knelt, broken.

* * * *

Pete had been inside an ST suit before, but never under such conditions. He had only used them in previous digs when the director needed a hands-on sitrep of the rocky makeup of the blast zone, in order to make last minute adjustments. They had always relied on his knowledge to make the right decisions and avoid catastrophe. A lot could go wrong when using high explosives. The suits were bulky and limited movement, allowing for very little peripheral vision. The visors easily fogged up which hindered visibility even further.

The lingering stink of the black air that emerged from the dig shaft was blocked from nose by the suit's hermetically sealed interior. He had trouble getting the suit on in such pain let alone moving freely inside it. The gloves were clumsy and awkward, the boots heavy. He could only imagine how the soldiers felt – on top of their gear they carried satchels with ammunition, along with their primary weapon and sidearm. It made movement awkward and difficult.

Teams of twelve men at a time were lowered hundreds of feet into the hole in the crudest of ways – a makeshift iron platform retrieved from the rubble of the explosion hinged on a pulley system suspended meters above the hole itself. The wires were attached to the back of a truck which slowly backed up along the desert, lowering the platform. It was lowered and raised every ten to fifteen minutes, ready for a fresh group of guns.

Pete's group was the last to enter. Accompanying his descent was Mr. Black and an elite firing squad of soldiers, all of them covered head to toe in their class BA-5 Sub-Terra suits. Pete took the time on the journey down to think. He wondered if he would ever make it out of the desert alive. If he did, how was he going to explain to Ernest' daughter what happened? Would he be forced to secrecy? Too many questions needed answers. He thought best to focus on the situation – even the soldiers were silent, seemingly cautious and aware of the dangers that could lie ahead. His prime directive now was simply to stay alive.

"So you want me to tell you what kinda' rocks are down there?" said Pete sarcastically, his voice muffled and distorted by the confines of his suit. He had trouble believing it was necessary for him to accompany the mission. If he had to guess, he'd say Black planned on leaving his body down in that hole. In that case he could make up any story he wanted.

"So to speak. You should be thankful. After all, not many civilians get to see what you are seeing, or do what you are doing, Peter."

Black asked very odd questions on the way down, while ordering one of the soldiers to make radio contact with their brethren already *inserted* in the ground.

"Sir I can't get a feed. Nothin' but whispers and fuzz. Must be some kind of electromagnetic interference down there" Said Private Bermudez as he continued to attempt contact with the squads below.

"What did you make of the gas cloud, Peter?" asked Black, this time in a false, unusually friendly tone.

"I didn't make much of it. Haven't seen anything like it before Black. I hope you know what you're getting us all into." Said Pete, to the dismay of the soldiers who seemed on edge, as if they expected an authoritative, reassuring answer from Black.

"Probably just a methane vane." Piped one of the soldiers, clearly uneducated on the intricacies of geologic rock formations. Pete didn't want to admit it for fear of alarming everyone, but no such rock, not in his decades of digging into the planet, had yielded such a reaction when struck. He too was baffled by it, and sought refuge in his denial.

"You have a family, Peter?" Black asked, with fake cheer.

"Go fuck yourself Black." He muttered in response. Some of the soldiers chuckled, sympathizing with the civilian.

"Almost there, bout' 15 meters."

"Alright men, ready up. Chester, Lancome, you're in first. Bermudez, Sanchez, I want you securing our exit. Set up a TRANSCOM relay. You should get line of sight signals. Clear?"

"Roger that sir".

The lift began to slow. Pete looked up, adjusting the bulky confines of his facemask in order to see the entry point. The gaping tear in the Earth was now the size of a dime. His view shifted to beneath his feet. A speckling reflective surface came into view underneath the steal weave.

"That ain't no rock, sir."

The lift jolted to a sudden halt, nearly bringing Pete to his knees. He clung to the steel cable in the middle to keep his balance. The soldiers carried out their orders with precision, turning on an array of powerful flashlights – one mounted on their gun and one on their head. When they landed on top of the 'rock' it felt cushiony and soft. Black knelt down, and glossed the floor with his hand, revealing a sticky, ooze-like wetness that stuck to his fingers.

"What the hell is this stuff Lieutenant?" Asked Sanchez, a physically small soldier with a big mouth.

The Lieutenant simply looked at Black unwaveringly, who let the goop pass through his fingers. They turned to face the busted drill shaft. Pete's prototype was embedded, twisted and conformed to the gelatinous surface, as if the two were fused together. The Titanium was worn down and metal spikes protruded from the wall from when they had been stripped off and flung.

"Switch to IR scopes. Chester, get yourself through that hole. Chester trained his lights on the gaping hole that had been carved as a result of the drill still half-stuck in it. There was barely enough space to fit a man so they had to be careful as not to tear their suits apart on the way through. A rope fastened by the soldiers that had previously entered helped them to rappel into the cave.

At least *my* baby was the one that cracked this sucker. No other bit could have managed that, Pete thought, momentarily impressed by the sacrifice of his prized invention.

The black ashy air that exploded upwards out of the hole was streaming freely through the breach, rendering the soldiers that entered nearly invisible almost immediately.

"Your Turn Peter" said Black, gripping him by the shoulder and helping him enter the gaping tear. He grabbed onto the rope and was guided into the hole by the soldiers below, who had already created a 5 meter perimeter, guns aiming, scanning the black mist for signs of other soldiers.

The only thing visible was the white, rocky floor, which crumbled to dust under the slightest pressure. Ridged footprints rallied and wandered into the abyss that lay in front of them. After Pete came Black. The two remaining soldiers stayed behind to guard the entrance. *Lucky bastards*, Pete thought.

The environment within the cavern was creepy. The powerful lights adorned by his group penetrated only a few feet into the blackness.

"IRs are no good down here sir. Visibility is extremely limited. Let's link up with the other squads ASAP"

Black seemed confused. "Shouldn't they be down here waiting?" He asked impatiently.

"Yes sir, they should, but they're not. Lancome – spread flares every 15 meters. We're gonna' need to find our way back out of this mess." Snapped the Lieutenant.

Pete knew better than to trust the soldier's reassurance – that they would inevitably leave this place without hindrance - he knew they were trained to be confident no matter what.

The slightest pressure of wind could be felt rushing past them and out of the hole. The black air continued to gush out of the small crack in the Earth with no signs of slowing down.

"I'm catching a faint broadband signal sir. Could be coming from anywhere. Recommend staggered search pattern. They gotta' be down here somewhere." Said Chester, fidgeting with his metallic communicative headset.

"Roger that."

The Lieutenant fluttered a string of hand signals to his men that Pete didn't understand. He looked up at a patch of the ceiling that his light could reach, just barely. It was scarred with vein-like ribbons, opaque multicolored and glimmering with no definite direction. The veins branched off in all different vectors, receding back into the walls on either side. As they proceeded, the cavern walls veered outward, the ceiling climbed higher until it was no longer visible. The floor took on a downward slope, leading deeper into the earth.

What the hell is this place? He thought, befuddled by his surroundings. If he had to make a guess, he would say they were inside the belly of some giant, living creature. But of course that was impossible. The gas poured out of the cavern like smoke bellowing out of lungs. *Rocks don't breathe,* he thought.

The pain in his ribs was dim and unimportant now. Adrenaline kept his eyes from blinking, and his constant shaking was dulled by an inert, hormonally induced focus.

"Sir! Look!" Shouted Lancome, as he popped a bright flare and held it close to the floor. Lying there was an m-16, its magazine half empty with bullet casings littering the ground. The chalky dust revealed what looked like drag-lines into the darkness.

"Barrel's still hot sir. Looks like someone dragged him away. . ."

Just then, a razor sharp scream bellowed through all of the soldier's radios, sending a chill up their spines. The message was choppy and hard to decipher, but they got the gist of it.

"This is TAC-COM 2-11 . . . urning fire . . . ultiple casualti . . . . they ca- . . . . . of the walls . . . of nowhere . . . . . inging squads two and four back . . . . . I repeat, unknown hostiles . . . . . . epare for imme- . . . extraction!"

Pete understood *extraction* loud and clear.

"Holy shit sir, *what the fuck* was that!" shouted Lancome. Before he could answer, the Lieutenant spotted something peculiar, moving hastily in the darkness just meters in front of the boundary of his headlight. He could not be sure if it was a thick cluster of gas or something real.

"Possible Contact, stay sharp! Diamond formation! Lancome, get a hold of Sanchez and Bermudez let em' know we're on our way back!" the quartet of soldiers huddled to within arms length of each other as quickly as they could, corralling Pete and Black in their midst with weapons trained intently on the invisible area surrounding them. For a moment there was silence, save the sounds of a losing battle careening through their headsets. Bullets being fired, shouts of retreat and haunting screams of death entered their headspace.

"Sir we gotta' find em, we can't just sit here!" Shouted Chester, momentarily losing the focus of his scope.

"Negative Chester, too risky. We'd be walking into the same trap they did. Lancome, take the rest of your flares and heave them as far as you can in that direction!"

The Lieutenant pointed along the barely visible wall they had found themselves pinned against, their only guideline back to the cavern entrance.

Trap? What could he possibly have meant? And how was the Lieutenant so calm? Pete used his reason, assuming there was a great deal of information being kept from him. Maybe he didn't want to know. His mind was already filled with things he didn't want to know.

"Whaddya' mean trap? What the fuck is waitin' for us down here LT!?!?" barked the soldier, as panic began to set in. The LT remained straight-faced and calm as his training and instinct kicked in. A brief moment of silence ensued. The Lieutenant had a moment to regain his composure and make a decision.

"Alright, send a distress signal for back up. Heavy weapons, clean up crew, everything. Let's get the fuck outta he-"

Before the Lieutenant could finish his order, the cavern lit up to the tune of a bright blue light. They couldn't see what it was coming from, only that its source was concealed by a large rock pillar a hundred meters in front of them, which was suddenly and momentarily visible. The cavern was *huge*. Between their group and the fleeing soldiers, the plain dipped twenty meters and back up again, like a giant bowl.

The light was followed by more screams on the radio – but this time they could be *felt*. Chester removed his headset, realizing that the screams were now close enough to be heard by his own ears. A second burst of bluish-white light emerged, and a third, brighter than the two previous followed it.

"What the hell is that!?" Shouted Dixon, pointing towards the giant pillar. A quintet of soldiers scurried from behind its shoulder, some turning back to return fire at whatever was attacking them. As Pete looked on in terror, he witnessed something impossible.

A bright bluish-white colored corkscrew of what looked like lightning emerged from behind the pillar into the cavern, all but vaporizing a hapless soldier who stopped to cover his fleeing squad mates. Two more men emerged from the area but were cut down by similar attacks.

"Return cover fire!!" Shouted Lancome and Chester simultaneously. They unleashed two full clips into the general area, focusing on the breach point coming around the corner from the pillar. The bursts of their rifles added more noise to the mayhem. The only good shots they could take were when the cavern was lit up by whomever – or whatever was attacking their friends. Many bullets were being fired into the darkness aimlessly, but the soldiers had few choices.

His team occupied, the Lieutenant had a few seconds to collect his thoughts, devise a plan and issue more orders.

"Alright, secure that squad, suppressive fire on our way out, let's move soldiers!!"

By now, streams of soldiers blanketed the cavern floor, sprinting, stumbling and fumbling their way back to the orange burn of the signal flares. They were running up a slight tilt in a sandy, slippery formula, firing their guns inaccurately at the expansive area behind them. Every time the cavern lit up, more soldiers lay dead and dismembered on the floor. Lancome, Chester, Dixon and the Lieutenant provided what little cover fire they could, but it meant nothing.

Fixated on covering the fleeing squads, the four marksmen lost security in their flanks. At the very edge of his lateral vision, Pete noticed something moving ever closer in the darkness. At first he could only decipher a tall rectangular shape. A large, skinny figure emerged briefly, still half-shrouded by the blackness of the cave. It began to wave its abnormally long, bony hand in front of its chest in a circular pattern, creating a distorted blue light that grew brighter with each rotation.

Pete wasted no time. He leapt from the wall and Mr. Black's clutch, grabbing the Lieutenant's firearm from its holster. He instinctively aimed and squeezed the trigger, missing on his first shot. He fired again, this time catching the tall creature in the left shoulder, which knocked it off balance. Two more bullets pierced the creature's wiry midsection, dropping it. A pool of purple blood oozed from the holes in its body as it collapsed and went limp.

What remained of the soldiers, about fifteen in total, made it back to the signal flares that Lancome had tossed. Some had abandoned their guns, others remained engaged. It became obvious quickly which of the remaining soldiers kept their composure and which could not.

"HELP ME!" Shouted one of the survivors, exhausted and unable to breath. He stopped.

An easy target.

A blue beam pierced the darkness and struck him square in the back, opening him up as if a bomb had exploded inside him. His flailing body became a projectile aimed at the other soldiers, knocking two more to their feet.

Black stood up, seemingly oblivious to the firefight occurring around him. He remained silent and calm, his eyes locking with Pete's for one last time. They were empty, lifeless, and unafraid.

The broken and defeated group moved at a frantic speed, some electing to tear off the hindering confinements of their suits, risking the inhalation of the gas in order to gain mobility. Only eight of them made it back to the hole alive, with an unknown menace presumably in hot pursuit.

"Johnson what the hell happened? Where are squads three and five!?"

"Dead sir, and we will be too if we don't get ou-"

"Stow that shit soldier! Who attacked you?"

"I don't know sir, they look like big bugs . . . they came out of nowhere, we were drawn deeper in to the cave . . . they took two members from 5th platoon soon as we created a perimeter. . . . Baker and uuhhhh"

". . . Stanhope."

"Alright calm down soldier"

The LT gripped his shoulder firm and dug into Johnson's eyes with his own.

"Speak"

"Sir they're not human" was the only reply Johnson could muster.

The Lieutenant realized he had only seconds to make a life or death decision.

"Schlesinger, grab that rope we'll give you a lift. The rest of you provide cover fire, toss any and all flares on your person we need to increase visibility!"

The orders held a warming notion for the remaining soldiers, lending credence to the belief that they might actually make it out alive. It occupied their mind with a task, instead of fear. The Lieutenant's strength added to their own, if only briefly.

Frantically, Pete positioned himself directly beneath the hole and grabbed the rope. On his way up, the Lieutenant nodded his head, acknowledging that Pete had saved his life just moments earlier. Pete thought this must have been the reason for allowing him to leave first. He admired the Lieutenant for his courage and selflessness.

He gripped the slimy outer edge of the cavern and pulled himself closer to the platform waiting there for him. There was no sign of Bermudez or Sanchez, not even a single bullet casing. He keeled over onto his stomach, reaching his hands back into the danger in order to help pull more men to safety. He made sure to lock his leg to the platform so as not to fall back in to Hell.

I hope you're left till' last, Black, he thought to himself. However, as he looked around at the remaining soldiers, Black was not among them. He had vanished.

Pete firmly grabbed Lancome's arms, but it was too late – a bolt of raw blue energy split his body in two pieces, leaving only his charred forearms to be grasped. Pete could feel the sting of heat emanating from the bolt on his own skin. Blood and bone fragments smeared his visor, causing him to wale in agony. He rolled back over, in an attempt to save one more life, but it was too late. The soldiers were being overrun.

Perhaps on different terms, in a different location, they would have stood a chance. They did manage to kill a fair amount of these horrid creatures, but there was just too many, and it was too dark. Every reload left them vulnerable to an attack, and there were too few of them left to cover each other while the other reloaded. A soldier carrying an M60 light machine gun stood up, screaming as he squeezed the trigger, spraying a hundred spikes into the darkness. He simply could not wait for visible targets any longer, frustrated by the cowardly manner in which his enemies fought. "COME ON YOU BASTARDS!" He shouted.

One of the beams came from just feet in front of him, blowing off the whole left side of his body, splattering blood onto the cavern walls. Accepting death, he reached for his sidearm with his remaining hand. As his body folded and crippled, he exacted his revenge on the creature by unloading a full twelve-round magazine into it's torso, yelling fiercely as he died.

"Grenade out!" Yelled an infantryman carrying a submachine gun. It was a last ditch effort – the other soldiers responded in kind, emptying their pockets and satchels of every last piece of ordnance they brought with them. The fragmentation grenades exploded ferociously, dismembering and obliterating a dozen of the tall, gangly monsters. Hot bubbling purple blood covered the floor and made its way onto the soldiers, who for a moment, believed the tide was turning. The bright explosions gave them a quick view of other silhouettes, other targets – of which there were many.

A rifleman who had elected to remove his suit made a brave dash over to the smoking m60. The team's lights overlapped over it, revealing a creature lurking in a crouched position. The soldier swung the butt of his rifle, letting out a grunt as he did, cracking the creature in its oversized head as hard as he could. Even in crouch, the creature was the same height as the soldier attacking it. The blow was followed by a knife rained into the chest, which he had pulled out of his belt. He reached as high as he could, slightly jumping as he thrust the blade as deep as it would go. The LT shot two more creatures, revealed in close quarters by the signature blue balls of light.

The soldier got down and hid behind the obliterated body that lay next to the m60. He grabbed it hastily and dove back into the line of soldiers covering him, and began to assist them but it was not enough to stop the advance. The sheer number of these things was overwhelming. Continuous effigies of blue death rained on the soldiers from everywhere. The men began to run out of ammo; nestled into a corner. They were too occupied to even think about climbing the rope out, one at a time . . .

The Lieutenant went into prone position as his men fell to death around him. An explosion from one of the bluish-white blasts just barely missed, forcing him to roll over, his eyes pointed upward at the hole – at Pete, arms dangling. He lip-synced his last two words:

"Get out."

Pete climbed onto the platform and gave the steel cable the mightiest tug he could muster, looking down at the hole as the platform ascended. He nervously aimed the Lieutenant's pistol at the hole, supporting his shaking wrist with the other hand.

The Lieutenant, still staring up at him, managed to conceal himself in a dusty divot created by one of the blasts. He knew his fate was sealed in that cave alongside his dead brothers. He reached into duel satchels around his waste extracting a grenade in each hand as the creatures were now almost on top of him. He crossed his arms over his chest and let out a lung-busting roar, slammed the lids of his eyes shut and pulled the pins.

* * * *

Topside, a fleet of paramedics, choppers, and a fresh contingent of soldiers were waiting for Pete. They had a plethora of questions to ask but he could not answer. Two medics peeled him off the metal platform – the tail end of the explosion from the grenades was powerful enough to melt part of his suit directly to the steel grate. His left arm, torso and part of his hip suffered intense burns. Once again, he was very lucky to be alive. The pain, understandably, was too much for him. Although he stubbornly tried to communicate with the nurses, his mouth did not form words. He was a heartbeat away from going into shock.

The last glimpse he recorded of the site was that of a festering, smoldering ruin. No more black gas spewing into the air, no more bluish-red flames.

He had done it. The Lieutenant sacrificed himself to save Pete and probably many others. Moments after Pete was pried from the platform, the entire hole collapsed, leaving no possibility of another team being lowered and slaughtered.

It's over, he thought, as he fluttered in and out of conscious. He did not feel pain – in fact he did not feel anything. The one image pasted in his mind's eye – like a recurring nightmare was the creature he had presumably killed. Not a human by any stretch, but with distorted humanlike features. *What the hell* was that thing? Some kind of deformed man? A robot? An alien?

In that moment, he realized the bigger picture. This was the plan all along. There was no base to be constructed, no expertise needed, no "geological information" required, as Black had put it. This was a military operation from the outset, and he was a damned fool to have believed otherwise. He and Ernest were lured into a trap – under the guise of paying customers, Black and his crew tricked them into giving their lives. Had the director known the whole story? How deep did this lie go? He felt like a government guinea pig; his life's worth akin to an expendable tool. It was a most unpleasant and sickening feeling.

None of that mattered now, because they were dead. All of them. Even Black. He was left with a burning desire to find out what really happened that day even if it required his life. He owed that much to the Lieutenant and his men.

Before he passed out, his friend flashed before his eyes. He would probably have to go along with some bullshit story conjured up by the army, denied the right to speak truthfully to Gale about how her father died.

"I'm so sorry Ernest," He murmured, as his last sliver of consciousness faded.

Pete woke up on a medevac chopper hours later, with young nurses tending to his myriad wounds.

"Wh-where am I?" He managed, using every ounce of strength he had to squeeze the air from his lungs.

"Just outside Dulce, New Mexico. Don't worry Mr. Schlesinger you're safe now." responded the nurse, who made Pete feel slightly better. Her beautiful young face reminded him of one of his nieces.

"Wh-what's the date?"

"August 29th, 1977. You were hit by an explosion, Mr. Schlesinger. Right now you are experiencing temporary amnesia because of your wounds. But you're gonna' be just fine, ok?" Said the nurse reassuringly, placing a folded towel underneath Pete's neck and skull. He tried to get up, but the pain came back immediately.

"Please Mr. Schlesinger, stay down. You're in no condition to go anywhere."

Bits and pieces slowly returned to his memory. Chief among them, the terrified faces of sixty-six crack soldiers who were now gone.

Who gave their lives to save *his* life.

"Buncha' god damn heroes" murmured Pete, half-asleep and feeling the effects of sedatives.

"Yes Mr. Schlesinger, you are a hero." Said the bewildered nurse, playing along with his drug-induced ramblings like a supportive mother to her child.

"How long till' we reach the hospital, pilot?"

"Twenty minutes ma'am" He replied sternly.

The chopper and five others like it flew towards the fading desert sun, headed towards a faint cluster of lights nestled in a small formation of mountains on the horizon.

Chapter 1

HOUSE PARTY

Anthony Stall and five of his best friends convened on the deck at a local House Party. It was St. Patrick's day in Boston – among the wildest party days all year. Not even the most blindly dedicated soon-to-be government agents could avoid the drunken slander. The night sky was clear revealing all the familiar constellations and the air was brisk; just cold enough so that people's breath could be seen leaving their body. Kegs of cold ale lined the rails, ready to be emptied and guzzled by jovial college students.

"Bottoms up guys!" cheered Anthony's best friend Thomas, who signaled the group to empty their throats and guzzle their first pint of the night. Anthony had just finished one of his last training exercises for the FBI, and was more than ready to indulge in a few (too many) cold ones. It had been nearly four months since his last drink, sworn to discipline by his strict uncle. Despite his abstinence from partying, he knew how to throw them back. He polished his topped off glass seconds before any of his friends, which is more substantial a timeframe than it may seem. He embraced the cumbersome drink, enjoying not just the taste as it bypassed his tongue and entered his throat, but the loose feeling that entered his body along with the beverage.

"Looks like our boy here still has it!" Said Thomas, slapping Anthony on the back. He had to reach quite high – Anthony, being six foot three to Thomas' five foot eight. He hit Anthony quite hard, but he barely budged. His wide frame could handle such a small hand quite easily.

"Man, there are lots of good lookin' broads here. I hope you still have that legendary touch, Stall." Said Jonas, a scrawny, frail amigo huddled in Anthony's shadow.

"Another round gentlemen?" Piped Thomas, not really asking but assuming as he collected the glass mugs and cracked the nearest keg.

"So, Stall, tell us a bit about your training. You shoot any guns yet?" Asked Jonas excitedly, the rest of the group focused intently on Anthony's answer. The decades-old boards beneath creaked and groaned as he shifted his weight uneasily, trying to think of something wise and prophetic to say. He had their full attention and did not want to disappoint.

"Of course." He said conservatively. The reality was that most of his training was the 'boring' stuff – chalk talks, countless hours in the classroom learning tactics and strategies. Only once every two weeks was there weapons training.

"Of course? That's all we get eh? You stoic son of a bitch always so –"

"Shut-up Jonas, let the man be. It's St. Paddy's, the last thing he wants to do is think about all that boring shit." Interrupted Thomas. Thomas was and always had been Anthony's de facto translator. He loved to talk, be loud and garner people's attention, while Anthony was naturally quiet and introvert. Even with women, Thomas would initiate the conversation, while Anthony relied on his clean cut good looks and soft charm. Some things, as his Uncle always used to say, were *better left unsaid.*

Truthfully, the firearm training was anything but glorious. Anthony thought better to let his friend's imaginations do his bidding rather than spoil their minds with boring stories. He neglected to mention that in terms of weapon proficiency, he was at the top of his class.

"It's ok Thomas" Anthony rescinded. "I don't mind talking about it. There's not much to it really, a lot of classroom time, when we do use guns it's pretty simple stuff. Target practice, mostly."

Jonas, Alex, John and Nick all looked at him with cheeky grins put off by Anthony's overly humble explanation, as if their expectations had been let down by the boring truth.

"Sure, Stall, you're just saying that. You're probably on some secret mission right now you bastard!" Shouted Nick, already intoxicated and spilling his third beer. All six of them laughed in unison.

Anthony swung his glass into the middle aggressively then raised it back down. He opened his coat pocket, revealing a pack of Marlboro reds, unopened.

"You gotta' be kidding me man, you smoke now?" Said Nick, pointing at Anthony like he was guilty of something. Anthony held his composure, and spoke.

"I don't smoke Nick, you know that." Patting the fresh pack. "But I'm smoking tonight."

He peeled off the wrapping expertly, bit a cigarette out of the package and lit it.

His friends simply stood there in awe at Anthony puffing the stogie, half-entering the house but caught in transition. Anthony truly was the envy of his friends and they reveled in microscopic ways at everything he did.

"I'll be in after this guys." Flicking the ash from his cigarette.

Anthony walked over to the edge of the balcony and rested his elbows on it. He gazed up at the stars, which were particularly visible. He finally had a moment to himself. It's what he had been used to for the last four months – very little social communication. His life had become dedicated, strict and precise. The style he once carried years ago had all but worn off.

But maybe, he could unlock it somehow, and what better place to do it then a pre-St. Patrick's day party?

Anthony looked up at the stars again, and remembered what his uncle had told him when he was a small child. He told Anthony stories about his parents and one was about a particular set of stars in the sky.

Those ones right there, Anthony. That's your parents looking down on you.

The words of his Uncle so long ago seemed like silliness to him now. Although very far away, Anthony still knew exactly where to look to find those stars. They were just barely visible between much brighter ones.

He took a few more swigs of the watery keg draft and a dozen more puffs of his cigarette until it was gone.

He turned from the stars and looked back at the house. Each window revealed a sea of green. Young people packed tightly into each room conversing while drinking plastic cups full of green beer. The floors were sticky and black from people neglecting to take their shoes off.

This truly was a *Rager,* he thought, as his friend Steve used to say in high school.

Anthony walked confidently into the house, ready to loosen up a bit. The beer began to take its effect. A quick spray of of less than eloquent cologne and he was ready to mingle.

Everyone inside had green on. Everyone but him. Big dumb foam hats, giant star-shaped glasses, even legwarmers, all of it green. Needless to say he stuck out like a sore thumb; his manicured brown leather jacket and stiff black shirt a slap in the face to this pseudo-holiday's color code. He flashed a smile and marched nonchalantly into the living room, towards his friends. And then he saw her.

A perfectly rounded golden goddess, from the souls of her feet to her longest lock of curled hair. Anthony couldn't help but give her an obvious up-and-down, like a hungry dog to the sniff of blood. He didn't care if it looked awkward, or if she noticed. In fact he wanted her to see, if only for a second, just to acknowledge his presence. She wore glittery white shoes and tight, dark blue jeans all the way to the top of her hips. Her pierced, perfectly tanned belly showed, and then a green, slim-fitting shirt to prop up her breasts. She had green eyes and bright red lips that Anthony wanted to kiss.

Her length was displayed beside a plant nestled in the corner of the room, next to which she stood. The natural curves of their bodies played against one another, the leaves of the plant and her skin and hair glowing similarly under the light.

She broke eye contact with her friend to observe Anthony, with a cozy grin on his face, towering over his friends and looking back at her. Anthony tensed up, but was relieved when she broke and flashed a quick, friendly smile while chattering away to one of her friends. Anthony engaged his circle of buddies, pretending not to notice.

Got her, he thought.

"Did you see that over there Anthony?"

"Oh I saw. I think she saw me too."

"You know her?"

"Not yet," said Anthony. "But I'd like to."

"Oh yeah? Let's play a game of cat and mouse. I'll go and introduce myself then you slide in all smooth, kay'?"

"If you say so!" said Anthony, not knowing if it was a good decision. Anthony had seen reckless drunk antics from Thomas in the past and how they usually crashed and burned, or ended up with both of them looking like fools. He also knew that Thomas was trying to impress him, as if he had developed uncanny pick-up skills in his brief absence. By traditional standards, the girl was way out of his league.

Thomas broke formation and plastered a visibly nervous smile on his face. He walked over to the girl and stuck his hand out awkwardly, reciting his name and greeting her. To Anthony's surprise, her face lit up and she emphatically grabbed Thomas' hand and shook it vigorously. He pretended to pay attention to his friends' conversation about the latest HBO shows and other nerdy jargon, but he was biding his time waiting for the right time to pounce.

Thomas asked her a question. She was stunned and blushed. Anthony moved in. Before he could get there, the girl's friend was tossed into Thomas, who flung his drink all over the girl's shirt and collided with her. A fight broke out. Two drunken hooligans in a pissing contest over a mouthy exchange.

Anthony reacted without hesitation quickly identifying the bigger man in the fight. He dove in to the entangled pair, pulling and yanking on a hand, which came with a body. The kid flung himself around, carrying a heavy uppercut with his right hand. It was too slow. Anthony avoided the punch, simultaneously wrapping the extended arm into a lock with his own arms, forcing the kid's own hand into this throat, exposing his ribcage. He used his leverage and height to raise the kid slightly off his center of balance, quickly stepping in and throwing him over his leg into the ground.

Meanwhile, the other guy, just moments ago wrestling the same person, stood in awe. He didn't know whether to throw a punch or run away, observing such an efficient subduction. He was probably lucky, being outmatched in size and tenacity as he was.

Anthony assumed full control, thrusting the brunt of his forearm into the brawler's neck. He pushed his entire body weight onto him. He looked into his eyes and talked very slowly.

"I'm going to let you up. Then you are going to apologize to me, him (as he nodded towards the other stunned fighter), and my lady friends over there." As he pointed towards the corner of the room, eyes still fixated.

"Blink twice if you get me" Said Anthony.

The kid blinked twice quickly. The first takedown was far too precise and tactical. He didn't want to fight again.

Everyone in the room was silent and stared as Anthony made his stipulations and finally let the kid up. He made his promised apologies and shook hands with the owner of the house over a communal beer. Anthony looked like a hero.

"So what's your name cowboy?" Asked the beautiful green eyed girl, grabbing Anthony's arm before he could sort himself out after the tussle.

"A-Anthony" He stammered, mentally kicking himself. It was far from what he had rehearsed in his mind just moments before.

"A Anthony? Ha ha! Well I'm A Jennifer, nice to meet you!"

"Nice to meet you too. Finally." Anthony said.

Thomas stood there observing, and then at the girl's perfect chest, covered in his drink. She seemed oblivious to the stain, enthralled by Anthony's moves. He scrambled to find a cloth. Although his plan didn't work perfectly, the end result was the same. His best friend Anthony was now one on one with the hottest girl in the house, and she seemed interested in him.

"Jennifer . . . Jennifer. I'm so sorry you had to witness that, I'm really not a violent guy. But I felt bad when my frie-"

"Awww save it, ya big pussycat." Jennifer interrupted as she laid a hand firmly on Anthony's chest. "That was awesome. Ya think you can teach me some of those moves?"

"Definitely." He replied, his grin widening. He slowly moved in closer, eyes locked and grasped Jennifer's other hand. She seemed up for the taking, so he leaned in for a kiss. She abruptly turned her cheek, but did not back away.

"Not here", she whispered. "Somewhere else. Take me somewhere else."

Anthony did not waste any time. The music was back on and everyone had forgotten about the fight within minutes. He gently grabbed her by the hand and led her toward the stairs which led down to the main door of the split entry. On the way there, he wrestled with the notion of whether or not he was sober enough to drive.

"You sure you don't wanna' stay here any longer?" Anthony asked, trying to reaffirm that he really was a nice guy. He felt stupid for asking in case she thought he was scared and couldn't handle her, then decided against leaving with him.

"Nope, I think I found what I'm lookin' for" said Jennifer as she planted a soft kiss on Anthony's neck. The pick-up seemed a little bit too easy. Anthony began to second guess the girl's character, surprised that she'd be so willing to leave with him.

How many other guys has she done this with?

But this girl was intensely beautiful, and his doubtful thoughts were superseded by primal urges.

"You like Camaros, sweetheart?" Anthony asked, his soft smile emerging once again.

"Of course, any right-minded girl should! Why, you gonna' show me yours?"

"Follow me," Replied Anthony affirmatively. He noticed a southern tinge in Jennifer's accent that he hadn't noticed before.

The two made their way down the stairs and out the door onto the concrete path that led to the street. Thomas and Nick noticed Anthony's tall silhouette brushing through the crowd next to a bright poof of blond hair. They looked at each other in awe, then began to weave their narrow, scrawny bodies toward the front of the house to catch a glimpse. They stopped at the door, huddled behind one an another so as not to be seen, but they could not escape Anthony's legendary awareness. He peered over his shoulder to Thomas, winking at him as he left.

Anthony led Jennifer up to his old, busted and broken ford pick-up from the 70s. Tattered blue paint chips and a worn-down chassis covered in rust.

"This isn't a camaro?" said Jennifer, disillusioned.

"I didn't say I owned one, I Just asked if you liked them!" said Anthony, quite coyly.

The small lie could have broken the deal, but she was encapsulated by his smile and demeanor already, caught in his web of masculine appeal. Jennifer hesitated for a moment but let out a chuckle, looking at the hunk of scrap metal, then back at him with a smile she tried to hide.

"Hop in. Don't worry, I invest more into my home then my car."

"Come on Thomas, let's go find some for ourselves!" Said Nick, pulling at Thomas' sleeve.

Standing slack-jawed, with a sense of satisfaction and accomplishment coursing vicariously through him, Thomas slowly turned back to the party.

"That man is not human," He said, sipping his green beer.

* * * *

Anthony's Uncle had raised him from infancy. He was the only parent Anthony had ever known. He found himself sitting in his favorite diner, sipping a deep glass of frosty beer.

"World's goin' to shit Cap. Too many people, too many mouths to feed. Just wait til' all the Asians start piling up over here. I'm tellin' ya', they're gonna' be the US majority within ten years!"

"I don't know bout that, Jim."

"What's not to know? Our government's in the shitter, and theirs is boomin'. Plus, they already got four or five times as many people as us. I'm telling ya', it's only a matter of time."

"I heard the economy's back on track."

"Well where the hell'd ya' hear that? Yer buddies over at Langley know something I don't?

Jim leaned in close, ogling a toothpick in the midst of his lips.

"I'm telling ya, I don't have buddies over in Langley, or the Pentagon, or god-damn NORAD for that matter. You and all your dumb paranoid ideas, Jim, I swear . . . "

"Aha, Ha ha ha! You know I'm just pullin' your leg Cap. Nothing wrong with a little bullshit here and there. You could lighten up too, ya know? Matter of fact – Scuse' me, waitress? Get my friend here a bottle of Rolling Rock and a shot of Jack, if you don't mind."

"No problem hun."

The pretty waitress smiled and turned on a swivel, holding a tray of drinks in her hand which were unaffected.

The bar was filled with delinquents – not young but old – the smell of welfare checks and bad decisions lingered in the air. The waitress scooted by, placing the shot and beer in front of the Captain at lightning speed. It was a very busy holiday for any bar.

"Thanks sugar," said the Captain, revealing his charred, unaligned teeth in a dainty smile.

"You hear about that, Cap?" said Jim, pointing at a television mounted several feet above their barstools.

"What the hell. . ."

A young female reporter was on the news, with a headline that said *"Space Race back on"* beneath her.

"The recent end to NASA has come at a cost for the US. It has now been confirmed that the Chinese have set aside an extra forty-billion dollars for their Space Weapons program which is being perceived worldwide as a direct countermeasure to the US' new Heaven's Gate program, purportedly set to launch in July. Although former NASA spokesman Daniel Triche neglected to be interviewed, he did admit in brief press statement that NASA has no ties to the Heaven's Gate program, which is still being shrouded in mystery by Washington. The President is expected to make a press release of his own concerning this and other things to do with the economy on Wednesday, later this week."

The reporter had Jim and the Captain engaged. No more information regarding the subject followed.

"And now for our forecast, here's Mark —"

"Wow!" Jim exclaimed, slamming his sloshed beer mug on the countertop. "Heaven's Gate? The hell does that mean?"

"I don't know Jim. Probably some lie conjured up by Grovelman to make us look tougher than we are. You may actually be right about the Chinese. They ain't fuckin' around anymore."

"Damn right they ain't!"

Although the Captain didn't like to admit it, he was as curious as Jim was when it came to secret government information. Both of them held jobs which positioned them next to a continuous drift of tidbits and rumors from the top, but they were far from it and only ever caught scraps. Being director of the FBI, it was inevitable, but Lester's time had passed in the old-fashioned era, where secrecy and espionage were repugnant and secondary to a blazing-guns, smoke em' out attitude.

Jim took a big gulp of his beer in the silence, and looked at his watch.

"It's late, Cap. I gotta' retire. Want to catch a cab? I'll get off at Fenwick and you'll go home from there."

"What's the rush, Jim? It's St. Pat's!!"

"Well Anthony's back, and I told him I'd cook him breakfast tomorrow morning. I haven't seen the kid in a while and I don't wanna' be too hung over . . . and sleep in."

"Alright. I'll come with ya." The Captain looked around the bar as he replied. Another sea of green, and no one else that he knew, or desired to associate with, even on a holiday.

"By the way Cap, you've been around him for the last four months. How is he?"

"Funny you didn't bring that up earlier, Jim."

"Funny indeed. But seriously how is he?"

Jim yearned to know how Anthony's training was going. There was an unspoken sense of pride which resonated between members of the FBI about professionalism, intelligence and who could seal the biggest cases. He wanted to hear how Anthony was doing there. He wanted to hear about how perfect he was for the job.

"He's quiet in class." Said the Captain, hesitantly.

"And his marks?"

"Top Notch."

"And what about the gadgets? And guns?"

The Captain momentarily reverted to his at-work persona, reliving the events of Anthony's training while he was there. His speech became perfect and unblemished by curse words, as if he was reading from a well-prepared document.

"Well actually, he shows a very keen knack for the utilization of short and medium range firearms. His rifle skills are also best in the class. In fact, sometimes when we do target practice, it's the whole rest of the class against him."

Jim's face came to a slow smile as he listened, but tried to hide it.

"Mmhmm. What else?"

"Well, for starters, he recorded the highest mark ever on the tests we did on thought recognition patterns."

"Explain."

"Well, basically, each candidate listens to a story told by a random, then interviews them after. They have to indicate whether they are lying, and if so, what the real story is. But there's a kicker. The candidate may only ask ten questions."

Jim spent many years in the Bureau and trained his fair share of recruits, but had never heard of such a test. For a moment he was inspired for the future of the FBI and impressed they had developed such simple, yet awesome ways of measuring intellect – ones he could have benefited from during his training.

"So how'd he do?"

"Well, we repeat this process with each candidate about three times a week, sometimes more. Most times, the candidate wastes all their questions without even realizing it, then asks for more time. Sometimes they guess, sometimes they can figure it out. . . But Anthony. . . the first eleven times he guessed on an average of four questions, right every time. In fact, Jim, the kid was never wrong. Not once. It became like a running joke amongst me and the other teachers. I'll be damned if I've met anyone with a built in bull-shit detector like that, or if I ever will again."

"That's my boy!" Shouted Jim, thoroughly impressed.

"I don't think you understand, Jim. That kind of awareness is unprecedented in . . . well in any human being. Sometimes he didn't even ask questions, he would simply lay down the real story right back to the person, always accurate. We honestly didn't know what to throw at him next . . . The tests are designed for the students to fail, and then learn from their failures for next time."

"Yeah he's been like that since hes' a kid. Never could lie to him about anything"

As Jim spoke, he looked down at the ground, realizing that what he said wasn't entirely true.

"I mean, we've done this with hundreds of guys, no one is even remotely close. He's gonna' make one hell of an agent. You've done a good job raising him, Jim.

"Thanks Cap, means a lot to me."

And it did.

"Hey that must be ours," Said Jim.

Their taxi screeched around a corner and came to a stop right in front of them. They hopped in and made their way home, each with a sense of pride resonating from their conversation about the prodigal son.

* * * *

Anthony woke up in his bed naked, half of the sheets wrapped tightly around his body. The ceiling fan raised the hairs on his moist back. His eyes opened wide. Flashing before them were the images of a dream he had been having since he could remember, one of his parents that he never met.

It seemed no matter what he dreamt about it, his dream would always end with him in his coffin. His eyes are closed, but he is awake, and aware. Somewhere outside the coffin is a woman, tall and beautiful, that he can almost see clearly in his mind's eye. She whispers the words:

"Wake up . . .

. . .Wake up, my child."

This is where his dream ends. At first, he didn't know how to react. He began to ignore it, thinking nothing of it. His life demanded his attention towards other things.

Lying next to him was Jennifer, fully naked and clinging to the edge of his bed and a pillow, her midsection covered by the smallest sliver of sheet. Her skin had the same glow as last night but her hair was a tangled mess. The dimples on her lower back accentuated a tribal tattoo that worked with the curves of her figure.

Anthony turned over to her and pulled a frock of hair from her face. She opened her eyes slowly, then smiled.

"Hey handsome."

"Right back atcha' babe."

The two giggled together and shared a passionate kiss.

"Wanna' get some breakfast? I know a great place down on Queen's. My treat." Said Jennifer, which took Anthony by surprise. He expected her to be on her way out soon, like a lot of the girls he entertained.

"Damn girl, I'd love to. I really would. But I promised my Uncle I'd have breakfast with him. In fact I was supposed to be there ten minutes ago. I'm really sorry, how bout another time?"

Anthony wasn't sure what Jennifer's reaction would be. He wasn't lying but what he said would certainly sound like a quickly conjured lie.

"Well I figured since you made me orgasm multiple times last night, it's the least I could do. Girl's gotta' hold on to something like that."

Anthony was relieved as Jennifer's bright smile lit up. He was also relieved that he performed admirably, because at that point he couldn't quite remember.

"It's alright stud. But you better call me!" She demanded, pointing her finger firmly into his chest.

"Oh don't worry, I'm all over you. What are you doin' tonight? I wouldn't mind taking you out to dinner somewhere fancy."

"I have no plans, but I'm a country girl. Fancy isn't my thing. Take me to a burger joint and I'll be happy."

"Wow. That might be the sexiest thing I've ever heard." Said Anthony, quite honestly.

"Get dressed, I'll give you a rip home. Where do you live?"

"On campus at Boston U . . ."

"Bit of a detour but I can do it. Let's roll! But wait, I have to find my keys."

As Jennifer covered her perfect body with her clothes, Anthony frantically searched for his car keys. They were nowhere to be found. He closed his eyes and focused on where they might be. Images popped into his head from the night before, specifically of being in the kitchen, and the keys falling from his pocket – he remembered not by sight, but by the sound of the keys hitting the tile floor. While Jennifer was wrapped around and kissing him, one of his feet must have . . .

The heat vent in the floor. He must have kicked them in there accidentally. Bingo. The keys dangled underneath the grate, barely clinging to where he could reach. Anthony was impressed by his own sleuth abilities. He also knew he was lucky they didn't fall deeper into the vent.

The drive over to the University didn't take long at all because no one was on the road. They must have been either too hung over, or still drunk. Jennifer nestled herself in Anthony's bosom the entire ride, clinging to his outstretched arm that wrapped around her as he drove with the other hand.

This girl is really into me, he thought. And she was. But he had always remembered what his Uncle told him about one night stands – *One night stands shouldn't be followed by plans!* He would always say. But maybe Jennifer was different. Maybe she wanted something more meaningful.

"Alright gorgeous, we're here. I wish you could cling to me all day, but we both have our lives to attend to. So get on'!" said Anthony, leaning across her and popping the passenger door open.

They shared one more kiss before she left – something to keep her mind occupied in the meantime.

"Here's my number Tony. Can I call you Tony?" said Jennifer as she peeled a piece of paper out of her tight jeans and handed it to Anthony.

"Babe you can call me whatever you want. I'm gonna' call ya' later, okay?"

"You better!" Said Jennifer, pointing her finger once again authoritatively. Anthony enjoyed her bossy tone. He had no quarrels with spending more time with her.

Although he enjoyed Jennifer's company, he also enjoyed having personal time to relax his outstretched mind. He hadn't seen his uncle in months and was looking forward to conversing with him over a delicious breakfast. His bustling blue truck hacked and wheezed as he pulled away from the border sidewalk of the campus, Jennifer's scent lingering; a welcome memory for the senses. However, unbeknownst to him at the time, Anthony would never see Jennifer again.

He arrived at his uncle's house; an old, brick building with dull blue shutters for the windows. Overgrown hedges lined the front, twisting and spiraling in front of every window. His house was in desperate need of a makeover. The grass looked like it hadn't been cut or serviced in years. Yellow and white patches covered his yard, which was marred further by mounds of dirt and rocks. The roof was bent and beginning to cave in on itself. Spotted missing shingles covered it all over.

You need to find a woman Uncle Jim.

His uncle met him at the door before he could raise his hand to knock, smiling and in his underwear.

"I figured you'd be late, bud! Lemme' put on some pants. Have a seat, food's almost ready."

"No problem, got a pop for me Uncle?"

"In the fridge help yourself."

Anthony entered the kitchen, which was filled with the aroma of maple bacon and sizzling fried hash-brown paddies. A pan full of cheesy eggs cracked and bubbled on the stovetop. He looked over at the table; adorned with placemats, cups of fruit and perfectly stacked cutlery on top of napkins. Oblong pitchers of orange and apple juice glittered in the sunlight entering the window at the end of the table. Anthony's favorite breakfast sausages lay steaming between two pieces of paper towel on top of a plate. He no longer wanted a beer.

"Now I finally feel like I'm at home, Uncle Jim!" Said Anthony, removing his coat and placing it on top of his chair. The feast for his senses was a familiar, warming welcome.

"Need help with anything?"

"Naw, you just sit tight and relax. So I talked to Director Desjardins last night. He had nothing but good things to say about you. How's it been for ya'?"

"It's been . . . long. But to be honest, I thought it would be a bit more challenging, you know?" Said Anthony, as Jim tossed everything onto plates with a spatula, listening.

"But other than that, I'm enjoying it. They said they might have an assignment for me within the next few months." Anthony gazed upon his plate full of food. "Wow, you weren't kidding. This is gonna' be delicious!"

The two of them picked up their cutlery and began to eat. The food was indeed delicious, and he was glad he ditched Jennifer to enjoy it. Jim took a moment to look at Anthony, shoveling egg into his mouth with a piece of buttered toast in his other hand. His dark, usually sharp hair was messy and frayed. He had subtle bags under his eyes. Jim had seen the same look when Anthony was in high school and he knew what it meant.

"So what was her name?" Jim asked with a smirk on his face.

"Uhhh what? Oh. . . Jennifer. Her name was Jennifer" said Anthony, caught off guard. "How did you know?"

"You know nothing gets past me Anthony. Nothing. Besides, young strapping stud like you? Even if I didn't know, there was a good chance that I could guess correctly."

"You're funny."

Anthony continued to eat, but at a slower pace. He remained silent but had a peculiar disposition, like he wanted to say something but didn't know how.

"Something buggin' ya' kid?

"Well, Uncle, I've been having this strange dream lately. I can't seem to shake it"

"Explain?" said Jim, becoming intently focused on what Anthony had to say.

"Well, it's hard to explain . . . I always end up in a coffin . . . and no matter how hard I try, I can't muster enough strength to break out of it. It's like I can see myself inside . . . but I'm utterly helpless. I can't really tell if it's a dream or nightmare, ya' know?"

"Anthony, I used to have dreams like that. There was this one where I'd always end up on the edge of a cliff, and I had two options. One was to jump, the other was to walk back into the jungle full of beasts, where a certainly horrific death awaited me."

"Also, if I focus hard enough I can hear a voice . . . it says 'Wake up' . . . and that's usually when I wake up, after struggling to get out of the box. I don't know what to make of it. But lately the dreams have become so real . . . so life-like. Sometimes when I wake up I feel like I'm still inside the box . . . I have to throw water in my face just to make sure." Said Anthony, as his uncle listened carefully.

"Uncle, I know I've asked you before, but what was my mother like?"

The question caught Jim off-guard. There were a thousand good adjectives he could use to describe Anthony's real mother, but he didn't want to go down that path again. He had told Anthony since he was young that his parents were killed just after he was born during a highly classified operation.

"She was a beautiful woman, Anthony. In heart and mind."

Jim reached across the table and placed his hairy, thick hand on top of Anthony's and locked onto his eyes.

"You are the same. You inherited everything good about her. Don't let these dreams get to you Anthony, I'm sure they will pass. In the meantime, finish your breakfast. There's something I want to show you outside."

Anthony followed his Uncle outside onto the back deck after satiating himself to an overly full stomach. It was overgrown with uncut hedges and untended, wildly blossoming gardens. Nestled into the back left corner of the fenced-in yard, a shack painted light blue stood amongst hip-high weeds. It was obvious by the perfectly upkept condition of the shack that Jim had been spending most of his time there.

"In here."

Jim marched up to the shack and swung its door open with a quick pull of the metal wire hanging from above him. As the chain links went end over end, the shed revealed a smooth looking vehicle.

"No fucking way, you did it Uncle?"

"I've been talking about it for years, finally got around to it. She's striped up and down like an Oakland Raider. Decided to go dark with the colors"

"I knew you had something going on. I had a dream about i-"

"Yeah she's got a special 10 cylinder block, reinforced chassis. Bulletproof glass too. Why not, I said to myself. Old men like me need to have hobbies to keep us from going crazy."

Anthony stood in awe of the perfect looking Camaro as his uncle rambled on about the upgrades and adjustments made to the car. When he played basketball in the driveway as a youth it was nothing more than a rusty pile of junk absent wheels. A weighted tarp covered it's ugly, decrepit exterior. Now, the pristine garage held a hidden gem that could light up the neighborhood.

He ran his fingers across the smooth exterior, admiring the craftsmanship involved.

"This your operating vehicle now? Get rid of the Toyota?"

"Nope. Still got the Toyota."

Jim observed Anthony admiring the machine and reached deep into his pocket, fiddling its contents about. His hand slivered out of the pocket, and with it dangled a set of keys with a small 8 ball attached to them.

"Heads up" said Jim, as he tossed the keys towards Anthony. He caught them in his right hand, snapping them out of the air as they sailed.

"It's yours, Anthony. All yours."

"You can't be serious? I mean, you love this car! I don't know if I can accept this."

"I don't remember giving you a choice, youngblood. Now lets take er' for a spin!"

"I don't know what to say?"

"Let your lead foot do the talking ha ha ha!" Laughed Jim as he popped open the car door, barely fitting his body between it and the edge of the shack.

Anthony stared at the keys for a moment. He couldn't wait to hop in that beast and take the reigns. He hopped in the driver side and placed the jingling keys in the ignition, being careful not to miss the ignition slot. It wouldn't matter, but he wanted to let his uncle know that he wouldn't treat his hobby like a toy. The engine revved ferociously, as Jim let out a jovial holler and patted the front dash with his hands.

Anthony could feel the power and torque rustling through the chassis, and he grasped firm control of the wheel, vibrating. A few floors of the petal jacked the engine up to its full capacity – the car was extremely powerful. He felt and heard its itch to leave the garage.

"Thanks, Uncle. This means a lot to me." Said Anthony, in all sincerity.

"Well I couldn't let ya' pull up to work in that embarrassing piece of shit." Said Jim, as he looked into the rearview mirror which displayed Anthony's truck on the front curb. The two looked at each other and shared a laugh.

"Can't believe that hunk of junk is still running."

Anthony kicked the beast into gear and slid it out of the garage, down the driveway and out onto the street.

"I could get used to this, Uncle."

"I bet you could, Anthony. I bet you could."

"Whaddya' say we christen this beauty with some cold ones?" Asked Anthony, uncharacteristically. He wasn't the type to drink on Sunday afternoon. Jim didn't expect Anthony to ask, but he was willing to do whatever Anthony wanted. After all, he'd be a full blown agent in no-time and too busy to spend time with his weary old Uncle.

"Yeah, we'll just extend the holiday. I know a great place down a couple blocks, they got shuffleboard. You're on."

"You don't even know what you're getting yourself into old man." Anthony joked, always eager for a challenge. He never shied away from any type of competition.

Anthony kicked the vehicle back into gear and screeched the tires, peeling the sleek muscle car out of the quiet neighborhood.

Chapter 2

LIAISONS

The west wing of the pentagon had just received a much needed facelift. A dozen new offices and a brand new lunch room, lined with stainless steel coffee machines and brand new appliances. Down it's wide hallways, a clean-cut, handsome man clad in a tidy Versace suit strolls. His fast pace is made evident by the loud clamoring of his Italian-style shoes. In his hand he carries an important stack of concealed documents – ones that hold a valuable secret.

After traversing half of the gigantic building, Gary Jones finds his destination. To his left, plaques and commemorative scriptures remembering those fallen and injured in the 9/11 attacks. Across from them on the outer periphery of the building is the office he is looking for. Written plainly on the door is the man's name – 'Mr. Grey'.

He knocks gently on the door.

"Come in, come in" replies a voice from the interior.

The rectangular office is bigger than most in this part of the building. It is fitting, because Mr. Grey is a huge human being. At least two meters tall with shoulders nearly as wide. Gary enters the office as Mr. Grey sits silently, reading over a document pried from an envelope which reads "CLASSIFIED."

"Have a seat, Gary. How's Martha? And . . . Taylor?"

"Tyler, actually sir. And they're both fine."

Gary didn't like the fact that Mr. Grey knew him so personally. He was told this was all business. But these bigwigs in Washington always knew the whole story, even if they pretended not to.

"That's good to hear. I understand you have an important piece of information for me?" said Grey, removing his glasses.

"I have no idea, not my place to comment. I'm just the middleman here. I was told I'd be compensated. . ."

"And indeed you will, providing what you carry is useful to me. . . to ussss." Mr. Grey lingered on the last syllable, creating a sort of hiss.

This kind of thing was not Gary's forte. He had been a straight and honest man his whole life – the kind of man not easily corrupted. The surreptitious aura surrounding this particular task made him feel very uneasy. The sooner he got paid and back to his administration job at the FBI headquarters, the better.

"Here it is, sir."

Gary handed Grey a thick envelope, marked 'FOR YOUR EYES ONLY'.

"Now Mr. Jones, you've heard of the Heaven's Gate program, haven't you?"

"Yes sir."

"Then surely you've heard that we are in search of America's finest and best – in all aspects of physical performance. . . . as well as mental . . .and emotional . . ."

"Supersoldiers. I caught wind of something like that. But I don't pay any attention to the rumor mill, sir. I simply do my job." Said Gary, making Grey fully aware that he did not care to know more than he already did. He also wanted to look professional – this little backdoor maneuver could get him fired, and even worse, thrown in jail for treason. But it was worth it. He didn't like the feeling associated with betrayal, but it paid well.

Too well.

"Loyalty, Gary, is hard to find. I trust that you are a loyal man. Going behind the backs of your superiors is . . . not seen as an honorable. But let me assure you, that you are helping America to prosper."

Grey opened his desk and pulled out a thick envelope glued shut. He put it on the table and slowly pushed it across the mahogany desk towards Gary.

"I think you'll find that to be more than enough to pay for your loyalty, Mr. Jones."

Gary looked at the envelope. It was thick. Thicker than he was told it would be. He went to grab it — but Mr. Grey reached for the wad of paper simultaneously, his sausage-sized fingers smothering Gary's, and said his final piece.

"You know, Gary, it's hard to find a good man these days . . . one you can trust. I believe you are a trustworthy man. Thank you for your effortssss" Said Grey, this time his eyelids lowered with a cold, emotionless blank stare etched on his face. The prolonged hiss, Gary thought, must have been a lazy reflex of Grey's — or something he did on purpose because he liked the sound of his own voice. After all, everyone in Washington loved to here themselves talk.

"Ill be in contact. Good luck . . . with everything."

Gary abruptly left the office, stuffing the brown paper wad into his pocket. It barely fit, so he kept his hands in his pockets to cover it from prying eyes. His pace quickened — he did not want to be seen leaving Mr. Grey's office, or the pentagon, for that matter. It would only take one suspicious colleague in the wrong place at the wrong time to catalyze his undoing.

Gary was also a good liar. He wasn't sure if Mr. Grey believed him – he had heard many things about the Heaven's Gate program, and how the upper tiers of the military and air force were trying to handpick groups of talented Americans to be inducted into their secretive programs . . . and made into some sort of supersoldiers. At first, the rumors seemed like hapless jargon between lower-tier agents and officers. But now, he had reason to believe there was some truth to the rumors.

Also, Gary didn't particularly care about what he'd done, at least not to the FBI. If Grey really wanted that information, he'd have got his hands on it somehow. What really made his stomach twist was the feeling of personal betrayal – he knew what was in the classified envelope.

Mr. Grey wasted little time. He carefully peeled the tightly glued envelope open and let its contents over the desk. A stack of papers, which held every piece of information about a single human being you could possibly imagine. Hair color, weight, size, proficiencies, weaknesses (of which there were virtually none). Finally, Mr. Grey had exactly what he wanted. His lips formed a sleazy, evil smile.

He picked up the black phone with his right hand, covered in strange tattoos. On his pinky finger, a grey, metallic ring. His fingers mashed fifteen digits in succession. A deep-voiced man replied on the other end, to which Grey replied.

"We've found him."

Chapter 3

ANTICIPATION

Before he knew it, Anthony was back at the office. No time for Marlboros or cold beers with his uncle. No time for Jennifer, whom he neglected to call back. He realized they were in different spots and he didn't want to impose anything on her. He regretted not seeing her again, but that sentiment had a place waiting for it on some unreachable storage shelf in Anthony's heart and mind.

The booming sounds of Beretta handguns filled the gun range with deafening noise. All six shooting slots were filled with candidates, eager to show their instructor that the short break they enjoyed did not affect their accuracy. Anthony was a rock – his bullets never went anywhere but exactly where he wanted them to. He felt so natural and calm with an instrument of death in his hands it was like an extension of his arm. Other students, supposedly waiting for their turn to fire, couldn't help but huddle behind his wide shoulders to catch a glimpse of his work.

"Hold your fire!" bellowed a voice from the end of the row, barely heard. A green light on the back wall of the range turned from green to red, signaling an end to the target practice. Anthony lowered his weapon, clicked the safety button and placed it on the table in front of him. All sixteen recruits watched as the instructor, a fat, bearded man with a toothpick jostling around in his grill, walked out onto the range. The targets were set at twenty-five feet – standard body and head targets, with points assigned to each spot for accuracy. The instructor started at the other end, examining the targets one by one.

"Not bad" He said, as he ran his hand over a bullet-riddled rectangle. Most of the shots were centered around the heart and lungs, with a few stragglers lingering on the periphery of the oblique and upper shoulder. A single shot flew through the edge of the neck.

"But these ones aren't lethal, Jackson. If this guy was wearing body armor, you'd be a dead man I think."

The instructor pointed his fingers to the missed shots as the rest of the class pertinently observed Jackson's failure.

"But still, not bad. How bout' you, Williams?"

The next target in line was a mess. Only one or two bullets touched the heart region, while five or six others strayed in all directions – the arm, shoulder, lower torso, neck – and one lucky shot to the top of the cranium.

"Williams, you still drunk? What a fuckin' mess. This just isn't gonna' cut it."

The whole class chuckled.

"Sorry sir. Won't happen again." Snapped Williams, eager to be out of the spotlight.

The instructor nodded his head quietly at the next three targets, giving advice and assessing each candidates' accuracy, until he came upon Anthony's at the end of the row.

There were only two distinctly visible holes – one in the heart, and one in the head.

"You only fired twice Stall?"

"No sir. I shot em' all. Full clip"

"So you missed everything, except for these two shots?" the instructor pointed each hand toward a hole.

"Actually sir, I just kept on shooting the same place."

The instructor looked closer. He noticed that the holes were not the tell tale perfect circles that a single bullet would make, but staggered, overlapped Venn diagrams that unless careful examination was given, would look like single shots.

"I don't believe you. Damn showoff."

"Needless to say sir, he was dead before he hit the floor."

The rest of the class peered in close to Anthony's target. He was so precise with his gun that he could make bullets disappear into impossible spaces. Some of the class was jealous, but mostly they were in awe.

"Fine, you asked for it Stall. Gunney, give him the test." Barked the instructor, yelling into a closed circuit television mounted above the firing slots.

"Sir, the test?"

"Yeah Stall ya dummy, the test. It'll tell us all if you're really that good . . . or just the luckiest son-of-a-bitch I've ever seen. Let's go!"

The test was something the Instructor had developed himself. He had an extensive resume in dealing with firearms – from his stint in Vietnam in the seventies to the gulf war. If anyone in the room could devise a challenging shooting test, it was him.

"Choose your weapon, Stall. Any of these three. Obviously, each one has strengths and weaknesses. Choose wisely."

Lying in front of Anthony on the table were three assault rifles. A G-36 semi-automatic rifle with an extended barrel and padded shoulder mount for reduced recoil. Next to it, a standard M4 carbine with detachable front grip. And of course, Anthony's favorite – the long-barreled, always trusty M-16 with adjustable firing options of single shot, fully auto and three-round burst. The choice was easy.

"I'll take this one sir."

Anthony raised the weapon and popped the banana shaped clip where it belonged. He holstered the weapon against his shoulder, making sure the sights lined up properly.

"Ok, Stall. Here's how it works. Shoot the targets. You have four clips in front of you, don't waste bullets. The test will end on its own if you miss two or more targets in a row. You have to be extremely fast on the reload. Good luck."

"Huh?" Anthony asked, barely catching the gist of the instructor's explanation. Well before he was ready, an alarm sounded and two circular bulls-eyes lowered from the ceiling 10 feet in front of him and began to criss-cross very quickly in front of each other. Anthony instinctively squeezed the trigger twice, hitting both targets dead center. Before he could regain his stance, two more targets, this time at the very edge of his periphery emerged from the floor and began to coast backwards toward the wall. It was child's play. The targets dropped as Anthony aimed them down, rapidly. But it wouldn't stay easy forever.

Before the second set of targets disappeared, three fresh targets were already in view, two on the ceiling and one on the floor. Anthony's arrogance got the best of him – he misused his time. They zigzagged back and forth two or three times. Anthony missed one before it ducked back into a hole.

Dammit! He thought, but there was no time for that.

More targets began streaming wildly across the range – some far, some close. Some were smaller and harder to hit than the others. Some turned sideways for only a split second, giving him the slightest chance to mark them. By the time he had emptied his second clip, only 15 seconds had passed. The targets popped up frantically. 20 seconds down, three clips down. Anthony was so quick on the reload it was as if nothing happened. His hands moved with the precision of a robot, fresh clip in hand, ready to go, not a moment after the empty one fell out. He reaffirmed his grip each time he pulled the cumbersome firing mechanism – the only real and obvious disadvantage of the M-16.

Last clip, I hope I didn't waste too many bullets he thought, as he punched the final belt of spikes into the weapon. The last eight targets were exceedingly difficult – and small. They popped up four at a time against the back wall, twenty-five meters away. Anthony tried his best, but couldn't be sure if he hit them all. The clip wound down to its last projectiles. The floor was littered with hot casings, the air filled with the loud blasts of the weapon. Anthony squeezed the trigger furiously four or five times after the clip was empty, making an unwelcome clicking sound.

Usually he had an exact count of the remaining rounds in his clip at all times. This time, he was way off. Lowering the weapon, he let out a sigh of relief that it was over. It was a very intense thirty seconds, to say the least. Beads of sweat trickled down his face.

"How'd I do?"

The instructor walked to the far right corner of the firing room. Standing at hip level was a case with a glass box covering it. He popped the case open, revealing Anthony's score.

"Good god . . ." He whispered under his breath.

"Sir?"

The Instructor did not respond as he walked over to the firing slot, where Anthony stood, waiting. The rest of the class behind him stood just as eagerly.

"Well, Stall, I still think you're just lucky. But fact is only a few aces have ever made it past the third round, or the third clip. I thought you were done for on that first miss for sure . . . but you held your composure. Good job."

The class jumped and cheered around Anthony, as if he had saved their lives.

"You're somethin' else, Stall." Said the instructor as he walked towards the sound-proof titanium door to the facility, four stories underground.

"Chalk talk in forty, gentleman. Get a meal and a coffee into ya."

The class turned to face the instructor, who wasn't done speaking. He was normally stern and unrelenting in the mantra of his teachings, but Anthony's performance shook him. He was visibly proud of one his students, something they hadn't experienced from him.

"Stall, I Think you might just be ready for your first mission!" Said the Instructor as he swung the thick door open and left the room.

But for Anthony, it was a mixed emotion. He couldn't help but dwell on that miss. That one, single error that almost cost him the whole round.

The whole *mission.*

I can't miss like that again, he thought. *Not ever.* His perfectionist attitude, although it kept him focused like a laser beam, was also his biggest weakness. He was not good at accepting failure, especially from himself.

Now was the time for work, and to show everyone that he was the best agent in the whole organization.

* * * *

The last time Mark was on a normal jet plane he was visiting his parents. Their trailer home in St. Petersburg was overgrown with thick green grass and an assortment of flowers. He remembered playing cribbage on the front lawn with his mother and 'remembering' moments throughout their lives. The visits never lasted long, but were probably better like that. Each time he saw his mother, she would pester him about why he never chose to start a family. She wanted grandchildren, and the window of opportunity to grant her wish had all but faded.

This trip was much shorter than the four-hour flight to Florida – In fact he took *this* flight everyday. A quick jump over the mountains from McCarran International Airport - The jets leave at approximately 6:20 am and arrive just before 7:00, not a bad commute by any means.

When the planes took off, they faced due east then did what seemed like a full one-eighty. As soon as he got on the plane and until he landed, all Mark knew was that they were flying west, directly into the desert.

Everything was dark. The inside of the cabin was lit up by very dim, white lights, which had nothing to catch on. All the colors inside the plane lacked enough hue or brightness to be illuminated. The windows had covers that were bolted shut.

Mark reaches for his phone, which is vibrating. Once, a text message, twice, a phone call.

He fumbles the phone to his ear frantically.

"Hello?"

"Mr. Brathurst, this is Man Under the Mountain. I am henceforth enacting security codes Vector Alpha Boy Sigma, Boy Beta dash one-one-nine and Charitable Prize three-three-four-eight dash Alpha."

"Understood."

The phone call was brief and precise.

To any normal man, the lingo would sound like senseless babble, but not to Mark.

The first coded message meant that the plane was being diverted north to a different location for one or more of three reasons: The plane was having technical difficulties and needed to divert, but that didn't make sense – they'd have turned around earlier. Second, because a Rhyolite-level security lockdown of the facility had just been ordered, or three, because they were under attack by inbound fighter jets.

None of those things seemed like possibilities to Mark, although he had been trained to understand them. Neither did the second security code, which translated quite simply, despite its length. These codes were designed based on a mixture of two things – ability to relay a well-deciphered message to an employee, whilst also limiting their knowledge of the situation.

Telling them *just enough*.

"Charitable Prize" basically meant "Highly Valuable Technology" and the number sequence relied on the subtract 2 rule – 3 3 4 8 meant 1 1 2 6. If the decoded numbers added up to ten, which they did, every employee must then destroy every shred of evidence they carried pertaining to that technology. If deemed necessary, Mark could also face a polygraph to determine if he mentioned anything incriminating to any outsiders.

But then there was *dash Alpha*.

Any time a dash and then an Alpha appeared in code it meant one thing and had no connection to any other sequence of code previous, or after. It stood alone, translating as a universal "HUGE CONSEQUENCES IMPLIED" or "EXTREMELY SERIOUS."

Every time Mark heard *dash Alpha*, he began to think he wasn't being paid enough.

The short detour brought Mark and 14 other passengers to a purely secretive location, nestled deep within a rocky mesa. It had many names, but to him, it was known simply as 'S4'.

There was no communication between any of the passengers, ever. The secrecy of Mark's job relied on as little communication as possible – the information readily available to everyone there could spell disastrous outcomes in the wrong minds.

As the plane neared the base, the edges of the shutters gave the slightest hint of daylight. And then, all at once, darkness. The slivers of gold quickly turned jet black.

Seconds later, the thudding of the plane's wheels against the ground rocked Mark almost out of his seat. He reaffirmed his grasp of the armrest and let out a sigh.

Outside of the plane was a massive hangar, larger than any above-ground hangar on the planet. The ceiling rose a hundred and fifty meters high, and the 'runway' itself spanned 6 lengths across. Almost invisible were glowing neon signs above hollowed out doorways chiseled into the distant walls. Yellow and black arrows directed planes, as well as foot traffic. Even more interesting to Mark was that there was no visible entrance from which to come in, let alone fly a plane through. Just massive rocky walls.

Mark followed the painted angular path towards the wall in front of him, carrying his jacket and a briefcase cuffed to his wrist. It took him past a series of planes being guided and controlled by men waving fluorescent batons dressed in blue jumpsuits. Finally, he reached one of the doors, which was much bigger than it looked from so far away.

The message from the plane still reverberated in his mind but there was nothing more to be heard of it. Guards lined a stairway leading down through the door, encouraging everyone leaving planes along the route. Mark complied, making his way down the spiral along with two dozen other government employees.

Something must have happened, he thought. He also remembered the first time he heard security codes implemented – in training he never believed they'd actually be used.

. . . Vector one-one-zero "Resolute Prometheus" dash Beta . . .

A simple code, meaning that he'd have to stay an extra night, either because the planes couldn't make it, or because of something "ABOVE SECURITY CLEARANCE".

That's what *dash Beta* meant.

Mark had become so good at telling secrets, and keeping them, for so long, that it became part of his very soul. His parents believed he was an airplane mechanic at the airport. His few real friends knew him as an outgoing, fun-loving brother.

It was all a charade. The truth was, he himself believed he was the type of person his friends saw him as, but that his true self had been all but destroyed by the nature of his job. It was beginning to get to him. The secrecy and security of this place ran too deep for his liking, and he was beginning to feel a tinge of uneasiness about it all.

He wanted out.

* * * *

Anthony stood up straight in his chair at the front of the classroom. He could feel a different mood in the class than the usual, humdrum group of lazy-eyed observers paying half of their attention to the instructor. Everyone was on edge, for they now had badges. Every one of them, at any time, could be plucked and thrown into a mission, domestic or international. Anthony could not wait for the opportunity. Whatever it was he would be assigned to do, he was going to do it with utmost precision and focus.

After a few moments of silence, the burly, shaded instructor entered the classroom which was filled with sunlight – a welcome benefit denied in the subterranean firing halls. It lit up the prickly stragglers of facial hair that escaped his beard. He adjusted his belt and eyed down the classroom full of students.

But they weren't students anymore. The instructor's normally blank expression was replaced with a smug look of self satisfaction, as if he was singly responsible for the success of the cadets – like a father taking off the training wheels.

Maybe he was. Anthony didn't care. He was eager only to hear whether or not he would embark on his first mission. There was a surmounting anticipatory tension in the air that could be cut with a knife.

"Okay, you slugs. Time to look sharp. Williams! Put that shit out and pay attention!"

Williams, ever the troublemaker, waved his shaggy blond hair to the side as he took one last drag of his cigarette. Part of his locks covered a scar hidden on his left upper cheekbone and over his eye lid.

"Alright, here's the situation. We've got a particular target this time boys."

Everyone's ears perked up, their postures shifted.

"Recent Satellite footage shows the location of a high value target. The DEA and ATF have suggested we get further intel before a joint-ops pursuit is ordered."

The Instructor pinned pictures onto a board as he spoke.

They revealed a crowded European city with narrow streets and few cars.

"Ahmed-Al-ak-a . . Al – ak – aaaa"

"Al Akazawhi, sir." Said Anthony, who quickly made memory of the name, written sloppily in black marker next to his profile.

"Thanks, Stall. Ahmed Al Akazawhi. We have good reason to believe he may have ties to a North-American corporation called DynaTech.

Alakazawhi runs a drug and gun smuggling operation with laundered money that DynaTech writes off. First off, I'm gonna' need four volunteers, 24 hour surveillance at the dock site over the next ten days. You'll be assisted by four or five DEA guys in UC. We believe Al Akazawhi has it set up so that everything runs smoothly, hidden through the docks and their takin' a cut."

The class looked at the instructor stunned, as he pointed to various pictures and targets, then at each other. They were shocked into the realism of their first mission.

"I'll go." A voice barely spoke from the back, belonging to Jim Durst.

"I live right down by the docks, have my whole life. I know the area and some of the people pretty well."

By now, most of the *agents* in the class began to take notes with pen and paper.

"Excellent." Replied the instructor, still scanning the ranks to find more volunteers.

"Ramirez, Stiltzy and Barritzer. You three will go with him."

The Instructor didn't have time to let them figure it out for themselves. After all, he was there, now, to issue them orders.

The agents accepted them. Some of them wrote it down.

"Perfect. I'll explain the situation a little further tomorrow morning. But as for now, we need to implement part B. . . "

The Instructor put his hands on his waist and looked into the floor, enveloped in deep thought.

"We're sending a surveillance team over there. This guy likes to stay in the Middle East but for some reason, we got lucky. We think he might stay here for a while, and it's fully within our reach."

"Sir, got lucky?" Asked Anthony.

"Yeah. Fortunately for us this dumb fuck went on vacation, or so we think. Not too often world-class criminals decide to do that. He practically gift-wrapped himself."

This sounded juicy. A nice trip to Europe, some easy surveillance work. Not bad for a first mission.

"Stall, you up for it?"

Anthony was ready for it, regardless of what it was. The instructor could have asked him to walk on the moon, and he'd have said yes.

"Absolutely sir." He replied affirmatively.

"Good. Then you'll be paired up with Williams. Keep an eye on each other out there."

Anthony turned and locked eyes with Williams, who was already fixated on him. A wild card, for sure. Someone he didn't know very well, and maybe didn't trust - at least not yet.

"You got it sir," piped Williams from the back of the room, still focused, eyes unwavering, on Anthony's.

"Alright then. Class dismissed. Dock crew, I want you guys all here at 0800 tomorrow morning. We'll go over the specifics."

The agents acknowledged as everyone began to pack their things and file out of the debrief room.

"Stall, Williams. You stay here for a minute."

The words caught both of them halfway to a stand. They looked at each other and sat back down.

The instructor sat on an empty desk between Anthony and Williams, and took off his hat.

"Listen guys, anything can happen overseas. It's very important not to be seen. The slightest hiccup in the field can hold huge consequences . . . death even. Remember your training, and come back in one piece, alright? And Williams, no hero stuff. You too Stall."

"Understood sir."

"You two are the best of the litter. I'm sure you'll do a great job. Both of you."

Anthony was an obvious frontrunner for the top cheese, but Williams, he didn't expect. He was overly opinionated, untrustworthy and tended to be ignorant. He also wasn't the best with weapons. The instructor's vote of confidence in Williams came as quite a surprise.

"And remember guys, this is not a drill. This is the real thing."

Anthony and Williams both nodded their heads, eager to impress and accomplish.

And so it was. Anthony would finally embark on his first mission as an agent, just like his Uncle, Mother and Father before him. He had waited his whole life for this – the moment didn't occur exactly how he had expected.

"Oh, and one more thing guys. Since we don't know exactly how long Mr. Alakazam plans on enjoying himself, we can't waste any time. Your plane leaves tomorrow."

Chapter 4

FRUITION

Mark waited, and waited, and waited some more. Time stood still in this place. No sun, no windows, no clocks. Some civilians had found quiet spaces to carry out mundane tasks, others remained cooped up just like him. The room he was in had extremely low rock ceilings, and branched off deeper into the mountain in four directions, four stairways. Half the people in this facility carried guns.

The message must have been for real. Something was actually happening. Something serious. Whatever it took, as long as it took, he knew he had to get out of that place and start looking for a new job . . . something less trying on the nerves. His parents needed him to be around more often. They were not long for this world. He didn't know if he wanted a family, but he was certainly willing to give it a shot.

But had he gone too deep? How would he leave, knowing what he did? It all started out as reverse-engineering a downed Russian spy satellite in order to decipher and intercept their transmission frequencies.

They needed his *abilities*.

He thought he was helping his country – but after a few years he realized he was only helping the corrupt powers that be maintain their secretive, informative grip on the natural world. Mark had seen and done things that would be considered impossible to the common man.

He had even been privy to the intricate details involving a few high-profile domestic and foreign assassinations. Like an awkward cliché, he pretended not to know when his inner circle talked about what they saw on the news.

All for the safety of my Country was what had been shoved down his throat. After many years, *All for the rich to become richer* was more like it.

If Mark had to assign a label to his profession he would say *traitor*.

I'm a professional traitor he thought. *And I'm damn good at it.*

Each of the four stairways began flooding a stream of people into the room. Who knew where they were coming from, or what they were doing. Two men dressed sharply in suits and polished shoes emerged from the edge of the stairs, bobbing their black-clad bodies from step to step. They approached Mark, who wasn't surprised. They held expressionless faces covered with black sunglasses. Rubber wires extended out of their ears and down their backs.

Both men towered above him.

"Are you Mark Brathurst?" Asked the one on the left.

"Y-yes, I am. W-who's asking?"

The two men looked at each other.

"Come with us sir. There's been a change of plans"

"Whaddya' mean?"

"Please sir, we have orders to take you back."

He didn't have a choice, which was always the case anyways. The men escorted him back up the long, winding stairway, and out onto the expansive platform. They walked over to a set of elevators meters away from the doorway. One of the suited men flashed a paper-thin card in front of a holographic scanner mounted on a metal, hip-level pedestal. The elevator slid open and they entered.

Even if he wanted to ask, the guards probably wouldn't answer him. They were doing their job, and they never messed up. Mark admired their dedication but their demeanor was thoroughly frightening.

The buttons in the elevator went from 1 to 6, all going down.

Once again, the tall guard looming over Mark's right shoulder revealed the paper-thin card from before. He waved it gently over the holographic button pad. When he did, fifteen more holographic buttons appeared with a bright yellow lining.

Always so secretive.

The guard pressed the very last button on the pad, as the elevator descended into the depths. Mark felt the grip of descent warp his stomach.

The elevator was as bleak and boring as the guards escorting him, but its ridiculous speed made up for it. The gravitational distortion came to an evening point, and the metal contraption came to an abrupt stop. Mark felt his feet come back underneath him, his g-force induced tunnel vision disappear.

The metal door slid open quietly, revealing a relatively small room, compared to the earlier environments. The floor was made of an interesting red and white marble that made footsteps loud and echo. Rows of columns made of the same material extended into the uneven ceiling, lined decoratively with circles and pegs. Past the columns, a bigger cavern – a drop off.

Mark hesitantly walked through the room towards the edge, the suited guards giving him the slightest guidance.

Are they gonna' throw me off? He thought. It certainly looked that way, as if they had a designated floor just for tossing people when they needed to. As he neared, he noticed – a slit in the floor – something peculiar.

Stairs. Invisible from the elevator, until now. Death would have to wait.

The white metal and glass railing lining the perfect edge created an optical illusion. Geometrically centered in the middle of the edge where the stairs lay, there was an extra protrusion only visible upon nearing approach. The stairway entrance, narrow and curved, was angled in a way as not to catch any light.

The stair way went straight down along the right side of the edge in one direction for quite a distance. The opening at the end revealed a smidgen of sandy-colored floor. He was compelled to look over the edge but it might alarm the guards unnecessarily. The long descent fatigued Mark, more in mind than body, but it all made sense when he got to the bottom.

More red and white marble pillars, these much thicker and taller, planted into the ceiling. The wall opposite the edge dipped down, then horizontally, revealing a roof and small chamber.

Just beyond the massive pillars which reminded Mark of giant cedars were two sets of trains. Long, stainless-steel colored reflective cars linked by a very small black rubbery section, every hundred feet. The nose and sides were curved perfectly. No windows, except for a shiny blue surface wrapping the end of the cylinder – the cockpit. It looked like a visor on a helmet.

As the trio approached the vehicle an invisible door sunk in then slid across on its own. The shiny outside lining of the train retracted like skin. Mark was startled – and he noticed no wheels, no tracks. Underneath the train was a flat, skinny slab of shiny alloy scarcely lined with encased bulbs and metal levers.

"Enter, Mr. Brathurst."

The guards followed him inside the train. To his left, sitting on a bench with a guard of his own, Eugene Spelnyk. A flight simulation engineer he recognized from days earlier, and to his right, a very dangerous looking man. Dressed from head to toe in nothing but black with all black sunglasses to match and perfectly straight hair. Every extendable limb carried a strap with a weapon on it – each thigh held a handgun and a knife was strapped sideways to his belt. A large sling diagonally across his torso supported an assault rifle on his back. Thin, strange looking body armor lined his waist, neck and ribcage, which bolstered magazines and who knows what else. He leaned over a row of chairs, poking a swab down the barrel of a Desert Eagle with its various parts spread out in front of him. Mark didn't want to look him in the eyes.

"He will escort you both from here."

Both of Mark's escorts and Eugene's left the train. He and Eugene couldn't help but stare at the ominous black assassin. The train kicked and pulled, Mark grasped a pole for stability. The assassin was unaffected, as if he was used to it.

"Train's moving. They go up to nine hundred miles an hour you know." Said the black-clad character.

"We'll be back to homebase soon. You two just sit tight."

His tone was calm and sounded sincere – like a sheep in wolf's clothing. Mark tilted his head back and closed his eyes as the train began to pick up speed.

* * * *

One thing Anthony didn't expect was how soon everything would fall into place. Finally, a challenge for him. Finally, his anticipation and awareness were being tested.

Williams reached for the ceiling and turned on the overhead light. He revealed a thick book, reading glasses and shut the window next to him. In front of Anthony was the retractable platform full of pictures, documents, even notes he had taken in previous classes. His writing was always clear, precise and meticulous. He had even stopped and made smaller versions of the evidence – making them concealable. He peered carefully into the folder, wearing glasses of his own. Only split second refreshments were possible. He did not want to risk letting someone on the plane or one of the stewardesses see what he was reading. The old lady across the aisle . . . asleep. Next to her, an even older man, eyes closed. Stewardess just made her rounds. Perfect time for a peek.

Ahmed Al Akazawhi

5'8"

Brown hair/brown eyes

Born: 23/05/1974

Profile: Suspected international drug and weapons dealer

- *Known ties to Hezbollah, Taliban, ISIS, NRA*
- *Suspected ties to North American Corporation DynaTech, suspected ties with European drug lord Cezar Luis.*
- *Known to employ one or more 'decoys'*
- *Al Akazawhi has a large scar on his right forearm and a tattoo of Fidel Castro on his left calf muscle.*
- *Walks with a slight limp, due to injury sustained during the Gulf War.*

Notable Events: Suspected involvement in hotel bombing in Republic of Congo, 2015, although only circumstantial. Suspected supplier of US armaments to foreign national aggressors in China, Libya, Russia, Afghanistan, India, and 11 others.

Danger Level: Serious

Threat Level: Serious

Target Acquisition Importance: Extreme

Al Akazawhi has been rumored to carry fully automatic machine guns on his person. He rarely goes anywhere without multiple armed guards.

A businessman a few aisles up raised from his chair and turned towards the back of the plane. Anthony quickly shut his folder and removed his glasses.

"What are you reading?"

Williams flicked the paperback around. On its cover read "ART OF WAR" –Sun Tzu.

"Good Book?"

"Absolutely. Very insightful. You ever read?"

"Only textbooks and reports, ha ha"

"Well this kind of relates to our job. It's about more than just fighting, but also deception. And tactics. Ya know, all the other boring stuff."

Anthony didn't think any of that stuff was boring.

"I'll have to try it out some time," Said Anthony, hiding his sarcasm. Williams was different than he thought. Or maybe he was just trying to look smart. He seemed to have extensive knowledge of all the equipment they brought with them, so maybe Williams would be useful.

The plane landed. Anthony and Williams caught a cab to a hotel, and set up shop. The first order of business, at least to Anthony, was to coordinate a birds-eye map with the evidence photos. He popped open a high-tech laptop which came out of a Styrofoam-studded suitcase, and peeled open a city map that he had grabbed on his way out of the airport.

"I'm hittin' the bar. You comin'?"

"Are you kidding me?" Anthony asked, entwined with paperwork and electronics.

The two looked at each other, completely differing mindsets clashing.

"Suit yourself. We got plenty of time for that later. Try to enjoy yourself once in a while, Stall."

Williams thudded out of the hotel room and made his way to the elevators. Anthony went to work, typing addresses, street names and coordinates into a group of different specialized programs on the laptop. It didn't take him long to match all the pieces together. Within minutes he had enough information to make a plan, down to the minute intricacies. A gust of wind rushed in a window that Williams had opened to blow smoke out of, sending a neat stack of papers into disarray. Anthony leapt to the window, annoyed, and shut it. Above the skyline rose the signature silhouette of an upside-down golf tee – the Eiffel Tower. Anthony took a moment to admire its beauty, which had a calming effect.

Maybe he should enjoy himself a bit, he thought. Consider it a job perk.

After all, there wasn't much he could do today. Tomorrow would be different. Anthony grabbed his suede jacket and left the room.

Williams was exactly where he said he'd be, entrenched firmly on a barstool in the lobby venue. He was taking his time to examine the variety of females in the room while sipping an elegant mix of ice and brandy.

"I decided to take your advice, Williams. Get me one of whatever you're having."

"So you've come around! I figured you would Stall. Always so stern. Like a robot. We're in Paris, Bro!" Said Williams with a smile. "The mission will handle itself."

No it won't Anthony thought. *I will.*

"I've organized the gameplan for tomorrow. I'd like to go over it with y-"

"Yeah, yeah. We'll figure it out." Interrupted Williams. "By the way, call me Eric."

It was the first time Anthony had heard Williams' first name since the first few roll calls. He felt like he instantly knew him better.

"Alright, Eric. We'll do it your way. As long as you promise to do your job tomorrow. This isn't a game anymore." Said Anthony, as the waitress stopped to take his order. She noticed how serious Anthony looked, virtually ignoring her.

"Il veut la meme que moi, s'il vous plait" said Eric as he downed his drink. "Un autre pour moi aussi."

The waitress smiled and closed her writing pad. Eric turned and faced Anthony, all joking aside. The muscles in his face became devoid of creases and limped to a lifeless, cold stare.

"I'm an agent too, Stall. I know what I'm doing. Just because I'm not a god damn superhuman doesn't mean I can't do my job, and do it well. I know how to read a situation as well as you do, so maybe you should start looking at me as an asset rather than an enemy, got it?"

Anthony was quite surprised by Eric's boast, and he respected him for it. He also resented being called a superhuman. The situation was a tricky one to build a trusting relationship in so he would have to make some sacrifices in order to build that trust. Eric was his only friend here.

"Alright, Eric. I have a meeting later with the contact Head Instructor James gave us. I'm going alone, it'll draw less attention." Said Anthony. Eric did not say otherwise, nodding his head habitually.

"Oh and Stall, one more thing. You notice him?" Eric referred to someone, without pointing or looking.

"Who?" Asked Anthony. He truly had no idea.

"Him. Over there. Don't look now, at your 7 o'clock just past the doorway, on his cell phone. Gray suit. Tall."

Anthony slowly turned his head to make it less obvious. Eric had spotted something he had deemed a worthy target. More importantly he had spotted something crucial that Anthony missed.

"Missed him, Stall? Thought you had that profile stitched up. He was leaving when we showed up this afternoon."

The man looked familiar — one of Al Akazawhi's errand boys. For a second he thought the man may be onto them, but his presence seemed to be a random occurrence. Eric's perceptive ability surprised him a great deal.

"You think he's onto us?" Asked Anthony, quietly.

"No, I don't." replied Williams. "If he was, I think he'd have tried to kill us already."

The two looked at each other and Williams slowly began to develop a cheeky grin. He started laughing out loud in Anthony's face. Anthony laughed as well. Stoicism had it's drawbacks in espionage, it made identification easier for anyone who was looking. Keeping a relaxed, normal-person attitude was as important as anything technical for blending in as a regular civilian.

"I think it's another gift. Maybe we can tail him. Go have a cigarette outside, or make a phone call. Try to see what he's driving, and get the plates."

Anthony caught Eric's drift loud and clear, and added his own insight.

"What about a mobile tracker?"

"Good idea. I've got two of them upstairs. I'll try to make it back down in time before he leaves. When I come down, try to stall him."

"Whaddya' mean, stall him?" Asked Anthony, confused.

"I dunno, just get in his way!"

Williams left before his second drink arrived. It looked peculiar, but not many people saw. He walked nonchalantly toward the elevator.

Maybe he's not so bad Anthony thought, surprised by Eric's style and ingenuity. The man didn't seem to be going anywhere. He spoke in Arabic, a most recognizable dialect, over the phone. Anthony, well versed in the ancient language, wasn't quite close enough to make out what the man was saying. He decided to get closer. On his way outside he caught a series of throaty syllables.

Eric twiddled his thumbs fervently as the elevator lights went from one to the next. Finally, the 11th floor arrived. He shot out of the elevator, and down to 1107. The trackers were in a pseudo-compartment on the outside of the suitcase that held the crypto-laptop that Anthony brought.

Anthony waited outside the glass doors of the hotel, a row of sedans and station wagons lining the curb in front of him. He peered back inside, giving the man a quick up-and-down. There's no way a man dressed so sharp would drive anything regular. Directly in front of him, a Volvo – and another. Next to them, a BMW sedan with rust on and around the tailpipe and in the wheel wells. Not a chance.

Anthony walked several meters down the valet sidewalk, lighting a cigarette to seem less suspicious. Two cars in front of the parked BMW sat a brand new pearl-colored town-car with a silvery – chrome colored band wrapping around the midsection. *Bingo.*

Before Anthony could get any closer, a driver popped the door open, wearing a tidy, blue three-button suit and a hat with a beak. He noticed Anthony but was oblivious. The driver looked around and began to march over to the end of the sidewalk and around the corner of the building.

Anthony assumed he was taking a leak. He peered back into the glass windows lining the building, the man still on his phone. And also, Eric, trudging down the hallway from the corridor of elevators with the slightest pop in his step, only noticeable if someone was looking for it.

It was perfect timing. Eric burst out of the building and made his way toward Anthony. Concealed, he flashed one of the palm-size trackers in his left hand, and then quickly covered it from sight again. But there was a problem – Anthony looked around, to make sure the coast was clear, but the man was not there – he was already on his way out of the building and back to his car. He noticed a flash of grey in between the gap in the windows. He was moving fast. Anthony would have to improvise.

"Do it." He said to Eric. "I'll distract him. Driver's around that corner." Eric didn't quite know what to do, so he followed suit, feeling like a sitting duck.

Anthony was nervous as well. His legs began to move hastily towards the door. He locked onto the flashes of grey passing through each staggered window. As he approached, he picked up his pace just a bit.

Eric knelt beside the car. It would only take one person's eyes to reveal him. He placed the device under the rear wheel well, unwrapping a foil surface that revealed a sticky rubber adhesive – but it wouldn't stay stuck.

Anthony had no choice. He collided into the man on a right angle, pretending to text on his phone as Eric frantically prodded the chassis for a better spot.

They both fell, Anthony to the street and the gray-suited man back into the glass door. A woman behind him shrieked, startled.

"Je suis désolé, un accident! Oh mon dieu, je suis désolé!"

Anthony tried his best to act like a Frenchman. The man recollected himself and got to his feet. He had a look of utter disgust on his face. His dark, thick eyebrows arched and firmed, his jaw squeezed tightly.

Nice! A flat surface. . .

Got it!

Eric rose to his feet and turned his head, lifting his legs into stride seamlessly. Seconds later, the driver emerged from around the corner. Eric hoped no one had seen him. He saw Anthony with his hands up, and the target staring him down with his fists clenched. What kind of half-ass diversion had Stall conjured up?

The man took a step closer, and another, as Anthony backed up. He spit at Anthony's feet, cursing in his native tongue as he walked to his car, which Anthony had guessed correctly. He and Eric locked eyes and let out a sigh of relief, realizing how close they both came to being exposed.

"Man that was arrogant. And bold."

"Yeah. Way too close. We need to be way more careful than that from now on."

"Yup. And what the hell were you thinking running into him? Honestly?"

"I had no choice. You needed the time. You should be thanking me."

Eric nodded his head.

"Maybe your right. Thanks."

Finally, Anthony and Eric were beginning to understand each other. They both realized that their petty differences would have to be put on hold. Screwing up in training meant a retry – there were no retries in the field.

"And let's not do anymore of that cowboy shit again. I don't plan on gettin' bagged on my first mission."

"I agree. Let's go get that tracker beacon online."

Although they fumbled, juggled and sloppily got the job done, they had done it nonetheless. Being an agent was more than it appeared, and certainly more difficult. There was no way to prepare for every situation in training. Not everything would be so precise, so tactical, and he'd have to deal with personalities like Eric Williams.

The air in the room was serious. Williams hadn't smoked a cigarette or cursed since the lobby, Anthony didn't speak. He was fully engaged with documents, pictures and a keyboard.

Mohammad Sharif Al-Rahim. The fact that Eric had noticed him before he did made him nervous. Were his skills as good as he, and everyone thought? One skill he would certainly have to learn on his own is to accept that he was human, and he too made mistakes. On the other hand, what happened was unacceptable. He would have to be better, stronger, and smarter, no matter what. Torn between ideals, Anthony's only escape was to focus diligently on the mission - To make sure things went much smoother than before.

"By the way Stall, how did you know that was the right car?" Asked Williams, emerging from his novel.

He *didn't*. It was basically a guess – an educated one.

"I don't know. . . . I don't know."

Eric chuckled in disbelief and returned to reading. His condescension annoyed Anthony but he couldn't do anything to remedy it. He hoped the contact he would meet later had a more compatible personality. Anthony looked at the clock in the corner of his computer screen.

"I'm leaving now. I'll be back later. You gonna' be here, Eric?" Eric did not respond, but waved his idle hand in a whimsical gesture.

Anthony put on his leather coat and grabbed a set of room keys off the wall. He could use some time outside, out of that room, away from Eric. The contact was two and a half miles away – a hefty scamper, but Anthony looked forward to it. He would have plenty of time to drive when he got back home and got a hold of his brand new Camaro. Maybe he could do some sightseeing on the way.

The roads and buildings all looked the same. A slight wintery breeze rolled through and disappeared sporadically. The chalky grit of stone streets scraped off his Italian boots with each step. The locals moved much slower and more gracefully, seemingly never in a rush to get anywhere. Wherever he went, the Eiffel's looming gaze followed him. It was like the North Star of Paris. Avenues and streets wound in diagonals and awkward splits made it more difficult than it should be to traverse his intended route. Street performers sang songs and played instruments. He even saw a mime. *Typical.*

Finally, after a series of short lefts and rights, he came upon a particular street corner, angled very steeply – like the Flatiron building in New York. Outside the building were multiple sets of wiry metal tables and chairs, some with umbrellas. There was a sign on the upper lip of the embroidered building, reading *"Souvenirs d'Italie."* This was it. He approached the building confidently, which seemed devoid of human presence. The lights were bright and illuminated the entire restaurant and some of the dark street – but where was the contact? Anthony pushed the creaky door open to the sound of jingle bells. Seconds later, a bald head poked out from an arched doorway from behind a row of barstools.

"Hey there, I'll be just a minute. Have a seat anywhere." Said a voice from the back room. The sound of crackling, popping and bubbling was accompanied by a most welcoming aroma. Whoever was back there was making something that smelled delicious. Anthony squatted into a wooden chair that groaned and creaked as he put his weight on it. After a minute of silence, the man emerged from the kitchen, holding a large plate full of multicolored linguini smothered in tomato sauce, vegetables and roasted chicken. He wore a long apron with a white t-shirt, all of it covered in grease and dirt. His bald, oily scalp shone underneath the light. The man had very kind-looking eyes and a wide, inviting smile. His back hunched badly. This guy really played the part – no one would ever believe he was an American.

"You must be Stall," Said the man, as he placed the steaming dish in front of Anthony.

"That's right. And you are –"

"I am." Interrupted the man. "Please, eat. I think you'll find that it's quite good."

Anthony wasn't hungry, but he also did not want to insult the man. He picked up a fork and began twirling noodles around it, lifting the fork for his first bite. He wasn't lying, it was delicious. Some of the best pasta Anthony had ever eaten. He wondered if the man was actually Italian, because he sure could cook like one.

"So they sent you after Akazawhi. Stupid man he is. Thinks he owns the whole world, thinks he can go wherever he wants, like we're not going to find him."

"You're right" replied Anthony, his words hindered by a mouth full of food. The food was so good, he couldn't help himself. He shoveled it end over end into his mouth like he was addicted.

"I hear you're at the top of your class" Said the man. Anthony was surprised he knew so much about him.

"Maybe. I don't really pick. I can shoot good." Said Anthony, still engulfed in the plate.

"I bet you can. Very skilled, just like your parents."

The words stopped Anthony dead in his tracks. The man looked at him with a barely-noticeable grin on his face.

"You knew my parents?" Asked Anthony, placing the fork down.

"I did. Two of the best agents . . . and human beings I had the pleasure of knowing."

This was all too abrupt for Anthony. He couldn't understand why this random person half-way across the world would bring up his parents. No one ever did.

"You look like your father. A spitting image. He was one hell of a man, Anthony."

"So I've heard. How did you know them?" He asked, intrigued.

"I met them years ago, before you were born. I dare say, your father saved my life one time."

"No way. . ." said Anthony. Besides the few things his Uncle told him, Anthony really didn't know much about his parents. He didn't live by any close relatives and none of his distant ones ever spoke about them, neither did the higher-ups in the service. Each word that came out of the man's mouth teased and intrigued Anthony's thirst for knowledge.

"What happened?" Anthony asked.

"Let's just say I was young and dumb, and he came to my rescue. . . Anyways Anthony I just wanted to say it's a pleasure to meet you."

The conversation quickly reverted back to focusing on the reason for the rendezvous.

"Please, eat it all."

Anthony didn't hesitate. He shoveled the last few bites into his mouth, devouring the meal.

"Now let's get down to business. Basically, everything you need to know is in here. Keep this close."

The man slid a tan-colored envelope across the table, big enough to fit regular 8x11 paper.

"That's it?" Anthony asked confused – he thought the meeting would be longer and more complex.

"That's it. And Anthony – be safe out there. You never know who is watching."

The man waited a minute to let it all sink in, then took the plate into the kitchen. Anthony sat, staring at the envelope. Images of pictures of his parents from his uncle's house streamed through his mind. He came to his senses, pocketed the envelope and left the store. All he was thinking about as he pushed the door open was how satisfying the pasta was and how full it made him.

The man waited until Anthony left. A corridor to his right, between the end of the counter and a stack of potatoes lit dimly blue held a freezer at the end of it. He made sure to lock the front door. He made his way back to the freezer and popped it open, revealing a variety of frozen foods – entwined with them, an equally frozen human body. The hand stuck up, fingers twisted and contorted and the face had a ghastly look upon it. The man bent over and shoveled a turkey and some vegetables out of the way. The corpse had an apron on as well.

He kept tossing food about until he found what he was looking for. A paper, silver-gray metal strap holding several vials of bright blue liquid. He bent the lifeless arm, cracking it back down into the freezer and recovered the body with bags of food.

Removing his apron, the man grabbed a hold of the white wall-mounted phone in the kitchen and began to dial. His fingers moved at a blistering pace, dialing a total of twenty-three numbers. There was no ring, but someone was there, listening . . .

"He is on his way back to the hotel. All is going as planned. I have not been compromised. I will be returning shortly."

Chapter 5

TWISTS AND TURNS

Ahmed Al Akazawhi turned out to be a much more interesting character than anyone could have guessed. The reports were accurate – he did always have a huge entourage with him, wherever he went, always ready for a gunfight. The locals and even police officers stayed out of his way. Among his daily stops were a deluxe French spa where high-class escorts awaited him, a few driving ranges on the outskirts of the city and countless stores to shop in. Every night he visited the most popular clubs and bought the most expensive wine they had to offer. He almost fooled Eric and Anthony by sending one of his identical decoys for a drive off into nowhere. After three full days of surveillance, the two new agents felt like they knew him personally. Despite his arrogance, he was smart. No outstanding warrants, no criminal record – and he never physically touched, or even came near any product. Anthony and Eric only saw him on the phone once.

The tracker on the vehicle turned out to be a worthless risk. It didn't yield any profitable information, and those things weren't cheap. It served only as a lesson learned.

Anthony and Eric were lucky and perhaps good enough, however, to witness one of Akazawahi's rare blunders. Never using a phone could also hold consequences, as he would learn. Proudly stowed in their luggage were two-dozen hi-res photographs of a face to-face meeting between him and a fat bald man in a suit on top of a parking garage. They had to make it to the 11th floor of an adjacent building and set up their equipment before the meeting ended. It was extremely incriminating – the suited man, a foreign accounts manager for DynaTech Inc., handed Akazawhi an Ipad before he left.

Luckily, Anthony had remembered to bring his crypto-laptop and an 84A *PATCHFRAME* triangulation device. Cruel and efficient tools, able to use orbiting satellites to pinpoint certain signals, so long as you had the password. The program link on his computer added variables like speed of movement, whether the device was a phone, Ipad, computer, a radius of up to 100 miles and as little as 12 feet, signal strength, even color. . .

It generated a list of every serial code in the area that could be tracked instantly back to the FBI, and other intelligence databases to see who bought it, where, and for what price. The satellite gave them a bird's-eye view on the laptop screen, on which they could zoom in, click on the icon which stuck to the device location in real-time. If Akazawhi moved, so did the Ipad. With the tools at their disposal, it was easy to hack directly into the tablet, knowing only as much that it exists.

After the meeting was over, both men entered all-black SUVs and left. Anthony and Eric took a moment to rifle through all of the files on the Ipad. It didn't matter how far away they got. With the stroke of the "F" key, the satellite would follow the target until "M" was hit – meaning simply "commit to memory." After that, any US satellite could pinpoint that exact device within seconds.

A particular file named clumsily enough, *"Desired Commodities"* seemed to be the smoking gun. Anthony and Eric expected to see a list of weapons, maybe prices, numbers, locations, contact names that would indicate some sort of drug or gun transaction. Instead, hundreds long, a list of names, ages, weights, heights with more icons that delved deeper into the personal profiles. Were guns and drugs not enough for Akazawhi?

Now he needed to transport *people?*

Perhaps even more intriguing was whatever the hell DynaTech was doing. Anthony decided best to let the brainiacs figure out the situation back at headquarters – he had already done his job. Before copying every shred of information from the Ipad, he did notice one thing – everyone on the list was almost 2 meters tall and weighed well over 200 pounds. Most had blue or green eyes and of course, there was not a single female. He needed to get state-side, and fast – the men on that list's lives may now very well depend on his actions.

"How you feeling man?" Asked Eric, as the two found themselves walking through the airport, bags in tow.

"I feel kinda' weird. Bit of a headache." Anthony replied. He let out a raunchy burp that tasted like tomatoes, and gripped his stomach.

"Gross, man! Something's definitely wrong with you bro!" Said Eric as he patted Anthony on the shoulder. Anthony looked up and to his right, on top of a pillar. Gate 23 – 2 more gates. Was he going to make it?

"Ya' know, we did a pretty good job. I'm looking forward to getting stateside, what about you?" Asked Eric. Anthony did not respond. His vision became narrow and elongated, his hearing dulled. He could feel the nauseous effects building inside him. They made it to gate 25, where Anthony half sat, half collapsed into a row of chairs.

"Wow, man! You alright?" Eric leapt to his side, supporting him to an even keel. "Whoa man, you don't look so hot."

"Excusez, est-ce que je peux vous-aidez?" Asked a rather large security guard who had seen Anthony's tumble. He couldn't form words – it felt like his throat was tied shut. He thought he might vomit if he tried too hard.

"Non, mon ami est . . . fatigué. Avez-vous un pillow?" Eric replied. The last thing he wanted to do was cause a scene. The security guard looked at Anthony, laying flat on the line of connected chairs, and then at Eric.

"Je pense pas. Il n'est pas prêt d'entrer un plane." The guard stepped in closer, but Eric stepped in front of him before he could get closer to Anthony.

And then in a moment of purely desperate brilliance Eric reached for his badge out of his pocket and flashed it. It could be the best or worst possible decision to make. The guard looked at the badge – he knew exactly what it was. He once again looked at Anthony, then at Eric, who put the badge back in his pocket.

"Allons-y." said the security guard. He turned and walked away as if nothing had happened.

"Wha-what . . who was . . .what"

"Holy shit man, you gotta' snap out of it quick, here take thi-"

Before Eric could finish his sentence, Anthony dozed off. His head hit the chair hard enough to make a sound.

"Whew, close one buddy. Just sleep it off." Eric sat back and slid his hand into his pocket, examining the cold metal badge with his fingers. That's the second time they got lucky on this mission. He wondered what would happen on missions when the luck ran out.

* * * *

The Magneto-Levity bullet train travelled for six hours in pure silence. Mark wanted to talk to Eugene, but given the situation, he didn't see it as a necessity. He dozed in and out of consciousness as the train rumbled through the Earth. The assassin sat in the next section of the train, his legs folded. His upper half was invisible from where Mark sat. He remained there the entire time like a silent statue. Finally, the deafening white noise and hum of electric vibrations began to dissipate.

"We are slowing down. Excellent." The assassin broke the silence and came into Mark's section. Eugene heard his clicking boots and peered around the corner, wide-eyed. From where he sat, the assassin looked like a walking gun rack. Mark stood up and looked outside one of the ceiling windows, still rock, but this time discernable from a dark moving blur.

"Mr. Spellnyk, come with us. We have arrived at our destination."

Eugene glanced at Mark and tucked his eyebrows, as if to look for his approval. Apparently Eugene didn't have as high of a security clearance as he did. He wasn't accustomed to the way things really worked down here. Mark gave the slightest head nod towards the door, Eugene followed.

Outside the train looked much different than before. Everything was a grayish white color, and it was cold. *Very* cold. The Assassin didn't seem to care, as he leapt out of the train. Once again, the door slid open like liquid on its own.

The uneven ground was layered with patches of ashy dust. Their feet kicked up plumes that melted out of sight. The jagged walls were lined sporadically with clumsy wires and vent shafts with a light every 10 feet. Most of them flickered and some were burnt out.

"This way."

The assassin veered towards a circular opening supported by broken lumber beams and stilts, which tilted downwards. As they approached it, a gust of cold wind hit them. It made Mark and Eugene tense up, curling their bodies inwards. At the bottom of the ramp Mark could see something white – it must be snow – but how?

More cold air streamed up through the corridor, growing fiercer and colder with each step. They finally reached the bottom. Standing before them, a gaping void of snow, mountain and howling winds. The corridor seemed to lead to absolutely nowhere but a drop-off, a hole in the side of a cliff. Mark spread out his arms and stopped Eugene behind him, making sure not to get too close to the edge. The assassin, unfazed, reached out with his right hand to the wall. A rusty, teal-colored box popped open, revealing a metal latch. The assassin yanked it downwards and held it there.

"Just wait" He commanded.

The howling winds grew calmer, the warmth began to return. A flicker of light shot up the metal pillar attached to the latch and turned on a bright red light. Mark looked out into the expanse, and he could see what looked at first like the reflection of the sun through a distant glass surface. It grew more powerful, and brighter. The winds were now virtually gone, the cold became heat. The light began to form a jagged tetrahedron so bright Mark and Eugene had to cover their eyes. It extended across the maw, to a now visible portion of a distant rock-face.

A bridge.

"Let's go" said the assassin.

Mark and Eugene were both hesitant. But they rose to their feet. The assassin stepped on to the white-hot glow, and it supported his weight.

"Come on, we don't have forever."

They were shocked by what they saw, but proceeded anyways. The brightness came to a dull tolerability and a cylindrical shield started to form around the long, narrow bridge, concealing them entirely.

"This is fuckin' amazing." Eugene whispered under his breath. Each step on the bridge radiated bolts of wiry plasma to the edge, which reverberated up the walls and through the entire construct. Mark had seen a lot over the years, but nothing quite like this.

The bridge took at least five full minutes to cross, but finally they arrived at the end. Mark made sure not to look down. Another random hole in another random rock-face. This time, it veered upward. He was very happy to be back on solid ground. Mere seconds after they got off, the light-bridge disappeared and the thick snowy mists returned. At the top of the entrance lay a metal grate – a platform, and a large, steel-reinforced window built into the mountain, overlooking the canyon. In the middle of the platform, a dozen or so computer screens with an array of buttons, levers and control modules along with an appropriate number of chairs.

"Welcome, Mr. Brathurst, and Mr. Spellnyk. How was your journey?" Churned a voice from just beyond the platform near a grouping of stalagmites.

"Actually, it was long. Very long." Said Mark.

"My name is Mr. Brown. Do you know where we are?" Asked the man as he emerged from behind the row of spikes. He wore a large parka, buckled at the waste and very thick. He clicked a device in his hand that retracted a larger part of the metal overhang covering the window. The extra sunlight carved the bony ridges of Mr. Brown's face and lit up his grey prickly hair.

"Uh no sir. We haven't been briefed. Can I ask you one thing?"

"What's that, Mr. Brathurst?"

"Is there a hard-line here? I can't get any service on my phone and I'm sure my parents are worried sick. I'd like to call and just let them know I'm alright, and that I'm on backshift." He asked, using his hands as he spoke. He hoped Mr. Brown was a reasonable man.

"I'm afraid that's impossible, Mark. You have been brought here for a very important mission. One that transcends family . . . and other commitments."

Mark moved forward, but the assassin placed his hand firmly on his chest, stopping him. He realized the futility of his plea.

"Please, follow me. You too, Mr. Spellnyk."

The two looked for the approval of the assassin, who nodded his head and laid his cumbersome assault rifle against a rock. He sat down and began relieving himself of all his munitions, a time-consuming task considering the amount of weapons he carried.

"I'll be on the SAT-NAV downstairs sir." He said to Mr. Brown.

"Good."

Mark and Eugene followed Mr. Brown past the window and metal platform. Mark noticed something familiar, from years ago, on one of the holographic screens on the console. Past the row of spikes was a carriage elevator just large enough to fit them all on.

"Here, take these." Brown handed Eugene and Mark both a phone-sized holo-card, similar to the ones the guards had used at S4.

"Put them around your neck, they will grant you full access anywhere. Make sure the guards can see them, they tend to be quite strict about these things."

Mark examined the card as he put it around his neck. A series of translucent nodes and circuits which ran into a rectangular conductor chip at the bottom. On the top was written "Rhyolite Level 33" – a security clearance Mark had heard of before, but believed it to be a myth.

"So, Mark, you must have heard the security codes?" Asked Mr. Brown.

"Yes, actually, is everything alright?" He didn't really care if everything was alright. He just didn't want Brown to know how he truly felt. He wanted Brown to trust him.

"Somewhat. Are you familiar with Starset?"

"Yes, but only vaguely. They stopped briefing us on its construction months ago. What about it?"

"Well, it was attacked. Certain things were . . . stolen. We couldn't risk allowing anyone without proper clearance to know the whole situation. The potential consequences could be catastrophic. . ."

The security card apparently gave Mark the right to know all of these things. Mr. Brown seemed to trust him.

"Attacked? By who? A foreign power?" Eugene bantered.

"You could say that." Mr. Brown replied with a smirk on his face. The carriage came steadily to the bottom, down to another confined rock corridor. The trio walked down and came upon another massive room, encased once again in a large glass dome with a steel-ribbed grid to support each hexagonal panel. It looked like a giant honeycomb shielding them from the fierce cold winds. Mark and Eugene both looked down over the rock lip adorned with multiple ladders. And then, Mark saw once again what was on the holographic screen, and everything started to make sense to him.

Years ago, he helped reverse-engineer a so-called flying saucer for use by the Airforce. Of course the intricate details of its recovery were way above his head at the time – but not anymore. Sitting ominously on the landing pad below him were four giant shiny Frisbees. An array of mechanics poked and prodded their undercarriages, sparks flew and pieces jostled.

"Oh my god, that's the T-IV B! And you've got four of them!" Exclaimed Mark, excited.

"Your memory serves you correctly. Now you must understand why I've brought you here."

Mark had an idea, but he wasn't quite sure.

"Well, we only ever managed to get these things off the ground using conventional aeronautic engineering . . . the systems inside were nearly impossible to figure out, and we couldn't ever produce enough of the craft's original fuel."

"Element 136, you mean."

"Yes! Dragon's Breath, they called it! Stuff was so volatile it only lasted for a millionth of a second! Our engineers couldn't harness the stuff so we had to install double-reciprocity Mark-3 Levity drives in er'." Mark said, momentarily excited to see that his old project had taken off the training wheels.

"We have plenty, now." Said Mr. Brown, as he clicked another button on his wand. A rock-covered door slid open from the floor in the middle of the quartet of saucers, revealing an extremely bright orange light source, encased in a briefcase-sized carbon fiber containment mechanism.

"Our engineers have finally synthesized enough of element 136 to use as a fuel source, the way it was intended.

Mark and Eugene looked on truly amazed, as the briefcase of pulsating light lit up the whole room.

"We've also weaponized the energy. Let me tell you, it is *extremely* deadly. And that is why you two are here." Said Mr. Brown, looking down at the craft.

"What do you mean?" asked Eugene. "Weaponized?"

"Yes, Mr. Spellnyk. Using diamond superconductors we've managed to funnel the core energy into a projectile weapon.

The two looked on in silence. Everything seemed alright until Mr. Brown said *weapon.*

"I'm not going to beat around the bush. Mr. Brathurst, you are familiar with how to fly these things from remote, am I correct?"

"Yes" replied Mark.

"And Mr. Spellnyk, I understand you personally oversaw the completion of the G-11 SYNCRO-wobble drive, just days earlier?"

The mystery of their presence there finally began to unravel rather abruptly.

"Yes" replied Eugene.

"Excellent. Now listen to me carefully. A plane is about to leave Paris International Airport. You arrived with minutes to spare. Aboard the plane is a high-value target, the importance of which could determine the outcome of the United States herself. We have been ordered to destroy the target, and you two are the best candidates I could find to operate the T-IV B."

Target?

"Remember, you are doing this for your country. And Mr. Brathurst, I've had a change of heart. There is a satellite phone in the office over there. Feel free to call your parents, but make it short. We launch in less than 9 minutes."

"Thank you sir."

Marked wasted no time marching toward the office overlooking the launch pad. He picked up the phone and dialed. No one answered.

" Hey Ma, it's Mark They needed me overnight to repair a 747, phones were down and I couldn't call. I'm so sorry. I'll be home tonight." He hung up the phone and walked back to Eugene and Brown.

"By the way, Brown, might I ask where we are?"

"French Alps. 600 miles North of Paris."

The assassin wasn't lying. The train moved extremely fast, and must have been extremely deep inside the earth to have managed such a short route.

He and Eugene were alive, he had been reunited with an old passion – but still, something wasn't right. He knew he wasn't being told the whole story. Groping his new security card, he decided to ask a question he would have never asked otherwise.

"So what's the target?"

"Oh, it's a piece of cargo. A very dangerous piece of cargo. One we can't let get Stateside."

Layers of deception permeated Mark's mind. He wasn't sure whether he believed what Brown said, or if he cared enough to spend time thinking about it. Memories flashed about building the T-IVB and how difficult their operation could prove to be, especially from remote.

Chapter 6

ABSOLUTION

When it came time to get up and walk down the long corridor to the plane, the attendant taking and verifying tickets called security on Eric and Anthony. The same guard from before was on the scene quickly to explain the situation to her. Eric was relieved. He didn't want to pull out his badge again.

"F5 and F6 and . . . .Right in the middle. Better get you seated buddy. . ."

Anthony was losing focus again, quickly. Eric felt the hang of his long, nearly lifeless body as he struggled to trudge down the aisle, flinging beads of sweat about the cabin.

"Hey! Come on man! Almost there! Sorry Miss," Said Eric, apologizing to a pretty blonde women horridly offended by Anthony's proximity. After a few more cumbersome steps, he managed to fling Anthony into the last seat under the F column. His body crashed into the armrest and folded awkwardly into the seats.

Man, he's really sick, maybe we should go to a hospital thought Eric. Despite his brash nature, Eric thought Anthony was a pillar of strength – a *beast.* Seeing him this sick was slightly unnerving. A stewardess observed and heard what he did and began to walk sternly. He quickly folded Anthony's lower half into his portion of the seat and jacked his body up.

"Se-Seatbe-"

"What are you trying to say?"

"Seatbelt." muttered Anthony, temporarily rolling his eyes open.

"Gotcha."

Eric harnessed the seatbelt and latched it together, just as the stewardess arrived. He was surprised Anthony could still somewhat communicate.

"Is everything OK here?," She asked with her hands on her hips, clearly unimpressed. Eric was glad she spoke English.

"Uhh, yeah. He's uhh . . . narcoleptic. Can't control it. I'm his guardian, everything is fine. Do you have a pillow and a blanket for him?"

Quick thinking, but she couldn't believe that. Anthony was breathing heavily, sweating, and mumbling furiously – far from asleep. His eyes rolled around but couldn't focus on anything. Eric felt the badge in his pocket. He'd do it if he had to. The stewardess looked around, bit her lip and leaned in for a whisper.

"Fine, I'll get you a blanket and pillow."

Evidently she didn't care to do more than she had to, which was lucky for Eric. The last thing he wanted to do was get kicked off the plane. He had mixed feelings of relief and guilt for taking Anthony's health for granted, hoping that it was just a really bad case of indigestion or food sickness. He was further put at ease as Anthony's breathing calmed, his posture relaxed. Eric made sure to prop his head firmly beneath the pillow and cover all of his extremities with the blanket.

"Whew! Sleep it off bud!" He said, patting Anthony's shoulder. "I'm gonna' get some shuteye myself.

Eric tucked his briefcase beneath his seat and leaned it back as far as it would go. Fifteen minutes later, the plane had shot itself into the air and was beginning to climb into the blue, up and away from everything.

It was a particularly clear day with few clouds and the sun shone very bright. As the passengers found ways to occupy their time, the pilot's voice came over the radio with instructions and notifications – in French first then English. The two pilots couldn't wait to get to their homeland, the States, to see their families. Joseph Zoraster Anderson conversed with his co-pilot, a long-time friend and co-worker.

"Beautiful day. I never get tired of seeing that."

"Seeing what?" Responded Blaise, visibly tired from a harsh night in Paris. He and one of the stewardesses had gotten to know each other after a half-dozen bottles of expensive wine. He wasn't in a talking mood – hoping the "new girl" who had been with them long enough to see him commit adultery wouldn't open her mouth. His wife was easy to lie to so long as there were no leaks. Joe didn't want anything to do with it. He was happily married and cherished his wife more than anything.

"The endless blue sky, the extended horizon. It really is beautiful."

"You're right" said Blaise. "We're at altitude. Send the beverages and refreshments."

"You got it."

Joe once again beckoned over the announcement system, telling everyone to unbuckle their seatbelts if they pleased.

Eric nudged Anthony, "You thirsty?"

No response. Anthony was still out cold. The stewardess finally came to his section of the aisle with a wide smile on her face.

"What would you like sir?"

"Uhh. . .Jack and Coke, no ice please."

"Certainly, and your friend?" Asked the flight attendant, as she tilted her head into the row to better observe Anthony.

"As you can see, he's in no mood for a drink!" Eric said, patting Anthony's shoulder.

"I see." The stewardess cracked open a can of Coca-Cola while plunging her hand into the metal trolley. It came out holding a shot sized plastic container with a peel-back lid. It wasn't Jack Daniels, but it would have to do. Her other hand cupped the drink with a napkin as she handed it to Eric – but just then, as if God himself had prevented his lips from touching the elixir, a stroke of heavy turbulence jolted the entire cabin.

It was accompanied with a fierce, deafening vibration which made all the lights flicker on and off sporadically. Eric was tossed out of his chair and into the next one, but he managed to cling desperately to the armrests and nestle his torso back into the chair.

The drink flew out of her hand and into the air as the stewardess was brought abruptly to the cabin floor, screaming in terror. The unattended trolley jostled violently, its corner striking an elderly man quite hard in the temple. Strings of blood spattered onto the lights and air vents above him as he keeled and gripped his face with both hands. Another shift in pressure and gravity yanked Eric back out of his chair before he could strap himself in. The lights flickered back on. The cumbersome trolley met the floor at an angle and careened all the way down the aisle to the tail section. A less fortunate flight attendant lay pinned between her trolley, which had jammed itself sideways in the aisle, and the speeding hunk of metal coming towards her. Eric could do nothing. He heard an awful shriek of pain as everything collided. Paranoid, he felt his body up and down for injury – all good. Anthony, impossibly still asleep, was unscratched as well, although his limp extremities flailed during the chaos.

As the plane righted itself and the lights came back on, the cabin was so loud with the sounds of pain and fright that Eric could not hear himself think. Everything happened so fast. He stood up in the aisle, wondering who he should try to help first.

"Joe! What the FUCK was that?" shouted Blaise, his hands still squeezing the flight controls.

"I-I dunno. Windspeed . . . normal. Some of the electricals are completely gone. I've lost control of the aft rudder and some of the left wing. We can't turn left." Said Joe in a panic as he flipped various switches and levers, yielding no response from them.

"This isn't happening. We've got injured passengers back there!"

Both of the pilots could hear the moaning and screaming.

"Uhh. . ok! She seems to be stable again. . .for now." Joe looked Blaise right in the eye. They registered pure fear. "You go back there, make sure everyone's ok. I'll be fine up here. Try to calm them down, got it?"

"Got it. You gonna' talk to em'?"

"Can't. Speakers' blown out."

Blaise unstrapped himself and leapt out of his chair. He peeled through the blue curtain and into the first section – *business class*. Unfortunately for these higher-ups, their chairs were bigger, more spacious, and thus offered more room to be thrown back and forth. A few lucky ones had their seatbelts on. He looked to his left. A once pretty woman lay crunched in between the floor and her chair, her neck badly twisted in the midst of her blonde hair. The man sitting next to her curled up into his chair, gripping his briefcase, shaking.

He needed to get to the aft – there were no sign of the trolleys, or stewardesses. A pregnant woman obstructed his path as he tried to wiggle past. She grabbed him only to yell in his face, but he didn't have time for her. He prayed Joe could keep the plane operating. Another blackout like that and he'd be tossed like a hot potato. He finally made it to the second curtain which opened. Eric was there, with his shiny badge flashing.

"FBI. I can help." He yelled extremely loud. "Quick, to the back. The stewardess. . .she . . ."

Eric couldn't finish his sentence, after he saw Blaise's jaw drop, his eyes widen. Blaise pushed Eric aside without resistance. Eric knew what was on the pilot's mind.

The back of the plane was a mess - Unconscious bodies and battered people trying to help them. He saw a high-heel attached to a leg underneath the metal trolley, covered in blood. He didn't want to believe it had happened, but his eyes confirmed the horrific truth. Blaise dropped to his knees in despair.

The stewardess meant much more than a one night stand to Blaise – her name was Jenna, she was beautiful, and he thought he may have been in love with her. Now she was dead.

On his knees, Blaise immediately felt rage dwelling inside him, then denial, then despair.

Pure, *crippling* despair.

The other passengers who needed his help seemed unimportant now.

Eric stood terrifed, but his instinctive mind kicked in. He corralled the panicking pregnant lady, found her a blanket and strapped her in.

"Shhh. Everything will be alright. Everything is fine. See? The plane is fine." He caressed her, but she pulled away, trembling. A young man sat in the seat next to her. Eric checked his pulse and found nothing. He noticed the man had a ring on his finger, much like the one the pregnant lady wore.

Two seats up, a trickle of blood seeped into the aisle. A very small hand lay on the floor next to the red. Eric didn't want to look – he couldn't. He rushed to the cockpit amidst trying to keep his focus intact. His mind searched for scenarios during his training that might help him – nothing specific about being on a doomed plane.

"Hey! FBI agent!" He yelled, before Joe could object to this presence.

"What was that uhh.."

"Joe. My name is Joe" He blurted while frantically checking the craft's systems and gauges.

"And your guess is as good as mine Mr. . ."

"Williams. Eric Williams."

"Nice to meet you Eric. How bad is it back there?"

"Very."

"Good God. . ."

"I know, Joe. But we have to keep our composure. Can we land?"

"I'm not sure, Eric. I've never seen the controls do this . . . .Half the electrical just gave out all at once, then came back on. And thank god it did or else we'd be in the ocean already."

Eric's mind raced. Talk about bad odds, and bad timing. On the desperate reaches of his psyche resided the possibility that this had something to do with Al Akazawhi. *Was he that good?* It could also just be a malfunctioning plane. *Lightning, maybe?* There were no clouds – that didn't make sense.

"Joe, can you send a distress signal?"

"Already tried, shortwave and broadband are both out. Check your cell phone too – mine is zapped, so was Blaise's."

"Blaise?" asked Eric, pulling his phone out of his pocket.

Joe didn't answer. Then Eric pieced together who Blaise was.

Eric's phone had no signal, no power.

Zapped.

During concealed weapons training, he remembered a certain segment referring to mini-EMP remote detonated devices, sometimes carried by techno-terrorist groups – small enough to fit in a briefcase, but big enough to knock out a city block's electricity.

Was it someone on board?

"Joe, I have to know. Can we land?" Eric wanted to search for potential suspects, if his hypothesis had merit.

"Maybe. Our best shot is a seaborne landing. I have no control of the rudder, or the left wing. We're just coasting. We have enough floatation devi – wait, what the hell is that?"

Joe peered out of the cockpit window and over the smooth nose of the plane. A thousand feet directly down and to the left, his eye caught a small, silvery metallic reflection.

"What do you mean, I can't see it?" Eric shouted, devoid of recognition.

"There! Down there!" Joe stood up and pointed straight down. The speckle of shimmer stood out like a sore thumb against the blue seascape.

"What is that?" Asked Joe, as he looked at Eric who was equally dumbfounded.

"I don't know. There it goes!"

As quickly as they had seen the object, it was gone, behind the plane and out of view.

"Do you think it's someone trying to help us?"

"Could be, Joe. But I wouldn't count on it. Keep this plane airborne, I'll try to calm everyone down."

* * * *

"Eugene! Little less juice on those capacitors! Flux drive is hard enough to handle as it is!"

"Yes sir."

"Don't call me sir!" snapped Mark, wrestling the interface in front of him. 4 screens gave him a panoramic view of the T-IVB's flight space.

"Yes sir. I mean, sorry uhh Mark."

"Why the delay, gentleman?" Asked Mr. Brown, overlooking the operation from a rail above his head.

"Sorry sir, target's in sight. Eugene, one more time. This time slow and steady, ok?"

"Copy that."

Eugene's hand's floated above two spherical holograms that shone onto his hands. He took a deep breath.

"Here we go. Raise disband propensity to 7/8ths"

"Raising now!" Said Mark. Was it bad that he was enjoying this a little bit?

Eugene slowly moved his hands forward over the surface, dragging the light with him. It molded to this finger tips and followed them tightly. To his left, a large flat screen displayed the plane zooming away and veering to the right leaving streams of smoke in its wake.

"We're in position!"

The winds howled and drummed against the complex, adding external stress to the compound. Time to execute.

"Wait. Eugene, wait!" said Mark, exasperated. "You see those markings?"

"What Markings?" Asked Eugene, as he felt Mr. Brown's gaze upon him.

"On the plane!" Mark yelled, angered.

"Continue, Mr. Brathurst." Said Brown. He stuffed the uprising before it happened. Also, as quickly as he had left, the assassin returned and was standing ominously camouflaged on the platform. This time, he had a katana in his hands.

Mark felt like a fool. Foolish to believe he had a choice. Foolish to believe what he was being told. Despite the taxing fatigue of his journey to his place, he still trusted his eyes – he knew the difference, by the strike of the eye, between a cargo jet and a commercial jet.

But the fear of death, and of losing his future family, cast a greater light in his mind. Images of his wife and baby dying surged through his synapses. Maybe he didn't know it, but Eugene's life may be forfeit as well.

"Eugene. Level the thrust and take us in. Let's get a good shot at this."

Eugene hesitated.

"DO IT SSSSSPELNYK!" Yelled Mr. Brown, in a throaty, loud and frightening voice. Slobber dripped from his jaw, and he clenched his bony hands.

"Yes sir!"

* * * *

When Eric returned to the cabin, it was even worse. The painful moans did not cease, in fact they grew louder and more numerous. The aisles were filled with panicking passengers – some trying to help themselves and others, some simply panicking with no direction.

I better get to Anthony Eric thought. He didn't have time to help everyone. He leapt on top of a chair, awkwardly squeezing his torso above while his hands pinned his weight against the overhead storage compartments.

He swung his legs around and back onto clear space. The curtain was within his reach.

"MOVE!" He yelled. One hand clutched his concealed beretta, the other motioned toward his hip – and his badge. Amongst the panicking passengers, no one showed signs of suspicion. Not one breathing soul inside the contraption was calm.

Eric didn't wait to push the shorter man aside, thrusting himself back into the commercial cabin. The curtain splashed over his head, revealing Blaise – much taller than his broken, anticipatory form from before – now standing tall, eyes filled with rage. It was the only thing he was left with. Eric couldn't help but notice a face; covered in blood with an equally destroyed body attached. Blaise stood over the mess as if to protect it, when in reality his hope was lost. Everyone's hope was lost.

In their last breaths, Blaise and Eric stood, staring at each other, accepting the harsh reality that there was absolutely nothing either of them could do. Anthony remained in row F. He didn't wake up. He didn't even move.

"Oh my GOD! EVERYONE GET DOWN!!" Joe yelled – Eric could barely hear it, but he turned to see the pilot, arms raised, emerging from the cockpit. And then, a blinding white flash illuminated the whole cabin, only to spur an incredibly brief silence.

It was followed by an explosion that ripped the entire aft section of the plane off flinging passengers and hunks of churning metal out into the inner atmosphere. Eric felt the immediate grasp of pressure. He flung around, smacked his head and slid down the aisle towards the end of the destroyed plane. His hand clutched and wrapped around an armrest, but he had no chance. The chair itself was ripped and flung out into the blue – it was over.

As Eric plummeted, he watched the burning plane light a fire across the sky. The wings both snapped off, spraying their fuel and adding a series of explosions to the fireball. He could barely see a piece of land on the horizon.

People and debris fell in his proximity – he was spinning too fast to see them, but he could hear faint screams. His life flashed before his eyes. Just beneath the doomed aircraft, Eric's eyes squinted long enough to catch a faint silvery glimmer zooming away.

Before they left, the instructor told him to make sure that no matter what, nothing happened to Anthony Stall – and Eric had failed him. Anthony was the best and brightest – the future of the FBI, and he wasn't able to save him. It was the last emotion Eric felt before he died.

Chapter 7

CATASTROPHE

"I-I can't believe we just . . ." Mark collapsed in a sigh, folding his shoulders into the awkward chair. He felt an intense sickness looming inside him, waiting to get out.

"Mark? What's the matter! Mission accomplished baby!" said Eugene, smiling and happy. His grin turned to a frown.

"Eugene. No, Eugene . . . the plane . . . the markings. . ."

Mark felt wooziness inside him. He could almost *feel* the plight of the passengers, as if it were his own. He couldn't stop it – the vomit forced itself up his esophagus and out onto the pad, jerking his torso into a crunch as he did. Another wave took him to his knees and hands.

"Oh man! You alright! Holy shit!" Yelled Eugene, as he leapt from the chair to help Mark. The orbs of light surging around his fingers disappeared, and so did the screen in front of him.

Eugene embraced Mark in his arms.

"You don't understand, Eugene. That was a commercial plane."

"No, no it couldn't have been Mark. It wasn't!"

Eugene looked up at Mr. Brown for approval, but he found none. How could he have been so naïve? He and Mark rose to their feet. What now?

The assassin leapt from the balcony above them, at least fifteen feet to the landing pad. He landed evenly on both feet, with a loud metallic clamor as his boots struck the floor.

"Take them to the machine." Said Mr. Brown. He looked Mark right in the eyes – cold and threatening.

"The machine? What fucking machine!?" Yelled Eugene as the assassin moved towards him. Mr. Brown turned slowly and walked out of view. Eugene was finally beginning to realize the truth.

"We have no choice . . . we never did . . ."

"QUIET!" Yelled the assassin. He had lost his will to pretend.

"What do you mean!?" Eugene asked.

"It's happened before Eugene, I swear it!" Mark squeaked out, before the armored assassin pointed his gun,

"They're gonna' wipe our brains!"

* * * *

"You know Cap, I'm proud of ya'. And I'm also glad you had such a positive influence on Anthony. He gets back today, can't wait to hear from him. But I digress. Lemme' end this speech with a bang."

Jim stood up in their favorite diner, all of Cap's best friends had gathered to celebrate his retirement. Everyone had a big mug of beer in their hands.

"To Lester Desjardins, aka Cap, the best goddamn boss, and the best friend I've ever known. Cheers Cap, we love ya'."

Jim clashed his heavy mug into the next one, starting a chain reaction of loud tings and spilled beer. Jim couldn't remember the last time he saw Lester this happy.

"Thanks for coming everyone. I'm having a blast."

An awkward moment of silence as Lester's face turned red – he noticed everyone looking at him, waiting for more.

"Speech?" Asked Lester's younger brother, a car salesman.

"Oh no, I can't. I'm not a speech guy."

"You better!" Piped Jim. He knew how to push Lester's buttons.

How to *get to him.*

"I'm gonna' chug this beer, and by the time I'm done, you better be talking!"

"No – Jim, I –"

Too late, Jim tossed the glass block to his lips and began guzzling. The gulps were heavy, each one pushing his already stretched button-up shirt to the breaking point. He continued to lift the glass, some of the brew trickling onto his face. He thrust his arm out and pointed right at Lester, snapping his fingers. A few chuckled as their attention was directed toward Lester, stunned.

"Well, if you insist. Hmm, where do I start. . ."

"AAHHH!" Jim mouthed, then let out an obnoxious burp, gripping his stomach. Everyone around the table laughed once again. Lester could get annoyed, but why? He knew Jim's antics were only a childish attempt to lighten him up. He didn't want his friends to see him get angry, because then Jim would win.

"I've lived a long and fulfilling life. I was married to a fantastic woman, god rest her soul."

Lester touched the four points of the cross to anoint his deceased wife. A few around the table did the same.

"We produced two beautiful daughters, who are off in the world getting educated. I miss them dearly. I've also had a fantastic career, no thanks to this goon over here."

Jim looked up and smiled while pouring himself another mug.

"Means a lot to me that all you guys came out here tonight. I mean it. Uhh that's it. That's all I got guys ha ha."

"Well at least you tried old man!" Said Jim, to the tune of more laughs. Lester couldn't help but join in. After all, it felt good to speak from his heart, as cold and remissive as it had become.

Back at Jim's house, he and Lester sat and conversed into the late hours of the night.

"So when's the kid back anyway?"

"Should be back by now. Haven't heard from him yet."

Jim could sense something about Lester. Something was on his mind. He squinted his eyes and stared deep into the table, entranced in a perplexing thought.

"Why do you ask?"

Lester didn't answer right away. He had to collect his thoughts.

"Well Jim, this case we've got him on . . . it's blowing up. NSA caught wind of it after info leaked about what we found at the docks."

"The docks?" Jim asked, intrigued. Lester usually liked to safeguard information. He could tell this was serious.

"Yeah. I had McClaren assign a few of the new agents to monitor the dockyards. We had a hunch that a Middle-Eastern drug lord named Al Akazawhi was running dope into the mainland through the dockyards, right here in Boston, and possibly in Baltimore. It was the last order I gave, and of course . . . sending Anthony to Europe."

It was hard for him to say.

"*You* sent Anthony? He told me he was at a training exercise in New York!"

"I'm sorry Jim. I should have told you before. He and another recruit named Williams were sent to gain intel on Akazawhi. It was a game-time decision and they were the best two we had."

As far as Jim knew, Anthony was in Langley doing a two-day course to determine whether or not he would be a possible candidate for the government's ultra-classified remote viewing initiative. His skills were so much higher above anyone else's that it warranted a real look into his potential psychic abilities. Jim was slightly relieved – he was old school, and didn't want his boy having his mind-warped by a bunch of psycho-scientists.

"Anyways, four months ago we were investigating a money-laundering scheme run through the docks. It led us to a series of phony off-shore bank accounts controlled by a North-American corporation called DynaTech."

"So DynaTech is distributing the drugs?" Asked Jim, putting two and two together.

"That's what we thought at first. That they were paying off the dock union-heads and subordinates to keep their little operation under wraps. But here's where it gets really strange."

Jim lit a cigarette and arched his back on the front of his chair.

"We managed to get access to a few of the crates . . . specific ones. Barritzer and Durst came across a crate that had no serial tag that we could trace. And there it was. But when they opened it, they didn't find any money, any drugs, or any guns."

"I'm not following you."

"Bodies, Jim. We found bodies. Not dead, but . . . asleep. Inside large cases attached to generators that said Dynatech on them. DEA's in UC gave our boys enough time to infiltrate."

"Oh my god. Wow. What did you do?" Asked Jim. What would he have done?

"Well, we got all the intel we could gather, pictures, videos . . . a few loyal witnesses. Barritzer was smart enough to realize that he couldn't be seen by anyone working on the docks with the smoking gun in his hands, or else they'd be able to tip off the union before we could build a case around them."

"So they decided to leave the people in that crate? Are they freaking insane?"

"We had no choice. If we came out abruptly the media would twist and contort the whole thing into a fucking fiasco. We had to Jim . . . the agents put an F-A6 surveillance block inside one of the walls of the crate before they vanished. Thank god no one saw them."

"I can't fucking believe this Cap! When did you become so damn heartless? And since when did the FBI put *intel* before human lives?" asked Jim, angered.

Lester looked at him, his eyes flattened into a serious gaze.

"Jim, you know as well as I do how deeply corrupt the whole bureau is. This is far from the worst. It's the lesser of two evils. The last thing we need is a national crisis on our hands about human popsicles stuffed inside a container. Especially on New England soil. Not on my watch."

Jim clenched his hands together, his cigarette hanging a tail of ash from his lips.

"Well Cap, I hope y'all know what you're doing. I just hope those people don't end up dead . . .*on your watch.*" Jim said, pushing his finger into Lester's chest.

Lester was too intertwined with the bureau to ever leave. Although he had officially retired, a man of his status could never truly leave behind his lifeblood. It's all he knew, and damn if they didn't need him there. The next director in line, a pompous, thirty-something with a clean-cut educated background, he knew, was not cut out for such a task. His lack of real-world experience didn't sit will with Lester, and he was the only one on the council who voted against the man's ascension.

"Well, wherever that crate goes, we'll hear and see everything. It'll lead us right to where we need to be. Yer' gonna' have to trust me on this one, Jim."

"What do I care anyways? I'm out of that scene." Jim retorted. Despite how he actually felt, his words were the hard truth. He pretended as if he too were devoid of desire to be close to the biggest case, to know what the average man never would. As if he had somehow transcended it.

"I had to tell ya' about this. I mean, I'll make sure things go according to plan, but this is the strangest thing I've seen in all my years. Bodies? What for? At first I thought they were smuggling the drugs inside the bodies, but that just doesn't make sense. I'm not sure if I want to know what's on the final leg of this investigation."

Jim rose from his chair and sat on the couch next to Lester, butting his cigarette in an ashtray on the coffee table in front of them. A moment of silence diffused the situation. They were men, they had lives outside the bureau, and needed to let their brains shut off every once in a while just to keep them sane.

"Anyways. Got this the other day. Guy went on and on about this OLED technology . . . Organic Light Emitting Diorama . . . or something. I had to buy it."

"Jesus Jim, how much this thing cost?" Lester asked, shocked by the size of the television a dozen feet in front of him. Jim fumbled around the lower perch of the coffee table looking for a specific remote.

"Let's turn this sucker on."

The massive flat panel screen lit up the whole room. The same female news reporter from the bar appeared.

"-saster has struck off the coast of France earlier this evening. A 747 transcontinental airliner crash-landed just off the coast, presumably killing all on board. Official details have not been fully disclosed to the public, as the investigation continues. Airliner officials say they will have more details for us later."

The picture came into focus, revealing a split screen with headlines flying through a bar beneath the two images. On the left, a helicopter hovering around the crash site – a smoldering scar digging half a kilometer into the green canopies. The forest burned wildly. Only bits and pieces of the disintegrated plane remained, the rest of it was a speckled fiery field tracing the curved line of the crash. Individual fires hundreds of meters apart painted the sky with ribbons of smoke.

On the right, a pretty blonde reporter detailing the situation.

"Here with us is Technical Engineer Jeremy Witherspoon from the National Aeronautics Safety Commission. Good day Mr. Witherspoon"

A 4-second delay distanced the man's response.

"You too. Good day." He responded, fidgeting.

"So, Mr. Witherspoon, what can you tell us about the initial response to this disaster?"

"Well, we are keeping all options open. If you'll notice on the images being displayed now, there is no visible evidence of the wings."

As he spoke, the split screen image compacted towards the top of the television. The headlines streaming before became the viewpoint from the encircling news chopper.

"Actually Mr. Witherspoon, to me it just looks like a bomb went off, I cannot recognize anything."

The reporter waited for a rebuttal, with a confused look on her face. She was right, the entire image was a smoking mess, completely devoid of recognition.

"Indeed, you're right, from this particular image it is very hard to make out anything really. However, we did determine where the nose hit based on where we found the black box. From the information we have gathered so far, it appears the wings were separated from the craft *before* it crashed."

"So, you did find the black box? Will it be released to the public?" asked the reporter, seemingly intrigued on a personal level.

"That is doubtful as of right now. I personally have no access, but I do know that the black box has been found." Jeremy's eyes drifted off camera for a moment. It appeared as if someone was trying to tell him something.

"Uhh as far as we know there were no survivors. I mean, you can see for yourself, it would be virtually impossible to survive something like that. It truly is a remarkable tragedy, one that we may never fully understand."

Once again, Jeremy looked off camera and shifted his posture. He was visibly uncomfortable.

"Thank you Mr. Witherspoon."

Lester's head tilted toward Jim. Both their mouths hung open.

"When did you say Anthony got back?"

"You don't think. . . "

"Jesus Jim, give his phone a call now!"

Jim stretched his body out to gain access to his tight pocket, pulling out his touch phone. Nothing but a dial tone, then the answering machine. He dialed again, and left a message.

"Nothing. No answer! Shit Cap, what do we do?"

"Let's go to the bureau. See if anyone there has heard from him or Williams. I'll call Williams now! Fuck! I don't have his number. Call the headquarters now, tell them we are on our way!"

"Wait Cap, we don't know if it was his flight yet. Maybe we should think about this for a sec-"

"No way, Jim, we're not taking that chance! Grab your keys let's go!"

Cap was right. They couldn't take that chance. But there was something else on Jim's mind. Something dark, deep, nearly disbanded from memory, but always there. A secret he held for the better part of his life – from everyone. His best friends, his co-workers, and sometimes even himself, out of necessity. He prayed that, above all other things life, the day would never come when his secret was revealed.

Both of them were too drunk to drive, but who cared. They'd be speeding too, vulnerable to a pull-over. But Lester had something for that. Something he had earned, but rarely ever used. They rushed out the door, jackets in hand. Lester sent text messages and looked for numbers in his phone.

"Wait!"

"What, Jim!?"

"We're not taking that." Nodding his head towards the old Toyota parked on the curb at the end of his lawn.

"Anthony left the Camaro here. Way faster."

Lester didn't take the time to deliberate, but changed his jaunt to a stride in unison with Jim, towards the garage in the back. Just a minute later they were almost to the freeway, ignoring multiple red lights and stop signs. Lester reached down to his ankle and pulled up his jeans. Strapped to his meaty calf was something that looked like a passport, shiny black. His hand brushed it, as if to make absolutely certain that it was still there.

"What *is* that?" Asked Jim.

"Protection."

"From what?"

"Everything. Let's hope I don't have to use it."

Jim reaffirmed his grip on the wheel. He busted the gearshift up a few notches, feeling the tires grip the pavement.

It only took them seven minutes to reach the headquarters, which lay snuggled in the downtown district in a high-rise. The Camaro screeched to a halt in front of the building. They didn't expect anyone to be there at this hour.

"Who's that!?" said Lester, holding a phone to his ear. He saw a face, barely. It was faintly familiar. As he got closer, the face was attached to a body, curled up into a ball and planted against the glass lining of the front foyer. It was a recruit he could just barely remember.

"Jones! Gary Jones! What are you doing here? What's wrong!?" Shouted Lester, as he marched quickly toward the man. He corralled his bent knees with his arms and burrowed his head in between. Jim and Lester knelt down next to him.

"Alright kid, what are you doin' out here?"

Gary lifted his head slowly. He shook in self-disgust, wiping streams of tears from his cheek.

"Sir, you must have heard. . ."

"Heard what, Gary, the crash? The plane crash?"

"Yes sir. That. I . . . I can't handle it anymore. I'm sorry sir. I'm so sorry."

Jim prayed that Gary wasn't going to tell him what he didn't want to hear. He felt sick to his stomach – barely able to breathe.

"Relax, son. There's nothing you could have done. Now listen to me. You work in the administration department don't you? That means you have access to the SATNAV database, am I right? You have a passcode don't you?" Lester gripped Gary's shoulder tightly.

"Yes sir but –"

"No buts! We need your help. We have to find out for sure if – "

"The answer's yes, sir. He was. Anthony *was* on that plane. So was Williams. . ."

His fears realized, Jim's knees buckled. He looked up to the sky, lost. Everything he didn't want to happen was happening.

"How do you know?" Demanded Lester.

Gary took a deep breath, but he could not hold his composure.

"I'm so sorry sir. I was terrified . . . they knew about my family . . . I had no choice!"

Lester didn't have time for Gary's rambling.

"What on earth are you talking about son?"

"They killed them. Sir . . ."

Gary and Lester locked eyes.

"I've done something terrible!"

* * *

The hospital walls were blurry and the linear geometry of the hallway blurred into indiscernible spirals. The wheels of the medical bed twisted around the hallways and into an elevator. It brought the team of emergency medics to the fourth floor. He couldn't speak, or feel his body.

A plastic bag full of nutrients jostled around his head, attached to a few tubes that waved streaks of white around. Anthony was alive.

Glimpses of consciousness mixed into his induced dream-state, bringing him to and from the recesses of his mind. As the elevator ascended a white light overtook his senses, propelling him back into his dream – it had been going on as long as he could remember. This time, he was in control. The coffin that confined him broke open with ease and he stood up from it. Surrounding him, nothing but blackness. Space, stars and complete silence, until a faint solar wind carried the slightest touch of sound. It sounded like a faint voice growing ever clearer the closer he listened. It came over his left shoulder from the utter abyss. As the voice got louder and louder, a faint blue dot grew bigger and brighter.

He could tell it was the Earth – his home. His senses pounded with millions upon millions of horrible screams which had overtaken the soft voice. The Earth turned from glowing blue and green to red and black. Cities and landscapes lay charred and utterly destroyed; lifeless. The screams dissipated, leaving only silence . . . was this the future he was seeing?

The geometric tiles blurred into focus as Anthony's conscious senses peaked, briefly. His hand gripped the plastic rail of the hospital bed tightly and shook it. The force was nearly enough to tip the whole bed off kilter. Two nurses shouted orders in his face. The one on the left grabbed his hand and tried to restrain it but to no avail. Their lips moved rapidly but were not accompanied by any sound that Anthony could hear. As soon as he started to feel his legs again, the black endless space returned, along with the faint voice. This time, a beacon of circular, blue light emanated from his chest and extended into the endless universe. What could possibly be happening to him? His mind had no control over what he was experiencing, as if he was outside himself, looking in. The stars, all at once, ceased to be shiny dots and became lengthy, streaking ribbons. His body left the Earth and began speeding into the blue stream of light at a speed he couldn't quite comprehend. His body blended into light, becoming a vessel of pure energy traversing the stars. Eventually, a faint bluish-purple circular mass grew larger and larger in his view, and lay directly at the end of the beacon. He was moving so fast, he felt like he was going to hit it – but before he did, his eyes opened abruptly. He knew where he was now. Hospitals tended to have a unanimous, unmistakable feel and look about them. The nurses guiding his cart flung the thing through a doorway adorned with dark brown paint. Anthony extended his arm from the sheets and wrapped his long fingers around the nurse's arm.

"Wh-where am . . ."

Anthony could only make out bits and pieces of what the nurse was telling him. He decided it was a better idea to read his lips.

You've . . .Been . . . Accident . . . Hospital . . . Calm.

Normally his lip-reading skill was impeccable. He could only make out certain words, but he got the gist of it. Lip-reading wasn't the only thing he couldn't do well – his reaction time was drastically impaired. He noticed the nurse's eyes flicker. He tried to react, but he wasn't fast enough. As his head and torso redirected to the left, the other nurse had already stuck the needle deep into his shoulder. He felt the fatigue permeate his veins. He struggled to keep his eyelids open, but the dose was too heavy. They shut, and his arms went back to limp.

One of the nurses let out a deep breath and wiped his forehead of sweat. They spoke with heavy French accents, glad to have Anthony restrained. He couldn't be sure, without the sedatives, if they could have restrained him had he regained his coordination. The nurse's arm had already developed a distinct finger-print bruise from Anthony's unnaturally tight grasp.

"Wow. Look at this, Phillipe. He fucking bruised my arm."

The nurses met at the end of the bed, examining the bruise.

"That doesn't seem possible. He was just unconscious, moments before..."

"Good thing you had that cocktail handy, ha ha!"

As the nurse rubbed his sore arm, both men looked at Anthony. Besides his ravenous sporadic behavior, he appeared to be fine.

"Grab those scissors. Examine the torso."

Phillipe handed him the scissors, and he began to cut Anthony's shirt down the middle. No sticky blood revealed any obvious injuries. His ribcage moved up and down naturally, inhaling oxygen as it should.

"What's wrong with him?" Asked Phillipe, as the nurse poked and prodded his torso.

"I don't know? Apparently he was in that crash and got rushed here. Did you see that on the news?"

"Haven't had time." Said Phillipe, lifting his hands into view. They were still covered with bloody gloves from the last patient he had been working on. During the panic, he hadn't had time to properly remove them.

"Phillipe, grab that remote. Turn on the television and enlighten yourself."

Phillipe did as he was asked, flicking on the small 13" television propped high above Anthony's bed – but not before peeling off the gloves and tossing them into a nearby garbage can.

"Channel 17"

Gleaming across the tiny screen were the same images that had been streaming on every news station for half an hour now, those of an utterly destroyed landscape marred by raging fires.

"My God . . . how did you find out?"

"They were talking about it on the radio in the lunchroom, before this guy showed up. Turn it up."

Phillipe's thick fingers mashed the squeaky rubber buttons on the remote. He angled it awkwardly after a limited response from the device, its batteries taped into place sloppily. A news anchor's voice described the situation as the helicopter circled the site. The headline on the bottom read 'Tragedie dans l'aire'. As the nurses looked on, it became impossible in both of their minds that anyone could have survived. They both looked at each other, and back at Anthony, who seemed to have no visible injury and to be in good health.

"So you say this guy came from *that?* How is that possible? I mean, just look at that mess, Claude!"

Claude could not think of a reason to disagree. It simply didn't make sense.

"Either someone gave me the wrong information or . . ."

"Or *what?*" Asked Phillipe, not allowing Claude to keep it in. Claude looked at Anthony with a bewildered look on his face.

"Or he's the luckiest son of a bitch, *still* alive."

Phillipe agreed – but how could it have possibly happened this way? And why was Anthony unconscious at all? Although he wouldn't admit it, Phillipe wanted to be there when Anthony regained his wits – he must have an incredible story to tell.

"Anyways, I don't think he needs our immediate attention. Seems to be fine. I got a gunshot wound two floors up. Stay with him, re-run the diagnostics, we don't want to take a chance and miss anything. There's got to be *some* reason for him being unconscious as he is."

"Agreed."

Claude grabbed a clipboard off of a counter lining the room near the door. He rubbed his bruised forearm, and looked back at Phillipe.

"Oh, and I'd strap his arms in. Wouldn't want a repeat of this, especially if there's only one of us here."

Phillipe nodded his head in agreement. Claude walked toward the door, but before he could get there, two rather large men entered the room. Their shoulders filled the wide doorway entirely, and the tops of their heads blocked out the ceiling light emanating from the hallway. It made the hospital room noticeably dimmer. The change in darkness seemed to match the aura that the men carried in with them. Both of them were clad in Black from head to toe, their shoes shining without any blemishes. Both men also wore sunglasses and had an earpiece traveling into their collar. Claude didn't know whether to try and pass them or stand still – the large, ominous men had a certain stunning effect about them. Curiously enough, they spoke in perfect French accents. It was off-putting since they clearly looked American.

"Uhh . . . can we help you? Sirs?" Claude stammered, nervously.

The guard on the right tilted his head towards the other one, nodding his head the slightest bit. He seemed to know what his counterpart meant. He abruptly left the room, with his hand touching the earpiece nestled in his head. The remaining guard removed his glasses slowly.

"This man is property of the United States Secret Service. My name is Agent Szczezniak. We'll be taking him off your hands now."

"What do you mean?" Asked Phillipe, baffled. "We don't even know what's wrong with him yet! You can't just take hi-"

"Please, Mr. Alain, trust me. It is important for the national security of France and the United States that we apprehend this man immediately." The guard interrupted, staring straight into Phillipe's soul. He hadn't the guts to ask, but he wanted to know how this man knew who he was. It was a frightening gesture. Claude edged his way to the door as the man in black loomed closer to the hospital bed, allowing his body the thinnest route of access. The man, still staring at Phillipe, didn't seem to care. He was going to get his way no matter what. Phillipe was no fool – he realized this quickly. His naïve desire to hear Anthony's story disappeared just as fast.

"O-Okay. Just uhh . . . sign the release papers when you leave . . . please." Phillipe managed, more for the health of his own conscience than any other reason.

"Don't worry. I've already spoken with Mr. D'Entremont. Everything is under control, Phillipe." Said the man in black deeply, hypnotizing the nurse with his endearing demeanor.

Phillipe didn't resist. Seconds later, the suited man from before returned with two others just like him – clean cut and silent. They formed a quartet around the bed and brought it out of the room and out into the hallway. Phillipe slowly trudged out to the doorway and peered a sliver of his head out into the hall. He watched as the four men escorted Anthony away. So did everyone else for that matter. Trailing behind the men and seemingly oblivious to the situation loomed a tall, perfectly groomed man with black hair and blue eyes wearing a doctor's coat – but he was familiar with everyone who worked there. He had never seen this man before. He decided, given what had just happened, that it was not his place to question the man's presence.

Thoughts racing, Phillipe sat down in a chair meant for guests, and turned the television back on. This time, the caption on the bottom read 'Pas de survivants'.

Chapter 8

REVELATION

"Cap! Your keycard! You still got one, right?"

"Here!" Lester tossed a lanyard attached to a plastic white card the size of a normal bank card directly at Jim. He snatched it out of the air and slid it in front of a holographic panel attached to a glass door. He and Lester filed through the unlocked barrier with Gary trudging behind them, still sobbing.

"Jones, the file room. Show me. Now." Jim demanded as he grabbed a firm hold of Gary's suit jacket. Gary was having trouble keeping himself together, but they didn't have time for his emotions.

"This way, sir. Follow me." He muttered. Gary brought them past a row of cubicles lining the wall and around a right-hand corner. At the end of the hallway, a larger than normal, ultra-thick vault-like doorway with a padlock on it.

"Through there."

Gary twisted his smaller body through Jim and Lester's as if he had gained some sort of confidence. His fingers danced across an indigo colored number pad that made beeping sounds as the buttons were pressed. After a few seconds, a loud bell tone rolled through the hallway as the indigo pad turned to green. A series of metallic thuds and clamors emanated from inside the large door. Gary waited a second, then edged it open. By now, a few agents, secretaries and paper-pushers began to observe what was happening. Jim and Lester didn't care – there was no hiding their intent at this point. It was not entirely strange – every time this vault opened, people tended to get curious. It held a great many valuable documents and files of which only a few trusted people had access to. Evidently, a breach in security could happen very easily.

The inside of the room was dark at first, but then Gary flipped a switch on the wall that lit up everything to the tune of a bright white light. The walls, ceilings and floors were adorned with square panels that glared white. Jim felt his eyes adjust to the abrupt change in luminosity. Aisles of filing cabinets traversed the room all the way to the back, where a series of high tech computers lay perched on a raised, semi-circular pedestal. Each filing cabinet had a number pad on its front, much like the large door that granted them access to the room.

"Jones! Where is it? Which one?" Asked Lester, furiously.

"This one sir. I took his file out of this one."

Gary's fingers went back to work on one of the cabinet's closest to the computers. After a few seconds, the large black drawer popped open, revealing a series of documents enclosed in paper folders. Right in the middle of the row of folders, there was an empty spot.

"I told you sir, they made me take it. And give it to them. There was only one copy." Said Gary. Lester shoved him out of the way and began to dig into the files himself.

"He's not lying Jim. Anthony's file isn't here."

Jim grabbed Gary by the scruff and shoved him up against the adjacent row of filing cabinets, nearly knocking them over.

"You fucking traitor! what have you done!" Yelled Jim, as he struck Gary to the floor. He curled up into fetal position and began crying again.

"Wait! Jim! We need him! Gary, get on that SATNAV right now. Send out a ping, see if we can locate Anthony's transponder signal. Williams too!"

Lester bent over and crunched his burly digits deep into Gary's jacket, snatching him up from the floor. He nestled Gary into his bosom and walked over to the computers, controlling his body and placing it more than helping him walk on his own.

"O-Okay. I can do this. Give me that keycard . . . please."

Jim tossed the lanyard right at Gary's face, it trickled into his hand. If not for Lester, Jim may have torn Gary apart with his bare hands.

"Whew. Okay." Gary slid the card into a port on the computer deck, illuminating an array of flashing and solid multi-colored lights. They could feel the hum of electricity as the contraption came to life.

Gary went to work. A specialized keyboard made for his right hand consisted of a smooth half-orb where his hand hovered and acted as the mouse. Around the peripheries of the sliced ball were a series of keys and notes that corresponded to certain commands. It left his other hand free to navigate through the many touch-screens that popped up on the screen itself. His hands jostled and bounced around the whole apparatus, momentarily impressing Jim and Lester. They were too old-fashioned to operate a normal keyboard proficiently, let alone this thing.

"Bingo." Said Gary. His mood had swung back completely, now he was focused.

"Bingo? Bingo what?"

"Williams transponder signal sir. I've found it."

"Well where the hell is it then?"

Gary did not answer their pestering. Instead he took his right hand off of the ball and used it to spread the holographic window as large as it would go. It showed a coastline – and a red dot out in the ocean. The image was easily understood.

They didn't want to believe it, but the standard TSS-14 transponders rarely ever failed. Thinner than a hair follicle and embedded deep in the agent's wrist, they emitted a constant, steady signal. Also, they kept a six hour memory of the agent's location, so that anyone observing could track their movement.

"Show me a two-hour time relapse."

Gary's fingers went back to work on the strange control device. A yellow line began to appear on the screen. It came from the coast, went out into the ocean, did a wide loop back towards the coast, then abruptly stopped over the ocean.

"There!" Lester pointed at the screen with his finger. "That must be where the plane got hit . . . or exploded. Williams must have fallen out of the plane before it came back to land."

"So you mean to tell me Williams is at the bottom of the fucking ocean?" Jim asked. He, Lester and Gary all looked at each other.

"I'm afraid so, sir." Gary responded.

"What about Anthony? Where's Anthony's!" Jim demanded, impressing his body weight onto Gary in his chair.

"One second. I'll run a double-patch through the system. I'll have to cross reference it with his last log entry. . ."

Once again, Gary's fingers went to work. A few seconds passed as their bodies huddled in a close, anticipatory perch around the console.

Another window popped up, glaring an unwelcome yellow bar holding the word UNKNOWN. Gary's body language said it all – his focus broke and his torso drifted slowly into the chair.

"I – I don't know sir. Can't even bring up his last entry! It's like someone erased it all!"

Erased?

Lester could sense his friend's anger boiling. Jim's face was red and his fists were now clenched. He feared poor Gary would bear the brunt of Jim's wrath, and he may not be able to stop him. He knew he had to act or Gary's life may very well be in jeopardy. At the same time, could Lester mindfully disagree? There would be a time for Gary to pay for what he had done, no doubt – but not right now. Right now they needed him.

Lester did something he was used to doing his entire career – he took control of the situation. Convincing Jim to play along would be his biggest challenge. He had seen Jim's legendary rage before, and was quite surprised he hadn't lost it completely.

"Jim. We need to get over there. Now!"

"It's over Lester. You know it as well as –"

"But we *don't* know that Jim!" Lester growled, clutching Jim's shoulders.

For a moment, he incited a spark of hope – he could see it in Jim's eyes. But there was something else to be seen in them as well, something he couldn't put his thumb under.

"Now we can assume Williams . . ." Said Lester, looking at Gary, blank in the face. "But Anthony, his transponder signal isn't red, it isn't red Jim! It was yellow!" He re-affirmed his visual focus and gripped Jim even tighter – he needed Jim to be onside mentally, just as much as they both needed Gary for what he knew, if there was to be any hope at all. In a soft, calm voice, "Yellow, Jim. Yellow."

"Red means dead. Not yellow."

"Red is dead." Replied Jim.

"Yes. Red is dead. Yellow is just yellow, Jim. Come on. We have to go, and we have to go now."

Jim weighed his thoughts while Gary twiddled his thumbs. Being unoccupied allowed his thoughts to return to guilt, fear, and self-loathing. Tears trickled down his shaking face as his mind retreated to a breaking point.

He's right. There *is* still a chance, Jim thought.

"You're right Cap'. You're right. I'm ready"

Gary looked up like a dog after it had bitten someone, his pathetic demeanor imposing, hoping there was some way out of his turmoil.

"Jones. You're coming with us. Jim, get the car ready, I'll meet you down in the lobby."

"Where are you going?"

"Nowhere. Just trust me. I'll be down shortly. I just need a minute with Gary."

Jim looked at Gary one more time, acknowledging all in one glance his hatred, pity and disgust. The chance that Anthony, his boy, may still be alive was the only thing worth focusing on. Jim marched back to the steel vault and slid between. He didn't bother explaining himself, or anything else, to the few graveyard paper-pushers who had developed an observational curiosity.

"Hey! Get back to work!" Lester shouted as Jim's thick shoulders brushed past. They all listened, scurrying back to their stations. As soon as they were gone, Lester grabbed Gary's chair and flung it around towards him.

"Alright Jones, listen up. I don't know exactly who you talked to, or where that file is, or what the fuck you were thinking. But you, Me, and Jim are gonna' get to the bottom of this whole god-damn thing. You get me?"

"Y- yes sir. I understand." Gary whimpered, wiping tears from his face and sniffling.

"Now I only have one question for you before we do this. And by god you better tell me the truth boy."

"Okay, sir. Okay." Gary had no intention of lying.

"Where did you bring that file?"

"The pentagon sir."

"The fucking pentagon? Are you serious?" He really didn't expect that one. A terrorist group maybe, or even domestic anarchists of some sort. He plunged his hands into his waist and reaffirmed his posture, his mind racing with the potential catastrophe that could be unraveling. Maybe he didn't want to know.

"We'll get to that later Gary. Get up!" Growled Lester as he yanked Gary from the chair by his shoulder and to his feet. "Lead the way."

Gary stammered towards the large vault door. Lester reached down his leg and peeled back the pant leg covering his ankle. Strapped on by a nylon band to his meaty calf was a tiny booklet. He fumbled it around in his fingers and opened it up. Inside was a small computer chip that had an oily glow to it.

"Jones. What kind of phone you got?"

"Uh, Iphone sir, Iphone 8." Said Gary, reaching into his pocket.

"That'll work. Give it here."

Gary tossed the phone over to Lester. He took the small chip and placed it on the back of the phone where it seemed to attach magnetically and began to dial a long sequence of numbers. Gary couldn't quite see what his fingers were doing on the phone but within seconds he held it up to his ear and moved towards him, and the exit.

"Vigilant Overwatch this is BlueTop 17, over. . ."

What now? Gary thought.

"I repeat, Vigilant Overwatch this is BlueTop 17, over!"

At first there was only static, but after a few seconds the chip on the back of the phone flashed a red light.

"We hear you, BlueTop 17. Is this a secure link?" Said a muffled voice over the makeshift walkie-talkie.

"I'm using a civilian's cell phone. I had no choice. We have a situation on our hands."

"Affirmative, BlueTop. Encryption codes please."

"Initiation code 777, I am located in sector 15-A. My hashtag is SEE AY PEE 1, spelling CAP1"

A few more seconds of fuzzy static ensued before the voice returned. Lester moved the phone from his ear to his mouth for when he had to talk and when he had to listen. Gary thought this made him look like an old man unfamiliar with modern technology.

"Roger that. Good to hear your voice Captain. What do you need?"

As soon as Lester heard the reply, his feet sprung into movement again. Gary did not follow.

"I'm gonna' need an empty flight to the European mainland for myself and two others. Fastest plane you got. And I'm gonna' need a black squad on the ground on standby for when we get there."

Once again, a brief silence ensued as Lester waited for his response.

"Copy that, Captain. Flight 46 is on the Tarmac now. She's all yours. Double-Engine Raven. I am sending the bookings to your mobile device now. There will be two agents waiting at Gate 23 to assist you. Will you be needing weapons?"

"Couldn't hurt. Pack a few of those new NR-MC submachine guns just incase. And body armor."

"You got it. Clarify, Captain, is this all pertaining to the plane crash that happened earlier today?"

"Yes, how did you know?"

"We received a direct order from the pentagon to an hour ago. There are squads en route to the location now."

It was the second time Lester had heard about the pentagon in the last five minutes. Before that, he couldn't remember the last time he had heard of it. Something big was definitely happening, but he would need to find more pieces to the puzzle to make some sense of it.

"What was their mandate?"

"Asset recovery, sir."

"And who issued the order?"

"Marcellus Grey, sir."

"Apparently there is a national security threat involved with the situation. They wasted no time sending in the clean-up crew."

"Alright, alright. Confirm Vigilant Overwatch, this stays off-record."

"Confirmed, BlueTop 17. Good luck."

Lester clicked the off button, removed the strange chip and tossed the phone back to Gary, who wasn't ready for it. His nerves had gotten the best of him, but he was beginning to fully embrace the severity of the situation. He wanted to help.

"Alright Jones, let's move!" Said Lester, as he crouched and placed the chip back on his leg. He looked around to make sure no one had seen him. The more people talking about what was happening, the worse off they would be — besides the possibility of Anthony's death, Lester also had an obligation to worry about what could become of Gary. He knew that he couldn't let Gary leave his sight — it was too risky. The last thing he needed right now was a nationwide scandal which was one authoritative confession away from happening.

Traitors on our own soil Lester envisioned, would be the headline.

Lester began to walk with purpose, but Gary remained, shoulders hunched, peering into the floor with a bewildered look on his face.

"Come on Jones! We don't have time to fuck around!"

"Wait! Sir, WAIT!" shouted Gary.

"For what?" Lester replied, angrily.

"There's something else. Something I neglected to tell you, and it may be important! I don't want to take any chances . . ."

"What is it, Jones?" Lester demanded. Time was of the essence; every second passing limited their chances of retrieving Anthony.

"The man I spoke with at the Pentagon . . . his name was Mr. Grey. The same Mr. Grey who ordered the cleanup crew, I would assume."

"I'm listening." Snapped Lester.

"Well, when me made the deal, he asked for something else — another file. But I didn't give it to him. I told him I could not find it . . . when in reality I was scared that I wouldn't get paid for it . . . I'm so sorry sir . . ."

Now Lester was truly confused. Another file? If it was Williams, Lester thought, or any other agent, he may have beaten him to the ground right then and there.

"Well, out with it Jones!"

"Follow me, I'll get it for you. If they wanted it, then it must be of some importance."

Gary moved back into the vault room without a gesture of approval from Lester, who was inclined to follow. Could it get any worse?

Gary rode his index finger along the row of locked file cabinets, all the way to the back corner of the room.

"Here, this one!" Gary said, exasperated. His fingers went to work on the keypad and within seconds the drawer popped open on its own. He began sifting through the files with his hands, and finally came upon the one he was looking for – he snatched it out of the drawer and handed it to Lester. The folder itself was tattered and worn. It looked very old, as if it had been stuffed in there for years. Even the writing on it was smudged and hardly discernable.

"That's the one he wanted." Said Gary, as Lester examined the front of the folder. 'These are some of the oldest records we have."

On the top there was a name he could barely make out.

P. Schlesinger.

"Who the hell is he, sir?" Asked Gary, perplexed.

"I have no idea, Gary. But we sure as hell aren't gonna' wait around here to find out. It's time to leave."

Lester pulled his button-up shirt from the confines of his belt and stuffed the file, folded, in the breach of his pants by his hip and covered it back up with his shirt. Gary was probably right. If Mr. Grey wanted the file then it must be of some significance. They would have to figure that out later.

"Come on! Jim is waiting for us downstairs."

They shut the vault door behind them as they left. Nearly everyone in the office area ogled them as they marched down the corridor and to the elevator – it was the least of their worries.

When they arrived at the airport, there were two agents waiting for them at gate 23, just like Lester had expected.

"Some friends from Langley?" Jim asked Lester, half-joking.

"No, Jim, not Langley. But friends indeed. Let's get on this plane"

Gary, Jim and Lester walked down the long corridor towards their flight – out of one of the windows Gary saw the plane. It was a small, sleek looking jet with smooth angular wings and very few windows on it, painted shiny black all over. They finally boarded it through a small hole near the cockpit attached to the docking walkway.

"There, Jones, sit down and strap up." Said Lester. Jim did the same.

"Open it" He said to one of the agents, referring to a metal cabinet just before the cockpit entrance. The agent revealed a metal key and plunged it into the lock – the door swung open revealing an armory – handguns, assault rifles, sub-machine guns and stacks of body armor that stuck out on rails which slid out from the wall from the push of a button. He took two vests and tossed them at Jim and Gary.

"Put them on underneath your clothes."

Jim walked up to the locker as well, strapping a handgun to his waist. His Kevlar had multiple slots to hold magazines. He filled a few of them while examining the guns.

"I didn't want to take any chances, Jim." Said Lester. Jim did not respond, but looked him in the eyes briefly, and continued to drape himself with gear. They both looked at Jones, among the sounds of clicking and cocking. His thumbs twiddled fervently and his knee jostled restlessly as he looked out one of the few windows in the plane.

"Can we trust him with a gun?" Whispered Jim. Lester pondered the question for a moment.

"Can we trust him *without* one?"

"Good point." Jim replied. "Strap him up when we land."

"There's a SATNAV console in the back, Jones."

Gary's ears perked up, his body wiggled around in the chair awkwardly.

"Go get on it, keep trying to get a signal." Lester pointed to the back of the plane. One of the agents moved to the back of the plane and pressed a button. A table slid open and a holographic screen lit up from it. Gary took off his jacket, bridged his fingers together and cracked them all, then went to work on the apparatus. "And Jones, see if you can find any information about Anthony's assignment. There should be a brief log somewhere in the headquarters database, you should be able to access it from there."

"How did you swing this, Cap?" Jim asked.

"Friends in high places, Jim. Call it a job perk."

Jim smirked, then strapped his shirt in on top of his Kevlar vest.

"Jim. Look at this."

Lester handed him the file from his hip. As soon as it reached his hands and he read the name, a cold, lifeless look swept over his face, as if he had seen a ghost.

"Have you ever heard of this guy?" He asked.

Jim ran his fingers over the document.

"Can't say I have." He replied, but Lester knew he was lying. Jim was good at hiding things, but this time he couldn't. Lester took a step closer.

"Jim, is there something you wanna' tell me?"

The two looked at each other for a moment in mutual understanding. Lester could tell that Jim's mind was stewing with something – something he wanted to get off his chest.

"We're airborne in two. Strap yourselves in!" Said the pilot, peering his head into view from the cockpit. They both sat down, Jim clutching the folder tightly.

"Jim?"

"Where did you get this?" He asked, intrigued.

"From the file room. Jones told me that a man at the pentagon was interested in obtaining it. Let's try to find out why."

The plane started to move away from port, the entry hatch closed on its own. Jim pried open the folder and began reading. He looked at the documents within the folder as if they were some kind of ancient relic; a one-way ticket to the past.

"By the way Jim, you really should strap yourself in."

"Why's that?"

"Because this thing is *really* fast."

Half a minute later the sleek, sharply angled plane was in the air and speeding toward the ocean. Lester wasn't kidding – Jim could feel the intense force of gravity pulling him deeper into his chair as the plane zoomed towards the stratosphere.

"We'll be there in just under two hours, sir." Said one of the agents coming from the cockpit.

"I told you Jim, these things are fast."

Chapter 9

PANIC

The hallways flickered in and out of vision. Anthony was no longer in the hospital, and no longer laying on a stretcher. He was being dragged by his arms and could feel his knees hitting the protrusions lining the poorly manufactured metal floor. Grates and panels formed a strange bumpy walkway littered with shards of detached steel. There were no windows anywhere, and no sunlight. Images blurred through his mind – some of them held brief instances of space, others with loud, fiery explosions, and Williams – falling. Was he dead? And what happened on the plane? Anthony' eyes felt like they were being dragged down by a thousand tons of sand. He struggled to open them for the briefest moments. The ceiling was covered in thick groupings of multi-colored wires that were harnessed together by plastic bands. Every dozen meters or so, a dim light glared against his face. He managed to look up briefly, catching a quick glimpse of the assailants carrying him. Two large men, adorned in all-black combat suits – guards of some sort. Despite all of his abilities, his strengths and his cunning intellect, he had no power, no control. There was nothing he could do to save himself. But there was one thing he could determine – these couldn't possibly be Al-Akazawhi's men. He may be an international criminal, but this was something entirely different.

The crooked hallway ended abruptly and Anthony was dropped to the cold, harsh ground. He struggled to lift his head to get a view of his surroundings. His neck muscles ached and quivered from the weight of his raised head. He could not hold the pose for long. In front of him was a perfectly angular metal table. On the other side, he could see two sets of legs and feet – perfectly coiffed black pants and shiny black shoes. The pressure on his neck gave way causing his head to thud against the ground. He was utterly incapacitated.

"Pick it up. Put it in the chair and give it a shot" Said a voice, presumably from one of the men sitting behind the table. "Tie its hands together."

The two guards yanked him from the floor and nestled him firmly in a cold metal chair at the table directly across from the two men, whose faces were rigid, stern and devoid of empathy. He knew, right away, that they were not there to help him. The men tied his hands behind his back firmly and to the chair, ignorant of the pain he was in. Anthony struggled to stay upright in the chair as they did. Before he could muster a pathetic resistance, he felt an intense burning pain in his shoulder. Seconds later he was fully awake – more awake then he had ever been. The burning pain invaded the rest of his body, searing its way into his muscles, deep into his aching bones and to the tips of his extremities. The men sitting across from him became very clear. Next to him on the table was a strange looking machine bolted and fastened into place. It was a shiny metal box with a series of red and yellow buttons in a row, with one purple button at the end – some sort of measurement scale, he thought. The closer his mind came to balance, the more questions arose in his fractured psyche.

Where the hell am I? And who the fuck are these people?

To his right and left, the guards who brought him there stood firmly against the wall, waiting. He couldn't turn his head far enough to see what was behind him.

"What the hell is going on here!?" Anthony yelled at the top of his lungs. He struggled uselessly to free himself from the chair, but he only made it inches off the seat before the guards planted him back by the shoulder. Their grip strength was unnaturally strong, and it hurt quite a bit – their hand felt more like metal clamps than bone and flesh.

"Calm down, Anthony Stall. We will be asking the questions here." Beckoned a voice from across the large table. It harnessed Anthony's full attention.

"How . . . do you know my name? The Bureau, they will find me! And your fucking boss, Akazawhi will get what's coming to h-"

"We know everything about you, Anthony Stall. We have been looking for you for some time. And now we've found you, and not a moment too soon. Although I must admit, you hid yourself quite well, managing to evade our best assets. Despite all of our efforts to destroy you, here you sit in front of us, still breathing."

Anthony was truly lost. He had no idea what was going on, or what these men wanted with him – but at least now he could piece together what happened on the plane by seaming together shards of memory that lay disparate and scattered in his mind's eye.

"Now listen to me carefully. You are going to tell us what we need to know, and your life *may* be spared. If you choose to resist, I can guarantee you will experience a most painful and excruciating death. Do you understand?"

"Wh-what . . . what's happening to me?" Anthony stammered.

"Ironic, isn't it? That you chose to become an agent of the FBI, that you were hidden underneath our noses for so long. I must say, I respect you for being so clever. Unfortunately for you, cleverness will not save you now."

"What do you mean?"

"Oh we both know what I mean, Anthony Stall. You're reckoning is at hand. You can answer us of your own free will, which I recommend, for your health, or we can hook you up to this machine in front of us, and the choice will no longer be yours."

Anthony looked at the machine, and to the side panel, where two wires protruded. On the end, metal spikes. No way was he going to give in. No way was he going to forfeit the *one thing* he had left. He looked back at his interrogators, and lunged forward as he spit across the table at them. One of the guards came from his periphery with a vicious closed fist, nearly striking him out of the chair. It was extremely painful, busting his upper lip open and jostling a few of his teeth.

"Fine. Have it your way." Said the man, nodding his head at one of the guards, who retracted the two wires from the machine and plunged them deep into Anthony's neck. Almost instantaneously, he felt the wooziness return to him.

Truth Serum.

The Bureau had all sorts of contingency plans for a captured agent, but none for this. He knew he had no choice but to answer everything honestly. He felt truly helpless.

The man across from him pushed down on the first red button in the row. Anthony felt the grip of truthfulness invade his mind. But he had to fight it.

"Now tell me. Where is the location of the Darmerian base on Earth?"

The words rolled through Anthony's mind like a pinball machine and left. *What the hell* is a Darmerian? They were going to need more powerful drugs to break *his* mind.

"F-Fucck youuu!" Anthony gargled, stringy, bloody drool and spit trickling from his mouth.

A finger reached over to the machine, pressing the last red button before the series of yellow ones. Anthony could feel the numbing effects of the drugs taking him deeper into a trance.

"Okay. Let's try this again. What happened to our liaison at the restaurant in Paris?"

For a moment, images darted through Anthony's mind. He could grasp what the man was talking about. They looked intently, and could tell he might have a reasonable answer for them.

"He. . ." Anthony whispered.

"He what? Tell us!"

Anthony raised his head, and came up with an answer.

"He fed me."

"Well he was *supposed* to kill you. Obviously he failed to do his job. Did you kill him, Anthony?"

He had to think about that one for a second. His mind was very hazy, and grasping any memory firmly required a high level of concentration. In this state, his mind worked only in truths. Anthony had never killed anyone in his life.

"No. But . . . but he . . ."

"But he what! Tell us now!" said one of the men, raising from the table and striking it with close fists.

"But he makes one hell of a pasta dish." Anthony said, somehow mustering a smile, if only briefly. This time, the guard from the other side closed his fist and prepared to strike Anthony again.

"Wait!" said the interrogator. "We'll show this comedian who tells the jokes around here."

His finger hovered along the row of yellow buttons then rested above the last one in the line – the purple one. If this didn't work, then they would need something more powerful, or they might not get the information they were looking for at all. He hesitated for a moment, but eventually pushed the button in. Two cylindrical implements rose from the top of the machine. Inside the glass tubes was a silvery metallic liquid substance. He twisted one with his hand, depleting the case of its contents, which were injected straight into Anthony's body. It was a risky choice – there was more than enough Amenithol in the case to kill a man, should there heart rate dip too low.

But he's not a man, thought the interrogator.

"How does that feel, Anthony Stall?"

The other interrogator decided it may be a good idea to ask some control questions to make sure they weren't looking for something that could not be found. Perhaps he actually didn't know? It might serve as the only explanation as to why, despite the immense power of the drugs, Anthony was able to dodge the line of questioning. Given the uptake method of the serum, it seemed to be physically impossible for him to be lying. He began asking a few questions of his own, whilst allowing his colleague to regain his calm.

"Are you currently strapped to a chair, Anthony?" He asked, to the dismay of his colleague.

"What are you doing?"

"What if it doesn't know?" He whispered, covering his mouth from view.

"Yes." Anthony replied, interrupting their conversation. They both looked at him, then back at each other.

"What do you mean, doesn't know?"

"I mean, what if it doesn't know what it is? What if no one ever told it? It would explain why we aren't getting anywhere."

The Interrogator pondered the question and decided his colleague may be right.

"It would also explain why we were never able to record any attempted contact between him . . . and his brethren. None, for the last 23 years. Nothing. Besides, have you ever seen this stuff *not work*? You know as well as I do that's physically impossible. For humans *and* exos."

"Yes, but if it had done it in secret then we wouldn't know anyways!"

"You may be right, George. But then again, you may very well be wrong."

For the first time, the interrogators revealed their humanity – they had names.

"Fine. Do it your way. I'll get Gordon down here, he's an expert with this type of thing."

George rose from his chair and walked toward the exit of the room, but was greeted by Gordon, who somehow knew they needed him there before he was officially summoned. He was an average sized man with Grey hair and glasses to match a thick grey moustache. His small, brown eyes hid behind a pair of glasses stooped on the ridge of his nose. Although everyone else was covered from head to toe in black, he wore normal civilian clothes – a checkered gray and white button up shirt, tucked in at the waist. He also wore khakis with a belt and his shoes were anything but formal.

"How did you get here so fast?" George asked him, confused. "This is quite a large complex. It would have taken you at least ten minutes to get all the way here?"

"Fifteen, actually. But now I am here. I've received a direct mandate from L-Block. I am to take this prisoner to the machine."

"Are you sure? We've already been questioning him for quite a whi-"

"I'm sure, George. I can take him from here."

"By all means." Said George. He stooped over Anthony condescendingly, running his hand across his forehead. Slimy sweat dripped from his hand and to the floor after he wiped it on Anthony's jacket.

"Filthy creature."

"Release him." Gordon said, pointing. He stood firmly in the room, owning what limited space the small room offered him.

The guards moved with precise unison, unshackling Anthony from the chair, each grabbing an arm, and hoisting him to a standing position. His hands were still confined, but at least he had the freedom now, to walk on his own. Gordon gestured towards the door nonchalantly and led him out of the room, and back into the hallway. After a few steps, Anthony seemed to be exponentially regaining control of his senses. Things were different now. The fear that had coursed through his veins and paralyzed his will had left him. The sight of a normal-looking person, detached and unhindered by the ominous, ruthless coldness of his interrogators, brought him back to a vaguely familiar place. The calmness of his nerves gave him the physical strength to transcend his fear and finally lift his head, and to examine, with unbiased vision, his surroundings.

The layout of the hallway baffled him, and made him feel slightly claustrophobic. It was everything *except* for a perfectly angled rectangle – protrusions, square and oblong shaped jutted out randomly, forcing both he and Gordon to maneuver their heads around. There were black and white spherical nodes attached to more bundled wires dangling from the ceiling – presumably some sort of arteriole network of electricity and power – normal buildings weren't constructed like this. Bare, unprotected arrays of what resembled the silicon chips inside a computer acted as myriad transformers, dispersing arteries and veins in every direction. Once his mind had deterred far enough from that room, and the confusing questions, and the plane . . .

A *clue.*

A large portion of wall blended into a scarred, jagged rock formation. Anthony's investigative mind sparked all at once. It searched for reasonable possibilities. There was only one that sifted to the top – he must be underground. And if he was, his transponder signal (which he also abruptly remembered) would do him no good, barring the chance that his captors hadn't already disabled it somehow. A primal urge to stay alive governed his thought process, urging his mind toward a solution – an *escape.*

When they had reached safety from listening ears, Anthony inherited the ability to speak. By the looks of Gordon, he may even answer honestly. Gordon looked at the watch on his left hand quickly. His body language displayed a mixed feeling of anxiousness, awareness. Anthony recognized his demeanor. He had seen it many times before. Someone must have been breathing down his neck as well.

"Where are we?" He asked pertinently. The response could have gone either way, or been nothing.

"Underground Installation ES-13. Quickly, Anthony, There is no time. We must hurry." Said Gordon, adding another point of reference for Anthony's mind to work with, and build on.

"Wait, what? What is this machine you are taking me to anyways?" He asked. There was a split in the path ahead, one direction veered upwards to the right, the other diagonally down the left, presumably deeper into the Earth.

Gordon's pace quickened and he looked at his watch again. Anthony struggled to keep up, throwing one leg in front of the other as his shoulders tumbled awkwardly from side to side. Why was he in such a hurry?

"They call it the MM. The Master Manipulator. It can pull long dormant thoughts out of your mind. Ones you didn't even know were ever there." Gordon admitted. It sounded terrifying. "But we're not going there Anthony." He said, looking up. Anthony looked in the same place and mounted firmly, nestled to a bent girder between two stalactites was a CCTV camera, directly above the fork in the road.

"What do you mean!?" He asked, absolutely intrigued. Gordon grabbed his wrist and pulled him into the path to the left, just in time to avoid the circulating camera from seeing them. It was the first time their skin touched – and something unexplainable happened. Anthony's eyes drifted into a direct line with Gordon's, as if he was hypnotized. All of his thoughts narrowed and focused into one, laser-like concentration.

Sensations both physical and emotional rushed into his hand, up his arm and throughout his whole body. In that moment, he felt safer than he ever had. Like nothing could hurt him.

He felt utterly invincible, and none of his fears could hold him back.

"Follow my lead, Anthony Stall. We're getting out of here."

He understood loud and clear even though, as he realized seconds after, Gordon's lips did not move at all.

The downward path was made of nothing but rock. Some parts were narrower than others which made quick travel more difficult.

"Wait." Whispered Gordon, crouching. Another camera. They'd have to be very fast this time. It loomed high above, with a light attached. They darted underneath it's gaze during its turn with milliseconds to spare.

"This way. We should be out of sight now." Said Gordon, once again checking his watch.

The pathway opened up and became vast. They finally reached a wide open room. The jagged walkway ceased to exist, becoming a solid, marble rock shiny floor which turned into a wide stairway. Large, smooth pillars pushed into the ceiling, supporting an otherwise unstable rock roof, twenty meters above their heads. The cavern was vast. Anthony ducked his head and followed Gordon down the stairs to another platform, and another set of stairs. The roof curled downward at a sharp angle, limiting their view beyond the second stairway until they were half-way down it. It was completely silent, other than the echoes of their shoes hitting the floor. Once they had reached the last few steps, the bottom chamber of the cavern came into view. Anthony tilted his head up for a moment to see where they were going. The first thing he saw was a tall guard, much like the ones that carried him into the interrogation room, except this one had a large assault rifle in his hands that he didn't recognize – which was a surprise, given his extensive knowledge of firearms. Part of him wanted to test it out, but a larger part wanted nothing to do with it, and nothing more to do with this treacherous place. In front of the guard lay two more pillars, shorter and wider than the previous ones. Gordon took him by the arm once again. Invoked by nothing but tactile sensation, instructions flooded his mind.

"Don't say anything." Was the gist of the message. He felt the urge to look at Gordon's lips to see if he was speaking – and to make sure he wasn't losing his mind.

Behind the guard was a smooth, metallic silver train resting on a carved out section of the cave that extended, in the back, deep into an orifice farther than he could see. The front of the train was curved and oblong with a blue angled window attached on the front. It had no windows anywhere else. He wondered how such a thing could be engineered and constructed down here.

"Halt!" Beckoned the guard, holding his hand up to Gordon meters before they reached the side of the train. "Who is this? Where are you taking him?" He demanded with authority, clutching the handle of his cumbersome rifle slung across his body with his other hand.

George had almost made his way back to L-Block. It was quite a jaunt from the interrogation cells. On his way, he passed a research laboratory, a weapons testing facility and the main foyer – a massive hollowed out cavern used for storage and the transference of heavy machinery. The installation wasn't finished – gargantuan worm-like digging machines dozens of meters high and hundreds of meters long laid in rest scattered kilometers apart in the huge cavern. They were so big he felt like he could reach down through one of the port windows of the walkway and pick it up like a child's toy.

Walking by these monoliths of secrecy and invention, George felt a sense of pride in himself, and in his job. He had to consider it a job, a calling even, because he certainly couldn't call it a career.

Counterbalancing the innate urge to blow the whistle and live a normal life was very difficult for everyone, but never spoken of. George did it by trying to realize the bigger picture. He truly believed in his soul that what he was doing was just, and for the good of his country. He existed in a place where tax dollars were relevant to thin air, where every blink of the eye revealed long-held secrets, where normal human beings are forced to live a double life, and where time seemed to disappear unseen into endless tunnels and dark chambers.

All for the *bigger picture.*

He passed a series of elevators and reached the administrative headquarters of the facility. Waiting there, as a testament to what things were like on the surface, was a pretty brunette woman sitting at a fancy mahogany desk with antique lamps and pen docks. It looked as though someone had transplanted an entire office room from the 1950s and copy and pasted it right there. It served more as a reminder to the employees of the installation that they would once again return to the "real world" – extended forays underground could yield harmful mental effects that could severely hinder the well-being of less-than strong minds. The rocky walkway gave way to a series of metallic grates that acted as an access platform to a grouping of office cubicles suspended high above a hollowed out floor – so deep he couldn't see.

"Hi there, hun', how have you been?" George asked, leaning over the edge of her expansive desk.

"Oh ya know. Just working the day away. If you can even call it a day. It's easy to lose track of time down here without any windows . . . any sun." Said the woman. it was probably a good thing that she knew very little of what really happened in the facility she worked in.

"By the way darling, did you happen to tell the engineers about the problems we've been having with the fusion coils in R-Block?"

"I did! But if you'd like to tell Gordon yourself, he should be in his office."

George was immediately confused.

"What do you mean? You just sent him down to us, did you not? Direct mandate?"

The girl had a baffled look on her face.

"Umm . . . not that I recall?" The words came out of her mouth slowly, without certainty.

"But he just . . ." George stammered. He instinctively leapt onto the platform beyond the desk and ran down the metal grate walkway towards Gordon's office. It was locked, the blinds were down, and he didn't respond verbally from within. A most terrified and guilt-ridden feeling permeated his senses. If what he thought was happening actually was happening, his life was now forfeit. The security of this installation was *his* responsibility, his prime directive – and there was no grey area, no second chances in the eyes of his superiors.

"Gordon! If you're in there, I'm coming in!" George yelled. He backed up and unleashed a powerful kick straight into the door, detaching it from the hinges entirely. He couldn't see anything – but then the desk inside the office jostled. He ran around it only to find Gordon, hog-tied by a strange, extremely smooth rope he didn't recognize with duck tape over his mouth, frantically struggling to break free of his confines. Above his head, an air duct was wide open. Its cover dangled by one screw still attached.

"Oh my God . . . Lucy! Sound the alarm! We have code black security breach!" He yelled, rushing out of the office and back down the metal platform.

"I am taking this prisoner to Starset. Direct mandate from L-Block." Said Gordon, slowly edging closer the guard as he spoke with impunity.

"I was not informed. Let me confirm with L-Block."

The guard turned toward the pillar closest to him, which had a computer pad and screen embedded in it. Before his fingers could reach the device, the alarm went off. It was extremely loud like a fire engine and red lights lowered from hidden compartments in the ceiling. Anthony quivered and hunched his shoulders in shock, realizing he may die right then and there.

Gordon leapt forward towards the guard, covering more ground than seemed possible. The guard tried to swing his gun around, but Gordon was somehow much too fast. He grabbed the barrel of the rifle and used it to strike the tall guard in the face. He responded with a cumbersome right hook that Gordon easily dodged by sinking underneath and delivering a heavy blow to the guard's midsection – it shattered the guard's armor and blood spattered from his mouth. Gordon finished off the guard with a hard kick directly to the chin, carrying him off his feet and into the pillar. He let out a painful whimper as his limp body folded and crippled, unconscious. Anthony was amazed that a frail man such as Gordon could deliver such a deadly blow – it seemed to be literally impossible.

"Come on Anthony! Let's move!" Gordon yelled. They huddled close to the train. A piece of its side retracted, allowing them access.

"Where are we going!?" Anthony yelled, shimmying his back against the wall of the train to regain his footing.

Gordon rushed to the cockpit. His hands flung around frantically pressing an array of buttons and levers. In front of him rose a pedestal, and then a holographic screen. More Guards were already making their way down the marble staircase. They opened fire on the train, but it was too late.

The energetic hum of the magneto-levity platform brought the train to life as it slowly began to move forward. Gordon then sprinted to the back of the train. On his way, he removed his dress shirt, revealing a series of instruments and devices strapped to his body, ones that Anthony had never seen before. From a distance, he looked like a suicide bomber with explosives ready to blow. Who was this man?

"Hold on to something Anthony!" He yelled, before pulling down a console that slid down from on a metal rail from an overhead compartment. His fingers danced across the holo-pad screen at lightning speed. A small, man-sized hole opened up at the back of the train, from which Gordon could see a squad of guards rushing down toward the track. Some of them kneeled to get a good shot – a few tracers flung through the hole and around the cabin, just barely missing Gordon's torso. He loosened and removed the jacket full of coils and tossed them through the hole out onto the track. The guards seemed to recognize what he was doing.

"BOMB!" One of them yelled, faintly heard but definitely discernable.

"Anthony! The lever next to the holo-pad! Crank it up to full!" Gordon yelled, huddled in the back corner. Despite the resonating tings of a few accurately placed shots that had managed to enter the cabin and ricochet throughout, Anthony summoned the courage, on impulse, to leap forward to the control console. He kicked the lever as hard as he could, jamming it up as far as it would go. He felt a powerful jolt that his legs could not compensate for, bringing him back to the ground. It was probably a good thing. Lying prone, he looked back at Gordon, who held something small in his hand. Gordon waited mere seconds until the loud tings stopped as the train curled downward, giving the guards no angle. Barely clear of the blast radius he pressed a white button on the device.

The shockwave reverberated through the train, lifting it slightly, but it remained on the track and continued to pick up speed, propelled forward by the blast. A fiery cylinder shot through the hole, accompanied by a deafening blast that caused Anthony to curl up into fetal position. He foolishly tried to cover his ears with his hands as the searing heat of the fireball extended above his head, singing the tips of his earlobes. The explosion did what it was intended – the rock ceiling collapsed in on itself, making any pursuit impossible. On the other side, shards of jagged rock flew toward the squad of guards. A few lucky ones managed to hide behind whatever they could, be it the pillars on the marble platform or the side of the track itself. Most of them were riddled with makeshift missiles or outright dismembered –a gruesome sight left in the wake of their failure.

The fireball dissipated from the cabin just as fast as it had entered, leaving most of the interior of the train scarred black. Some of the seats toward the back were melted pools of gooey, bubbly plastic dripping on to the floor. As soon as the impulse to retrieve Gordon crossed Anthony's mind, he was there, standing tall, untouched by the blast.

"That was a close one, Anthony. We bought ourselves some time."

Gordon went to the front again and with his bare hands, tore off a metal panel that revealed a complex group of wires, nodes and circuits. Using a piece of half-melted railing torn from one of the benches, he smashed the bare panel until it sparked and fizzled.

"What are you doing!?" Anthony asked, using the same shimmy strategy as before to regain his footing.

"Making sure the manual shutdown from the base is disabled. We should be fine now."

"Are you sure? Where are we going?" Anthony asked. His voice trembled with fear and uncertainty, his body shivered and ached. Gordon grabbed the cable wire harnessing his hands together and ripped it apart, freeing him. It seemed impossible, but Gordon made it look easy. He knelt down, impressing his presence onto Anthony and looked right into his eyes.

"Home, Anthony. We are going home."

"Home? What, you mean Boston?"

"No Anthony, not Boston." Gordon said as he took Anthony by the shoulder. It was a reassuring gesture that dulled the looming sense of danger and fear of annihilation. "Have a seat, it's going to be awhile before we're there." Gordon looked at his watch again, which had somehow remained intact.

"But how . . . What do you me-"

Anthony was interrupted not by Gordon's voice, but something far more fantastic.

'Beep Beep, Beep Beep' he heard, the sound of the timer on Gordon's watch running out. What he witnessed next was more than he could bear. First, a flash of light so bright, that it blinded him even through his closed eyelids. It died down slowly, allowing him to catch a glimpse, and there, before his very eyes, Gordon shrunk half a foot, his arms and legs grew skinnier, his torso narrowed and his hips widened. His head tilted back and jostled about as his shoulders became less angular and smaller. His hair grew rapidly down his back, changing to blonde. His eyes changed from brown to blue – even his skin became softer, smoother and began to glow. Within half a minute, the man that stood before him had transformed into an incredibly beautiful, blonde haired, blue eyed woman. She removed the watch and threw it on the floor. It disintegrated into thin air seconds later.

"Hello Anthony." Her voice was soft, and soothing. "My name is Aremis."

Anthony was terrified. Given everything he had just experienced, this was the icing on the cake. His mind's attempt at a logical explanation overwhelmed his synapses – he collapsed to the floor, eyes rolled back, and fainted.

Chapter 10

MOLE

DynaTech Incorporated. The third biggest company in the world, although they were good at keeping that a secret. Their contracts included everything from military, to commercial, to domestic. They had a presence in nearly every country and on every continent. Front-runners in nano-technology, genetic research, with tendrils extending deep into every branch of pharmaceutical and neurological science. The mainstream media dubbed them "The Wal-Mart of Science" – a moniker they lived up to in every imaginable way. By 2024, 65% of every consumer technology item sold in the United States at one point, was either conceived, regulated or upgraded by DynaTech. Lately though, all of their projects had taken a back seat to *The Initiative* as it was dubbed, mostly by low-level employees who didn't know better, who were there just to do what they were told.

"The Initiative" had a real name, and real-world practicalities, although half the people involved in the project would never know the real objective. Stacey Peterson, a mid-level bio-research analyst found herself stationed at a remote research and development outpost located in Alaska. Hand-picked for her unique skills in designing genetic alterations in living creatures, her gift, unbeknownst to her, would be her curse. After an ex-boyfriends father, who happened to be a high-ranking military intelligence officer read her 230 page thesis on non-birth related transgenetic mutation, her fate was sealed. Her story rose through the ranks through secret telephone calls and undisclosed meetings until someone, in some institution, decided they needed her. Exactly what they needed her for, she was never really told. But what she knew for sure is that $500,000 for six months of work was worth turning a blind eye to.

Churning snow leapt and bounced off the tetrahedral treads of the MTV- 3a. A fierce snowstorm chased them in right off the tarmac and was beginning to catch up with them. The pilot, nestled in the egg-like appendage suspended beneath the chassis, demanded updates from his navigator, who rested prone, on top of the chassis, with binoculars. All 5 people on board were safely covered by a rigid twinkie-shaped dome encased in a rigid steel cage structure. Stacey sat with two other scientists, one a bio-molecular physicist, the other an advanced weather pattern analyst with a keen knack for accurate predictions based on self-created mathematical algorithms. They were so complex and divergent, only he understood them. Stacey wondered why he wasn't somewhere else, like Harvard, revolutionizing the world with his talents. The massive, buoyant angular treads mounted to the vehicle ripped and roared through two-meter high snow banks making for a bumpy ride.

"Johnny, what's our ETA?"

"1600 meters and closing sir. We'll be at the fence in under a minute."

Johnny's binoculars were designed for this sort of situation. The built-in thermal scope detected the invisible flags on top of spires in the mist and marked them at distance. He then looked at the screen mounted on the binoculars' bridge to confirm their position via GPS. The map on the screen showed no fence, no buildings, only a waypoint – only a blinking dot on the screen.

Stacey was both nervous and excited to see her home for the next six months. It was going to be a long journey, but to her it was worth the benefits it would yield for her career. She was young and talented; eager to embrace the obstacles in her way.

"400 meters, take her down to 3rd we're comin' in a little hot"

"Roger that."

It seemed peculiar to Stacey that Johnny would give the pilot orders. She had always known it to be the other way around. These guys operated more like a team, which was good, she thought. The vehicle was far too crowded to fit anyone's ego, and judging by the way they plowed through the treacherous Alaskan tundra she understood why they needed to be so cautious. Flipping one of these monsters definitely wouldn't end well.

The pilot grabbed a latch directly in front of him and pulled it down a sliding track. A subtle growl came from the engine as the land borne catamaran slowed, lifting the passengers up and forward out of their seats, enough so that they had to dig their feet into the floor to compensate.

"100 meters, Gate bearing two-thirty-six degrees, take er' in slow."

"Copy that" the pilot responded.

The engine purred and vibrated as the MTV-3a crept along, crunching two feet of snow underneath each tread.

"I Got Visual. There's the edge of the fence. Let's get the flare gun out, doesn't look like there's a gate here. No wait, there it is! 231 degrees, hundred meters!"

"I see it!" the pilot responded. His vision wasn't as sharp as Johnny's. He had to squint to see the outline of the fence, like a far away sail hidden in thick ocean fog. Clutching the two hand held levers that controlled the treads, he righted the vehicle and took a straight line to the gate, which opened not a moment too soon, as if some computer, or someone watching, had timed it perfectly.

"We're here folks. It's been a slice. Make sure to get all your belongings from the undercarriage, there will be a team to assist you." Johnny got to his feet and unbuckled his orange coverall jumpsuit. After lighting a cigarette, he slid open a hatch on the inside of the steel contraption and pressed the big green button that emerged. Beneath his feet, the floor slid open, folded and a ladder slid out and extended to the ground.

"Time to get cozy and warm!" Said the quirky weather analyst. Stacey could already tell he had a very strange personality and wasn't too keen on getting to know him – but he would be there for six months either way. She would have to communicate with him through the language of science, it was the only thing she could think of that they might have in common.

Stacey climbed down the ladder first. Before she reached the bottom there was a squad of men in heavy blue jumpsuits with gasmask-like appendages covering their faces ready to greet her. She could barely hear the crunching snow underneath rubber boots over the howling winds. One of them spoke through his mask in a raspy, distorted voice.

"Hello, Miss Peterson, we will escort you to your quarters."

The men had already removed all the luggage from the storage compartment tucked underneath the chassis. Just faintly, she could see a grayish structural outline above the distant horizon. It could have been 50 meters or 250 meters, she couldn't tell.

Just meters in front of her stood a circular capsule clad in smooth, shiny metal big enough to fit 10 people. The masked men and the three passengers stepped inside. At the push of a button, the capsule's doors slid closed, snapping fiercely as they came together. Stacey felt pressure on her ears as soon as the capsule locked. After a slight jolt, the capsule descended into the ground.

The capsule slowed after half a minute, making everyone's guts quiver. The metal doors slid open revealing the central inner chamber of the complex. It was dauntingly massive. Stacey walked out onto the granite floor with her head postured skyward, fixated on the ceilings that must have been fifteen stories high. A hexagonal, raised glass dome structure separated the rocks that constituted the 'unfinished' areas of the roof. The roof itself, as well as the walls, were ugly. Hanging wires sprung out like vines on a dying tree covered the interior of the chamber. Makeshift metal grating attempted to cover the awkward, decrepit innards of the base but they were still very visible. Nonetheless, the entire structure was something to be in awe of. The others that came with her shared a similar awe-struck look on their faces.

"How deep-"

"A hundred and seventy meters, miss Peterson. Follow me to your quarters." Said one of the suited men, who could not remove his mask because his hands were full of gear.

A vast expanse of marble and granite lay between them and a series of hexagonally carved out passageways that went in all different directions. The biggest one lay directly ahead, about the length of two football fields away, by Stacey's estimate. In front of them was a semi-circular pedestal of descending steps. She felt like helping the suited man with the load, they had a long walk ahead. As soon as the man's foot reached the last step, a square shape about the size of the elevator lit up on the floor. It looked magical to the eye, as if pure rock was somehow being instantly melted into glass.

"All aboard!" He said, releasing the luggage onto the shiny surface. Everyone but the guards hesitantly placed their feet onto the plat form.

"Okay. Now everyone sit down." He said, after removing his mask and revealing a thick beard and long shaggy hair.

"This thing is pretty cool." He chuckled. "Just try not to fall off. It's like being on a horse carriage." His cool demeanor stood in direct opposition to the aura of the facility.

The man then removed his glove and placed his hand firmly on the floor beneath him. It looked hot to the touch, but felt as cold as granite should. A rectangular panel beneath his hand turned blue, and was followed by a very loud beep. He raised his hand, and they were off. The installation's new occupants could not believe their eyes as they felt their bodies begin to move. The operation of the mechanism played tricks on their proprioceptive perception. A clear cut path lay ahead of them in the form of bright lights that extended across the chasm in alignment with the rectangle they were sitting on. The pace quickened gradually, until they were moving quite fast – at least as fast as Stacey could run. Her peers looked around, giggling and marveling at the flying carpet they found themselves on. The end of the lit trail brought them to another uncovered elevator which took them two stories up onto a raise metal platform built into the rock. Meters beyond was posted a sign that very clearly and visibly said "LEVEL 1 LIVING AREA/RECREATION" Above a long door. The font used for the lettering carried a very serious tone. Through the doors were more steps that eventually led to a wide hallway lined with rooms on each side. They were about the size of a decent hotel room. Each one had a bed and dresser, a shower with a sink, various other pieces of useful furniture, and a personal fridge stocked full of water, juices and alcoholic beverages. There was a flatscreen television and video game console inside of a wall unit in each room. Despite the drab appearance of the walls, the rooms were quite comfortable. After ten room-lengths the hallway led to the recreation room.

If it could be seen from above, the room itself would look like a giant dollar inserted into the ground.The walls were at the same angle all the way around, and it was massive. The outer perimeter was lined with all the amenities to keep one alive and entertained – a full gym with a kitchen on each side lined the far wall. After the kitchen was an enclosed pool, then a small library full of books and desks with laptops. Rounding out the right side of the room's perimeter was a theater-style projection room with plenty of seats, and even a popcorn machine. To the immediate right upon entering was a duo of butlers, which was made obvious by their white gloves and polite manners. The middle of the room held a basketball court and a tennis court side by side. Almost the entire left wall consisted of a bowed, heavily reinforced window that peered onto the ocean. The crashing waves of the ice shelf allowed the dwellers a glimpse of the outer world – a small reminder to keep them feeling less confined. Everything inside this massive room was designed for leisure, entertainment and comfort, and was facilitated by a team of helpers to cater to their every whim. There was even an all-hours restaurant right against the window. The menu consisted of whatever the inhabitants desired.

Stacey was relieved. This place was amazing – she could definitely get used to it. All of her future coworkers felt the same way, most of them enthralled by their new leisure. Considering where she had dwelled in the past, Stacey realized that "LIVING QUARTERS" was the nicest place she had ever lived.

"Not what you expected? Ha ha! All work and no play is no fun for anyone!" Exclaimed the bearded escort. "Make yourselves at home, pick any room you like they are all the same. These guys here will take care of you. There should be someone contacting you through the announcement system within the hour."

The trio of escorts left the group to their devices. They didn't have many questions. Before they disappeared entirely, the bearded escort told Stacey to come with her.

"Mormont wants to talk to you personally Miss Peterson, he's eager to meet you. Come with us."

No one seemed to notice that Stacey followed the men out of the room.

They returned to the initial huge room and then followed a stone stair way up the wall to another door that looked just like the one to the living quarters. The sign above it read "LEVEL 1A – BIOLABS 1-7." They entered. Another set of stone stairs brought them to a hallway shaped just like the one lined with their apartments, only the rooms lining this hallway were bigger and had windows. Most of them had tables in the middle with a wide array of tools and appendages hanging above and beside them. At the end of the hallway was a man-sized door with a label that read "CRYOGENIC STORAGE."

The room was cold, and everything was lit in a blue hue, much like the red inside photo development labs. A man in a suit stood at the edge of the room next to a raised platform with his back turned.

"Miss Peterson. It's a pleasure to finally meet you. We've been very excited the last few days." Said the man, smiling. He extended his hand to greet Stacey.

"You must be Mormont?" She asked.

"Yes, I am. You're an intuitive one, I see."

Stacey didn't quite know how to react. Mormont stared at her for a moment, smiling, as if he had found a long lost relative.

"Do you have any idea why I've summoned you here?"

"Umm, not really sir." Stacey responded. She really didn't know and hadn't bothered to formulate a guess. The luxurious setting of the living quarters was still fresh in her mind.

Mormont clicked a button on the raised platform next to his waste. The platform top opened like a casket, billowing steam out as it did. The casket was adorned with multiple insignias that were all too familiar to her and everyone who had ever watched a television, or heard a radio ad – the triangular logo that represented Dynatech. Inside was the body of a man, but not a normal one. It was extremely large, at least two meters tall, and it was not devoid of clothing like most cadavers. The entire body was covered up to the collarbone in a shiny metallic material that form-fitted and near the hands and neck, looked like it integrated with the skin. It looked more like a superhero costume than clothing.

"Wow. What is that?" Stacey asked, puzzled. It looked like a man, but she couldn't help but notice the subtle differences. The ears were slightly pointed at the top, and the skin had a peculiar glow to it. Also, the face lacked eyebrows and the hair looked like it was drawn on with a marker. It didn't flow in any particular direction like hair was supposed to.

"Well, that's why you are here Stacey. You are going to help us understand this individual as best as humanly possible." Said Mormont, as he walked over to a rack of surgical tools on the wall, taking a large knife. Stacey grew slightly unnerved. What was he going to do with that?

"You see, the average person would easily be convinced that this is the body of a regular man. But you are too smart for that Stacey, aren't you?"

"I guess so? I mean, the ears, the hair . . ."

"Indeed! Your observations are astute."

Although Mormont came off as friendly, Stacey's inner conscious told her otherwise. She didn't trust his unusual friendliness. There was just something off about him. She wondered if Mormont could pick up on her uneasiness.

"Go ahead. Touch it."

Stacey hesitated.

"Don't be shy! It's perfectly fine." Mormont assured her, using his free hand to caress the silvery outfit. Upon the touch, it lit up like a sparkling diamond underneath his hand. He ran his fingers back and forth on the suit, leaving trails of light that gradually dissipated after a few seconds. Stacey was astonished.

"Wh-what is that sir?" Stacey asked, baffled.

"To be honest, we don't know. But we do know one thing." Mormont said lightly, raising the knife in the air as he spoke. A spark of nervous tingling ran through Stacey at the thought, but before she could gauge her reaction, Mormont plunged the knife toward the cadaver. Amazingly, it did not pierce the body like it should. Instead, a fountain-like appendage of the metallic costume shot up to meet the knife, enveloping the tip, lodging it securely in place. After Mormont released his grip, the knife fell haplessly onto the torso and the metallic skin slowly retracted back to the body.

"It is one hell of a defense system." Mormont looked at Stacey who was astonished.

"We haven't been able to even scratch the stuff. Knives, bullets, even explosives – it shields the body from everything. We have had minor success with high frequency electromagnetic distortion, and some very strange things happened when we pumped high amounts of gamma radiation into it. But other than that, this suit is basically impenetrable."

"Wow." Stacey remarked, truly amazed by the material's capabilities.

"So who made this stuff? The Russians? Chinese?" Stacey asked, curious as to the origin of the incredible body armor. Mormont looked at the escort, who had remained silent the whole time, and chuckled.

"No Stacey, not the Russians, nor the Chinese."

"Then who?"

Mormont looked at the ground. His smile disappeared, his demeanor changed instantly. Stacey could tell he was very serious.

"Miss Peterson, we handpicked you for this job. Do you know why?"

"Well, because of my thesis?"

"No, Miss Peterson, no. Your thesis, although impressive, was not the basis with which we selected you. It is because of your distinguished record of silence in past contracts. Your ability to work successfully without letting your imagination get the better of you."

Stacey wondered where he was going with this. Her mind began to narrow down an unlikely possibility. If not the Russians, nor the Chinese, then there was really only one possible answer. But it was so farfetched . . .

"Miss Peterson, laying in front you of you is an extraterrestrial lifeform." Mormont exclaimed, without emotion or any kind of indication as to what he was trying to imply by telling her. Hands tightly concealed behind his back, he gazed at her like a scientist observing a prodded rat. She was flabbergasted. All at once, she had just become privy to the answer of a question that held monumental implications for all of mankind.

"Are you serious? I mean really?" She asked, excited. After all, it's not every day you come face to face with an alien.

"Yes, Miss Peterson. A real alien. We captured him and three of his friends earlier this week. They were trying to infiltrate this facility.

"Infiltrate?"

"Yes, infiltrate. Luckily our security team was able to thwart the attempt. Unfortunately, we lost a great deal of men in doing so. These . . . creatures, as we have come to know, are extremely dangerous. Able to shapeshift into different people. You could see how that could fool even the most advanced levels of security."

Stacey was amazed, confused, excited and slightly scared all at once. Too many questions raced through her mind for her to collect her thoughts. This truly was unbelievable.

"Before I go any further, I must know something Stacey."

"What?" She asked quickly.

"Can we trust you to keep this a secret? From your peers, your family, from everyone?"

Stacey pondered the question. Could she keep this a secret? One side of her desperately wanted to enlighten the human race, to let them know what they have been missing out on. But the other side knew that the idea alone would result in the termination of her life.

"Yes sir. You can trust me. I will not tell anyone. I promise."

"Good! I am glad to hear that Miss Peterson. I knew picking you was the right decision. Starting tomorrow, it will be your job to unlock the mysteries surrounding this individual, and the others we have in cryo-storage."

"Others?"

"Yes Miss Peterson. In some ways they are just like us. In others, they are as different from us as white from black."

She couldn't help but ask what was on her mind.

"Where are the others?"

"They are dead, Stacey."

She should have known. It's not like they would have been allowed to leave of their own free will. What was truly amazing to her was everything that she knew was being held from her. How deep did the situation go? Asking questions was not the right thing to do – it would not yield any answers for her – only punishment. She knew the routine. The irony of her situation entailed the fact that she would never be able to tell another soul about what she was about to engage in over the next six months.

"I know this is a lot to take in so abruptly. But we had no other choice. It is imperative that we figure this out as soon as possible."

"Why?" She asked, although she knew she wasn't supposed to. But Mormont was leading her on.

"Well, we know that they are hostile. And extremely sophisticated technologically. Unfortunately, these facts alone pose a threat to us."

"I see." She said in a perplexed gaze. Mormont took a step closer.

"I will be frank with you, Stacey. There is a war going on underneath our cities, underneath our roads, deserts and forests. And in our atmosphere. It is very real. And the frightening aspect of it all is that we are monumentally outgunned. You could very well turn the tides of this war. We need your brain, Miss Peterson, and your commitment. You could save hundreds if not thousands of lives." Said Mormont quite seriously. Both of them stood there for a moment, milling over the situation in their minds.

war?

"That's enough for today. Return to your quarters. We begin work at 0700 tomorrow morning."

And that was it. Her escort brought her back to the living quarters where everyone else was fully immersed in the entertainment prospects at their disposal. She laid supine in her bed, staring up at the ceiling, pondering the severity of the situation she was now in.

* * * *

"We're fifteen minutes out guys, I've got a grassy field located on GPS, 23 miles outside Paris. Sound Good?"

"Yeah take us down. Nice and quiet."

Lester and Jim were almost there. During the flight they scoured the back channels with telephone calls and intelligence updates. Anything they could somehow design into a possible scenario in their minds, playing the game of mental numbers.

"Uhh, Captain?" Said Jones, weakly.

"What is it Gary?" Replied Lester, leaning over and intently examining a series of maps.

"I've got something."

Everyone in the cabin looked towards Gary, even the agents who typically remained silent. He sat in his chair uneasily. His knee bounced like lapdog's tail at the sniff of food.

"What is it Jones?"

"You're gonna' have to come and look at this sir."

Both Lester and Jim huddled around the SATNAV screen.

"I cross-referenced Peter Schlesinger with the NSA, and CIA databases. A contact from the pentagon was able to provide me with an encryption code that gave me access to the departmental mainframe." Gary said, clearly and concisely. He had been busy for the last hour and a half. "He was officially listed as deceased in 1997, found dead in his apartment with lacerations around his neck."

"Murder?"

"Officially listed as a suicide sir."

Jim and Lester looked at each other, mentally agreeing on what they both knew.

"Anyways that's what I got from the CIA. Also, they monitored him as soon as he got back from a job in the Nevada desert back in '77 where he was badly injured, they considered him non-threatening by '85. Not much right? Well here's where it gets really weird."

Gary clicked a few times and pushed some buttons. A series of windows popped up. Jim and Lester perched even tighter to Gary's shoulders.

"This is from the NSA database. And it's only from two weeks ago. Apparently Peter Schlesinger is alive and breathing, and the NSA has been watching him for months. Supposedly he is a cyber terrorist, he is somewhere in Europe and is considered a 'target of extreme priority' which, incase you guys didn't know, means they really want him dead."

Lester wondered who this 'contact' was, and how Jones had slithered his way into their pocket, but that wasn't as important now.

"We'll figure that out later. What about Anthony?"

"Well, I ran a search. But not just a normal search." Gary raised his hand and placed it on what looked like a common USB storage device sticking out of a port next to his knees. However, it was far from that. He tapped his finger on it lightly. It was an awkward moment for him, not knowing if his tricks would yield the respect of a good impression, or anger.

"Get to the point!"

Jim and Lester had seemed to accept what Gary was, and what he was all about. They didn't have time to get mad at him. He hoped that somehow his guilt would be given a reprimand, a way out. Maybe he could somehow make up for what he had done and regain the pride he once had, as well as the respect of his mentors.

"This thing lets me tap into the grey areas . . . the things that are usually hidden, ya' know, compartmentalized. Anyways, here is Stall and Williams' mission record."

"Where did you get that thing?" Asked Jim.

"Sir, how do you think I keep everything so hidden?" Gary asked, then rolled around in his chair. "So *sneaky?*"

Gary dodged the question and went to work on the screen with his hands, expanding a window as wide as it would go. It showed pictures of Akazawhi and his henchmen, a stack of writing pertaining to the mission.

"So what are we looking for Jones?"

"One second sir."

Gary held down a series of buttons on the keyboard which opened up a black window. Then he started issuing in commands and prompts. The green hieroglyphs danced across the screen faster than Jim and Lester could read them. They looked at each other, acknowledging the fact that neither of them knew just how corrupt Gary Jones had become. Were there more leaks inside the bureau?

"Here it is." He said, pulling another flat window into view with his nimble fingertips.

"This document was attached to Anthony's file with an Ariolhyte-level encryption code just hours before he left. Whoever wants to see this file needs a security clearance way above mine. Above both of yours, too."

"Someone at the headquarters?"

"I don't know sir, I don't. But I might be able to run a satellite-blowback test, it doesn't always work but sometimes you can trace signals back to certain radar towers. It's a long shot, but I've done it before."

Lester wondered what would happen if someone else in uniform got their hands on Gary. What would happen to him, and Jim, and to the pilots. These were some serious security breaches happening, and he was allowing it. For a second, the thought of regretting his decision to embark on this hapless journey crossed his mind. To turn back and regroup in the States. He pushed that thought so far out of his mind, indulging his self-earned belief in his own instinctual strength that he knew it would never return. If his career – his life was on the line, so be it.

"Do it."

"Okay, I'll do it. There's one more thing though guys."

Gary had their full attention. His normal jitters stopped and he clenched his jaw. The kind of serious look that usually denotes a deep, entranced thought coming to the surface in a moment of self-realization, and admission.

"I can pop that file open sir. I can do it. But if I do, a carrier signal is gonna' broadcast back to The Pentagon, and to Mr. Grey. It will be considered a complete breach of national security and I will be prosecuted, and so will anyone with me. Even the pilots"

He pulled the device out and tapped it with his fingers again, waiting for Lester or Jim to tell him what to do.

"You've gotta' be fucking kidding Jones. What else haven't you told us!?" Jim yelled, angered. "What the hell is that thing and where did you get it?"

"Mr. Grey gave it to me. He didn't even tell me. When I left his office, he gave me an envelope filled with money. This thing was in it wrapped in a piece of paper that said 'USE IF EXPOSED' written on it. But he tried to trick me, sir. I was too smart for him. I had this little thing analyzed and found out its real purpose for myself. I bet he didn't expect that, not at all . . . by all means if work my magic, I can crack that code and see that document. We all can. But it's gonna' cost us"

Lester weighed the options in his mind. He weighed *everything* in his mind. They all may very well be already in jeopardy of treason, and the best recruit the FBI had seen in years was most likely dead. He wasn't sure he could trust Jim anymore, but he was far too committed now to give up.

"Do it Jones." Lester said. He had to know what was in that file if it meant Anthony's life. Jim quietly agreed.

"Alright. Here we go."

A green hexagonal window popped up in front of everything after Gary held down a sequence of buttons on the keyboard. Quite simply, it said 'INITIATE?' in the middle. He clicked on it, making it disappear in lieu of a flood of documents and pictures that spewed onto the holoscreen. He was able to select one that had big bold red lettering stamped on it that read 'TERMINATE'.

"This is the one we want. Look. Someone, for some reason, wants Anthony dead. And look, here's the plan. This is the hotel him and Williams stayed at. He was supposed to meet someone at a nearby restaurant for intel on Akazawhi. But that was just a cover. A CIA assassin . . . here read this."

Lester scrunched his eyes together and read a paragraph under Gary's finger.

Kill and dispose of informant, pose as him in the restaurant. When target arrives, poison his meal with 50mg of Serum3. Transport corpse back to headqaurters ASAP.

It was cold, and tactical. He wasn't surprised – he knew how these things worked.

"Can you find out who attached the file?" Jim demanded furiously. In front of his face was proof that someone ordered Anthony's death, and it shook his nerves greatly.

"Not the exact person. But I've seen documents like this before, and they have Pentagon west wing written all over them."

"What does that mean Gary?" Lester asked, once again commanding him.

"Well sir, if I had to guess I'd say it was Mr. Grey himself. He's a very sketchy individual, let me tell you. He's the one who got me involved in all this backhandedness."

"That's what I needed to know Gary."

Lester knew that going after someone in the pentagon was political and literal suicide and success was very improbable. But his hand was forced. He rapidly envisioned a trial in an American court, a scandal in the news, or maybe, a sniper rifle on top of a parking garage. Either way, this Mr. Grey was going to feel his wrath.

* * * *

Anthony's eyes struggled to open. He felt the singe of exhaustion weighing them down, irritating his exposed eyeballs under the bright lights. He subconsciously hoped he would wake up in his bedroom, or in the hotel in France with Williams safe and sound – but it was not to be. Everything he had just been through was as real as the cold floor of the train beneath him. The woman who was once Gordon and called herself Aremis kneeled above him. When he came fully to, he lunged forward in a panic as everything resurfaced in his waking mind. He tried to thrust his arms into Aremis to push her back, but they touched nothing. She was much faster than she looked. Anthony thought about getting ready to defend himself physically but then he remembered what Aremis did to the guard outside the train. His ribs were already sore enough.

"It's okay Anthony. I'm not going to hurt you. But I must tell you, we are in danger. We must leave immediately, those guards are undoubtedly hot on our tail already."

"Wait . . . how can I trust you? And what the fuck are you anyways? You were a man, then turned into a fucking woman right in front of me. Explain that please!!"

"Anthony, we don't have time. I promise, there are answers to all of your questions where we are going."

"Yeah, because I've definitely got a few. And where the hell are we going exactly?"

Aremis smiled slightly, moving closer.

"Home, Anthony. We are going home."

Aremis extended her hand toward Anthony to help him up. He reluctantly extended his own arm and allowed Aremis to pull him to his feet. As soon as their hands touched, he felt relieved. A warm sense of joy, relaxation and utter bliss washed over his body. He felt safe in her clutch. There was another feeling apparent – Aremis was incredibly beautiful. Her eyes seemed to stare right into his soul. It was an intoxicating feeling that he couldn't describe, although he knew, somehow, that she could feel his emotions.

"This way."

Aremis led Anthony to the front of the train.She kicked a section of sheet metal as hard as she could and amazingly, the thing flew off and onto the ground below. The environment outside of the train was dark and dusty. Swirls of subterranean winds twisted plumes of ashy sand around the interior of the train, forcing Anthony to cover his eyes. Aremis leapt several meters down to the ground surrounding the track, which consisted of soft, flakey white sand that seemed to glitter like a hologram. Her feet kicked a cloud of dust into the air.

"Give me a moment." She said as Anthony watched on from the train. Her silvery metal outfit began to glow. She rubbed her hand against her hip, to which a piece of her suit detached and formed into a ball that fit in her hand. She grew brighter and brighter, until a luminescent aura surrounded her entire body. Her skin became almost transparent, her eyes became bright white. With Anthony observing in amazement, she flung the orb high up into the air towards the ceiling, simultaneously glowing brighter herself. Her aura made the dust particles stop in midair, at the mercy of her movements. It ascended for a long time, giving them an idea of how high the roof was and just how massive the cavern was. On the roof, by his estimate about three hundred meters high, the orb slowed to a stop. It's bright glow illuminated a series of angular lines connected to circular divots in the ceiling. The spider web of connected lines and dots resembled a neighborhood of roads and cul de sacs if viewed from above. Hovering feet from the roof, the shimmering orb stopped, and sat.

Glittering diamonds strewn across the black expanse of rigid curves and orbs seemed to adorn the road map, as Anthony perceived it. Some were as big as a Volkswagen Beetle and they hung precariously from stalactites that were part of the structure. It became quite obvious to Anthony that he must be underground, and that Aremis is looking for a set of directions. But his mind couldn't search for the answers to a million other questions – like how diamonds could be that big, and who could have built what they were looking at. But most pertinent to his struggling psyche was how he had convinced his own mind to accept what he was currently witnessing and subsequently perceiving as reality. Subconsciously he knew this was all impossible, but he had to bury that thought deep. Letting his mind wander during an experience such as this could quickly lead to insanity.

Engrained psychological knowledge from his training retrieved itself from the deep recesses of his fractured mind, allowing him to revert to a non-emotional state where he could be an observer – devoid of the "weaknesses" of emotional rationalization. It was a coping mechanism, taught to all recruits in his division as a last ditch-effort in a torture situation. Depravity of the mind or DOM mode auto-engaged itself to keep him from going into shock. A weaker mind would not be able to handle this.

The warmth of Aremis' touch lingered, dissipated and left as he watched the spectacle before him. He realized that he would have to take control of himself and stay calm no matter what happened next.

Aremis' posture shifted. She kneeled, and flung her hand towards the sky. On cue the glowing orb exploded furiously into a thousand rapid ribbons of light and glitter, the brief burst lit up the entire cavern for a split second, the same way a bolt of lightning shutters the expanse of the skyline for the slightest instant. The ribbons collected, spiraled together and wrapped themselves around the largest diamonds. They appeared to absorb the light itself and harness it. The glitter fell slowly to the floor as the diamond nodes grew more luminous. After a few seconds the ceiling no longer looked like a road map, but a star constellation painting the night sky.

"Good. I know where we are. Come on, Anthony, over to the other side of the tracks. we must move quickly. Stay close to me."

Aremis' glow dimmed until she looked relatively normal again. The ceiling dimmed along with her as if they were connected. The other side of the tracks looked the same. It was pitch dark except for the few meters of shine that was provided by a similar orb of light from Aremis suit that detached and autonomously followed them around. The two of them jogged down a tilted slope, a beach that never met water. Anthony's worn body ached with every stride.

After a few minutes, a subtle rumbling abruptly began; barely noticeable but definitely there.

"What's . . . that?" Anthony asked, puffing each word out with an exasperated breath.

"You feel that?"

"Yeah, a rumbling, don't you?"

"Yes, but . . . my senses are fine-tuned to such a vibration . . . yours should not be . . .yet."

"What do you mean 'fine-tuned'?

"I'll explain later. It is a good thing though, you're body is beginning to accommodate much faster than I expected. Come on! We haven't much time."

Their pace quickened. Anthony was growing tired. His aching knees began to quiver and shake. A raised dune clipped his foot and caused him to tumble face first into the dust. It was painful. He groaned loudly, struggling to get back to his feet. His arms could barely push his torso upright again. Aremis noticed and proceeded to pick Anthony up by his collar. Barely able to stand, he leaned on Aremis' shoulder who was quite a bit shorter than him, but she bore the weight easily.

The rumbling grew louder.

"We aren't going to make it! Hold on tight Anthony!" Aremis said loud and clear. Anthony barely managed to wrap his hands around her neck before she squatted and leapt a hundred feet down the slope with him in her clutch. Anthony drifted between consciousness and paralysis as Aremis skipped bounds across the sandy tundra. They were moving much quicker now, but the rumbling was beginning to shake the entire cavern.

"Hold on tighter!" Aremis yelled, feeling his grip weaken. They landed from a jump, creating a sizable divot in the sand. Aremis squatted and began to glow once more. Anthony could feel the energy emanating from her and surrounding them in an aura of protective light. She leapt one last time – Anthony felt the grip of gravity pulling at his stomach like he was on an elevator. They got so high that the cavern floor became invisible. Behind them, a spectral trail of light followed them like the tail of a comet. He turned his head to what lay in front of them. A rockface rapidly came into view, Anthony screamed and buried his face into Aremis shoulder, thinking he was about to die. But his breath remained – Aremis attached herself to the giant wall and began to climb with Anthony holding on like a monkey. They managed to roll themselves onto a horizontal pedestal just barely wide enough for both of them to fit their bodies on. Anthony wanted to lay there, exhausted and broken, but the rumbling was about to become an earthquake. He opened his eyes in time to see a spike from the ceiling falling right for him. Aremis flung her hand into the air and the stalactite shattered into a thousand fragments, saving his life.

"Come on! Down the path!"

Above the raised pedestal was a jagged set of climbable protrusions, and beyond them, a circular hole carved into the side of the rock wall, big enough to walk down. The jolt of adrenaline that surged through Anthony caused by the falling missile gave him the energy to get to his feet. Each step was cautious and painful – the vibrating cavern wanted him to fall to his feet.

"What the hell is causing it!" Anthony yelled as he and Aremis descended down the narrow winding path. She clutched his hand and pretty much dragged him.

"It's a Rhakthfer!"

"What the hell is that!?"

"It's a massive subterranean creature! They normally don't come this far from the core unless . . ."

"Unless what?"

"Unless it smells food! They consider us delicacies! Hurry Anthony!"

The path winded and became narrower and narrower. He wasn't sure if they were going to make it and Aremis, despite her power, seemed afraid as well. The roof was beginning to cave in piece by piece. They had to dodge falling spikes as they descended. The path came to a point where they had to crawl through. The narrow confines made it extremely difficult to move, but Aremis insisted they go through it. The man-size tube looked like a death trap. He looked at Aremis as if she must be kidding, there's no way he'd make it through there. A piece of the wall next to him slid off, nearly landing on him, causing him to impulsively launch his body into the hole. He made it only a few feet before the jagged rocks confined him. He began to panic. Aremis grabbed him by the foot and yanked him out of the hole to the ground – and then, she put her hands together next to her chest and began to glow again.

a circular beam of light shot out from her midsection into the hole. It instantly burned away the jagged protrusions, making the hole slightly bigger.

"Go now!" She yelled, as the cave began to deteriorate around her. Anthony wasted no time leaping back into the hole, shimmying down it as fast as he could. The freshly glassed rock was barely cooled – it singed his forearms as he wiggled through. Aremis got in behind him, urging him to move faster. The hole began to widen after about thirty feet where he could see the end of the passage. Once through, beneath him was a platform barely wide enough to stand on and in front of him, a pitch black expanse of nothingness going straight down. He exited the hole so fervently that he nearly fell into the abyss. Luckily, Aremis was there to grab him by the shirt and pull his body flat against the rock.

'We made it!" She said, smiling, as if the torment was over – as if they hadn't reached a dead end. Seconds after she rolled out of the tunnel, it collapsed completely, sending bits of rock and dust flinging into the gaping black hole beneath their feet. Anthony watched them plummet, wide-eyed, until they disappeared. There was nowhere left to go now.

"What do we do now?" He asked, desperately clinging to any jagged rock he could get his hands on.

"I must ask you to trust me now Anthony."

He knew what she was thinking, and he didn't like it one bit. She couldn't possibly be serious. Before he could argue, she grabbed him by the hand. He tried to pull away, but her grip was like a vice.

"On the count of three!"

"No wait! We can't!"

"1"

"You're fucking crazy we'll die!" Anthony yelled, desperately trying to yank his hand away to no avail.

"2!"

"LET GO!"

"3!" Aremis yelled, and then, with Anthony in tow, she leapt clear off the platform and descended into the black depths. In that moment, Anthony's life flashed before his eyes. He never should have trusted this crazy beautiful woman.

* * * *

The familiar click-clacking of shiny dress shoes echoed throughout the corridors of The Pentagon's west wing. A short, fat, balding man with glasses wiped sweat from his face as he paced nervously down the hallway carrying a file folder in his hand. Finally, he reached the door to Mr. Grey's office. He readjusted his tie, wiped the sweat off of his brow and took a deep breath. People walking by noticed how out of place he looked and the pools of sweat blotting his dress shirt. He raised his hand to knock, but a voice beckoned from within before his hand met the wooden door.

"Come in Cullen." He heard.

He opened the door slowly and entered the room where Mr. Grey sat in his chair at an angle where Cullen could only see the right side of Grey's body. The air inside Grey's office was filled with tension.

Grey slowly turned to face Cullen, holding an utterly disgusted look on his face, as if he was looking at a corpse.

"The file, Cullen." He demanded, extending his arm. He was trying to make it perfectly clear that he was not interested in any further discourse but the task at hand.

Cullen was so nervous that as he extended his arm to place the file on Grey's desk, his shaking limb dropped the file all over the floor. Pages scattered throughout the room, to which Cullen awkwardly scurried on his knees to regain the strewn pages.

"I'm so sorry sir! I-I didn't . . .I'm so-"

"Cullen! You are WORTHLESSSSSSS!" Yelled Grey, standing condescendingly above Cullen as if he was going to beat him senseless while he was down. He struggled to bundle the pages back together with Mr. Grey berating him. His face turned beat red.

"This is why you didn't get that raise Cullen. You pathetic, worthless, waste of skin. You are disgusting! GET OUT!" Grey continued once more, to which Cullen struggled to get to his feet, slipping clumsily out of Mr. Grey's office. People in the hallway stood and laughed, some walked on in ignorance. He didn't care about them – he was just glad to be about of there. He let out a deep sigh and laid his head against the wall. But then, from within the closed office,

"GET BACK TO WORK YOU PIECE OF SHIT!"

Cullen immediately sprung to his feet and began marching at an uncomfortable pace back to his cubicle on the other side of the building.

Mr. Grey carefully bent over and picked up a few pieces of paper and shuffled them back into the folder in the right order. After reading it over for a few moments he waved his index finger. The deadbolt on the door to his office clanged into place, locking it. He then picked up the phone on his desk and began dialing. An upbeat secretary on the other end answered.

"White House Foreign Affairs department, how may I help you?"

"Authorization code KOMODO2 put me through to Mr. White's office please."

"One moment sir."

After a few seconds, Mr. White answered.

"Hello brother. I've been expecting your call."

"So you have been briefed then . . . what is the statussss of the Darmerian?"

"Escaped. We have multiple tracking teams en route right now. We expect–"

"Escaped? ESCAPED? How did that happen?" Grey interrupted, slamming his massive fist quite hard on the desk..

"He had an assailant. It was . . . a complete breach. An intruder stole him and escaped in the maglev train, destroying any chance of retrieval."

"Hmmm. Red will not be happy about thissss brother. Who is assigned to bring them back?"

"The newest blend. They are quite un upgrade over the last batch we produced."

"Good. And what about the FBI Director and the Uncle?"

"They must be silenced as well. They stole a very important file . . . one that they must not make use out of. And I personally want to see that little rat of yours fry for his betrayal."

"Oh, he will. I will handle them, you make sure that filthy creature is captured and under our thumb. We cannot allow our enemies to awaken him, under any circumstances."

"Agreed. What did Mr. Brown do with the pilots?"

"He sent them to Starset for neural therapy. It should not be a problem. And speaking of Starset, has our package from Mr. Akazawhi arrived there yet?"

"Indeed it has. Our plans are moving forward brother. Stay vigilant."

Both men were silent, holding the phone for a few seconds, then hung them up in unison. After Mr. Grey buried the phone into it's pedestal, he picked it up and started mashing the buttons again. It rang twice.

"Authorization code KOMODO2. I'm going to need a tactical squad ready for deployment in Paris immediately."

Chapter 11

PURSUIT

It took thirty three and a half minutes for the cavern left behind by Aremis and Anthony to begin rumbling again. It started as a whimpering groan but as seconds passed, became a considerable vibration. Within a minute, the vibrations peaked into a violent shake. The massive diamonds strewn across the ceiling slowly shimmied out of their embedded grooves as a result of the increasing reverberation, eventually dislodging completely and falling toward the cavern floor. Most of them plummeted haplessly into the thick plumes of sand creating a deep thud that flung fresh, buried flakes into the air surrounding. Others positioned directly above the train fell, pulverizing massive sections flat into the tracks beneath. Huge electro-fluorescent explosions of energy and fire filled the cavernous air, leaving behind smoldering heaps of twisted burning metal and the snapping sparks of severed electrical wires. Fireballs flung into the reaches of the descending cavern floor, dissipating into nothing in the flakey sand.

A meters-wide circular section of the roof began to turn red. It grew hotter and hotter until it glowed burning hot. The rock literally melted and dripped like water to the floor below, settling and cooling into steaming piles of goop. Someone, or something, was already hot on the trail of the escaped hostage and his assailant.

The melting rock formed a hole that expanded rapidly – something was coming through. The spinning teeth of a sophisticated digging machine bored their way through rock into the thick air of the cavern with no regard for what lay beneath them. The jagged protrusions lining the cone shaped nose of the contraption ripped through solid rock as if it were water. Four spiral shaped rungs on the bullet-nose of the vessel culminated in awkward, smooth and jagged spikes formed by a unique carbonite element crafted under immense pressure and heat with the precision of lithium-diode nano-lasers. Carbonite3, as it was labeled, had a density four-hundred times stronger than diamond, and took on a precarious wispy form that did not conform to the rigid lines and angular curves of the vessel it was attached to. Microscopic holes embedded in the nose itself released a gelatinous mixture of chemical elements that broke down the rock on a molecular level. The carbonite shards looked more like the teeth of a ferocious monster than a mechanical digging instrument. The digging apparatus allowed the entire vessel to fall through the earth at half free-fall speed.

The nose of the machine emerged clearly from the rock, and its rapid spinning began to slow down. Attached to the nose was a giant cylindrical metal capsule that held the vessel's cargo. Once it was half way through, two more spots on the ceiling began to heat up and melt. And then another, and another. In total, eight of the metal hulks breached the cavern ceiling.

Once half way through, the spinning nose stopped entirely, retracted, and locked itself into place. The superheated carbonite teeth held a momentary glow that dissipated after a few seconds. The entire vessel fell into the cavern. Once free of the rock ceiling, it plummeted unapologetically towards the cavern floor, ready to destroy anything in its path. About thirty meters before it punished the sand beneath, four panels exploded off the side of the cylinder, revealing jets that immediately burst bluish flames toward the floor. They succeeded in slowing the vessel to a reasonable pace before impact. The precaution lay not in the effort to keep the digging nose from being ruined – it would destroy any earthly element that crossed its path and still maintain structural integrity – it lay in the necessity to protect the cargo residing within the cylinder. Although sturdily built for war, the intense impact could potentially kill them.

The nose slammed into the sand, embedding itself firmly into the ground and remaining upright. The other machines fell and landed throughout the dark cavern, all of them plunging violently; perfectly as planned. A circular pedestal on the very top of each cylinder raised itself, revealing a single heavily armored soldier. However, it would take a few seconds for them to become active. In unison, all of the capsules burst into life with a series of bright blue floodlights that made the light flakes on the floor speckle and shimmer. And then, each soldier came to life. Their heads tilted back, and their extremities began to move. Next to them, a holoscreen full of buttons on which their fingers went to work. Vents of steam erupted from sectioned metal panels, which then detached and flung perfectly in unison onto the sandy floor below. Another sheath of metal retracted and folded, revealing the contents of the capsules. Confined firmly to harnesses attached to a centrifugal pillar were more soldiers, who seemed to be asleep. After their captain above pressed a series of buttons on the holopad, they were all awakened. The lights on their helmets turned on, their arms spread out and detached the harnesses that held them in place. One by one, they left their makeshift chairs and climbed down a ladder on the middle pillar to the sandy floor below.

Each capsule held twenty four soldiers plus their commanding officer, each with individual distinctions. Eighteen of them were Expert Marksman Subterranean Shocktrooper – EMSS for short, and had light body forming armor designed for easy movement and increased agility. Four of them were heavy assault troopers – these ones stood well over seven feet, adorned with thick plated armor and a large chaingun that would over-encumber any normal human. The remaining two were the commander of the platoon and his delegate. Even for a genetically enhanced cyborg, simlutaneously issuing orders to 23 different brains proved to be difficult.

A four foot tall section between the capsule and the drill cone held their armaments. Long-barreled rifles, rocket launchers and side-arms as well as a full complement of fragmentation and stun grenades filled the compartment. They removed the weapons at a frenetic pace and by the end they were all armed to the teeth. Each and every soldier stood at least two meters tall, except for the communications officers who sported no weaponry. More robotic than human, these engineered supersoldiers moved and operated with a level of lethal precision that did not allow for error. Carved into the armor directly above their hearts was the triangular insignia of Dynatech, the company that created and owned their souls, if it could be said they had souls at all.

Without any words spoken between them, the squads rallied in straight lines to a point next to the train. Footsteps in the sand led further in to the descending darkness. The swirling winds of the cavern hadn't the time to fully cover Aremis and Anthony's trail. There they all waited in silence, standing upright, looking forward. Orders were not issued verbally, unless necessary. Each soldier had a device implanted in their neural cortex that received orders through radio frequencies, and each and every one of them would follow their orders unquestioningly, even if it led to their certain destruction. One of the capsule's team leaders handed his huge rifle to a grunt next to him and walked to the front of the pack, bent down and examined the barely-covered tracks. The cavernous winds in front of him coiled ribbons of sand in and out of the subtle divots left behind amongst the almost indistinguishable dunes. *Almost.*

The group commander's helmet was painted red for a reason. He had a unique ability among his peers – the ability to think. Only the best soldiers were given this ability, and for a specific reason. He was not a clone, but a real man. Although perceived as perfect soldiers, the ability to think rationally, or at all, had its merits in battle versus being a brainless killing machine. No matter how strong, quick or accurate they could be, they lacked the most powerful weapon on any battlefield. Because of this, there had to be someone with an actual brain down there, or the soldiers may become obsolete and inefficient.

He stood up from the trail and as he rose, the steps became more clearly visible as the angle changed. He began marching down the track on his own while issuing a series of radiofrequency orders through his headset. The soldiers organized into a long, staggered line behind him. The commander's robot brain could also send and receive messages from above. A constant link between his neural and nano-cortexes and those of his troops allowed their brains to see what he saw. The information transferred and downloaded instantly along with a list of worded instructions.

Because of the massive vitrified tubes left behind by the metal monsters that brought them, a neural network link could be shakily maintained with his superiors above. Images from his mind's eye traveled back to them where they could dissect the information in rooms full of monitors and headsets, then send orders back down. If need be, unbeknownst to the robotic drones, their owners could override their brains and assume complete control.

The commander took a few more steps, then stopped and knelt. A soldier appeared from behind him and detached a device from his back. It looked like a VCR before he deployed it for operation – it shapeshifted into what looked like a hand held satellite. He held a series 4 spectrometer, designed specifically to trace resonant energetic trails left behind by living creatures. It was a long shot, but they may be able to sniff something out, given the strong spectral lifeforce inherent to the creatures they hunted.

As they knelt and waited for the device to take hold, the line of soldiers was already forming a circle around them. The peripheral squads pointed their guns into the darkness, covering every possible angle. Their helmets lit up, giving them a dozen meters of vision-targeting to work with. Together, with an eerie sense of monotonous, simplistic brilliance, every soldier marched perfectly down the slope, ready without hesitation to destroy any threat that came close. The sum of its parts created a single tactically lethal unit that protected the commander and the officer that followed him.

Eventually the reach of their powerful indigo headlights shone the freckled surface of the cavern wall. And then, the silence broke.

"Signal confirmed. Seventeen meters dead ahead. Extremely faint. 0.8 spectrohertz and lowering."

Blurting information out loud was often the most efficient way for the drones to communicate rapidly.

They had a sniff. The massive swiss-cheese wall, however, gave them nothing more than a series of dead ends with only one narrow possibility of finding the right path again. Almost every hole went immeasurably deep into the Earth in a different direction, and there were hundreds of them.

On cue, teams of two, one regular EMSS and one heavy shock trooper approached the wall together while the rest of the contingent of warriors created a protective semi-circle around and connecting to the wall. The smaller, lighter-armored soldiers detached a cylindrical gun from the gadget-filled broad backs of their heavier counterparts, and aimed them up at the wall. The guns fired grappling spikes into the rock attached to ropes for them to climb. One by one, the soldiers began to systematically detach from their protective enclosure and ascend the ropes which were scattered at different heights. Everything in their plan was expertly coordinated, meticulous and scientifically pre-ordained – but in this case they would need some luck if they were to ascertain the whereabouts of the escapees. It was only a matter of time now, and they had a limited number of spectrometers to give them valuable hints.

As the regiment coordinated their efforts, the rocky ceiling of the cavern tucked a few kilometers away began to rumble again. A ninth and final digging machine made its way into the dark depths of the earth, much bigger, and moving much faster than the ones that preceded it.

* * * *

Six fully loaded extended cab black suburban SUVs nestled between pedestrians and small cars made their way through the streets of Paris, en route to the last known location of agents Stall and Williams. The tinted windows provided solace for those dwelling within the trucks, which screamed American. Everyone who walked by stared, and every car they waved out of their way crept slowly, gawking. Amidst the thick metropolis of foreigners, Lester and Jim devised a plan to find their lost son. Along with them, a few handfuls of the best trained assassins on the planet, cordoned from childhood and trained in the ways of death. Unlike the robotic quasi-humans produced by Dynatech, these soldiers could think and feel. They had memories and emotions, despite how hard they tried to conceal them. Conventional scientific thought dictates that emotion, and more specifically fear, can be a soldier's biggest downfall. However, these men pervaded scientific thought with their galvanized brains and hearts, built through years of camaraderie with each other through secretive combat training and education. A hard-wired emotional attachment to their country, the world itself and more specifically *each other* gave them the strength to do things normal men would not dare. The men of spec38 were modern day ghosts, since no one who engaged in combat with them had ever survived to tell of their existence. Clear and obvious deployment in such a densely populated area was a risk that Lester was all too aware of.

"The building is just around that corner. Get these civvies out of the way we gotta' move." Beckoned Lester, to which the driver of the vehicle they were in slammed on the horn and aggressively stepped on the gas pedal.

When they reached the building, there was no chance for discretion. All six SUVS pulled into the semi-circular paved area in front of the plaza, and the troopers filed out of the trucks within seconds. Their commander took a moment to look around and analyze their surroundings. It didn't take him long to start issuing orders.

"I want two sniper teams, one in that building over there, one in that perch just across from it." He said, pointing to each location.

"Roger that sir."

"Squads 1 and 2, secure the first floor and lobby. Squads 3 and 4 with me, we're going up to the room where Stall and Williams stayed. We're going to set up shop there." Said the commander, as he looked for direction from Lester, who had his focus buried deep in the file locked in his hands.

"Everyone else, take up perimeter positions around the building. Constant communication, I want eyes and ears on every individual who leaves and enters the area. Understood?"

"Confirmed sir."

After the orders were issued, a few men paired off and headed toward different corners of the building.

"Jim, Gary, let's go. First stop is the front desk, ask every attendant, service person and bartender if they remember Stall or Williams being here. Jones, I want you upstairs on that damn computer, call every police station and hospital in France if you have to. Find out whatever you can and speak to whoever you need to. If Anthony is alive in this city, we are going to find him. And remember, Akazawhi has in his employ a large number of spies in this region. Everyone stay frosty."

With that mentality, the remaining soldiers entered the building as the suburbans peeled out away and disappeared. The commander stayed close by Lester's side.

"Sir, my team at the airport has some new intel. They confirmed that Agent Stall and Williams *were* on that plane."

"And?"

"I had a CIA contact visit the nearest hospitals immediately after you sent the request for support. None of them showed any records of Anthony ever being there. The crash officially listed no survivors sir."

Although the severity of such a crash warranted nothing but death, Lester knew when he smelled a rat. Someone at the hospital was hiding something, but it was far across town and finding the exact individual or individuals he would need to press would be akin to finding a needle in a haystack.

"Of course it did." He muttered sarcastically.

Standing in the spacious lobby as his armed escorts searched every nook and cranny and interrogated the hotel's staff, Lester weighed his usefulness – what was he doing here? Was he on a wild goose chase? Once again, he had to stow that feeling and bury it. The decision was made.

"Contact all field agents in the area, prioritize their efforts at the hospitals. Do whatever you have to in order to find the information we need."

"Sir?"

"Anthony is alive. I have to believe that. His transponder signal was not activated like Williams' when he died. You must believe that too, soldier. Do you understand?"

The soldier hesitated for a moment then nodded his head.

"We're with you all the way through Lester." He responded affirmatively.

"Good. I am going to go check out that lead at the restaurant, maybe I can sniff out a few clues. We know Anthony was there, alive. Once we're done here we'll hit the hospitals."

"Roger that sir. I'll keep my men on point. Be safe."

Lester didn't spare a moment.

"Gary Jones!" He yelled, like a mother scolding her child. Gary and Jim turned from their paths to the elevator to listen.

"I'm going over to the restaurant. Alone. Send the coordinates to my phone immediately. Understood?"

"Yes sir!" Gary said enthusiastically. Jim hadn't said much since they entered the city and looked on without any input. Lester didn't have time to get to the bottom of his ordeal at the moment. After all, he was staving off the possibility of a dead son as well. Jim tended to get silent when he was feeling vulnerable.

Lester left the building, staring down at the GPS path laid out for him on his phone.

"What are you doing Lester?" Screeched a voice through his earpiece.

"I'm going to the restaurant Jim. I have to do this alone. I have a real weird feeling in my gut about this whole thing. Like it goes a lot deeper than I think."

Lester's pace quickened as silence pervaded his listening device.

"Yeah." Jim replied daintily, a few seconds later.

"Is there something you want to tell me Jim?"

"Just . . . Be safe Lester, that's all."

With that, Lester took his earpiece out and stuffed it in his pocket, thinking it might help clear his crowded brain. If he needed to, he could contact the spec38 captain via walkie-talkie. He passed a series of patio-restaurants, wineries and busy street shops. Almost everyone noticed his large frame bustling unapologetically down the busy street. He made it to the restaurant quicker than he had assumed he would. There it was perched on the corner, littered with tables and chairs outside, full of people enjoying a meal. Bottles of wine, vases with flowers, and tightly coiffed waiters wearing gloves. After a small Volkswagen passed him, he took his first step onto the street. As his shoe struck the pebbled stone, he thought of something – something he didn't think of before. Something he *missed*.

He plunged his earpiece back in.

"Jones, wasn't there supposed to be a contact meeting Anthony at the restaurant?"

"Yes sir, there was. I checked it when we were on the plane."

Another car forced Lester back on to the sidewalk.

"And?"

"He was supposed to do a mandatory detail brief on the status of the mission after his meeting with Anthony but never did. Give me 20 seconds I may be onto something."

"Hurry up Jones."

Lester took his hand off of the radio on his belt. Across the street past the triangular restaurant, he noticed a glimmer in a window on the fourth floor corner of the building. The same kind of glimmer that reveals a scope in the sunlight. Lester's training taught him never to be in a position where the sun could give you away. To stay in the shadows. Was someone watching him?

"Got it Captain. Strange thing is, I looked up previous mission brief reports by this 'agent'. He has no callsign. Every agent has a callsign. If I had to make a guess, I'd say whoever this person was, they're not around anymore."

"Oh yeah? And what makes you think that Gary?"

"Just a hunch sir."

Lester knew Gary was right. The fact that the thought arrived in his own mind simultaneously with Gary's meant it was true. He just wished it wasn't. His eyes scanned the distant windows and stone embroidered rooftops frantically.

"I think you're right. Keep digging see what you can find."

"Roger that sir."

"And Gary, next time you get one of these hunches, you tell me. You always tell *me*. Understood?"

"Roger that sir."

Lester yanked his earpiece out and let it hang on his shoulder.

And then, to his surprise, his phone rang – he wasn't expecting a call under any circumstances. The number was blocked. Normally he would ignore such a thing, but his gut told him to answer.

"Hello?" He answered.

"Hello Mr. Desjardins. I've been waiting a long time to speak with you." Said a raspy, slow-talking voice, recognizably of Middle-American dialect.

"Who are you? How did you get this number? If this is some telemarketer I am not in the mo-"

"I am not a telemarketer, Director. My name is Peter Schlesinger."

Lester's heart nearly dropped out of his chest.

"How is that possible?" Lester demanded, confused.

"I cannot stay on the line very long, there are prying eyes and ears all around us. I'm sure a man of your status can understand."

"I'm listening . . ." Lester said, waiting intently for the next bit of information.

"I have few resources available to me, but I am close. Close enough to meet you. Is that possible?"

"Yes, absolutely. When and where?" Asked Lester, hastily making his decision, although he knew he could be walking into a trap. But he could not deny his instinctual foresight – the chance that this man may help him find Anthony was worth the risk.

"I'm sending the coordinates via GPS to your handheld device. There is an encryption code to see them. It's ERNEST, all capitals."

"Understood." Lester replied. He began walking again.

"And Mr. Desjardins, one more thing. Make sure you are not being followed."

"I understand."

"The coordinates are en route. I will meet you there in one hour."

The line went dead as Lester stared down at his phone. Another awkward jigsaw forcing its way into the scattered puzzle tormenting his mind. First treason, now meeting with a potentially dangerous cyberterrorist. His instincts had served him well in the past, but he had *better* be right this time.

The coordinates arrived on his phone within seconds. He looked down at his phone, then toward the window harboring the potential spy. Someone had shut it. By the sloppiness of their operation, he assumed he was safe, and that Schlesinger's phone call coincided with those watching him. It was reassuring to feel like he had the upper hand, whether he did or not. Left alone, Lester operated purely on instinct. He put his hand on his hip to make sure his gun was there if he needed it, situated himself with the map in his palm and proceeded to the objective.

Meanwhile, Gary and Jim scoured a network of files, sent and answered phone calls. Every piece of information they could find could be valuable. After ten minutes, Jim paced back and forth in the room while Gary did most of the work, oblivious, emerged in his technosphere.

"You alright Jim?" He asked, finally.

"Wha-. . . huh?"

"I said are you alright? Maybe you should take a walk, clear your head a bit."

Annoyed with Gary's tone, Jim scrunched his eyebrows and clenched his fists to remind him of rank.

"Ah-em, Sir. Sorry. Sir." Said Gary, eyebrows raised.

"Maybe you're right Jones. Keep at it. I'm going down to the lobby to see if our guys found any new leads."

But Gary knew better, they both had radios to contact anyone in their contingent. He could easily ask from where he stood. He didn't say anything. With time by himself, he could pry into a group of files that held answers for him. He coded a 7 letter encryption-blocking command into a software program he illegally downloaded onto a SIM disk. Within 30 seconds, he found himself in the FBI database, making sure to enact protocols in a sub program that hid his presence there. It took a lot of finger work but he found Jim's file and began to analyze it, sporadically checking the door with his eyes.

A spec38 rifleman waited in the main floor lobby for Jim to ascend the elevator.

"Anything new to report soldier?"

The soldier didn't acknowledge him physically whatsoever.

"One moment sir, there are policemen outside. Stay here."

The rifleman walked outside to meet the police, but there wasn't just one – 4 squad cars in total were in the vicinity. Three of them parked conveniently around a corner supposedly out of view, but a reflection in the opposing window gave them away to the rifleman's trained eyes. A single officer exited a small urbanized squad car in front of the building and walked toward the entrance to the building. But something was wrong.

Jim's headset buzzed.

"Perch 2 reporting, I've got something."

The sniper's calm, steady scope rested perfectly on a pedestal 8 feet back from the window, giving him a clean view of everything on the long avenue below. His partner scanned the adjacent window while monitoring a series of screens that showed him the hallway and the front lobby of the building.

"1800 feet out. Three armed men getting into a cop car. They don't look like cops. Regulation assault rifle for the pigs around here is the FAS36, they all had m37s. Looks very strange."

All of the soldiers heard the information. If they weren't alert before, they certainly were now. They waited intently for their commander's voice. But before he spoke,

"Paul in the main lobby. I've got up to twelve cops out here. One is moving towards the entrance now. Sidearm only, but his friends are hiding around the corner. Contact in fifteen seconds. Perch 1 can you get eyes on them?"

"Roger that Paul. Suspicions confirmed, I see 7, 8 of em' they're getting ready! They all have silenced m37s."

"10 seconds." Said Paul.

The commander sat in a room two doors down from Gary, on the corner of the building with a group of soldiers and an array of surveillance equipment. His tech operator was busy doing facial recognition analysis on the assailants seen through his fellow sniper's scope, cross-referencing the faces with those of the Paris police department database. Every spec38 in the building waited for his word.

"5 seconds sir, what do I do?"

"Analysis complete, confirmed threat! Engage targets they're disguised as police officers!"

Jim abruptly realized what was happening and removed the pistol from his waist. Paul waited until the officer's view of him was blocked by a pillar next to the door, for only a split second. When his sightline returned, he was staring down the barrel of Paul's assault rifle. Two shots from the silenced weapon shattered the glass panes and struck him in the chest, and another one caught him directly between the eyes before his body fell to the ground. Civilians and bartenders shrieked in terror, dropping to the floor and scurrying into corners.

"Stall! Upstairs now!" Yelled Paul, retreating behind a group of leather couches a few feet away as a hail of gunfire entered the lobby. The attackers moved like they had been trained for this sort of situation. Normal police officers wouldn't have seen that coming. They took up defensive positions and looked for new avenues of attack, coordinating their shots with each other, limiting clean shots to be had by Paul and his companion.

Jim hid as much of his body as he could behind a stone enclave next to the elevator, aiming his gun at the entrance. He fired a few times, but the shots had no chance of success. Another soldier burst through a maintenance door meters from him, weapon drawn, and began firing. The fake police officers filed into the front courtyard, taking cover behind cars, concrete slabs, and whatever would block incoming fire.

"Engaging targets." Said the sniper. "Perch 2 cover our flank I have a target rich environment down here." As he pulled the trigger, the pinpoint accurate cannon erupted into his shoulder, forcing him to regain his balance. Jim raised his head to see what was happening – one of the police officers stood up to fire his weapon at the spec38 soldier in the lobby but before he could pull the trigger, the massive spike from the sniper's rifle hit him in the chest, turning his body inside out and flinging his mangled carcass half a dozen feet down the street. His blood sprayed everywhere, completely engulfing an officer standing next to him. Before the fake officers could regroup and return fire on the sniper, four more 50 caliber rounds hit their targets, knocking off the attackers one by one, making a mess of their once intact bodies all over the street. It occupied their attention, allowing Jim and the spec38 soldiers to make it to the elevator safely.

"We gotta' move Paul now is our chance!" Yelled the soldier, kneeling on the marble floor to steady his shots and conceal himself, bullets flying past his head. "MOVE!" He yelled, as Paul leapt from his cover, grabbed Jim by the scruff and launched him into the elevator.

"Perch 1 this is Aaron and Mike, we're coming around the other side of the building to engage, don't shoot us."

"Roger that." Replied the sniper, who continued to suppress the officers. One of them raised his gun above the hood of the squad car he was hiding behind to fire randomly – but it was an ill-fated idea. The sniper carefully waved his crosshairs, held his breath and fired, completely eliminating the officer's arm and sending shrapnel from the destroyed m37 he was holding onto the street. Seconds later, Aaron and Mike emerged from the opposite corner of the building. Carefully positioning themselves – one high and one low - they aimed their weapons and engaged. Within ten seconds, there was a bullet in the head of each remaining attacker, who were all too concerned with the sniper to see them coming. A minute-long gun fight left the lobby riddled with bullets, but staying true to their reputation, not one spec38 officer had been killed. The street was strewn with corpses, weapons and shot-up police cars, their lights still blaring, sirens still howling.

"Perch 1 this is Jasper1, SITREP!"

"All targets eliminated sir. No casualties on our side. Wait, sir, I hear something. . ."

The sniper's spotter tapped him on the shoulder and told him to be quiet. They both looked ominously, using their ears instead of their eyes. They both recognized the faint drumming of rotors drawing nearer. The spotter stuck his body out of the window and looked up at the impending doom looming towards them.

"Sir it's not over. We have multiple attack choppers inbound, they seem to know our location."

"Roger that soldier, rema-"

Before the commander could issue the order, there was an attack chopper already on top of them that had descended rapidly from the sky. It's dual chainguns ripped the walls of the building to pieces. Shattered glass, bullets and shards of wood flung violently in all directions. Four Spec38 rifleman were instantly shredded while the remaining three, one of them the commander, leapt for corners of the room and all somehow evaded the lethal mayhem.

"Where the fuck did that thing come from! PERCH 1 we've got heat on our ass can you get an angle!" Screamed the commander into his headset as the gunship's lights flashed in the window. One of the fallen riflemen had a rocket launcher on his back. Vinh saw it, intact. He wasn't trained to hesitate. He leapt across the window, giving the machine a good angle but he was quick enough to survive it's guns – a small missile flew in the window, and into the interior wall, exploding ferociously. A leather couch flung by the explosion into him and the commander, pinning them against the wall but also acting as a shield. Eric, pinned in the adjacent corner behind a granite kitchen counter turned on his infraVIS to draw a line of sight through the smoke and debris.

"Roger Commander we've had problems of our own, we are en route to provide support ETA 35 seconds stay alive!"

The sniper and his spotter popped through the door. They would have to travel the extent of the long hallway spanning the broadside of the building to get an angle on the enemy.

The constant adjustments of the chopper's blades sent gusts of fresh air billowing into the room. The smoke cleared briefly. The commander saw Eric. He fluttered a unanimous hand signal – shaping his hand like a gun and drawing an invisible line. *Drawfire*. The commander nodded his head and stood up, bringing Mike to his feet alongside of him.

"Get ready to fire that thing!" He yelled, pointing at the gaping hole where the window was before. Given the right angle, it could be an easy shot, provided they survived long enough.

Eric popped up as quick as he could, hip-firing toward the hole, then his long legs carried him out of the door and into the hallway, barely dodging the stream of spikes flying at him. But it worked – he drew the helicopter closer to the hole during its failed pursuit, giving Mike the slightest angle – just enough. His thumb slid a button from auto-lock to manual fire.

"FIRING!" He shouted, squeezing the hand-sized trigger mechanism. The rocket shattered the front of the helicopter and sent it into a plummeting spin. The rotors caught into the cement blocks of the corner of the adjacent building, knocking it back to level, but it fell, burning, down to the street and exploded. Pedestrians had already fled the area when the machine guns began to fill the streets with hot casings, but a few cars left behind added to the inferno. The fireball could be felt by the soldiers in the destroyed room.

"Let's move! Secure the tech!" Said the commander, referring to Gary Jones. The three of them huddled shoulder to shoulder and moved carefully down the hallway.

"This is Jasper all squads SITREP!"

A flurry of replies flooded through the commander's headset.

"Commander I'm coming down the fourth floor hallway with Stall and Jamie hold your fire." Said a voice, loud and clear over the radiospace. It was Paul.

"Roger that Paul."

Paul popped out of the seam at the end of the hallway, followed by Jim and the other rifleman. Everyone lowered their weapons and ran toward the room Gary was supposed to be in. When they reached the door, more floodlights descended upon them, this time from the window at the other end of the hallway – this time, they were all lined up with nowhere to go. The helicopter had them all directly in its sights.

CRACK!

CRACK! CRACK!

They heard - The sound of the sniper's uranium depleted shells pounding into the helicopter's rotor shaft.

It immediately spiraled out of control as the chain guns started to rev up. Bullets scattered all down the building as the helicopter lost its balance and went belly-up. One of the pilots tried to escape, but another fifty-caliber spike struck him in the chest as he was deploying his parachute. Red mist sprinkled to the streets below, engulfed seconds later by the devastating explosion of the helicopter.

"That was a close one Ray, good shooting!"

"Roger that. We are compromised. Recommend rendezvous at extraction point Charlie."

"Affirmative. Securing Gary Jones. En route in 8 minutes."

"What about the others?" Asked Jamie, pointing to the room full of their dead brothers.

The commander hated the idea as much as everyone else, but it was up to him to make the hard decisions.

"We don't have time Jamie. Burn it. Burn everything. Make sure you grab their dogtags."

"Roger that." Jamie responded, stowing his reluctance. The danger was not over yet – the mourning would have to take place later.

Paul kicked open the room with Gary Jones inside. He wasn't at the desk.

"Jones! Gary Jones!" He yelled, waving his rifle around the room.

Two sets of trembling fingers rose slowly from behind the desk.

"I'm a-alive," A voice whimpered.

"Come on we gotta' leave."

Gary scurried out from behind the desk and joined the troupe, who began moving down the hallway and towards the stairs, ready for anything.

"Sir the real police are comin' in hot. They're filling the streets they'll be on top of you in 60 seconds. Recommend taking the back exit and making your way into the sewer system. That's your best route."

"Roger that Ray thanks. Get yourself clear of this mess we'll see you soon."

"Roger sir."

Ray and his spotter packed up their gear and made a similar escape from the building they were in, out of sight from the hounding police motorcade. The individually assigned pairs like Aaron and Mike found their way into the sewers, using GPS locators to meet up with the main group. They jogged through the murky waters for a half hour, taking a series of turns and climbing a half dozen ladders before stopping to regroup. It allowed the soldiers the slightest reprieve from the task at hand – enough time to think about the compatriots they lost. Enough time to think about the reality of their situation.

"Soooo, anyone got a good idea on what the fuck just happened back there?" Touted Paul.

"Has anyone heard from Captain Desjardins?" Asked Jasper, the leader of the group, who had been trying to reach him on the radio since they left.

"I don't know sir, all the concrete and steel could be interfering with our signal. Lotta' fuzz on the line." Said Jamie.

Jasper turned and locked eyes with Jim, straight-faced. He was silent. Although he hid it well, the commander's aura reeked of anger.

"You are in command now Mr. Stall. What's our next course of action?"

Jim didn't know what to tell them. They all waited for his next decision, but he hadn't spent any time planning – he always left that to Lester, who was now missing.

"Well, we can assume they wanted to hide their identity so they could capture Me, Lester and Gary. And do it safely, ya know, out of the public eye. Maybe they didn't know you guys were gonna' be with us?"

"What about the choppers?" Jasper asked sternly.

"They must have been a last resort incase the guys on the ground ran into any problems."

Jasper and Paul exchanged a glance.

"Sound familiar?"

"Yeah." said Jim. "Sounds American."

"Wow. They really want you guys dead huh?"

"It would appear that way. Let's find a safe place to hide for now, Lester may try to contact us. And Commander, our group is too big. Gonna' be hard to stay hidden."

"I agree. He's AWOL at the moment. Paul, you and I are going forward with Stall and Jones. Everyone else to the extraction point."

"Copy that sir." Responded Paul. The rest of the group wasted no time in proceeding toward their destination. Their boots splish-sploshed down the unlit chasm and quickly dissipated beneath the sound of flowing water.

"So Mr. Stall. What's our next move?" Jasper asked as he took a step closer.

He pondered the question for fifteen seconds, holding his chin and squeezing his brow to make it fully recognizable what he was thinking. And he *was* thinking. If Lester needed to contact them, he would do so. He must be doing something important and for now they could not rely on him to call the shots.

"Let's see if we can get back on Akazawhi's trail, try to sniff out a lead. We can't give up on Anthony."

Jasper nodded his head in agreement, although he knew the plan was shit. Luckily, Gary had committed a few useful facts to memory before the choppers attacked.

"I know where we could start!" He blurted, looking around for approval.

"We're listening."

"Well I managed to remember the name of a processing plant run by Akazawhi's criminal enterprise when I was searching through his file. It's not far from here at all. Uhh, just under 3 miles."

"Can we get there through the sewers?"

"You bet. There's a hatch in the main bilge dump for the entire sublevel of the building for maintenance."

The commander looked at Ray, whose slung rifle covered most of his body. Paul didn't like it either, but at least they had regained a purpose. This was outside of the mission objective but Akazawhi *was* an international terrorist. If anything, they could gain some intel on his operation during the process. Anthony and Williams were as dead to him as the members of his squad left in the hotel.

* * * *

Lester made it to the dot on his phone. He had spent the last quarter hour traversing the subway system, winding through tunnels and sneaking through maintenance stairways. A flat screen at the end of the scarcely populated waiting platform gained the attention of a few people. As Lester drew closer the sounds of the television reached his ears. His French wasn't up to par, but the gist of the images was unmistakable. Hordes of police officers surrounded multiple smoldering ruins in the city streets; fire trucks, ambulances and helicopters surrounded the hotel. He couldn't believe what he had missed. He reached for a tile-covered pillar next to him for support, almost falling to his knees. He immediately fumbled through his jacket for his phone to try and contact Jim. A text message simultaneously popped up on his screen.

'We made it out. Whatever you're doing I hope it's important.'

A flash of light emerged a hundred meters down the subway tube. It flashed again, and Lester could make out the silhouette of a man holding a flashlight. The Parisians remained fixed to the television set, some calling their loved ones to make sure they were safe. Lester slipped by them and shimmied his body on to a narrow walkway leading to the light.

"Come in." A voice whispered.

He shut the door behind him. The man holding the flashlight double checked it to make sure.

"Hello Director. He is waiting for you. Come this way."

Lester followed the man down a set of stairs to another large, metal locked door. The deadbolt releasing made a loud sound as the door opened. It revealed a small room lined with very old rusted and broken down lockers which no longer held anything. In the middle of the room was a table, dimly lit by a cone shaped bulb hanging from the ceiling. A burly man with grey hair sat at the table, his faced ensconced by overlapping shadows.

"Have a seat Director. We have many things to discuss."

"You're damn right we do. I just found out that my friends were involved in a huge firefig-"

"At the hotel?" Schlesinger interrupted. "Are you also aware that you and your colleagues are wanted for treason?" He said condescendingly as he used a remote to turn on a television in the corner of the room. On it, Lester's mug shot alongside Jim and Gary's with a headline that read 'Enemies of the State' in bold red letters. Lester's heart nearly dropped through his chest. As soon as he grasped the situation, Schlesinger turned the screen off.

"I can provide you with protection. For now. I would advise getting Jim and Gary off the streets immediately, there are sweeper teams looking for all of you at the moment."

"I figured as much." Responded Lester, who seemed prepared for the news.

"Not your first rodeo Lester?" Pete asked, smirking.

"No. Not by a long shot."

A moment of silence ensued as the men let the situation sink in.

"Let's get down to business. I have some very important things I want to tell you."

"Let's hear it."

"Well, you must have heard something about the Heaven's Gate program in the news recently?"

"Yeah, but I haven't thought too hard about it."

"Well you *really* should, Director. Your superiors have been neglecting to tell you the truth."

"Yeah? And I suppose you are going to tell me?"

"It is a giant cover for what they are *really* planning. My cyber teams have been busy intercepting and decoding government transmissions for the last three years. There is a military installation in Alaska called HEAR - Hyper Energy Auroral Relay, are you familiar with it?"

"Ummm, no, I'm not. But not too long ago my guys were hot on the trail of a shipment bound for Alaska, with suspected ties to the international criminal empire perpetuated by Ahmed Al-Akazawhi."

"Ahh yes, a container full of live bodies?"

Lester was surprised for a moment by how much this man knew about what was happening. He was living up to the branding imposed on him of a cyberterrorist. It made Gary's actions seem not so distant, not so criminal. More than anything it made him feel old – like an outdated cog in a technological infrastructure that had made his old-school methods obsolete. However, Lester's inquisitive, detective mind was already starting to fill in the blanks.

"Well let me tell you the bare bones, Lester. The Heaven's Gate program is a front for something far more sinister. Why do you think Akazawhi has been so elusive? It's because the American government has been working with him. They needed someone with close ties to the black market that could operate outside jurisdictions. They needed to keep their hands clean because if anyone found out what they were planning, they might have a third world war on their hands. The HEAR is also a front – they claim it is just a research program, but in fact it is a weapon – one capable of manipulating and controlling the earth's magnetic field and ionosphere. If they wanted to, they could turn that thing on and create a level 5 hurricane anywhere on the planet. The government is claiming the Heaven's Gate program to be a response to a similar program by the Chinese, but in reality, the upper tiers of both governments are working cohesively to carry out a master plan. Let me tell you as a first-hand witness, the destructive application of the device itself is virtually limitless."

"So what does it all mean.?"

"Well, based on some of the intel we've been receiving, mind you, we have lost many men to ascertain that information, the shipment full of human beings and HEAR, and the Heaven's Gate program are all connected. As far-fetched as it sounds, they are breeding an army of perfect soldiers using the genetics of those captured men. You'll notice that all of them are nearly perfect specimens."

"This is all fucked up. Who authorized all of this?" Lester asked.

"Certain divisions of the American defense infrastructure have been infiltrated and compromised by exo-biologicals. Dynatech, DARPA, even the Pentagon."

"What, you mean Aliens? Are you fucking serious right now?"

Pete didn't budge. Lester could see the seriousness on his face, he wasn't kidding. Schlesinger paused for a moment, realizing his story would not be so easily believable, especially by an experienced intelligence officer. He took a key out of his breast pocket and plunged it into a lockbox he picked up from the floor and took out another group of files and handed them to Lester, who began to analyze them.

"I know it sounds ridiculous, but it's true. In 1977 I was involved in an underground firefight with extraterrestrials during the construction of an American Military Installation in New Mexico. They were big, ugly and numerous. I barely made it out alive."

Lester scanned the files in front of him which held pictures and profiles of the dead troopers, and an official mission report with huge sections of the script blacked out. He flipped one of the pages for Lester and put his finger on top of a picture that displayed a tall, gangly big-eyed creature laid out on an infirmary bed.

"That is a Zeta Reticulan. That is what attacked us down there. However, they are not calling the shots. We have strong evidence to support the idea that they are being controlled by the Alpha-Draconian race."

"Alpha-what?" Murmured Lester, unable to keep up with all of this new information as it was presented.

"Alpha-Draconians. They control the Zeta Reticulans. The 'greys' do their bidding for them. They are large, scaly, lizard-like creatures. We believe they evolved here, on Earth, during the early Triassic period and ventured out into the void to colonize other planets. Now they're back, and they believe the Earth still belongs to them. They have an undeniable, hard-wired hatred for humanity and want nothing more than to extinguish them and retake Earth for themselves. With their super armies and HEAR as their weapon of choice, they plan to do just that."

Lester was shocked to hear all of this, but somehow, from some dark nook in his mind, he was begging to believe.

"So you said these lizards have taken over our government?"

"Yes. Certain sections of it, although we don't know exactly who."

"What do you mean *who?*

"Well, we've categorized over 83 different exo-biological species. Some of them have the ability to shapeshift – to take on a human form to disguise themselves. You could see how that would help them manipulate their way into positions of importance."

The dots began to connect in Lester's brain.

"Mr. Grey!"

"What? Who?" Pete asked, surprised.

"Mr. Grey! Jones mentioned a man working out of The Pentagon named Mr. Grey. He convinced Gary Jones to relinquish Anthony's file. I've never heard of him before, but Jones insisted he was there, and made him commit treason. I ordered an arrest warrant on him just hours ago."

Finally, something Schlesinger didn't know. Now Lester was feeding *him* information.

"That's only going to the stir up the hornet's nest even more. You must understand how *deep* the corruption goes – they control everything. If I were you, I'd call off the dogs. Don't let him know that we are on to him, that way we can still hold some leverage."

"*We?*" Lester remarked, reminding Pete that they were not on the same side – not yet.

"Yes, we. Whether you like it or not Director, these things are real, and you and your ilk are now wanted men. I'm sure you understand the gravity of that fact and if you do, you know that I'm your best shot at getting to the bottom of this."

Pete handed Lester a series of files with CLASSIFIED imprinted on them in bold letters.

"The one on the bottom, Director." Said Schlesinger, pulling the file out from beneath the stack. The file had Anthony's name on it with a picture of him and Williams entering the hotel.

"Now, what I'm about to tell you has to be met with open ears, and an open mind. Can you do that Lester?"

"I guess we're going to find out."

"First of all, when you make contact with Jim Stall again, you are going to have to pry the truth out of him. Let me ask, how long have you known him?"

"Decades. He's been nothing but a good friend and worthy asset to the FBI, as far as I know. But since we left the States he's been acting strange."

"Not surprising. Jim is not who you think he is. And neither is Anthony."

"I'm listening."

"The universe is full of malevolent forces, but among the stars, there are races that seek to help humanity. Races that are not evil, and are incredibly advanced technologically and spiritually. One such race, as we have come to know them, call themselves Darmerians."

Chapter 12

ENLIGHTENMENT

The stars were spinning too fast. They were too far to ever be near, but lingered on his fingertips. He could feel their energy on his skin, in his body – in his soul. In the distance, fixated between two glittering constellations, a luminous violet orb tugged at his focus. His hand reached for it – the tips of his fingers lengthened, into long strings as if they were caught in the gravity of a black hole. He was almost there . . . the glowing violet jewel radiated serene joy and energy that permeated the very essence of his existence. The stars around him ceased to be dots, becoming long strings of light. Before his long fingers touched the growing planet, the brightness of the stars took over the blackness and the planet in front of him began to glow as bright as the sun. In his waking moments, a soft voice grew louder in his mind . . .

"You are almost there . . . Embrace the light . . ."

The trail of the soft voice led him into consciousness. The stars disappeared, the endless space became white. The beautiful aura of the planet transformed into a circular light on the ceiling. His eyelids slowly peeled open. He was awake. He was *alive*. The bright light on the ceiling cast a silhouette over three tall people standing over him. To his right, a familiar face. His memory took a moment to jog itself, but he could not forget the intoxicating lure of her gaze. Her face was perfect, her beauty stunning, just like he remembered. The faint vibrations of voices slowly became more familiar to his ears.

"You are alive Anthony." Said Aremis, although this time, he was sure to notice that her lips did not move. The voice happened *inside* his head.

"How –" He muttered, regaining control of his motor functions. He tried to say the words but they were scrambled in his head.

"It's okay. You have been through a lot. You must rest now."

As his vision adjusted to the bright lights, he got a good look at the other two 'people' standing over him. They were both tall men with rigid, perfect faces and large eyes – but they seemed to do more than just look at him – he felt as though they could see inside of him. Inside of his *mind*.

Aremis turned from the raised platform Anthony was laying on. As she did, Anthony aggressively grabbed her arm and pulled her back, as if he had forgotten how much strength the woman possessed.

"I've rested enough. You promised me answers." He said sternly. The men did not seem concerned, rather they looked at Anthony ominously. They appeared to be in awe of his presence. He could *feel* the sentiment as much as he could see it in their eyes.

Aremis looked at the other two, then back at Anthony.

"You are right I did. I owe you an explanation. How do you fee-"

"I'm fine." Anthony interrupted, keeping his focus on her. He tried to get up and to his feet, but he could not move more than a few inches in any direction. Aremis nodded her head to one of the men standing over him who pressed a button. The light above him turned off, simultaneously lifting an invisible weight from his chest. He could move. Despite the pins and needles that filled his entropic body, he stubbornly struggled to his feet.

"Well done. You heal quickly Anthony Stall."

"What is that thing?" He asked, motioning toward the dissipating light on the ceiling.

"It regenerates your energy."

"My energy?"

"Yes, your lifeforce. The energy that makes you a living being."

"Hmm." Was all Anthony responded with. He could ask a thousand questions but not be any nearer to fully understanding what he was going through.

"Come, Anthony, follow me. I will take you to the Elders."

"The Elders?"

"Our leaders. They are very old, and very wise. They will explain everything to you. But I hope you are prepared."

"Prepared? For what?"

"The truth, Anthony. Let's go."

He looked back at the two large men once more, who had nothing to say, still holding a bewildered, awe-stricken look in their eyes, like a parent seeing their child for the first time – or perhaps the last. He couldn't quite tell.

The two exited the room which didn't have any familiar structure or architecture. All that could be said about it was that it was a room – no right angles, no beams or girders, no wood or metal anywhere. The walls looked like a much smoother version of stucco – they felt warm on Anthony's fingers. The hallway followed a similar structure. Only the ground was flat, the walls spiraled into circles and avenues that went in all different directions.

"This way." Whispered Aremis. The floor beneath her feet lit up as she gracefully glided along the path. Now that they were alone and for the moment out of danger, the questions began to flood into Anthony's mind again.

"Underground. Remember? Very deep underground. Somewhere underneath what you would consider the North American plate." Said Aremis, without turning her head or slowing her stride. She had answered the question before Anthony could ask it.

"How did you-"

Aremis stopped and turned.

"I am telepathic, Anthony. I can read your mind. Do not be scared."

"And why *wouldn't* that scare me?" He asked pertinently.

Aremis put her hand on his arm reassuringly and looked him dead in the eyes.

"Because, Anthony, you can also communicate this way. It will take time, but it is definitely within your capability."

"I'm not so sure about that."

Aremis simply turned and continued walking. The hallway began to grow wider, the ceiling grew taller. Still, no architectural angles to denote any human presence. Along with it, the slowly increasing sound of many voices. They turned a corner which led down a stairway. At the bottom, Anthony could see a shiny, glassy floor at the end. The sounds of an atrium full of people conversing filled his ears.

"Don't be scared Anthony. You're home now."

He didn't know what she meant by home, but her words brought a certain comfort with them.

"Come on, they're about to enlighten everyone."

"Enlighten?"

Anthony followed Aremis down to the floor – it was the bottom of a giant room holding thousands of people. A stadium-like grouping of seats led up one side of the huge chamber, all the way up to the stalactites hanging from the cavern. There were thousands of them, and their heads began turning towards him. The voices became silent as they gazed at Anthony, as if they were witnessing a life-changing event. A gripping sense of reality hit him hard in the chest – his heart pounded furiously as more and more of these perfect-looking people quieted their thoughts and stared into his eyes. He couldn't handle the pressure. He was going to fall. Aremis was there, in time, sensing his distress, to grab his hand and save him. The stress disappeared instantly, replaced by a calm, soothing sensation that slowed everything down. Just like the feeling he had when they were escaping, he could feel the vibration first in the nerves of his fingertips, then up his arm and throughout his whole body. Without the threat of death imposing on his mind, he could grasp the sensation and hold on to it.

They sat in an empty spot of the front aisle. Before them, the twenty feet of glassy reflective floor and then a raised platform that had a distinct groove all the way around it about a foot from the edge. The whole chamber, massive in size and scope, mimicked a movie theatre.

"Because my lifeforce is very radiant and I have trained my body to send positive energy directly to others through tactile sensation."

This time she spoke out loud, to remind Anthony that he wasn't the only one inside his own head. He wanted to ask her why her hand felt so good, and received a scientific response. But Aremis looked at him and smiled slightly. There *was* something else there.

"Try to focus. This is very important Anthony."

Silence swept the room. All that could be heard was the dull lingering vibration of electromagnetic energy rippling through the molecular air. The groove lining the front of the stage started to move. All at once, the floor of the platform separated into hundreds of individual triangular shaped panels; lines of light separating them and glowing bright. The light dissipated abruptly, but the hum of energy vibrated more intensely. The panels turned, twisted and contorted in multiple directions, clattering and clicking in a symphony of crudely coordinated transformation. Eventually, a visible hole formed in the middle of the platform as the metal plates spiraled into a raised vortex then peeled away like a retractable sunroof.

A tall, smooth cylindrical spire emerged from the floor and slowly rose higher and higher. Incredibly complex series of nodes and smooth metallic sculptures supported the spire in a continuously widening base. After about ten feet, a large set of bluish-white eyes emerged that glowed so bright they sparkled. The spire loomed over a throne-like chair that continued to rise. On each side, more spires poked through the almost even plain of vision where Anthony could see. When they all rose, there were seven chairs in total, each holding a robed person with large, bluish-white eyes. But they weren't normal people – discernably humanoid, but their skin in ribbons and hair white as a cloud and longer than the robes that encased their frail bodies. They looked old, older than anyone could ever possibly live to be. Their skin resembled that of a lizard more than a man; rife with rigid creases and sagging pockets. Despite their overtly weak physicality, each creature held a vibrant, visible glow that resonated from their being and was amplified by the sparkling glitter of their robes.

"Who are they?" Anthony whispered to Aremis. She responded in kind by putting the answer in his mind telepathically.

"They are the elders of our race. They have lived very long lives and are gifted in the art of foresight. Their minds are able to reach across the energies that most of us cannot. Listen closely, they will enlighten you."

The hum grew to a point that was audible.

"Let us collectively envision our futures, children of Darmeria. As the enlightened before you, we bestow our knowledge of the present, and of the future, upon all of you. We give you this gift so that you may act in accordance with our goals on this planet."

The voice seemed to fill the entire chamber, but come from nowhere in particular and somehow, Anthony knew that it was the voice of the wrinkled creature sitting in the middle throne. Seconds later, the old 'man' raised his hands into the air, tilted his head and closed his eyes. The other six to his left and right closed their eyes and bowed their heads forward, entering a trance-like state. As the energy of their collective aura amplified, the room grew darker, as if they were sucking the energy directly out of the air and into themselves. The cylindrical top of the spire peeled open and out of it came a long mechanical spear with two shiny rings wrapping it. It locked into place and the shiny rings began to spin very fast, becoming brighter as they did.

The elders' aura continued to intensify, becoming a luminous shield that glowed burning white. Sections of the ringed spear popped open one by one until the end of it spread open like a blooming metallic flower, revealing a small shard of bluish-purple crystal that looked like it had a light inside of it. One of the spinning rings of light detached and hovered down to the orifice of the spear, locking itself in a spot where the crystal was directly in its center. In unison, the shard and the spinning ring became extremely bright, so bright in fact that Anthony raised his hand to his brow. A finger-thick beam of red light emerged from the tip of the spear and shone straight into the crystal. The pure energy surrounding everyone on the stage culminated to the spire and forced its way into the quickly fracturing crystal . . .

To Anthony's disbelief, the crystal began to vibrate violently, deteriorate and transform into something else. Its edges roasted off and became an ever-growing mass of thick gas that looked like a cloud made of steel wool. He thought about squirming, but Aremis' hand was already on top of his own. The metallic substance tumbled over the rocky walls, completely encompassing everyone's range of vision.

"Be calm, and listen." He heard in his mind.

Once the mass covered the walls entirely, the remainder of the blue light clinging to those on the stage left them for the crystal. The burst of energy shattered it into a thousand glowing fragments which, in a coordinated fashion, dispersed rapidly throughout the sheath of metallic gas.

"Close your eyes Anthony." He heard, softly.

"What's happening?" Anthony asked, but not with a whisper. He simply thought of Aremis and the question in his mind simultaneously, and was dignified with an answer.

"Close your eyes. Your mind's eye will become as big as the room . . . and you will see what they see."

Anthony closed his eyes. The inside of his mind became a projection screen for the thoughts and images the elder's had prepared for them. He felt comfortable, as if he had done this before. Sure, the method of delivery was different, but nonetheless he felt an oddly familiar feeling – that of sitting through an FBI debriefing.

He saw a battle. Hordes of monstrous-looking soldiers covered with weaponry and armor, attacking cities on the surface; killing innocent people – and those that tried to valiantly resist the onslaught. He saw the Earth, standing on the moon, watching it burn. The blue and green faded into black and red, the planet scorched and besieged.

What looked like northern lights on steroids rippled through the arctic circle, throughout North America and sporadically in every continent. Massive hurricanes tore through the oceans and continents, creating tsunamis higher than city skylines. Tornadoes ripped through jungles, deserts, cities, and barren plains. Volcanoes erupted ferociously, spewing fiery plasma high into the crowded atmosphere. The ferocity of the raised oceans encroached on every landmass. Japan, most of Russia, Upper Canada and the entirety of southern Europe were completely covered with angry ocean tides. All the while, those still clinging to what little life they had left constantly struggled to get to higher ground, avoid storm supercells and survive the extermination squads.

Humanity was being annihilated.

And then, the entire image turned white and disappeared.

As the white light dissipated, Anthony could see the outline of a body – of *his body*. His eyes opened wide, his extremities reached far, and then pulled in close to his torso, like a child. His skin began to glow as his body seemed to fall to the surface of a planet – but not the Earth. He could not feel the familiar stomach-churning yank of gravity. It was the purple planet he had seen in his visions before. Although no verbal explanation was given, his feelings told him what the images meant.

Finally, the next series of images showed sporadic glimpses of a remote installation nearly covered completely in snow, with arctic winds howling fervently. A grid of antennae hundreds of meters long lay next to the base, covered from the harsh thrashing of arctic winds by a protective energy shield, only visible when shards of ice or large clumps of snow were catapulted against its boundary. Anthony opened his eyes briefly and looked at his hands, which were extremely cold. His breath was visible, as if the room temperature had dropped to below zero in an instant. He felt like he was there, at the facility, freezing. He waded through the thick snow and up to the fence surrounding the facility, looking in at the grid of instruments encased in the perimeter. They filled with energy and power, so much power he could feel it on his face and fingertips. And then almost instantly, the images disappeared, and he was back in the amphitheatre with Aremis and the elders in front of him. He looked around to notice the metallic gas evaporating into thin air, disappearing completely. The glow that emanated from the elders slowly became nothing as they came out of their trance and opened their eyes.

"This is the fate of the Earth as we have foreseen. Malevolent forces intend to deprive humanity of their rightful inheritance of this planet. We must act hastily before these events become reality. This is now our priority." Said the frail man in the middle chair, as the implement retracted back into the spire above him.

"We have been blessed with the return of one of our own. Long have you been separated from your history, Anthony Stall, and now you are reunited with your lifeblood. We are enthralled to have you back in our embrace." He said, looking directly at Anthony.

"Go, children of Darmeria, and prepare yourselves for the coming war. Our race has protected the peace in this galaxy for countless generations, but now our hand has been forced. We must sacrifice our peaceful ways in order to proliferate the positive energy our galaxy has granted us. It is up to us, the beings of light governing the blackness of the endless void, to solidify a future for our more primitive relatives. This is our mission."

Everyone in the stadium rose from their chairs and began filing towards the large exit arches on either side of the platform. Aremis did not move, and Anthony knew not to.

"Come, Sagittarius, let us get a better look at you." Said the elder, pointing at Anthony.

Almost every departing Darmerian in the room made sure to glance at Anthony up and down before they were gone. Child-sized versions of the robust adults bickered and whispered like they were forming rumors in the schoolyard at lunch time.

"What did he just call me?" Anthony asked, looking for an explanation from Aremis.

"He called you by your real name. The one given to you at birth. Come on." She said, taking Anthony by the hand and standing up. "In human astrology Sagittarius is the archer, the marksman. Since you were born on Earth, your parents saw fit to name you after an Earthly constellation. It is fitting for your situation as well, as Sagittarius is half man, half beast. You have only known of one half of your own existence for your whole life so far – that of a man. A *human* man." She explained. As crazy as it may sound to any normal person, it actually made sense to Anthony. When he heard Sagittarius, images of his mother flickered in his mind, holding him as a child. He could not be sure if the images were from his imagination, or if they were real memories coming to the surface. And he was quite the marksman; he would never accept missing any target.

"I'm sure you have many questions. And by now, you may have found some of the answers on your own." Said the man, with Anthony looking bewildered.

"Or maybe not." Said the elder, his eyes shifting to Aremis. "Aremis is quite beautiful, isn't she? And one of our finest assassins. Thank you Aremis, your efforts are far more important than you could ever know."

"And I believe you have already met Tarliss." He said, motioning towards the left of the platform, where a familiar figure emerged. It was the man from the restaurant in Paris who fed him the delicious pasta. But what was he doing here? How could it be? In mid-stride, just feet away from them, the man ceased to be an Italian chef, and became something else. He grew almost a foot, his shoulder's widened and his face became more rigid. His bald scalp covered with perfect looking shiny black hair that looked like it was drawn on with a marker. His clothes became a body-fitting silvery metallic suit that reflected brightly. One last ripple of light ran across the entirety of his figure as the amazing transformation finished.

"Hello Anthony. It is a pleasure to officially meet you, in my real form." Said Tarliss, who held a certain authoritative aura. Anthony could tell right away that he was a warrior. His eyes told the story of strength, and of enduring through pain. They were deep, cast under a slight shadow created by his pronounced eyebrows. It reminded him of the many heroes and war veterans who had been his trusted instructors over the years. They told a story of unwavering dedication and a certain masculine perseverance.

"We sent him to make sure you survived the plane crash. The contact you were supposed to meet with as part of your mission in Paris was sent there to kill you. Luckily, Tarliss made it in time to keep you safe." Said the elder.

"So is that why I was so sick for the flight?" Anthony asked, trying to make sense of things.

"Yes. You're intuition serves you well. We couldn't risk exposing ourselves to our enemies, so it had to be that way. There was an ingredient in the pasta that interacted with the energy dormant within you. During the flight, it created a protective barrier around your body. That is why you survived. Unfortunately, since your body is as of yet unaccustomed to dealing with such energies, it reacted with an intense sickness. A by-product of your survival." Said Tarliss, moving closer as he spoke.

"What about Williams?" Anthony asked, still somewhat confused.

"He is gone. There is nothing we could do to save him. I am sorry for your loss. After we thwarted their initial attempt to kill you, their second attempt was much more desperate . . . much more *destructive*."

The words resonated with Anthony's subdued consciousness; bits and pieces of the plane crash flashed in his memory, as if he was there again, observing the event during some sort of outer body experience. He saw Williams' face, the agony apparent in it, and the screams of helpless victims so brutally murdered.

"How do you feel?" Asked the elder, wanting to hear Anthony's thoughts despite all he had to explain.

"I feel . . . alive. Although I don't think I should be."

"Indeed you are. Your life is very valuable, Sagittarius."

"Well you all went through a great deal of trouble to save me, so I guess it must be. But why me? And why are you calling me that? And for crying out loud, what the hell is this place? Who are all of you?"

"It is your real name. The name your parents gave you when you were a child. You are a Darmerian, as much as anyone of us. You just haven't realized it yet." Tarliss said affirmatively, his deep voice carrying a powerful notion of truth. "We are Darmerians. We hail from a planet called Darmeria near a binary solar system human telescopes have named Canis Majoris S-IV. I could tell you everything, but instead, I will show you."

Before Anthony could reply Tarliss was a foot in front of him, with his hands placed firmly on his neck. They quickly cast a white, hot beam upon his skin. He tried to struggle but it was pointless. He couldn't do anything but stare straight into the shapeshifter's eyes, as they immediately became blindingly bright and his body was gripped by entropic paralysis. His vision blinded, his perception warped and fizzled away until . . . nothing.

And then everything came back instantly. The perceptive reality of his senses exploded into focus once more. He and Tarliss stood side by side. He felt oddly calm, fully aware that he shouldn't be. Everyone else was gone, and so was the row of chairs. The room they were suddenly in looked and felt eerily similar to the rooms in the base that he and Aremis escaped from. A hundred meters in front of him, the sound of feet descending a stairway lingered in the distance.

"Don't worry. We are not actually in this room right now."

"W-where are we?"

"I pulled you inside of my mind. You are seeing my memories. Well, at least memories that have been shared to me by Rikthinius. Our bodies are safe."

"But . . . but this feels like real life! Someone's coming!"

"You can be sure they *won't* see us. Listen to me now Sagittarius."

The click-clacking of shoes echoed through the expansive chamber.

"Our race has maintained a peaceful pursuit of knowledge and wisdom for thousands and thousands of generations. Our goal has always been to seek enlightenment through a greater understanding of these things. When we ventured into the void, we found other intelligent races. Some like us, and some hell-bent on destruction and self-gain. And of course, some in the middle. Humanity was one of those races."

Three men in suits made it to the sublevel and continued walking. Tarliss was right – it would have been impossible for them to remain unseen, but the group of men stared straight through them like ghosts.

"During the Second Epoch of Enlightenment, our leaders created guidelines prohibiting the interference of natural circumstances elsewhere in the universe. Any Darmerian known to tamper with developing races or other developed races in a harmful way would be punished. We kept to ourselves, despite what we knew could happen if we did not intervene."

"Which was?" Anthony asked, as the men stopped and sat in a circular formation of chairs which arose out of a hole in the floor as they approached.

"The other races. The other *Malevolent* races. They look at the human species as a bag of loot for plunder. To make it worse, some of them joined forces. For the last seven thousand Earth years, the Draconian-Reticulan alliance has been constantly manipulating humanity. Abductions, genetic experiments, tyranny and war have all beset mankind from its inception. Some of us could not simply stand and watch as the Draconians mercilessly exploited them."

Another series of clattering shoes echoed through the huge room. One more group of three walked toward the circle of chairs. The women walking in the middle carried something in her arms.

"Your father was one of these Darmerians. He pleaded with the high council to change their laws so that humanity could be saved. All but one of the high council members disagreed with him, denying him and his followers the right to intervene."

"My father?" Asked Anthony, intrigued.

"Yes. Your true father. His name was Arektharius, the appointed leader of our seldom used military. That one member he convinced came here, to Earth, with him, your mother and many of his followers – the Elder, Rikthinius, is the one you just met. Despite the punishment they would incur from the high council, he had the courage to do what he believed was right."

Anthony got a better view of the walking trio as they neared. The chiseled facial features and sharp demeanor of the man made it clear.

"That's him isn't it. And that's my mother. Is that–"

"You? In her arms – yes Anthony – you are beginning to see the truth. You were just an infant. Your father was privy to the plan laid in place for the human race. A high concierge of the Zeta Reticulan race struck a deal with the humans, who were already corrupted by greed and the thirst for dominance of the planet. The agreement was made so that certain members of the human government would ascertain extra-terrestrial technology in order to weaponize it and take full control of humanity. In return, the Zeta Reticulans would be allowed to abduct and experiment on the human population as they pleased. Unfortunately, the whole thing was a lie – the Reticulans, in concordance with their masters, the Draconians, planned to annihilate most of humanity and turn the rest of the population into a slave race to do with them as they pleased. Reticulans get a euphoric high from the Amino Acids of human beings."

"Wow. This is all so . . . unbelievable."

"Believe it, Sagittarius. It is the truth your heart has been looking for your whole life. That one thing you knew in your soul, but couldn't quite grasp. I know you have had dreams. Very strange dreams that you were never able to understand."

The other man escorting his alien parents began to look familiar. Not his facial features, or his hair, but the way he walked and the way his burly forearms swayed in his gait. It was his uncle Jim.

"That's my uncle Jim. What is he doing here?" Asked Anthony.

"When the Zeta Reticulans learned of your father's intention to enlighten the corrupt human alliance, they knew above all things that they must destroy him, for fear of the humans finding out about their lies."

The circle of chairs before them were now full, and the two groups engaged in conversation.

"Your uncle served as an agent under a covert wing of the military, and he was appointed as a bodyguard to extraterrestrial liaisons. In this case, his job was to monitor your parents during their dealings on Earth. The humans told your parents that they would be given safe passage back to Darmeria, but they were betrayed. The humans decided to align themselves with the Zeta Reticulans. Your mother and father were killed."

After conversing for about a minute, the two groups stood from their chairs. Anthony's father extended his hand to the suited man sitting across from him, shaking it. After the handshake, both groups rose and walked toward separate exits.

"This meeting took place in 2001, just days before the terrorist attack on the World Trade Center in New York. The attack was part of a much larger scheme to initiate a global war that would solidify America as the globally dominant superpower. Every war they have perpetuated since then has been based on a lie, the end goal being complete dominance of the planet. It is all a giant system of psycho-political manipulation designed to divide humanity and distract them from the real issue at hand."

"What issue?"

"Interstellar war with hostile alien species. The Draconians knew that the Earth would be much easier to control if humanity was divided and scattered than if they came together under the knowledge of the truth. Despite their infancy, the humans proved to be excelling at a rate that alarmed them. They tried to avoid this problem by destroying their hope before they became self-reliant, before they could embrace the light. . ."

"But why?" Anthony asked, "Why do they want to destroy us? I mean, destroy them?"

"Fear, Sagittarius. Their race is fear-driven. Our race follows a different direction, embracing the light. Although we strive for peace, our race has been forced to engage in war for the greater good."

Anthony tried to absorb and make sense of everything he was learning. One question rose to the front of his mind, and Tarliss could sense it.

"They fear *you*, Sagittarius. They fear us. They fear what our race is capable of. That is why they killed your parents. I have one more thing to show you."

Once again, Tarliss took Anthony by the neck and warped both of them to another location. They stood in a familiar-looking room – the maglev train was being loaded with a contingent of soldiers along with three civilians.

"There was nothing they could do to save themselves once the humans were convinced that they must die."

Just after leaving, the train exploded ferociously. Torrents of heavy rock collapsed in on them killing everyone on board, along with Anthony's parents.

"Because of their fear, they cowardly assassinated your parents. But luckily, you were not on that train."

"Why not?" Anthony asked, intrigued.

"Your father was a very smart Darmerian. He made sure you were safe. Although your uncle Jim was ordered to kill you himself, he could not bring himself to do so. Before your parents got on the train, they entrusted you to Jim, making him swear to keep you safe . . . until it came time for you to realize who you really are."

"So you are telling me that my uncle Jim knew about all of this my whole life and never told me?"

Tarliss looked him right in the eyes and responded firmly.

"Yes. Do not be mad at him. He had to. Looking down on you as an infant in his arms, he could not bear the psychological damage of knowing he murdered an infant. Instead, he took you and went into hiding. With the help of his knowledge of deception, he created a false alias and blended into the population perfectly, knowing that one day, you would grow up. One day, the truth would set you free."

Anthony saw Jim carrying him as an infant away from the explosion, ensconced by a shadowy pillar away from prying eyes.

"Ever since that fateful day, the Reticulans have been searching for you. Fortunately, we found you before they could finish the extermination of your family. If your Uncle was here, now, we would thank him. For twenty-three years he managed to keep you safe – long enough for you to mature into adulthood."

"I-I don't know if I can handle this . . . it's just too much . . ." Anthony said, as his perception skewed and he began to feel nauseous. His inquisitive mind was used to dealing with evidence, facts and truths – this was a completely foreign element to his engineered thought process. Although it all seemed impossible, part of him knew that he would have to come to terms with this new information. Subconsciously he knew that failing to embrace what Tarliss was telling him would lead to his death. It was a most daunting and terrifying feeling. But at the end, an invisible, untouchable light at escaping the tunnel of disbelief and sorrow, there was the slightest infectious glimmer of hope.

Tarliss reached for him, and almost instantly they were back in the massive chamber with Aremis and the elders. The room was fully empty and ominously silent.

"I hope that was not too much for you, Sagittarius. Unfortunately we haven't the time to allow your mind to adjust to these changes." Said Rikthinius, his soft voice barely audible.

Anthony waited for more mind-blowing information, unsure of whether or not he was going to be able to cope with this new reality. He was however, thankful that he had been through such extensive training, knowing that a normal man would not be able to handle what he was going through. He still hadn't fully come to grip with the situation – half of him was expecting to wake up any minute, safe and sound on the plane, with Williams, ordering a drink from the stewardess. Seconds passed, and the thought faded. This was now his reality, whether he liked it or not.

"It's okay. I'm okay. Will I ever get to see my uncle again?" He asked, expecting to hear an answer he didn't like. Despite the mixed sentiment he now felt for his uncle, the *liar*, he wanted to see him – to know he was alive.

"Anything is possible, Sagittarius. But there are more pressing issues. The Draconian plan is nearing completion, and we are but days from the balancing of energy. Tarliss and Aremis will escort you to your chamber, where you can rest and grow accustomed to your new living environment."

Anthony wanted to know more. He didn't care about rest.

"What do you mean, *balancing of energy?*"

Tarliss and Rikthinius looked each other in the eyes, and Anthony knew they were having a telepathic conversation he could not hear.

"Come Anthony, we must –" said Aremis, clutching Anthony's hand, but was interrupted by Anthony's desire to know more.

"No. If I am who you say I am, I'm going to have to figure this out eventually. What does it mean?"

"He is right, there is no point in holding it from him." Tarliss argued. "On most life-sustaining planets we know of, there are certain times during the rotation around its sun where there is a balancing of energy in the atmosphere. On Darmeria, it falls on our 33ʳᵈ day, which are considerably longer than Earth days."

"And?" Asked Anthony, demanding a more thorough explanation.

"The humans have constructed a device, in concordance with the demands placed upon them by the Reticulans with the ability to harness this power. They plan to use the Earth's natural energy to create destruction on a level which humanity has never seen. So powerful, it will consume them all and destroy everything they have ever known."

"Is that why we are underground right now?" Anthony asked. He was beginning to connect the dots. Something he had failed to do for the last few hours, failed to achieve, was calmness of mind. His training kicked in instantly, his focus became narrowed. He could sense, feel and embrace his soul accepting the truth of its own existence. Even with the imposing slew of impossible realities grinding into his overcrowded brain, he was thankful for having been given some tool – some coping mechanism during his time as a human. The psychological tests they battered him with as part of the extensive FBI training were proving to be of use to him as he tried to bring together his mental equilibrium. It was a reassuring feeling among so many uncertainties.

"Yes, in part. Our refuge here has also kept us hidden from those searching, wishing to destroy us." Responded Rikthinius. "If we do not act soon, they will turn on their machine, and it will be the end for humanity."

The intensely vibrant creature calling himself Tarliss placed his huge hand on Anthony's neck.

"Yes." Anthony said out loud, to a question passed into his soul through a merging of flesh.

"I am ready. I can handle it."

His spoken word resonated through the minds of everyone, every *creature* in his proximity. They believed him. He could *feel* it.

"Very well then, Sagittarius, you have little time to learn what you must learn to survive this transition. Tarliss, show him our assassins, we must prepare for the Equinox."

* * * *

"We have to destroy it, or warn people somehow, or both." Said the man with the crispy-crittered hand and thick southern accent.

"And how do you plan on doing that?" Asked Lester condescendingly, as if the idea was a delusion.

"You have resources at your disposal at the FBI, don't you?"

"Not officially, since I *am* officially retired. But I still have some control. But what do you suppose we do? We can't just waltz in the front door guns' blazing! Not to mention we'd need approval from the board of directors, assuming they would believe what I'm telling them rather than arresting me on sight. And we don't even know where this place is!"

Pete walked over to a locker on the wall and pulled a thick file out. He tossed it across the table for Lester to view.

"What is this?"

"That is the result of a year's worth of surveillance and espionage."

Lester opened the file. It was filled with pictures. Most of them were too blurry to clearly make out what was in them, or what the photographer intended to capture, but Lester's trained eye could discern what he was looking at – a military base, fences, ensconced in an intense snowstorm.

"Wait a minute. Before we left the mainland, I assigned two of my newest agents to a shipment linked to Al-Akazawhi." Said Lester, his detective mind at work.

"And?"

"Bodies. A container filled with bodies. *Live* bodies. All men, all in good health. When we last conferred, they told me they traced the package to some base in Alaska."

He caught Schlesinger's attention. They both knew immediately that it was no coincidence. There was no proof, but that's how these things worked – the proof they needed never presented itself perfectly, and what they *knew* never coincided with the written facts. Lester knew immediately what he had to do.

"So why didn't you seize the package then and there?" Pete asked, as if he was privy to the tactics and strategies of the FBI.

"We thought it better to lay a trap — like we could nail Akazawhi and Dynatech to the wall with one giant red flag."

"I see. Let me tell you, those men are being harvested for their genetics. The ones that survive the genetic modification will be used as soldiers for Dynatech's private army. Those who don't, well, they won't be heard from again. By now you must have realized Akazawhi's place in this whole thing. He was simply a puppet, a scapegoat — a face for the media to focus on. To deter everyone's attention from the real agenda. If their plans had gone exactly the way they wanted, Anthony would have been in one of those shipments."

Lester's phone rang. It was Jim. He prepared himself mentally for what was about to happen between them. He didn't answer the phone, knowing that it may very well be traced by those trying to find and kill him. He walked up to the door leading to the train tracks, without any permission from Schlesinger. Before he could turn and reach the door to open it, he felt a dime-sized piece of cold metal push into his spine. It was Paul emerging impossibly from the slightest shred of darkness in the barely existent corner of the room. One of the many features of their body-forming combat suits was the inclusion of Vantablack - A carbon nano-tube material with the ability to absorb 99.9% of visible light, rendering the wearer nearly invisible. The only give-away would be the whites of the eyes and shimmering speckles upon their exposed knuckles.

"Confirmed. It's him. Feel free to come through the door Jim."

Like ghosts appearing from thin air, Paul's two accomplices suddenly were present. Pete marveled at how they could remain hidden in such a confined space and how on earth they got through the heavy door without them hearing. He was very covert in his dealings, but it became very clear to the whistleblowing veteran how vulnerable they all were, in that moment, in that place.

Tax dollars at work. He thought to himself.

"I have to ask sir. Why did you leave us?" Jasper demanded, lowering his rifle and stepping forward into the light dimly cast from the ceiling fixture. The shadows denoted a very serious look on his face.

"I had to. I'm sorry. There are things going on here that are much bigger than all of us." Lester said convincingly, in a way that reminded the spec38 assassins who their boss was, and what their priorities were. He also hoped they hadn't seen the local news on their way over, since there were other higher-ups that could perceivably pull them in a different direction.

"Sir we are with you either way. You have my word." Jasper said.

It was a welcoming reassurance. The spec38, if they decided to, were more than qualified to apprehend everyone there and bring them back for sentencing. Lester was going to have to decide very quickly how much he wanted to tell them. Sanctions and regulations were out the window – assets as they were considered; their loyalty now relied on the values they held as living breathing men.

The loud deadbolt lock on the door unhinged as Jim hastily entered.

"You've got some serious explaining to do Jim. Come on there's someone I'd like you to meet."

Jim said nothing. He held the door open for Gary, who scurried in with an armful of computer equipment and his jacket. Jim seemed relieved, as if he had lifted a giant weight off of his chest. Lester could tell he was eager to let it go.

"This is Pete Schlesinger everyone." Lester said, and almost immediately after, Paul and Jasper drew their weapons on Schlesinger and began screaming intensely.

"Whoa! Whoa! Lester yelled, as Pete, terrified, fell back into his chair. The spec38 officers seemed intent on killing him.

"GET DOWN NOW! EVERYONE GET DOWN!" They yelled, and it worked. The group had no choice. Gary curled into his jacket and buried his head into the corner of the room, whimpering, and everyone else hit the floor when the barrels were pointed at them.

"Explain yourself very clearly Director. This man is on our red list. We have a mandate to KILL on sight!" Paul yelled, squeezing his gun tightly.

"OK! Okay! Calm down, what is your red list soldier!?"

"Classified operating protocol. Certain individuals are on a classified list we all share. If we come into contact with such individuals we are supposed to waste them on sight. You better tell me why I shouldn't." Paul responded rapidly, poking Schlesinger with his gun to reaffirm how serious he was.

Holy shit, Lester thought. No wonder Schlesinger had to be so secretive. His mind worked fast to prevent a bullet from going into the man's cranium and the subsequent aftermath that left little to the imagination.

"You've been lied to soldier. For a long time. He is not your enemy! Lower your weapon let me explain it to you. Better yet let him explain!" Lester yelled, pointing unmistakably at Pete.

"What do you mean lied to? How do I know you're not lying? I've got dead men back there. And we were attacked by fucking Americans! No one else has that kind of coordination or hardware, nor the fucking balls to attack us like that. This piece of shit better not have something to do with it!" Paul yelled, pushing his gun barrel harder into Pete's chest. Lester was surprised Jasper did not step in to calm his soldier down but he understood why – they operated as brothers, not a hierarchy.

"Relax soldier. He's right. I'm *not* your enemy. Jasper, is it? Paul?" Pete said very calmly, raising his eyebrows as he looked at them, unafraid. His calm displacement seemed to indicate he had looked death in the face more than once. He reached into his pocket for his cigarettes and a lighter. The tension in the room slowly dissipated as he got up, took a seat at the table and lit his cigarette.

"Obviously you know who I am. Who I'm *supposed* to be. By the way please lower your weapons it's very hard to concentrate." He said, pulling the poisonous cloud deep into his lungs.

Jasper gave the nod, and the guns were down. But just incase, they waved their hands above the holstered pistol on their waste to make sure it could be drawn quickly.

"The reason you're men are dead back there is because you were onto something that was supposed to be covered up."

"What do you mean 'covered up'?" Paul demanded, impatiently.

As the soldiers became engaged in the conversation, everyone slowly rose to their feet, eventually finding a seat at the table.

"There is a monumental conspiracy happening on this planet as we speak. I am not a cyberterrorist, nor am I a murderer. I'm not the least bit dangerous; well at least not to the common man. But I do know the truth, and that's why I'm on this 'red list' of yours. Based on what me and my followers have found, the majority of the American government has been under exo-biological control for the last 60 to 70 years. Anthony Stall –"

"Is an alien." Jim interrupted. Every head at the table turned to him.

"He is an alien creature, an extraterrestrial, whatever you want to call it. Not from Earth."

"I'll let Jim explain, since you *already* trust him." said Pete, verbally putting Jim in the hot seat and delineating the burden of mistrust from himself. It threw the soldiers for a loop, making them reconsider how justified they were in this whole scenario – as if a double-locked evidence compartment in their brain had suddenly been blown open and was now re-opened for analysis.

Before he spoke, he looked Lester directly in his worn, caved-in eyes. He saw a fatigued pain. But it was time to come clean, to reveal what he had been hiding. Although the words didn't come Lester knew what he wanted to say.

I'm sorry.

Jim readjusted his seat and stared into the table, his voice held a robotic, monotonic and truthful resonance.

"Three months before 9/11 happened, and two years before I met you, Cap, I was on contract under The Air Force as a bodyguard to what they called 'foreign ambassadors'. I didn't know at the time, since they look basically just like us, but these foreign ambassadors were actually extraterrestrials from a planet in the Canus Majoris star cluster. For months, I lived in underground bases, constantly monitoring and acting as a chaperone for these creatures. My superiors told me they were from Austria, and I foolishly believed them. It was actually a perfect cover."

The Spec38 soldiers looked at each other, then at everyone else around the table. Jasper threw his rifle on the table and took off his combat helmet, Paul leaned back and kicked his feet up.

"Wha-" Lester stammered, surprised at how quickly the soldiers swayed.

"This just sounds so crazy that I don't think he could make it up. We're listening." Jasper said.

"Good. Thank you soldier. I eventually befriended these creatures, and they told me things. They told me about the reptiles, the greys-"

"Alpha Draconians and Zeta Reticulans." Pete interrupted while placing the files full of pictures in front of Jasper.

"Yes, whatever you want to call them. They told me terrible things. Like that the government had made an alliance with evil aliens, who wanted to take over the planet. At first I didn't believe them, but I came to know it as the truth. On September 7th I was given the order to assassinate them, but I couldn't do it. Not to mention they already knew about the plan because they were very advanced telepaths and had been reading my mind from the beginning. They didn't know the whole thing, however, only what they could harness from my mind. And I certainly didn't know everything."

"Compartmentalization." Murmured Paul, shooting a glance at Jasper, then at Lester, letting them know that there was a legitimate term for this sort of thing, and that he was privy to how the government used it to limit what people knew.

"So what happened to them?" Gary asked, who listened like a child hearing a fairy tale.

"Well, they must have liked what they saw inside my mind, because they entrusted me with Anthony. I got the feeling that they knew there was nothing they could do to save themselves. So I took Anthony and left. I created a fake alias, a fake history, grew a moustache, got some plastic surgery, put on forty pounds and blended right in."

"Blended in by joining the FBI?" Lester asked, annoyance underlying his tone.

"Yes, Lester, surprisingly enough I thought that was the last place they'd look for me, and I had never known anything else than to be a man of service. And I was right - until now."

Silence filled the room for half a minute, as everyone tried to conceptualize what they had just heard. It was like having their minds hit with a freight train and trying to pick up the pieces during a snowstorm.

"So you mean to tell me that aliens are trying to kill us all and take over Earth?" Asked Paul with an oddly agreeable tone.

"Not trying, succeeding. They are almost there. You've heard of the Heaven's Gate program, yes? Well because of our numbers they knew they would need some sort of superweapon to speed up the killing process. Heaven's Gate is a giant geo-political cover for a program called HEAR, a weapon that has the ability to control the energy in Earth's ionosphere. With it they plan to decimate populations by creating unlivable weather conditions – hurricanes a thousand times more powerful than any we've seen, tidal waves as high as skyscrapers." Pete proclaimed once more, feeling like a broken record.

"How do you know all of this?" Paul asked.

"Years and years of extensive espionage and what you would classify as 'illegal activities'. I came face to face with the alien agenda in 1977, that's when I lost my hand. I worked as a geologist back then – I built underground bases for the military, that sort of thing. I later surmised what these bases were intended for." Said Pete, speaking fast, timing drags of his cigarette to make sure he had time to breathe.

"And what was that?"

"Some were intended for protection from the onslaught for a select few of the population. Basically anyone who knew about the plan – some for food production, and so on. Others were designed for military purposes, such as creating armies designed to seek out and destroy any alien refuges deep within the Earth. Namely, the Darmerians, whom they believed had been hiding somewhere in the mantle. After the event, bout' a year of recovery from my injuries, The Air Force made me sign an oath of secrecy. I held that oath for 8 years . . . .but I couldn't live anymore. I couldn't live . . . with what I knew."

"So if this is all really happening, then what the hell are we all doing here? Shouldn't we be doing something about it?" Paul said, knowing full well that they had a monumental task in front of them. His efficient killing mind always focused on an objective, a task to be done.

Lester sensed something else that Paul wanted to ask. It seemed peculiar to him that he would so easily believe what he was hearing.

"We have to act fast. Two days from now, that machine will turn on whether we like it or not." Said Pete.

"Paul. Is there something on your mind?" Lester asked him directly. Given the level of truth-spewing going on, he decided it was futile to hold back on expressing any innate impulses. Everyone froze and tensed up, eyebrows raised, as if Lester was challenging Paul's loyalty. But Lester's instincts, as usual, were infallible.

"Yes sir. Two years ago we were on a recon mission in Northern Russia. We encountered some of the 'grey's' as you call them, in combat in the depths of an abandoned nuclear facility. Damn things came up, I mean, from underneath us, through the floors. Turns out they were trying to steal large amounts of uranium buried in an explosion that happened years ago. We didn't put too much thought into it, as we were deployed in Australia three days later. But believe me, these things exist. I have seen them with my own eyes. So has he." Paul confessed, nodding bipartisanly at Jasper.

"Why didn't you tell me this earlier soldier?" Lester asked.

"Well, you didn't ask." Paul responded in a coy manner. And he was a right. Their deployment in Paris had its own set of complicated necessities and priorities.

Everyone took a moment to think. Somewhere among the rush of mind-blowing information infiltrating their heads, there was a solution that had to be sought out. It had to come from the combined, makeshift think tank in that room, at that time, before they went anywhere. And it had to happen fast.

"Well I may have an idea." Said Jasper. "I told Ray to stay at our last destination. We found lots of containers there, and we hacked the manifest. They were headed for somewhere in Alaska. I'd bet my ass they're going to the same facility. He's got trackers on him. All I'd need to do is radio him and tell him to plant a tracker on one of the crates, and we'd have an exact location."

"I like it. Tell him to do it." Lester said, authoritatively reconfirming his place as the leader of the group.

"As for the rest of us, it's going to be pretty hard to get back to the States without being seen."

"And why are we going back to the States?" Jim asked, looking at Lester like he was crazy.

"We are going to confront this Mr. Grey personally. We're going to squeeze him and make him talk. It's our only out right now. We need a confession from him in order to move forward, to convince those who need to be convinced in order to march on that facility."

"Are you sure that's a good idea sir? I mean, we have less than 48 hours" Piped Gary Jones.

"I'm not sure, Gary. But it's all I got at the moment. If you can think of a better one, be my guest."

"Well actually sir, I think I might." Said Gary, standing up confidently, brushing the dust off of his pants and fixing his hair. He garnered the attention of everyone in the room. He reeked of amateur, childish enthusiasm.

"Spit it out Jones." Grumbled Lester, lighting a cigarette from Pete's pack, expecting to dismiss whatever Gary had to say.

"Well, first of all I'm sorry Jim, but I looked into your file when I was by myself. I found out that someone wants you dead just as bad as agent Stall. The update was encoded, and was added to your file yesterday. And given what you just told us, I think it's pretty apparent why. They can't risk anyone knowing the truth letting it out."

Jim and Lester shared a glance. They both knew where Jones was going.

"What are you getting at Jones?"

"Well, I think we should make it public. I think, instead of being secretive and risking getting caught, we should blow this thing wide open."

The idea seemed crazy and legitimate at the same time. There was little to no chance of them being able to get remotely close to Mr. Grey, even if they believed they could. Despite Gary's antics, he may be right. After all, that was the *democratic* way, wasn't it?

"Let me guess, Jones. You want to use us as bait!" Jim exclaimed, rising from his chair, angered.

"Wait, Jim, let him finish." Said Lester, waving his thick hand. "Calm down."

"Well, yes. And I can make sure the whole world sees it. The last thing any of these bigwigs want is their plans being thrust into the public eye, right? So let's do just that! I'll tip the authorities to your location, meanwhile, a squad of news teams will be laying in wait! Trust me! I can make sure the whole world sees you get arrested! Then they'll be forced to give you a trial! It'll be the perfect place to tell everyone what's going on! To warn them! Can you imagine the media exposure!? I say we use this toll on your head as an opportunity to expose them!" Gary yelled, getting more excited as he spoke, darting around the room and using his hands to relay his emotion. Lester was surprised to see how enthusiastic he was – he was used to seeing Gary as a weak, sniveling reprobate scared of his own shadow. Despite that fact, he could feel Gary swaying the opinions of everyone in the room, even the stoic, emotionless Pete Schlesinger. The media, after all, is their biggest weapon. Without it, or at least control of it, their shadow-enemies would be dealt a huge blow.

As much as he hated to admit it, Gary's plan was better. The way it was now, they were all dead anyways.

"And what if you can't get the media's attention? What if they decide to shoot me on sight and hide all the evidence? I haven't survived this long by being a fucking tattle-tale, Jones!" Jim bursted, truely mad at the idea of being used as a pylon, but equally if not more upset that Lester would consider subverting his authority to Gary's outlandish plan.

Gary put his hands on his hips and moved his lips to one side, looking down into the desk. He had to think about this one.

"If I can somehow get back to the FBI headquarters, I can make it happen. All I would need to do is put out a fake APB in the system. I have done it before. Someone would need to make sure the news was already there, before they came to arrest you."Gary explained, revealing his plan. It was farfetched, but they believed he could do it, after seeing how crafty and useful he had been before.

"But how can you be sure Jones? What if they don't see the APB in time. What if I get shot and buried and the media makes up a story? What if I don't even –"

"We're doing it Jim. It's happening." Lester interrupted. Jim tried to object, but Lester simply spoke over his voice. "I never thought I'd fuckin' say this, but you're right Gary. Cept' for one thing. Forget about the APB. Paul, Jasper, if I can get us to the States, could you get Jim into the Boston Globe building?"

"Paul, what's the forecast for tomorrow in Boston?" Jasper asked. Paul was already checking it out on the SATNAV device attached to his forearm.

"Wind and rain."

"We could hot jump right on top of that thing. Probably the best way, avoid all the traffic on the streets."

"Good. Tell Ray to stick them tracker thingies on the crates." Lester said while grabbing his phone out of his pocket. "I've got one more favor to call in, should be able to get our hands on an EFF jet."

It was clear by the air in the room that no one really believed they could pull it off. Lester realized this, but he could not forfeit hope. The bigger picture, laid in front of them like a death sentence, was the only thing driving him at this point. He opened his phone and began dialing. A voice on the other line wasn't the least bit surprised to hear from him.

"You're a wanted man, Captain. But I know who you are, and I will help you. I'm sending the coordinates to your phone. Be safe, and make sure no one follows you." Said the voice, clearly and concisely. He noticed Pete giving him a peculiar look.

"You're not the only one with secrets Schlesinger."

Lester took a moment to give his best version of a pep talk to the group whose bowed heads and slumped shoulders denoted an entirely empathetic demeanor. His hands began to shake as the gravity of the situation weighed on him. He clenched his fist and remembered who he was and where he came from. The mental strain of forfeiting his life for the survival of the human race clenched in that fist.

"Listen guys, we're outgunned, outmatched and outnumbered. Sooner or later they're gonna' find us and kill us. We've gotta' fight fire with fire on this one." He said emphatically, trying to instill some morale in his followers. They were listening.

"We're with you Cap." Jim said.

"All the way sir. Let's do this." Gary Jones added. Lester waited for the acknowledgement from Paul and Jasper. They looked at each other briefly. It had to be like this, they had to have the final confirmation. Their brute force and tactical minds would be the most crucial element if this little scheme was to work.

"Fuck it. He's right. We're smoked meat here. Let's move like we got a purpose. Where are we headed?" Jasper asked, just as soon as Lester's phone chirped – the message containing their next objective.

"17 miles due North. We're going to have to blend in. There is an EFF jet waiting for us there." Said Lester, standing up. He looked around the table once more.

"Time to go. *Now*." To which everyone rose and walked toward the stairs. Schlesinger grabbed a handful of files and a jacket, then through a door to retrieve his assistant, who was peeking, frightened, from behind a table.

"Are the soldiers gone?" He whimpered.

Lester stared at Jim, right into his soul. They walked up the stairs side by side in silence, although they could both feel that the other wanted to say something. Jim tried to open his mouth, but Lester interrupted angrily.

"I can't *believe* you lied to me that long Jim. To everyone. I trusted you. *Everyone* trusted you." He touted, letting Jim know exactly how he felt.

"I'm sorry Cap, I-"

"You lied. You betrayed us all. Now our lives are in jeopardy. Those dead soldiers back there are on you now, I hope you understand that." He said furiously, throwing his hands around and slamming his fist into the concrete wall. They both reached the top of the stairs, where Lester breathed in a big sigh.

"I couldn't, Lester, I couldn't. I'm so sorry I lied. But you have to understand-"

"Oh I understand very clearly James Stall, if that is even your real name. 22 years of friendship, all a lie." Lester vented, holding his shaking brow with his hand and wiping the beads of sweat trickling down his forehead.

"Schlesinger is ready sir. Let's move." Paul yelled from the bottom of the stairs, waiting for confirmation to get tactical – waiting to raise his gun again.

Lester took a deep breath and swung the heavy metal door open leading to the dark train tracks. He held the door open for everyone to exit. Paul and Jasper, clad in black, disappeared into the darkness just feet away, weapons raised, checking for threats. The few seconds it took for everyone to file out allowed Lester to calm his nerves – to sort out his mind. He couldn't help but ask Jim what he really wanted to know, in his heart as much as his mind. In a much calmer manner, he turned his head slightly and barely spoke.

"Do you think he's still alive, Jim?"

"I hope so Cap, I hope so."

"You and I will sort out our differences later. Keep that hope alive. It's about all we have left right now."

*   *   *   *

Mother Nature's wrath was a constant reminder of the consequences that would beset anyone outside the confines of the compound. The snow and wind beat the atrium ceiling and walls like a worn snare drum. At times throughout the night Stacey believed the whole facility was going to collapse in on itself and bury her forever. Maintenance had run dry; fallen nuts and bolts sometimes lay scattered across the vast marble floors within the massive chambers of the facility. It was hazardous to anyone traversing the long pathways, but no one ever complained. Complaining was an unspoken taboo. *Speaking* was an unspoken taboo; at least, speaking about anything other than their work. When they arrived it was all fun and games, but slowly the pertinence of secrecy superseded, thwarted and crept on top of the right to communicate. Stacey and her colleagues were quickly beginning to learn how to cope with living in constant worry while managing to do the work they were assigned to. Hours filled with more work and less leisure. The distances of time in which one scientist would see one of his or her peers increased dramatically. Like a frog in slowly heating water, the workers in the facility were being conditioned for an extended stay. The entertainment facility became out of reach, their work became more serious and they were surrounded by an ever-increasing contingent of armed guards. Most of the workers accepted it as the law, refusing to ask questions about their circumstances. But not Stacey – she could *smell* and *taste* the fear in the air. Their superiors feared them – feared they would escape and reveal their secrets. Although they came with smiles and polite discourse, nothing so sadistic and evil could be hidden, no matter how hard they tried. After just a few days, the hand-selected scientists were living in complete fearful isolation, with no promise of anything getting better for them any time soon. Deep down, they all were in denial. They all knew they would not be leaving this facility.

Once again, Stacey found herself in the lab alone, except for the guards that never spoke and never left her side. Although they never told her, she didn't dare defy their imposing control, knowing full well what would happen to her. She was already gone from the world of man – the only thing she still owned was the oxygen filling her lungs and the thoughts in her head. In front of her, the mysterious human-like creature that lay in a state between death and life, lingering between breathing and decomposing. Behind her, five heavily armed guards - two more than her last visit to the table.

The silver-clad perfectly composed organism lying in front of her proved to be impenetrable. High RF emissions failed, carbonite saws connected to half-ton mechanical arms descending from the ceiling shattered and exploded. Stacey was beginning to run out of ideas – which scared her. What would happen to her if she couldn't get this thing open?

She was going to try her last idea. During the RF blasting tests, she noticed certain distortions in the heartbeat monitor. She was the only one who noticed and neglected to tell her superiors, as they didn't ask for any specific details – only if it worked or did not work. Given the level of security always present, she was quietly amazed that she was given even that much. She wondered why, if this thing was dead, there was a heart monitor in the first place. It lingered in her mind as one of the many questions she could never ask.

"Can you come and help me hold this thing?" She asked uncharacteristically, but she could not lift the reconstructed second mechanical arm into the holding mechanism by herself. It was very dangerous to use two RF emitters in the same vicinity, but she didn't care anymore.

One of the ominous silent guards robotically slung his gun around around his back and walked toward the platform. He easily lifted the two hundred pound extension into the circular modular pedestal next to the raised platform and locked into place. Without words, he turned and walked back to his position.

"Not much of a conversationalist, are ya'?" Stacey said jokingly, to no reply.

She walked over to the control board and turned a key. Another panel full of controls and switches came to life. Each of her hands rested on mouse-like palm-sized balls that allowed her to pivot, rotate, dip and heighten the mechanical arms. She pointed them right at the body and pushed a large yellow button on each panel with meters next to them. Slowly and methodically, she moved the levers corresponding to the intensity of the radio-frequency waves to the top, while keeping a trained eye on the heartbeat monitor.

The mechanical arms started to vibrate at seventy percent, no movement on the heart monitor. Seventy-five percent – still no response. Risking it all, Stacey placed her hands on the RF meters once again. She didn't look back, but she could feel the tension rise between the guards watching her ever so closely. She wanted to test them. When she finally did look back, two of them raised their hands to their earpieces. Someone was watching her, and feared she was going to do something they did not want her to.

With a spastic jolt of rebellious impunity, Stacey cranked the meters as high as they could go. The guards ran over to try and stop her but failed. The emitters did what they were designed to, and the mechanical arms that held them in place stood strong and sturdy, although one more megawatt might cause them to explode ferociously. The sheer energetic power of the devices created a loud hum that Stacey felt in her chest. Before the guards could rip her away as she flailed and kicked, the heart rate monitor spiked. The whole screen turned red and signaled a very loud and noticeable alarm, adding to the frenzy of moving parts surrounding the table. The two guards carrying her stopped abruptly to analyze the threat as the other three trained their weapons on the dead alien. To their combined surprise, the shackles that held its hands and feet glowed white, burning hot, and melted away. The creature erupted into consciousness, tearing away its confines and sprung from the table. The guards were already firing, but none of the well-placed bullets penetrated – one after another, several dozen .45 caliber rounds were stopped just feet from their target. Cylindrical strands of the bio-mechanical, impenetrable silver suit shot out and met the projectiles, catching them in mid air. The guards fired until their clips ran dry. The two carrying Stacey lost interest in her. She managed to scurry away to the periphery of the large room and curled up into a ball as her captors engaged the suddenly awakened, dangerously hostile alien. Their weapons proved to be utterly useless.

After deflecting and nullifying a barrage of gunfire from all angles, the creature went on the offensive – but it didn't move like a man. It moved so fast that it looked like it was teleporting. A streak of blue light trailed its movements, which were almost impossible to follow. In a split second it was behind one of the guards then viciously sliced his head clean off with a swift swing of its hand. The guard standing feet away was cut in half at the waste by a similar blow that happened so fast Stacey's eyes could barely make out what was happening. In the time it took this creature to destroy two men and leave their bleeding corpses falling lifeless to the floor, the third guard firing his weapon managed to get his gun halfway into the area where the creature's bioluminescent aura danced and darted. His finger squeezed the trigger, just as the alien leapt right over his head and landed feet behind him. A powerful straight kick to the abdomen struck him so hard Stacey could hear his spine snapping in half. His limp body flew into the robot-arm fixed into the floor, knocking the device off kilter. The explosive electric reaction it caused affected the powerful creature, knocking it to the floor – just long enough for the remaining two guards to get a clean shot off.

Weakened, the alien tried to block the bullets with its bare hand from a kneel but it was too much. In his last moment of conscious existence, his eyes locked with Stacey's, and everything slowed down – so much, in fact, that everything stopped entirely. Her vision, her attention became tunnel-like, until everything became dark and all she could see was the bright blue eyes of the creature controlling her mind. It used its last sliver of life to show her things that terrified her even more. And then, as quick as it happened, her essence re-entered the conscious plain. The guards squeezed their triggers and sent hot lead into the alien's body. The protective suit did nothing to stop the impending death. Blue, shiny metallic looking blood trickled from the many holes now in it's body and sprayed all over the floor beneath the creature.

The guards immediately corralled the panic-stricken, trembling civilian and dragged her toward the staircase where she could faintly hear the rumbling of footsteps. A plethora of guards were on their way down to secure the area. Tightly packed between a group of them was Mormont. He looked very angry.

"What were you thinking Miss. Peterson?" He asked, grabbing her by the neck and pinning her violently against the wall.

"I-I tried . . . I thought that . . . I –" She mumbled, unable to formulate full sentences.

"Is it dead?" He asked the guard.

"Yes sir." He responded, looking at the bloody mess spread about the room.

"Leave her with me. Take the rest of the squad and lock down the living quarters. No one gets in or out, understand?"

"Understood sir." Responded the guard as he fluttered a number of hand signals to coordinate the rest of the soldiers. They filed out immediately, leaving a few behind to clean up the mess.

"Well I can't say I don't admire your efforts Miss Peterson. After all you *did* manage to break through that suit." Mormont said, holding Stacey, barely conscious, close to his mouth. Slowly, her vision centralized and she could hear properly, although she let out a sizeable vomit that nearly covered Mormont.

"Get up, Stacey, there is something I want to show you."

She struggled to regain her footing, using one of the guards to climb back up to a stand.

"I am taking her to the surface dock. Follow us. And make sure she doesn't do anything stupid."

"Roger that sir." Responded the guard, grabbing Stacey by the shoulder and directing her towards the back of the room. Mormont revealed a remote control from his pocket and pressed a series of buttons to which a panel on the wall slid open, inside was a brightly lit elevator big enough for twenty people to stand comfortably.

When it finally ascended to the surface, the howling winds and snow were incredibly loud. It woke Stacey up immediately. Torrents of ice slammed against the thick plastic capsule, making the whole contraption vibrate.

"Just wait, Miss Peterson."

Mormont once again revealed the control from his pocket and pressed a sequence of buttons. Seconds later, everything began to shake violently.

"Hold on to something. You are about to witness the true genius of this place"

Stacey looked out into the white monster before her. At the edge of her vision, massive grey walls began to emerge out of the ground. Piles upon piles of churning white snow were pushed away, accumulating into dozen-meter high banks as the stone monoliths ascended from the ground. All around the concealed capsule, the walls continued to rise, until the white was snuffed out by grey. Abruptly, at about a hundred and fifty feet, they stopped rising, the snow covering them shimmied off the top. The howling winds disappeared completely, the capsule ceased to vibrate. Inside, Stacey could once again hear her thoughts returning to her.

Flashes of the images bestowed upon her by the dying alien raced through her mind, forcing her to the ground again.

"Are you looking, Miss Peterson? This is the genius of our invention – our crowning jewel." Said Mormont, to no response. The images in her head were too intense. Her eyes rolled back, she could barely breath. Mormont grabbed her by the hair and forced her to look on.

Several beacons popped out from the top of each wall surrounding them, glowing bright blue. They grew brighter and brighter until a grid of blue lasers appeared, connecting the beacons on the walls into a unified protective force field barrier. It encapsulated sound and wind until the air within the makeshift stronghold was completely calm.

"What-what is happen- . . . where am I . . ." Stacey murmured, unable to come fully to her senses. She could see Mormont in front of her, but there was three of him. If only she could narrow it down to one, if only she could stop spinning . . .

"Oh, Miss Peterson, it's not over yet."

The rumbling of mechanized moving parts began again. The snowy plain encased by the massive walls began to shake and vibrate. Several huge square-shaped platforms opened, revealing a huge series of antennae that looked like metal trees. Stacey's equilibrium was beginning to return to her. The three Mormonts formed solidly into one wobbly figure in front of her. She mustered all of her will into one narrow focus as the scenes transferred to her brain by the alien took hold of her.

"You liar. . ." She whispered, clutching the guard to try and get back to her feet.

"What was that?"

"You . . .liar." She gasped, "You are *evil*."

"I am *necessary*, Miss Peterson. We all have a part to play. I have chosen to survive what is coming. You must decide now how much your life means to you." Mormont growled, angered by Stacey's outburst. He sounded as if he was trying to convince himself as much as her.

He has to die she thought, enraged enough to act. The guard considered her incapacitated, incapable. But she had one last burst in her. Feeling around on the ribbed armor on his breastplate, she found what she needed. She ripped at the knife and it came loose. The guard swung his encumbered hand at her hair, missing. With every ounce of strength she possessed, she leapt across the capsule and used both of her hands to plunge the four inch blade deep into Mormont's body. Her aim wasn't perfect, the dagger landed awkwardly in his side – enough to injure, but not kill. Mormont shrieked in pain, quickly yanking the dagger out of his torso. A swift reactive kick into Stacey's stomach followed, causing her to curl up into a ball on the floor, starving for breath, hacking. He looked at the guard, furious, clutching his bleeding wound. His response was a mix between shock and fear, he stood there, raising his hands, as Mormont pulled out a pistol and shot him in the head.

"You fucking bitch look what you've done! I wanted to LET YOU LIVE and look how you repay me!" Mormont yelled violently as he stumbled and planted against the wall. He fired four more shots into the dead guard, yelling furiously, as an expression of his anger. He quickly pressed the lift button and the capsule began to descend once again.

Mormont continued to kick and curse wildly. The wound in his torso continued to spit out sheets of warm sticky blood that covered Stacey. A fresh squad of guards waited for them in the infirmary room, guns trained. They quickly assessed the situation and rushed to aid Mormont, and the guard. They obeyed orders without question and were completely unaffected by the murder of one of their own. They dragged the carcass away as if it was nothing but an unwanted mess.

"Should we terminate Miss Peterson sir?"

"NO! We need her alive. But she has seen too much, take her to the machine!"

"Copy that sir."

The guards instantly corralled Stacey, tied her wrists and dragged her away. The journey was a half-conscious, painful struggle for her, as the guards pace was much quicker than her own disoriented feet could manage. Every time she fell, she was either dragged back to her feet by her hair or prodded until she stood up on her own. Were the other scientists suffering a similar fate?

After what seemed like a lifetime of pain, they reached their destination. One of the guards forced her to her knees and spoke to a large man, clad in black and adorned with multiple weapons. His chest held two pistols, his back carried a large automatic rifle. A series of small blades lined his thighs and hip, with a belt of ammunition covering his waist. As he emerged from the shadowy blackness in the corner of the room, he sheathed a long, shiny katana and reassured the guards.

"I'll take it from here soldier. Return to the surface."

The assassin's tone was deep and irrefutable, leaving no room for the guard's own discretion. He took Stacey by the shoulder and walked her over to the adjacent wall, which held a series of cylindrical, human-sized containers connected at the top by various pipes and wires running into the ceiling. As they drew nearer, three of the capsules slid open rapidly. Two of them already held a man each inside of them.

"You'll be joining Mark and Eugene for some regressive hypnosis. Don't worry Miss Peterson, you will survive this." Said the assassin without the slightest hint of emotion; a hauntingly scientific description of what was going to happen to her.

Even though he sounded sincere, she still didn't believe him. It didn't matter what she had to do, or who she might have to stab, she was going to break free of these confines, reclaim her life and blow the roof off of this place - or so she thought. Once inside the capsule, powerful sedatives entered her bloodstream via two stiff syringes plunged deep into her neck. Accompanying the incredible pain; an overwhelming feeling of helplessness and despair - and then nothing but blackness.

* * * *

Anthony and Tarliss conversed as they wound through tunnels, making their way to what Tarliss kept calling The Den of Fire. Of course these aliens wouldn't have normal names, like barracks, or training room, it had to have some biblical, epic moniker. They had already passed The

Hall of Light, a place where Darmerians gathered in huge numbers to recharge their batteries, which was basically like meditating. Each of them had a cylindrical container that shone a bright light just like the one he woke up to on the medical bed. For two hours at a time, they lay at forty-five degree angle, closed their eyes and got a really intense tan. More walking brought them to The Solitary Abyss, which Anthony thought was appropriately named, since it was quite literally a deep black hole leading deep into the Earth. Just before The Den of Fire they passed The Elder's Row, which was akin to a human library. All of the records the Darmerians had were consolidated here and available to everyone for self-education. It was as if Tarliss had purposely taken the longest route, in order for Anthony, or *Sagittarius* as they knew him, to gain a better understanding of what would soon be part of his new lifestyle. It was a very brief crash course in just how incredibly similar, but also how incredibly different these creatures were to human beings. From more than twenty feet they looked as human as he did, but once they got up close, subtle difference became obvious. Their cheeks tended to be more robust, their skin lacked any sort of blemish or scar. Only extreme age denoted any creases or lines. The eyes were big and bright, but not from reflection. Their heightened luminosity seemed to emanate from within the eyes themselves. Most, but not all of their ears were pointed at the top and almost all of them were connected to the neck at the bottom, as if they were meant to extend the jaw line. It was much more noticeable when looking from the side. Every Darmerian Anthony walked past seemed to acknowledge or at least be aware of his presence. He felt like if he wanted to, he could talk to them without his lips. He could do what he did before with Aremis, and they would not be scared to engage telepathically with him. What struck him as odd was the scarcity of children – there were some, but not many. They seemed to be every bit as rambunctious and spastic as human children, but weren't interested in playing. They tugged at their parents, constantly asking them questions about anything and everything. Their need to frolic and pretend was replaced with a thirst for knowledge that was constantly being filled. Seeing a young one had a certain ethereal peripheral quality to it – if they were born, and grew, they could die. Just like humans. Humans who had managed to dispel the curse of egotism and the suffocating woes of materialism.

"I thought you'd have more trouble adjusting, Sagittarius. I am quite pleased with your progress so far." Tarliss said. Most of the things he said carried a sort of stern reassurance, as if he understood exactly what he was going through and understood him deeply as a person.

"Yeah, I. I guess I've sort of been trained to move forward, not backward."

"How so?" Tarliss asked, genuinely intrigued. He seemed to be just as curious about human nature as he was about displaying Darmerian cultures and practices.

"Well, I was in the FBI. Certain parts of our training were designed to help us cope with situations out of our control, and, well, to try and get back that control, ya' know?"

"Control of the situation, or control of yourself?" Asked Tarliss prophetically. The question made Anthony think deeper than he wanted to. "I think you'll find that in most instances, the two are one and the same." He continued, as he extended his right arm and opened his palm, waving it. His pace came to a halt and Anthony did too. The wall of the stucco-looking tube they were currently in became completely transparent, the air in the room gloomed over. It felt like the walls had a self-sustaining energy embedded in their atomic fabric, and at the wave of a hand, as if it was his personal magic wand, Tarliss could redirect the energy at his leisure.

"There they are. Working hard, just like when I left them. Have a look."

Anthony peered into the meter-wide band of transparent material that now looked like thin air, or a non-reflective glass. Below them was a room full of tall, muscular warriors. It wasn't hard for his battle-trained intuitiveness to discern that they were conducting some sort of military training exercises.

"How did you do that?" He asked Tarliss. The questions running through his head just a half an hour ago took a back seat to new ones sparked by his curiosity. He was still struggling with whether or not he believed all of this, but seeing things with his own eyes left him no option.

"My energy. It is in you as well, even if you can't feel it yet. In time, you will be as powerful as I am, Sagittarius." Tarliss responded without turning his head. Almost every word and sentence that came from his mouth sounded prophetic.

"OK, I understand. I am supposed to have some kind of superpower I don't know about yet. And by the way, just for now, can you call me Anthony? It just sounds a little weird when you refer to me as some horoscope."

"It is not some horoscope" said Tarliss affirmatively, turning his head to face Anthony, denoting a very serious inflection. His deep blue eyes carried a hypnotic aura of truth that could not be denied. Anthony found himself truly wanting to believe everything Tarliss said, despite how hard his dichotomized psyche was battling with itself. "The human interpretation of the astrological calendar is a remnant of what we left behind, thousands of years ago. Darmerians first arrived on Earth millennia ago, during our first Epoch – we wanted nothing but to learn, to seek enlightenment through knowledge. Our emissaries took a research vessel to Earth that landed in the North Atlantic, close enough to observe and evaluate mankind, but far enough to not risk . . . *contamination.*"

"What, you mean like a flying laboratory? Like we were some kind of experiment?" Tarliss took a breath, as if he needed to think carefully about what he said next. He placed both of his hands in a triangle facing the luminous band of wall then quickly spread his arms apart. The wall opened up on cue. But it didn't open, it more so dissolved and disappeared, or some strange mixture of the two. It looked like a 50 foot drop, but Tarliss stepped out anyways. Before he could think to react, his hand was already firmly gripped by Tarliss' huge mit. They didn't fall anywhere, but simply hovered, floated down to the room below.

"Not an experiment, no. But it was an age where many of our efforts were designed to learn more about other sentient life in the Galaxy. There are some human records of this contact, although they are skewed, and not entirely accurate. Some cultures called it Hy Brasil. Have you heard of it?"

"Can't say I have. Never paid much attention in history class." Anthony responded, displaying sarcasm. Tarliss did not play along with his joking attitude, a most useless human trait.

"Despite their best efforts, the curiosity of the human civilizations proved to be irrefutable. It was as much a part of their spirit, their essence, as it was their desire to acquire sustenance." Said Tarliss.

"So they broke the rules?" Anthony asked, trying to piece together, in plain form, Tarliss' cryptic, prophetic explanations.

"Yes. Contact became more and more frequent. They sent their crude ships, their merchants and priests. They wanted to know more. So we left abruptly, fearing our contact would lead them into an unavoidable confrontation between species." Tarliss said, taking a moment to let the story sink in. they had reached the floor. In front of them, a group of silver-clad, robust alien warriors engaged in some sort of training exercise but obviously enamored with their presence. They looked at Tarliss, who simply looked back. Anthony was beginning to catch on. The warriors turned and continued their exercises, having telepathically been told to do so by Tarliss. He didn't have to be privy to the invisible conversation to understand that much.

"One of the things the early human groups did acquire from us, before we departed, was an intricate knowledge of the stars, and of constellations. It became instrumental in their religious beliefs, as they viewed Hy Brasil, and it's inhabitants as god-like. Over generations, the idea of astrological signs took root, but were conceived into what you now know as horoscopes – a most crude and incorrect interpretation of divine knowledge."

"I see. So what do they mean *to you?*" Anthony asked, refusing to give up until his detective mind came to a full comprehension.

"Those names have existed for millennia in our society. When we arrived, we used Earth's constellations to navigate different parts of the galaxy, and thus named them with our own legends and martyrs. It seems that very small parts of our culture, when relayed to early humans, became very *large* parts of their engrained belief systems. It is precisely for this reason that we were banned from any further contact with sentient species considered to be of lesser intellect than our own."

"Sounds to me like you were scared to educate them. Like they might learn too much."

"Not scared Anthony, just cautious." Tarliss said, shifting his focus toward the warriors. They all stopped, turned and headed toward them. Their movement was inexplicably coordinated, perfect, as if a computer program was sequentially controlling them. "I'd like you to meet some of our assassins. They have been training diligently."

Anthony saw a myriad of warriors before him. Some small, some very large, but all of them at least six feet and anatomically perfect. The shiny silver suits they wore reflected the intense light in the room as they walked, which didn't seem to come from any visible light fixture. It was simply there.

"Venethon, this is Sagittarius. He will be joining you in training." Said Tarliss.

"I will?" Anthony asked, surprised.

"Yes, you will. I'd like to tell you more about our history, but time is short. I believe it will be in your best interest to accelerate your lethality."

"Well, I am already pretty lethal. You should see my tests results during FBI-"

WHACK!

Anthony fell to the floor, clutching his ribcage, the strike reverberated through his body, and it hurt. His bio-alarms went haywire, his defensive stance; fists clenched and back on his heels automatically kicked in to action. His focus momentarily escaped him, but quickly returned with a boost of adrenaline. One of the large alien warriors stood in front of the others with his fist held out in front of him. He was positive that he was looking in that direction when the blow came, but it happened so fast his eyes could not follow. All he knew for sure was that he was outmatched, and nothing he had ever trained for could protect him from such a blow.

"He's not fast at all." Said the seven foot, muscle bound alien, whose waist wasn't half as wide as his shoulders.

"What the hell? What was that for!?" Anthony said, gulping, scared. He couldn't help but realize his death only required a one-limb swing from one of these creatures. But amidst the pain and feeling of inferiority, there was a spark of something else. A primal, destructive force brewing inside of him – he wanted to fight back. He wanted to be powerful like they were.

Tarliss gave him a peculiar look, then looked at the warriors surrounding him, half intrigued, half unimpressed. The latter was the only expression Anthony could recognize.

"Very well then. We will integrate later. Come with me Anthony." Tarliss said, as if he was personally offended by what happened.

Anthony rose to his feet slowly, the slew of assassins judging his every move, like a pack of wolves teasing a wounded creature.

"Beldonor, resume your exercises. We will return." Said Tarliss. They seemed to obey his order unquestioningly, although he was not the biggest. Anthony could tell he was the stereotypical strong silent type. The type he himself tended to be during similar interactions throughout his life. For a moment, he remembered a lesson his uncle had always tried to relay to him, in his infinite wisdom.

Never underestimate the wrath of a quiet man.

He couldn't decide whether he ever wanted to see that wrath or not. He too would listen to Tarliss and abide by his wishes, just as the others did.

They had some time to talk again, as they passed into the next room, through another series of illuminated tubes that led deeper.

"Not what you would expect. Believe it or not, English is *our* language, as well as most of the languages of Earth. Another thing early humans inherited from our early contacts." Tarliss said, once again letting Anthony know that he could read his thoughts.

"Interesting. *What else* did mankind inherit from aliens?"

"Well, much of the current technological advance in human society came from Zeta-Reticulan technology. Fibre-optics, Wi-Fi, most of it designed from reverse engineered vessels shot down from intense RF waves. Humankind is quite literally a melting pot of different species in terms of their technological prowess."

"Wow." Was all Anthony could muster. His mind was working much faster than his mouth could handle. He also wondered why Tarliss wasn't calling him out on a thought that had been perpetually crossing his synapses since he arrived in this place.

"It's ok, Anthony. She is very attractive, it is only natural." Tarliss said, to Anthony's embarrassment. It was now painfully obvious to him that nothing in his mind could be hidden, and that it was useless to try. There was also a keen insight into the aliens. They weren't so different from humans. If there were children, then it must have required sex, right?

"Do you think she is interested?" Anthony asked, unapologetically oblivious to the ways of Darmerian courtship.

"Aremis is a valiant warrior. Her mind is not consumed with things that do not contribute to the improvement of her soul, and the souls of all Darmerians." Was all he got in response. Another cryptic answer rife with uncertainty, at least perceived through a human lens. Anthony took it as a firm *no*.

"We are here." He said calmly, stopping and waving his large hand through the air once more. Another barrier disintegrated into thin air, revealing a room. Anthony didn't have to step inside to know what it was.

"There it is, Sagittarius!" Tarliss said, this time actually perforating a slight smile, although it was definitely an expression of pride, delineating from his stoic aura.

"There is what?"

"Your instinct. It is beginning to supersede your fear and your doubt. Unfortunate remnants of naïve human intellect. I felt your energy there, when the door opened. It is growing inside you very rapidly, and soon," Tarliss said, gripping Anthony firmly by the shoulders, "You will realize it. You will become more powerful than you could ever imagine."

Anthony wanted so bad to believe him, but he didn't feel any different. He still felt afraid, and a large part of him wanted to wake up from this dream.

"Come inside. You mentioned you had *some* combat training?"

"Yes. I was the top marksman in my class. By a longshot." Anthony said without realizing he had tucked his hands behind his back and spread his feet, a firm, chain-of-command-obeying stance. "No pun intended" He said, seconds after. Tarliss didn't seem to pick up on the human joke.

"Hmm." Was Tarliss' response, as if he needed to see it to believe it. Anthony couldn't tell whether he was doubtful or impressed, or neither. It was a notion of curiosity. "Show me." He said, motioning his hand towards the right side of the square-shaped room – the first room they had been in that resembled angled, human architecture. Anthony turned to look over his shoulder. He saw a rack pinned to the wall that held an assortment of smooth, white objects. He knew they were weapons, maybe even some sort of rifle but they were entirely different from anything he had ever operated. The two of them walked over to the rack as Anthony's excitement peaked. It would be a welcome notion that would put him back in his element – to hold, control and fire a weapon.

"These are some of our small arms. Pick one." Tarliss, said. Anthony looked at him, but his expression did not change. "Primitive weapons, outdated, from a much earlier, much *bloodier* time in our history."

Carefully examining the smooth, white oblong-shaped instruments, he wrestled in his mind simply how to pick this thing up. One of them was sticking out for some reason, at eye level. It looked more like an artistically carved musical instrument than a rifle. It's back was cut at an angle that quite clearly nestled in the shoulder, while the front had no barrel or any sort of visible hole for a projectile to come out. It didn't have a magazine, nor did it have a cocking mechanism. Anthony placed his hand in it's narrow, skinny center and held it like a guitar. Blue streaks of light lit up when he touched it that resembled a circuit board on a computer and where his fingers touched seemed to light up as well.

"What the hell is this thing?" He asked, wondering how it could possibly be lethal. But he was intrigued.

"Like I said, it's much different than the firearms humans use. Let me show you." Tarliss said, taking the weapon from Anthony. He raised it to his shoulder, showing him how it was supposed to be placed, but he didn't hold it like a normal rifle. He didn't *hold* it at all. His right arm raised into the air, while his other hand hovered just below the wider back end of the thing. It floated between his hands and reacted to his movements. He swung his torso left, then right, and the weird looking gun followed. He looked at Anthony to make sure he was getting the gist, then turned out into the open room and fired a dozen shots in rapid succession. Not bullets, but burning hot beams of blue light that let out a subtle hissing sound.

"How did you do that?!" Anthony asked, excited with the device. "There's no trigger?"

"No Anthony, there very much *is* a trigger. But it rests solely in your mind. When you think shoot, it will. If you can focus enough". Tarliss said, as he tossed the weapon to Anthony, who caught it. But he didn't catch it. The thing hovered in between his shoulders as if it was thinking on its own. He raised his hands into a comfortable stance, a mixture of pretending and believing. But despite his hesitation, the 'gun' nestled itself in the area between his shoulders and hovered there like it was connected to him – an extension of his physical body. He didn't hesitate to motion his hand below the weapon as if there was a handle with a trigger for his index finger.

"Take this and put it on." Tarliss said, holding out a helmet made of the same material as the gun. Anthony did, but just like the gun, he didn't feel it touching him. It just hovered there. The screen lit up and a continuous wave of static energy rolled down it every four or five seconds.

"There will be targets." Said Tarliss, seconds later a loud hum of electricity sharply burst into his eardrums, and lights on the wall in front of him were suddenly very luminous. Anthony looked at him thinking there was more information.

"Try to hit them all." He said. There wasn't time. Quicker than he consciously thought about it, his body reacted. He immediately liked how light the weapon was, and how easy it was to point it exactly where it needed to go. No wavering barrel, no need to compensate for weight and muzzle velocity. The device seemed to move without the necessity of his muscles, as if it could read his mind as well. The first shot didn't fully process in his mind as a conscious thought that could definitely have existed. It was more of a pinpoint reaction. He could feel his reflexes amplified. With precise accuracy, the shoulder-nestled weapon aimed up and to the left, where a disc-shaped white target appeared for no longer than a second. It was more than enough time for him to wax the thing, but there was certainly no time to linger. Two more targets appeared just feet in front of him, one on a perfectly diagonal line to his right and just feet above the floor, the other in a similar position but over his left shoulder. Both targets vaporized into glittering speckles, then faded into nothing, as the recoil-less beam emanating from the gun struck them. He was enjoying himself. He could feel the power in his hands, in his body, connecting to his mind and calming it, enough to suppress every notion of thought, amplifying five-fold his reactive instincts and letting them take over. He knew the second he began to think too hard would cause him to miss. Then, a break, just long enough for him to flash a glance at Tarliss, who had a barely discernable smirk plastered to his rigid, emotionless face. A split second later, four small white discs blipped into existence ten meters above him, all in separate corners of the room and began a trajectory straight towards him. If not for his heightened level of situational awareness, he wouldn't have seen the two coming from behind him as they were completely silent. He polished off the two visible ones within less than a second. There was no wait time on the gun, as soon as it had the proper line of sight, the thing fired. It saved precious split seconds between pointing the gun and the small distance of time it took to squeeze the trigger. No normal human being could feel or record such an advantage, but *he* could. Instinctively, Anthony whipped his body around to shoot the third target – it disintegrated five meters from him. The last quarter turn of his body left just three meters between him and the last disc, plenty of time to take it down. He stood there for a moment, a bead of sweat trickled down his face, he exhaled, expecting the level of difficulty to increase.

"Good, Anthony! Now let's see what you're made of!" Tarliss said, his eyes remaining fixed, as he extended his right arm from being crossed on his chest and pointed it toward the wall he originally faced. Anthony was preparing himself for something more difficult. He took a deep breath, braced his feet and shook his shoulders out.

I've got this He thought to himself, wondering if Tarliss was still inside his head, feeling what he felt, judging his reactions and thoughts and evaluating his "lethality" as he had referred to earlier.

The wall began to light up in the upper left corner. Then the bottom right. Then two spots in the center. He was beginning to make sense of the drill, the discs were showing the order they would come in, and he had better not miss. It reminded him of some the mental acuity and reflex amplification tests the FBI had put him through. It brought him a calming level of familiarity that made him feel more comfortable. His posture loosened up – the muscles he held tight released, as he realized he did not need to expend energy to hold the weapon in place. As soon as he did, the first projectile came screaming at him. He was already aimed at it with one eye fixated on the next target, a strategy he had developed from years of shooting. At first he thought he made an error, but he did not. The mental surge pulsed through the gun and it fired, but he had not seen the projectile materialize yet – the streaking bolt from the gun impacted the disc just as it was barely emerging from the wall. Either a well placed pre-cognitive shot, or an extremely lucky blunder. He didn't have time to decide which. He aimed at the bottom right, waited just a fraction of a second until the lit section became almost blinding, then pulled the trigger. Once again, the disc-shaped target disintegrated just as it materialized; a perfect shot. The two in the center burned glowing bright, but not one after the other. They seemed to be burning together, meaning they would come together. His aim would have to be immaculate. He planted his back foot during the half-second break before the discs fired. He waited for the blinding brightness which seemed like a quarter minute to him, but in reality the entirety of the drill so far had elapsed in less than twelve seconds, including the three seconds he spent acknowledging Tarliss. But why did it seem to be going so slow? Anthony was intensely familiar with perceived time-distortion during high-adrenaline, stressful combat situations, – everything slowed down when your life could end the next instant. But this was different - not something that could be explained by perceptive differences because of increased adrenaline. The gun did a mixture of leveling itself and *being* leveled at the target on the right. Anthony held his breath as the luminous orb materialized into a disc and shot toward him at break-neck speed. He shot the thing and tilted the barrel just inches to the left with barely enough time to line the barrel up with the second disc. It fired, disintegrating the disc just feet in front of him, showering him with glittering speckles of vaporized light, or at least that would be his best explanation of the stuff if asked to describe it. But it wasn't over. Before he could turn to Tarliss to try and gauge his opinion, 6 more lights appeared on the wall. Two in the upper left corner, one in each other corner, and one just off center. This was going to be tough.

Like before, he waited the impossibly small amount of time for the projectiles to "heat up" before they fired. The first three came from the corners, easy kills. The fourth, fifth and sixth, however, came at the same time – one from the center, the other two from the top left corner.

The hard part. He didn't know which one to aim at first, or whether he'd have enough time to even hit them all. He was already thinking too much. Letting his instincts smash through the cloudiness of over-analysis, he raised the weapon to the top left corner, just as the projectiles came screaming toward him. Two rapid shots came much quicker than his finger could have pulled on a trigger, for lack of a better explanation simultaneously, but there was no time to keep his vision focused there to make sure they hit. The third disc was already just five meters in front of him and closing rapidly. He got the barrel of the gun in front of it just in time to shower himself with more glittering light-dust.

Expecting another series of targets, he raised his gun back to the wall. Nothing. Tarliss simply looked on, nodded his head as if to tell Anthony to be patient. Five distinct globules of light began to form on the wall, but they were in perfect order, and Anthony immediately knew something was wrong. It didn't make sense. It was too easy. He chained down the five projectiles as they sped toward him and then rapidly twisted his body to face behind him. To his semi-surprise, two more discs were already en route from a curved part of the ceiling above the door they entered the room through. He barely had enough time to aim them down. Four more light spheres emerged on the far peripheries. He would have to turn his body a full ninety degrees between shots to be able to get these ones. The first one came from the left, he nailed it. Then from the right, another hit. He turned back to his left expecting a disc to be almost on top of him but the circle of light denoting an emerging target was gone, and no disc to follow it. At the time he didn't know why, but his head tilted straight up toward the ceiling. Incoming was the disc he had lost track of. It took him off guard so much that he felt to the floor firing, needing three shots to hit the target just before it plunged into him. Lying on his back, his quick-twitch instincts subdued, he searched around the room for the last projectile. His eyes darted around – finally he found it – screeching towards him from just above Tarliss' head. It was coming too fast, it was going to hit him. He tried to move the weightless instrument into a firing vector but it was too late. In what he thought might be his last moment, a spastic jolt of ferocity coursed through his veins, propelling his supine body up and away from the floor. His leg swung high and long, its corporeal orbit connecting with the projectile. The thing shattered just like the others, as Anthony crouched on the floor under the rain of vapor-glitter in a defensive stance. He briefly looked at his own hand. He felt extremely strong, and extremely fast. Faster and stronger than he ever thought possible. He thought if he needed to, he could destroy Tarliss and break through metal barriers with his bare hands to escape. His hand was surrounded by some sort of aura – it reminded him of looking across a hot desert and seeing the distorted, wavy air caused by the scorching rays of the sun. It flickered then began to dissipate as he clenched his fist into a tight ball, the gray, smooth floor beneath his arm becoming visible through the distortion.

"That's how it feels, Sagittarius." Tarliss said, but not with his mouth. Anthony rose to his feet and shot him a glance that could cut through stone.

"What's happening to me?" He asked simply and frankly. "I feel . . . *different.*"

"As well you should. Your body is adapting much faster than I expected. Your soul is beginning to realize its own power, and it is helping you to become a very powerful creature, as you were meant to be. It is only a matter of time before you can do things you once thought impossible."

Anthony wanted to argue, to tell Tarliss this was all impossible and stupid, and he didn't believe anything he was being told. But he had witnessed it for himself just moments before, and couldn't deny the power he felt surging through his own body. Nor could he deny that his senses were fixated in this new reality, as much as he wanted to fall asleep and wake up in the back seat of his Camaro, or in the window seat of a commercial airliner with his partner, Williams, sitting safely next to him.

"Show me more." He said to Tarliss, but not with his lips. Before he even noticed, he was speaking fluent telepath. "I want to know everything. I want to *be powerful*"

"You will be, Sagittarius. But it must be for the right reasons. For now, you must rest. Allow your body time to regenerate. This sort of transition can be very . . . detrimental to your energy levels."

Anthony didn't argue with him. He didn't feel strange about being called Sagittarius, nor did he argue that he needed rest. Tarliss took Anthony by the shoulder and looked him in the eyes like he was meeting God himself. He trusted Tarliss, and he trusted the path he was on was the right one. For the moment he stuck everything perplexing his mind in the back of his compartmentalized brain, a useful trick during combat exercises he had learned as a human. Everything that was bugging him seemed to disappear and smooth out.

"We're going to the regeneration chamber. Not the hall of light, I have a specific room set up for you. Let's go now. You will need your energy for tomorrow."

"What's tomorrow?" Anthony asked, this time with his mouth. Tarliss stopped and looked at the ground, and spoke deeply as if the words coming out of his mouth were hurting him.

"One week ago, we lost contact with a squad of Darmerians sent on a mission to Starset, the largest base the humans have constructed thus far. Their objective was to gain knowledge on the humans' plan as well as destroy the facility if it was deemed necessary. They failed, and now we fear the worst. Normally we would be able to connect with them through neural transpositioning, but we have been unable to establish a link. I am taking a group of assassins there to find out what is happening and to destroy the HEAR facility. If we do not succeed, the images you saw during the Elders' enlightenment ceremony will most certainly become reality."

Anthony pondered the situation, as the images flashed before his eyes once more. Destruction. Death. Misery. *Genocide* . . .

It all became very real, very quickly once again. The people – the *humans* he loved, would die horribly.

"And where do I fit in with all of this?" Anthony asked, although he knew what Tarliss was going to say. He just needed to hear it for confirmation.

"The Elders believe you need more time to procure your abilities – and maybe they are right. But I want you there with us. I believe you are ready. And if I am wrong, Anthony," Said Tarliss, gripping Anthony firmly by the shoulders, locking with his eyes "Then you tell me now."

Anthony had no intention of backing down, or shying away from a fight. Whether it was something he had developed as a human being, or a Darmerian, it was there, inside his make-up, regardless. If he wasn't ready, this was the best way to find out.

"You know I'm coming with you." He responded in tongue, firmly and absolutely, as if there was no other possibility available.

"Good." Was all Tarliss said. "Let me show you to your quarters. Tomorrow is going to be extremely demanding both physically and mentally. Be prepared to see Darmerians die. There is an extremely high possibility of it happening."

Chapter 13

ACCEPTANCE

Holding the title of 'FBI Director' had its perks, even when the whole world wanted your head. Favors done in the past for those who had been back-turned by everyone else, who had felt the depths of loneliness and hopelessness dictate their lives, would always pay for themselves in the future. Lester knew this, and thanked himself for doing things off the official mission record the few times his instincts told him he should. Using derelict subway systems, less-than monitored regions of Paris and a few scarcely populated routes that Gary had found for them, they made it to the EFF jet that would take them home.

Waiting for them at an ensconced military hangar nestled between thick trees on the side of a rolling green French hillside was a remnant of one of those favors.

"He's sitting at a desk just meters from that door. Jones, anything peculiar on the SATNAV communication lines?"

"Negative. At least nothing I can find. I think it's safe." Gary responded through the communication headset linking him to Paul and Jasper, who held a four hundred meter scouting position atop a well-shrouded tree. The angular shadows and narrow visible cracks between its foliage gave them ample camouflage and a perfect line of sight to the target. Paul rechecked his sniper system to reassure himself of its operational capacity in case things went sour.

"I can't see any sentries. He wasn't lying, Captain. He's expecting you."

Lester, Jim and Gary waited behind a row of bushes fifty meters from the hangar, well within Paul's line of sight, waiting for the confirmation to reveal themselves. Schlesinger and his assistant loomed meters behind in a thicker grouping of bushes that hid them almost entirely. It looked sketchy – there was half a football field of barren, open terrain between them and the facility – a lot of space for something to go wrong.

"I don't like it Lester. I don't like it at all." Jim whispered, crouching behind his left ear with one hand hovering over the pistol on his belt. Lester didn't seem to care – there was something else still sticking to his frontal lobe.

"It all makes sense though, doesn't it Jim?" Lester said, "About Anthony. About how he's so god damn good at everything. Like, *too good.*"

Jim didn't know what to make of his words, but he felt reassured that Lester wasn't worried about crossing the field. Or maybe he was, and he just wasn't showing it. Either way they really didn't have a choice. Gary leaned in like a quiet child to overhear their conversation. He had some sort of workpad in his hand that garnered most of his attention. Jim and Lester didn't bother to ask him what he was doing, assuming he was trying to help in some way. They had finally began to trust him, but not because they wanted to.

"Sir." He piped up, "I recommend discontinuing the use of all cellular mobile devices and crypto-gear. I'm detecting heavy distortions and irregularities in the radar tower ping-back subversion matrixes within a 60 mile radius. Someone's looking where they shouldn't be."

Jim and Lester looked at each other for a moment and agreed. They both took out their phones and smashed them on a big rock embedded in the bush, much to the surprise of Jones, who thought they may be reluctant. It bolstered his confidence in believing that hardened agents would respect his insights.

"I have to destroy my computer as well Captain, I won't be able to –"

"Just get on with it." Lester interrupted, then raised a pair of binoculars to his face. It helped put Gary in his place – they weren't about to start being nice to him just because he was useful. That was just too much to ask.

"Paul says it's clear. We can't just sit here." Lester said, holding three fingers into view, slinging the binoculars into a satchel. "On three. One, two, three!" He whispered, on three his voice gargling a bit as he leapt through the bush and bustled across the field. He looked briefly to see Jim and Gary scurrying out behind his wake in tow. His attention then shifted to the building in front, just waiting for the huge hangar doors to open, and a rifle to be pointed in his face. He slowed for a minute, but then remembered Paul's sharp eye was covering him, and increased his gait considerably, confident. The trio reached a door that blended into the metal thatch-work frame of the building, its only discernable features being a doorknob and a very thin rectangular outline.

"Paul you got us?" Lester whispered into his earpiece, leaning carefully against the wall beside the door with Jim behind him, who had unholstered his pistol and drew it ready.

"Roger Cap, breach and clear." Paul responded. It was regular lingo for the trained killers, but Pete had no intention of shooting anyone. He carefully gripped the doorknob, slowly turned and flung the door open. He and Jim poured into the facility, guns drawn, and scared the hell out of the man sitting at a work desk meters away.

"WHOA!" He yelled, falling over in his chair. It gave the agents the split seconds they needed to scan the large room with their firearms, to see any potential threats. It was barren; the place was silent, but not empty. A man and a woman in civilian clothing held notepads and pencils, both of them dropped when their hands went flying into the air in a scared, don't-shoot-me motion.

"We're inside Paul, its safe." Lester said, lowering his weapon. "Relax you old spook, it's me."

The man poked his head over the desk to see Lester holstering his weapon.

"You scared the shit out of me Lester. Was that necessary?" He said, rising from his hole like a groundhog. He was considerably small, had rounded, narrow shoulders almost completely covered by a wizardly beard that must have taken deacades to grow. He wore thick glasses that hadn't been updated since computers were invented and his oily bald scalp shone under the ceiling lights. On the desk in front of him was a series of controls and screens that Gary was instantly drawn to. Jim had an inquisitive look on his face, he was curious as to how Lester knew this person.

"Guys his name is Terrence Solomon Whittaker. In his prime," Lester Said, looking at Terrence as if to distinguish himself for capturing him, "He was the best hacker in the world. He still putters around but I don't think he really knows what he's doing anymore." Lester said, jokingly. It made sense. The man didn't look the least bit threatening.

"Why thank you Director. You always had a knack for honesty." Terrence said, and then a brief silence ensued as they looked one another up and down. It was a momentary look into the past, when things weren't so complicated, when there were bad guys and the guys whose job it was to catch them. It was a very brief respite from their objective which only took seconds to kick back into their heads.

"This helpless yoke got an immunity deal . . . and became a hermit, thanks to my generosity. Which brings us to the matter at hand." Lester said calmly, his serious pertinence returning to him all at once. He walked toward the center of the large room. Next to the civvies who dropped their notepads, a huge tarp covered what Lester presumed they had come here for.

"Is that it?" He asked simply.

"Indeed it is Director. My team has been taking good care of it. Hasn't been used since . . . I last saw you." Terrence said, his voice trailing off as he finished. It seemed difficult for him to mention, or to even reminisce about the 'the last time they saw each other'.

After another moment of silence with Lester's hands firmly against his hips, they all heard a knock on the metal door they entered through. It was Jasper and Paul, who had somehow traversed through four football fields of thick brush, awkward hillside and a thick stretch of marsh in the time it took them to introduce themselves and lower their guns. Their abilities and actions had an eerie precognitive tendency attached to them; they must have timed it perfectly and sprinted the whole distance. Soldiers were going to be necessary for this mission. Lester and Jim were both happy they had the *best damn* ones on their side.

"Sir. We just received word from Ray. The tracker was successful. The package is en route now, halfway across Russia on a cargo plane. When it lands we'll have exact coordinates to work with."

"Good. Is he safe?"

"Yes sir, he fell back to rendezvous point delta and linked up with the rest of the squad. By the way sir I thought I should tell you . . ." Jasper waited for Lester to turn and acknowledge him fully.

"I told the rest of the squad to standby. They are waiting at a secure location with enough supplies to last them a week."

Lester was intrigued, but he already knew why Jasper made the order.

"You think we might need them again. Don't you." He said, realizing that things were inevitably going to get uglier, and that his team would most likely have to be prepared to kill again. It should have scared him, but it didn't. He felt confident, like he had a back up plan if someone found them. For a moment he felt bad about using the spec38 as his personal tactical unit, but then reality struck his synapse, hard. Speaking of Schlesinger, where was he?

"Schlesinger and his assistant didn't follow you in?" He asked Jim, expecting him to take responsibility for their absence.

"I didn't look back, I Just—"

"Dammit Jim, go get them." He grumbled, turning away immediately after he delegated the order. Seconds later, the door swung open. Pete and his assistant tumbled into the hangar on top of each other, panting.

"I'm sorry guys. Lungs aren't what they used to be." He said, mid-breath, laying supine on the ground and stretching his arms out to open up his chest. Lester walked over to him, unimpressed.

"No more hesitation Pete. That kind of thing could get us all buggered, you got it?" Lester said, leaning over him. Still catching his breath, Pete nodded his head once to confirm.

"That's Pete Schlesinger! Good graces, in the flesh himself! What a delightful surprise!" shouted Terrence, much to the confusion of Jim and Lester, who gave each other that brief what-the-hell look.

"How do you know who he is, Terrence?" He asked, although he knew exactly why. Terrence knew nothing else besides hacking – stealing files, breaking encrypted firewalls, causing havoc for the best military code writers. He must have undoubtedly seen traces of his file somewhere in some government database he had broken into.

"The man is quite famous. Well, not in the typical meaning of the word, but, ya' know, in the *right circles*. Before you so graciously ended all my fun, I was in the process of prying open his file. Mind you, the only reason I didn't succeed is because I had never seen an encryption code like that before, it really threw me for a loop, I tell ya'." Terrence said, the look of a six year old on Christmas morning plastered on his face. "The FBI, NSA, CIA, every three-letter agency in the world wants this guy's head. But to see him in person, well that's just-"

"Can it, Terrence. We're not here to tickle your nerd fantasies. Is this thing fuelled up and ready?" He asked sternly, leaning in close, impressing his size and bulk into Terrence' personal bubble. Terrence leaned back as if Lester's body generated a force-field that was pushing on him. Paul and Jasper had already began walking over to the covered jet, performing their own tactical reconnaissance of the supposedly empty hangar, weapons drawn and pointing to the various corners and walkways in the building. The two civvies awkwardly bumped into each other and quickly moved out of their way.

"It's all clear sir. Let's get moving." Jasper said aloud, filling the largely empty hangar with his grisly monotone voice. He began to pull away the shroud covering the craft. It's matte black angular hull glistened and bent the bright overhead lights into a dance on its shapes and reflected in every direction.

"It's an older model than the one we came on, but it's still fast as hell. One of the conditions of Terrence' amnesty deal was to keep him out of view of the public. Luckily for us, this hangar was the perfect place." Lester explained, walking toward the plane with everyone following him. He turned and laser-eyed Terrence. "I trust you've kept her in tip-top shape? We're not gonna' die in this hunk of bolts are we?" He asked Terrence, who nervously scurried over to his workdesk filled with screens and keyboards. The rest of the group could tell the history between them wasn't exactly favorable for the techno-geek. His fingers went to work rapidly. Curiosity got the best of Gary, naturally drawn to Terrence' handiwork. He peered over his shoulder to analyze everything he was doing.

"Everything looks fine-"

"What subsystem are you running" Interrupted Gary, pointing at a series of code inside a green box on one of the seven different-sized monitors in front of him.

"UltraReddox Mark Seventeen." Terrence snapped back quickly, quirkily.

"That's a lie. They only ever built those things until Mark 14."

"Not true." Terrence snapped again, this time with a nerdish twist of authority. Gary leaned back from his shoulder mount after the comment, squinted his eyes.

"How do you know?"

"Because I built the damn thing. And the first one, and every one after that." Gary simply stood back and put his hands on his hips. Their childish battle of wits had caught the group's attention. Lester looked to his left briefly to see Paul rappelling *up* to a balcony, not down from one. He popped up onto the metal-grate walkway and began methodically looking for targets from the views he had through sporadic, four-foot windows spaced twenty feet apart.

"We've got to go soon sir." Jasper reminded him, but he did not acknowledge.

"The 15 and 16, well they were quite impressive, I had to design them for the bigwigs because of *him*," Terrence said, pointing at Lester, then continued, "I'm kind of admitting to breaching my enclosures here by admitting this, but who cares, no one ever checks up on me. And then they'll just copy the Mark Seventeen and implement it anyways, and I'll get a slap on the wrist, and a silent thank you, and they'll let me breath some more."

As the geeks vented at each other in a game of I-know-more-than-you-do, Lester looked around at the people surrounding him, and it made him think. *Deeply.* Were they really going to do this? Was this the group of people that were technically going to save the world? And more than anything, could Lester even *believe* that he *believed* all this? No. he couldn't delve into those thoughts. No matter how hard they pulled at him. He realized he was going to have to make better use of his resources. Dropping directly from flight into the news building? Everything was beginning to unravel in his mind. But he had to make it work. He had to make a difference, somehow. This moment of doubt introduced new ideas into his mind.

"You two shut up. It's time to go-"

"Wait, Jim." Lester said, motioning his hand slowly and calmly. He formed his other hand into a flat spearhead and pointed it right into Whittaker's soul. "You said yours is newer? A better model?" He asked, unwavering, his hand didn't move an inch. Gary and Terrence stopped to look at each other, then answer Lester's question. They both knew what he was thinking.

"Yes, much better. I recalibrated the crystalline nano-matrix into sixteenths instead of eighths. The processing power is effectively doubled. I also improved the energy expenditure ratios in the Dendri blocks, which there are now *also* sixteen of." Terrence rambled, speaking with his hands by creating an invisible device with them. Gary folded his arms, quiet, attentive.

"Ok. In simple terms, Whittaker. This 'Mark Seventeen' is superior to the ones being used in the field by the government as we speak?"

"I can guarantee it, sir."

He didn't know always know why, but he presumed it was because of the way he spoke and carried himself that people, all types of people referred to him as 'sir'. People seemed to naturally trust his tone and intention, like they wanted to please him somehow. It was a gift he most certainly knew how to make the most of.

"Outstanding." He garbled beneath his breath, hands on his waist, deep in thought. Jim and Pete were beginning to get the gist of what he was thinking.

"I like it Lester. Just so you know. I'll be able to help with the planning part." Piped Schlesinger. They believed him – the feds didn't just throw around the term 'cyber-terrorist'.

"You are all coming. Can you make that whole setup portable Whittaker?"

"Yes sir, one of the many improvements over the Sixteen. I'll need about ten minutes."

"You've got two." Barked Lester. Terrence didn't waste time hefting the various gadgets and screens into a more portable configuration. A series of snaps, thuds and clicks emanated from the work desk. It seemed peculiar to the agents why Terrence was so eager to go with them, to risk his life. But one thought considering what his life must already be like made it all make sense.

"Well don't just stand there, help me!" He said to Gary. It was amusing to watch him toy with Gary like that, realizing that he was on the bottom end of the totem pole amongst the group and the only person he could reasonably tell what to do. *One snake devouring another* Thought Schlesinger, who took out his cigarettes, hesitated to pull one out and light it, then threw them to the ground and crushed them under his boot.

"What about the civvies?" Jasper asked, somehow just feet from the group although no one saw him coming. It always spooked Lester how stealth they could be, even in a brightly-lit, wide open room.

"They'll have to come too. We can't leave them here. If they get caught and interrogated, they are good as dead. And hopefully they haven't been watching the news in the last six hours." He said, turning directly toward them and looking right into their scared eyes. They looked docile, unthreatening.

"Terrence they're *you're* baggage." He said authoritatively. "Jasper. Radio your squad, tell them to get themselves Stateside, and be ready for anyth-"

"Can't sir." Jasper interrupted, "By now someone has almost definitely fixed a link on our transponders. I ordered radio silence when we got here." He said quite convincingly.

"Wait!" Terrence yelled, fumbling through the bottom right drawer of his heavy wooden workdesk. "I've got something that will help!" He said, pulling out what looked like a disassembled phone from the early nineties. The gadget consisted of a 6x2 inch processing chip with a series of attachments and nodes that lit up. A tiny keypad from a prehistoric cell phone was jimmy-rigged to the thing, and an insert block for common phones was screwed in at the top.

"This will block anyone from intercepting your transmissions." Said the mad scientist, handing the device to Jasper, who looked unimpressed. He was used to sleek, perfect equipment, not this half-ass, delicate science project. "Attach it to your com system."

Jasper did, although it took him a few seconds to figure out how to attach it.

"You sure this thing'll work?" He asked. Everyone else looked at Whittaker with skepticism in their eyes.

'I can guarantee it!" He responded quirkily, his shoulders bouncing with self-indignation.

"Make the call soldier." Lester commanded, walking toward the plane. "Same plan, but with a few quirks. This time we are going to have the upper hand." He said, stopping to take one last look at the group he was going to entrust with challenging a global conspiracy. They weren't perfect, but he had faith in them. Everyone had come this far and now, a strategic advantage.

We actually have a chance. We can do this Jim thought. He looked in Lester's eyes and saw the same thing.

Anthony's fate was now out of their hands. He had to make decisions now for the rest of humanity, and he'd better not make the wrong ones. The fact that they had survived this far was less probable than the Celtics winning the championship this year. He didn't know whether to be happy or terrified about that fact.

"No strange pings or weird sounds on the frequency. I'm through, it's working." Jasper said. Paul was already perched on top of the plane, naturally blending into its angular curves as if he was supposed to be a piece of it. His matte black armor and silhouette didn't look the least bit out of place, the only thing giving him away was the white spots of his eyes and face.

"Excellent work everyone." Lester announced. He had to be positive, for the sake of morale. They would need it; the task in front of them was daunting, and some of them could die.

"Terrence forget what I said, everyone in this hangar right now is in this together from here on."

"You don't have to cuddle me Lester. I *hate* this place anyway. To be honest, I kind of got excited when you called. I was looking at your mug on the television when it happened!"

For a moment, Lester managed a definite smile.

"Good." He responded, "I hope your enthusiasm can keep us safe."

"I can most definitely guarantee it!" Terrence touted, pointing his finger in the air. Lester didn't care for the gesture. Despite his vigor, nothing and nobody could guarantee their safety now.

"Everyone on the jet. We're gone in three minutes." Lester yelled, making sure everyone could hear. "Jasper. You boys can fly one of these things right?" Lester asked, realizing all too late there were no pilots, but it was something he purposely let slip his crowded brain, fully relying on Jasper and Paul to find a solution to the problem.

"Of course. Paul's practically an Ace." Answered Jasper.

"Good." Lester said, "Very good."

* * * *

The commander of a battalion of lethal cyborg warriors peeled his crimson-marked helmet off. Along with the human traits he was gifted came a slew of weaknesses that, as his creators alluded to, 'could not be fully tweaked properly.' It might be another glitch that he was even aware of this, or consciously aware of *anything*. His head was sweating, and his skin crawled with cold. Was this normal? The soldiers under his command could never feel like *he* could, nor could they think at all. But they certainly could carry out orders. For longer than he cared to note, his troops had been meticulously searching every nook and cranny embedded in the massive rock-face before him, without so much as a minor complaint or the slightest hint of fatigue.

He waited for one of the two-man squads to give him something to work with. He was aware. He could elaborate, *think*. Random thoughts popped into his head, from who knows where. His synapses weren't controlled, methodic and robotic like his lesser counterparts. His dichotomous robot and human cortexes allowed his mind to venture outside the box and inside of it simultaneously. Something told him that he would very much need this skill that he could not explain, and need it soon. He had heard mention of a word that his creators used, something he had heard over the sounds of a drill tearing into his skull – and the word stuck in his head, or at least the unaltered part of it – *intuition*. He knew what it meant – its dictionary description was inside his mind and he could explain it – but would he ever *feel* it?

His 'enhanced' brain took him for a journey deep into the answer for that question. Flickering green letters seered into the tip of his retina over and over again after one minute passed and thirty-seven thousand minute calculations occurred in his auxhiliary cortex:

<:// PROBABLY NOT

Probably?

That was a word he didn't see often, usually everything his tactical mind produced for him was irrefutably one-directional. Yes or no. Attack or fall back. It was another set of intricate calculations for him to process but it would have to wait.

His communication device scratched and hissed, alerting him. Perhaps the drones had yielded something useful. A few received messages about possible leads hissed and cackled over the COM over the last few hours, but they all ended up being dead ends. He knew, because he checked each one of them personally to make sure the brainless machines weren't overlooking anything. It was easy for them to do. Their orders were concrete and they followed them rigidly, sometimes *too* rigidly. It didn't allow them to elaborate on inclinations that a real human being might have.

"ST-01-04 reporting. Anomalous spectral resonance detected. Recommending further inspection." Said the monotone, emotionless voice over the microphone fused to his eardrum. Through an attached processing chip, the sounds became letters in his mind's eye, but it was rife with error - another bug that needed to be fixed in time for the next 'batch'.

The letters read:

<ANOMALOUS SPECTRAL RESIDENCE DETECTED.
RECOMMENDING FATHER INSPECTION>

Enough of his human cerebellum was intact to root through the errors and make sense of the message. He even had an *opinion* about it. Everyone monitoring from above could also hear, read and analyze every order and message sent during a mission. It was a good way for them to troubleshoot and work out bugs to optimize the performance capability of the next group of EMSS.

If his squad performed well and he was deemed 'optimal' as a UOW (unit of warfare) as opposed to 'detrimental', then he might just *survive*. It was not a word he was trained to have feelings about, nor was it something designed to be important. But it didn't stop him from knowing what it meant – from knowing the difference between existing and not existing.

His brain calculated a response. He wasn't going to risk the message being jumbled or misinterpreted, so he spoke loudly and clearly into his headpiece, simply thinking of ST-01-04. The technology would do the rest.

"Roger that ST-01-04. Send coordinates, I will head to your location." He said. Seconds later, a reply:

"Position confirmed. Sending coordinates now." He got in response, then a series of codes ran across his eyes and downloaded into his lithium-ion storage chip. He fluttered a number of hand signals at two ST troopers that had been standing in one spot for four hours straight. Dust from the cavern winds was beginning to collect and build up, working its way into the narrow crevices in their armor. A waft of dust shook to the floor as they unhinged like a statue coming to life. The larger, heavy assault Shock Trooper stuffed a grapple hook into a gun detached from his back; his movements anything but smooth and natural. The thing pierced the ceiling of a large circular hole more than a hundred meters above them.

The Commander strapped an electronic clamping device from his breastplate onto the taut cable and pressed a button. Seconds later, his body shot up the line, bringing him to the opening. The two soldiers followed him there, both landing harshly with a metallic thud as their cumbersome armor bucked and moaned.

After a long journey down the winding tunnel the helmet lights of the search team came into view. At first glance the commander thought it was going to be another false flag. In front of them was a dead end – a pile of rocks that abruptly ended the trail. But something was irking the Commander. If they'd had the ability to think, to elaborate, they would have noticed that the rock pile looked out of place. He looked up at the dented ceiling, deducing that the rocks must have fallen from it, that some sort of force moved the rocks there.

"Move the rocks." He ordered, and they did, after the split second delay it took to process the order. "Run another trace. Power set to full."

The marksman holding the spectrometer raised the power output as far as it would go. The commander wanted to make sure this wasn't another error, which he was growing accustomed to dealing with. He wasn't sure it would lead anywhere, but he could not deny what was willing him to keep going. It must have been what his creators were talking about – his *intuition*.

"Spectral anomaly detected. Faint reading. 0.6 spectrohertz." Said the marksman.

"Carry on. Notify me when the rocks are cleared." Said the Commander, who then removed his helmet to reveal his scalp; criss-crossed with scar lines and semi-healed stitches. He leaned up against the wall, and did something necessary to keep his flawed, human brain running properly. He closed his eyes and dozed off into an induced sleep aided by an advanced strain of valium injected directly into his bloodstream. Before he was fully asleep, his nostrils picked up a faintly peculiar pungent odor that he didn't have adequate references in his memory to identify.

* * * *

Anthony lay encased inside one of the modular, man-sized vessels the aliens called 'Regeneration Chambers.' Tarliss told him he wouldn't feel it, or have any indication of it happening, but the 'energy' inside of him was going to recharge, amplify, become more present. It wasn't the type of sleep he was used to, and it was hard to feel comfortable at such an angle. He complained about it, but was reassured by his new lethal friend that it was the least of his concerns and that it wouldn't bother him. The reassurance worked like a magic trick. Combined with the overall mental and physical fatigue he had been staving off it was easier than he thought it would be to fall asleep. Within two minutes of lying in the smooth, bright egg mounted into the wall he was in the deepest phase of sleep, and dreaming vividly.

It started like many dreams he had as a human. Sporadic, vague, and full of memories he thought were simple illusions. But this time, they were clearer to him they had ever been, and the images he always thought were redundant mimics of television shows he watched as a child and random psychological representations of his life had their own set of realizations which became much less vague in this state.

He saw his mother, and he knew it was her. She was right in front of his face, looking right in his eyes. Her eyes spoke to his and his to hers. Hundreds of questions were being answered with no words. Their conversation seemed to last forever, and he seemed to be fully aware that he was in an unconscious state, and that he would wake soon. It was like no other dream he had ever experienced – the type of surreal dream state you purposely go back to sleep for, hoping you can control your slumber-world a bit longer.

Will I die?

Everything dies. You have much time left.

But you died. You and dad . . . they killed you . . . why didn't you stop them?

We had to Saj, It was the only way to keep you alive . . . I am sorry

What am I supposed to do?

What you were born to do . . . bring light to the dark places . . .

Her hands wrapped around Anthony's face. Her flowing purple dress exploded into a million glowing ribbons, until all he could see was blinding light. . .

The intense glare formed into strange blurry circular geometry. He was awake. The glass sheath opened on its own. It must have been glass, but there was no common light reflections on it like there should be. As it rose, he had to squint to see the bottom of its outline, which may have existed in his mind more than the physical realm.

"How do you feel?" Tarliss asked, emerging from the regeneration pod next to him. It was the first time Anthony saw him without his form-fitting sparkly suit on. His fibrous muscle strands rippled under the bright light, and there were some things on his perfectly sculpted frame that looked very strange – he had no nipples, and his ribcage was not *ribbed* – it looked more like a ceramic plated shield underneath his tight skin. Anthony couldn't help but stare at the differences.

"I - . . . " Anthony trailed off, smiling. Tarliss also smiled. "I feel fine. I feel good." He said, honestly. He racked his brain to try and compare how he felt to previous experiences. Nothing rang a bell – beer, weed, sex, nothing was quite like it. This was new. It was *Different.* Is that what it felt like to be powerful?

He popped out of the 'bed' and did a twisting motion with his torso. It moved freely through the motionless, heavy air inside the half-cavernous room. A ledge at the bottom of a set of semi-circular rounded stairs looked out into a jagged, luminous black rock face across an empty vein of open air deep in the Earth. Carved angles reflected along the sharp lines; creating a freckled display of sparsely connected glowing membranes..

"Where is the light coming from?"Anthony asked, unconsciously walking toward the glittering tapestry as he spoke.

"Let me show you something." Tarliss said, walking beside him, guiding him with his hand. As he walked past, Anthony noticed another subtle difference in Tarliss' trapezoid muscles – rather than being split into two triangular shapes, they connected *over* the spine – the same thing was evident with his latissimus muscles in his lower back.

"It's an evolutionary thing. Extra protection for the spinal cord." He said, reading Anthony's thoughts again. It seemed almost normal to him now, like he was expecting an answer without having to actually ask the question.

"You also have no nipples. And your ribcage looks pretty unbreakable."

"Also adaptations, extra protection for the heart and lungs. Many times denser than human bones. Ask yourself – did *you* ever break any bones?" He asked, to which Anthony could not reply. He really couldn't remember breaking anything, ever.

"I always just thought I was lucky."

"Well you weren't wrong." Tarliss said, grinning slightly, "Do you see those worms over there?"

"What worms?" Anthony asked, confused. Tarliss pointed out into the silent chasm just below their waist line. Upon closer inspection, Anthony noticed a section of the glittering wall on the far side was moving. He looked even closer, able to make out individual dots that stretched and contracted to move in different directions.

"Even down here, life thrives. They feed off of the energy that resonates from the core. Resourceful creatures." Tarliss said, simply looking off into the expanse.

"My mother . . .she –"

"Spoke to you?" Interrupted the chiseled warrior.

"Yes. She helped me answer a lot of questions. Is this normal for Darmerians?"

"Absolutely. Her presence is embedded in your genetic code, same as your father." Tarliss looked at the ground as if he was actually having trouble finding the words to explain.

"The humans use a word called 'metaphysical'. Are you aware of it?"

"Yes, sort of." Anthony said. He'd be hard-pressed to recite dictionary verbatim, but he got the gist of the word.

"The subconscious is a valuable tool." He said, looking Anthony in the eyes, "A tool you must use whenever you can." Was all he had for an explanation. Anthony was beginning to realize he'd have to figure some things out by himself.

"We are not so different from the primordial slugs on the wall over there. Like all planetary creatures, their bodies are designed to maximize the usage of the environmental conditions within which they exist. Darmeria is much larger and more luminous planet than Earth. I suppose you could say it has a stronger *spirit*."

"Is that why you are – I mean *we* are all so fast? And strong?"

"Yes. Our bodies have adapted to use those energies to our advantage." Tarliss said, putting his hand on Anthony's shoulder while maintaining his forward gaze. "We've learned to enhance our abilities, both mental and physical. Things once considered impossible by our scientists are now real. It's time to get your suit fitted."

"What suit?" Anthony asked, intrigued. He liked the thought of testing out more of the alien hardware.

"The same one I wear. Let's go to the armory."

A few minutes later, they were in the armory. The room was barren except for them. Each wall was filled with weapons, although they did not resemble human weaponry. Instead of sharp angular designs they were smooth and rounded. Most of the 'guns' didn't have triggers and there was a slew of devices that defied a logical explanation until their use was demonstrated.

"The back wall. That is where the metal is contained. At least what we have left."

"What do you mean?" Anthony thought.

"The metal that comprises our combat suits isn't natural to this planet – or *any* planet." Tarliss explained, "Our scientists first came across it in space, while monitoring a nearby supernova. Even *our* sciences haven't been able to fully explain it yet, but the metal seems to be able to think on its own, although it has no brain to speak of. The best explanation we have is that the star's consciousness survives the explosion, the ensuing black hole, and forms this material."

The star's *consciousness?* What on Earth – or in space, was he talking about? It was another thing he didn't want to spend too much effort thinking about. If these high-tech extraterrestrial warriors couldn't figure it out, he wasn't about to ruin his brain trying to do the same.

"So what if it doesn't like me?" Anthony asked, somewhat worried.

"It will." Tarliss mumbled, although he didn't sound confident.

The wall did the same disintegrating/dissolving thing from before, but this time they walked right through it without breaking stride. On the other side was another Darmerian; brittle-looking and hunched over an oval control platform. In front of them, a very thick pane of bowed glass, or whatever material they used that looked like glass.

"Shaa'luth Darmas, Tarliss. I have been working tirelessly on your request. I believe this is my finest version yet." Said the homely-looking alien. He was visibly much older than the others. His ears were elongated and pointed. His skin looked like that of the elders and his eyes had lost almost all of their bright-blue pigment, giving them an eerie white-blue pale glow.

Anthony stepped forward and looked down into the chamber between them and the bowed glass. Bolts of blue energy rippled throughout the chamber, emanating from massive, smooth clasps that encircled a ten-meter squared area in the middle. The floor surrounding them was lined with a hexagonal outline that formed some sort of laser barrier all the way up to the ceiling, which became visible when streaks of energy burst into it, flickering waves of energy across its surface. One of the clasps retracted slightly, and then another across from it, revealing what was inside. Anthony squinted to see it more clearly.

He saw the edge of a polymorphous blob of silvery-gray metal – something like a mix between mercury and water – but it shone bright. It's surface shimmered and reflected brightly whenever the blue beams of electricity ricocheted and rippled through the series of clamps, as if they had to pass through the blob to get to the other side. Each ripple forced a protrusion out of it that bounced off of the clamps and back into the center of its mass.

"Like I said, it can think. It has a mind of its own. I don't think it *likes* being caged like a wild animal." Tarliss said, but Anthony wasn't really listening, he was too fascinated – and terrified by the thought of the stuff covering his entire body.

"Step in to the grid. It's ready to be transferred." Said the hunched alien, going to work on a series of controls. Tarliss guided him over to a four by eight divot in the wall where he stood, leaned back and extended his arms and legs.

"Don't worry. Just close your eyes and think happy thoughts. It'll all be over in seconds."

Anthony tried to be calm, but he couldn't help it. The capsule form-fitted the ridges and contours of his body. He could feel its grip tightening on his chest. He struggled instinctively, but Tarliss put his hand up to remind him, *just breathe.* A glass-like sheath slid down, sealing him inside. Seconds later, golden bands of a strange amorphous material shot across his chest and tightened, the same thing happened to his wrists, ankles and neck until his whole body was completely covered. He tried to deny his primal instinct to panic and break free, keeping his eyes focused on Tarliss, who didn't seem the least bit worried.

A tube slowly rose from the floor connected to the spherical grid of clasps containing the free-flowing metal. Sections of it continued to emerge and rise, leading to the outer wall of the chamber, and into the wall itself, where a thicker extension of it ran the length of the wall toward the control room.

"Are you ready Anthony?" said Tarliss, inside his head. "Think of your Uncle. Think of your parents."

And he did. He first felt the incredibly cold ooze soaking onto his extremities. His fingertips danced, tickled, and then were squeezed tight by the thinking-metal. Eyes slammed shut, he grasped the thought of his loved ones and held them front and center in his mind. The ooze trickled slowly down his arms and up his legs, stiffening and tightening as it moved. The cold sensation quickly became a dull nervous pain after the material solidified on his skin and continued to coat his body. When it passed his shoulders and hips the pain intensified. It felt like a thousand nails being continuously drilled into his body and twisting, pulling at the holes ripped in his skin.

The remaining strands burned across his chest, culminating near his heart. It was almost over. Anthony could feel something surging inside him, starting from his extremities and pulling in closer to his center, just like the oozing material . . .

It was going to *kill him*. No, it wasn't . . . it wanted out – the consciousness Tarliss was talking about – another thinking, fully aware mental essence inside of him, *testing* him.

With a ferocious, thunderous belch of a scream, Anthony's vocal cords seized up and he released all of the pain, fear, love and angst building inside of him, as the final crawling strands of the alloy painfully unified on top his heart which was thumping so hard he could hear it in his skull.

One last reverberant shock of sparkling bio-luminescent energy pulsed throughout the suit as it stopped, leaving a circular brim around the neck. The raw emanating energy hissed, dulled and fizzled away. The glowing restrictive strands snapped back into divots and the whole device tilted forward. He fell stiffly out of the thing, nearly unconscious until his torso almost slammed into the floor – but a lightning quick reactive jolt shot his hands out to catch him. It happened so quickly it felt like the suit was controlling *him*.

He took a moment to look at himself, kneeling and raising his arms. A few sparks and fizzles of light surged over his arms and across his chest. The same quivering, 'hot' air that he saw after Tarliss' shooting test surrounded his whole body, distorting the view of floor beneath his forearms. As he felt consciousness spike back into his synapse, it dissipated.

"Just like I planned." Tarliss said. "See for yourself."

Anthony knew what to do. He rose, walked over to the eloping wall near the exit. It reflected like a mirror. His ears – they were *pointy*. His eyebrows narrower, even his hair looked different, like it had never grown, and would never grow again – as he turned his back to the mirror, he noticed something else – a bulbous extension to his toned back muscles covered the spot where the rounded bones of his spinal column were supposed to be.

"How. . . " was all he could manage, a whimper at best.

"I'd like to explain it all to you now, but I apologize, Sagittarius, it's time to leave. The team is waiting for us near The Prophet's eye." Tarliss said, once again with that irrefutable, authoritative believability.

Another new thing to learn, another question to ask, but he didn't act on the impulse. Instead, he embraced Tarliss' words as *orders*. He was used to following orders – it was a familiar, comforting feeling. Also, he was eager to see what he was capable of. He was a Darmerian, an alien from a different planet, it was all real. His mind had finally come to terms with its own fate and now, he felt as comfortable as he would be in the front seat of his Camaro.

"Let's go." He mumbled, all seriousness.

Tarliss stepped forward and took him by the shoulder. Their suits shimmered together, burned bright and luminous until they both vanished from the room in an instant.

They materialized in a different room entirely, surrounded by the squad of warriors that were less than impressed by him before. They looked at him differently this time. Their firm brows furled down and bridged; the look of respect and a hint of elation plastered to their sturdy faces.

Anthony peered over his shoulder to see Aremis. They locked eyes, and she smiled. Her disposition stuck out like a sore thumb amongst the hardened warriors.

"You look good." She said, holding some sort of weapon toward the ceiling. Anthony felt joy and comfort in her tone, something he had assumed was a seldom expressed thing among Darmerians. The feeling instantly subsided, replaced with a polar opposite – *danger* – his body twisted and his arm flung into the air. His body moved quicker than his own eyes could see, until they gazed up on the same brute who had hit him in the chest before, right in front of him. Another attempted attack – but this time Anthony was quick enough to block the blow. He held his arm firm, until the large attacker also cracked a smile.

"I'm impressed." He said, grinning happily, then grabbed him firmly by the arm and looked deep into his eyes.

"We will do battle together, Earthling." He said, then turned to Tarliss. "I like him." He finished, grim and monotone.

"The Prophet's Eye will take us as close as we can get to Starset. We have just enough time left." Tarliss said, moving towards a large orb embedded in a wall of metal built into a slab of rock. Everyone followed. The thing looked like a giant eyeball, floating in some sort of transparent bluish material outlining it hexagonally.

"It's a teleportation grid. Like stepping stones on a path. Don't hesitate." Tarliss said, as the warriors ran and jumped into the thing one by one, disappearing into thin air. It was his turn. Aremis took him by the hand and pulled.

"Come on," She telepathed, "It will be fun."

Anthony broke into full stride – shocked by how quickly his thoughts became actions. It was instantaneous. The moment the thought occurred, everything slowed down except for him. Simply looking toward the metal sphere, seventy meters away, made him *be* there. As other extraterrestrial assassins moved in his peripheries they moved at relatively the same speed, and he could reach out to them – *talk* to their minds, mid-movement. He considered how fast he was traversing terrain for an instant inside this time-distorted reality, seeing a rock kicked up by a Darmerian in front of him. He should not have had time to think about it, but he did. The rock should have flung to the ceiling, but it only rose a foot, at a rate so slow only an after-thought polaroid of the event existed for a fraction of an instant in his head.

Am I really moving this fast? Or is everything else just slower?

Seven long strides during the synaptic strike covered half of the distance. Another voice, an *answer* was inside of his head.

"Both."

It was Tarliss, who he now knew was nineteen and half feet behind him and currently elongating his right leg for the next stride. He trusted it as much as if he were inside Tarliss' body.

So this is what it feels like to be powerful he thought, the last pulse that traversed his neurons during the 1.37 seconds it took him to reach the portal.

Chapter 14

JOURNEY

"Terrence, get us an update on the air traffic in the area, double-time." Shouted Lester, standing in the aisle of the cramped jet holding the top of a chair with each hand. The geeks had set up shop in the corner, constantly monitoring all the screens, feeding the team with intel.

"Already on it sir. Two commercial jets scheduled in our time slot. Nothing alarming." Gary snapped.

"Good. Pete, Jim, what's going on with the news feeds?"

"A lot of chatter about Paris. They're calling it a terrorist act and blaming a radical civil rights group from Russia. Total bullshit, but it seems like people are believing it." Schlesinger said.

"Boy are we gonna' throw a wrench into that." Said Jim, writing down a monologue on a piece of paper. He was actually excited. Lester could tell he felt self-assured, like hiding Anthony for all those years turned out to be the right decision, and this was the culmination, the final act to justify his efforts. His enthusiasm was infectious.

"Nothing on the long-range sensors up here sir, skies are clear for the next half hour, at least." Yelled Jasper almost inaudibly as he frequently monitored a series of controls in the cockpit with Paul at its helm.

"Is there anything we can do to help?" Said Terrence's male civilian assistant. He, the other civilian and Schlesinger's assistant had naturally bundled together at the front of the plane, silent, scared and befuddled. They were going to have to know the whole story eventually if they were to be considered assets rather than loose ends. The look on their faces was akin to that of an unwanted guest at a party. "Anything at all?" continued the civvie, shaking his head and scrunching his brow; a mix of worry and sincerity.

"No, there isn't just sit down and be still. Have a drink if you think it'll help you. There's scotch in the front cabinet." Lester said, barely acknowledging the man.

"Fine." He said angrily, strutted back to his chair and started whispering to the girl sitting next to him, who hadn't looked anyone in the eyes since they left.

"Look at this sir!" Terrence announced, "CNN and CBS both reporting on something strange. Look at the headline, what the hell does that mean?"

Lester and Jim both stood up and leaned over Terrence' shoulder, impressing the combined weight of their guts on him. A reporter spoke with a sincere look of awe on her face. The headline read:

"MYSTERIOUS 'NORTHERN LIGHTS' SPOTTED ABOVE MAJOR CITIES"

The screen split in two, one side repeatedly showing different shaky camera views from Beijing, Atlanta, New York, London and Moscow. Even in the places where it was night time, they all showed what looked like Aurora Borealis in the upper atmosphere – not rippling and changing, but hanging in the sky as stationary ornaments.

"It's happening." Jim said, "It's really fucking happening. They must have turned the machine on already."

Were they too late? Should they consider kamikaze tactics as a last resort?

"Jesus Cap', we're done for. We need to start warning peop-"

"No, we can't start thinking like that. Stay with me Jim." He said, but the tone of his voice had no emphasis, no heart. He fought off the despair like everyone else was trying to. Jasper leaned into the aisle to overhear what was happening.

Gary once again cut through the silence with one of his epiphanies. He could barely get the words out; his hands motioned off his neck like he was literally trying to pull the information from his throat.

"Sir, I have to tell you s-something." He bursted. Lester could tell it was valuable, an honest adherence to his request to be told anything and everything to do with these *hunches* that Gary often developed.

"What? Spit it out."

"The peace relations summit. *It's today.* Most of the world's national leaders, all in one room. If there was ever a way to cripple the opposition…" He paused, everyone in the cabin lingering on his last syllable, "Well if it were me sir, I'd put a big bomb in that room. Think of the confusion *that* would cause."

He was right, that would be a crippling blow for the resistance effort that would inevitably form once everything got crazy, unless their enemies already had a contingency plan for that, which seemed more than likely. He hated the thought of it, but Gary's intuitive thoughts were twisted enough to be accurate. He had learned from years of experience that the stranger and more unlikely a possibility was, the higher the chance was of it being true.

"Is there any way to warn them?" Jim asked, "There must be some way. How long do we have?"

Every eye in the room shifted toward Gary's lightning-fast fingerwork.

"Scheduled for . . . six o'clock. We have an hour." He said, taking his fingers off the keyboard. It was the most he could give them, the farthest he could bring them. The trained agents had to design a solution now.

"I have to take a risk here guys, and you might not like it. I'm breaking radio silence. I'm calling Barritzer and Ramirez, telling them to go to the embassy." Lester announced. "Terrence, hand me the phone on the wall."

"You don't have to sir. Here, give me the phone." Terrence said, revealing another appendage similar to the one he gave to Paul. It was connected to one of the DIV ports on the computer by a thick cord. "This thing will keep you safe. I guarantee it." He said, snatching the phone from Lester's hand and stuffing it into his contraption.

"Here. Dial the number."

"Wait Lester," Jim interrupted. "What are we going to tell them? They are fresh recruits and we're asking them to do something pretty damn difficult. It's —"

"I know what I'm doing Jim" Lester cut him off."Gimme' that thing" He said to Terrence. He looked through a contact list that Gary had brought up in a window on the computer, found 'Barritzer0177' and started dialing. After 6 rings he wanted to hang up, but Barritzer finally answered his phone.

"Captain! Where the fuck are you! You're all over the news-"

"Shutup Brendan and just listen to me. First I want to say everything on the news is bullshit, I hope you know that." He said. Barritzer hesitated for a second but responded.

"Of course sir. Are you in trouble? What can I do?" He rambled.

"JUST listen to me. Are you by yourself?"

"Yes sir."

"Ok. I need you to do something for me. Remember that trace I ordered you to do?"

"Yes sir."

"I need you to pull that file, give it to Ramirez and tell him to bring it to the news building, and expect a call from me, is that clear?"

"Yes sir."

"Good. When you are done, Call Stiltzenbacher. You two go to the foreign embassy and order a lockdown on the building."

"But sir, the national peace summit is happening there."

"I *know* it is recruit. Bring a tactical unit to search the building. That is an *order*."

It sounded extremely dangerous – he had to really think about it. Lester technically had no right to issue them any orders whatsoever. Barritzer could easily have reported the call to the right people and betrayed them. Once again he hesitated over the phone, but responded after a few seconds.

"Understood sir."

Lester wasn't even his boss anymore, but the level of respect he commanded wasn't aware of it. Barritzer *sounded* sincere enough.

"If anyone questions you, well, tell them to go fuck themselves. Is that clear?"

"Crystal." He responded. He sounded eager. "Just one more thing."

"What's that?"

"The rest of the class wants in. They know you and senior agent Stall aren't the bad guys."

"Do you trust them, Barritzer?"

"Yes sir, I do. They want to help." He said reassuringly. This time, Lester had to stop and work out the details in his mind.

"Good. Bring them all with you, there is strength in numbers. Good work agent Barritzer, when this is all sorted out, you'll be rewarded for your merit." Said Lester, once again assuming the role of encouraging father figure and leader. It was odd for the others to see him act that way, as if he had forgotten about their current circumstance and returned to being Director of the FBI. The sentiment reeked of uncertainty.

"Just *one more thing.*" Barritzer said as Lester was about to hang up, "Did you guys find Anthony? And Williams?"

A long pause thwarted Barritzer's suddenly apparent morale and trustworthiness.

"No. We didn't."

After another pause, an impromptu moment of silence for their fallen comrades, Barritzer acknowledged his orders and responded.

"That sucks sir. It really does. Let's make sure their deaths meant something. I'm sure there's a lot going on that's way above our heads, but those guys were our brothers. Whoever's responsible is in for a great deal of pain when we find them." Lester listened to his admission, shaking his head and phone during the whole thing in a can't-wait-to-hang-up gesture.

"I like it. Agent out." Lester said, pressing the end button on the wall-mounted phone. Everyone in the cabin heard his side of the conversation, assuming the risk of being triangulated was worth it.

"That went well." Said Jim semi-optimistically, an inflection of doubt in his tone. Part of him expected attack jets to be closing in on them within minutes. He looked out one of the starboard windows once just to quell his nerves.

Lester took a moment to acknowledge Gary, who was once again fully engaged with the array of surveillance equipment surrounding him. Lester took him by the shoulder and leaned in close. Gary was half-scared, leaning back, eyebrows raised, not knowing what to expect.

"Good Job, Agent Jones." He said, but it was *more* than that. He was acknowledging Gary's status as an agent –a compatriot – a *friend* even.

Does he finally trust me? Gary thought, as a feeling of elation swept over him. Now, the floodgates were open. He was going to make everyone fully aware of the many ideas that had been running through his head, since everything he had already shared proved to be useful, if not *crucial*. Lester's faith in him gave him the confidence he needed to realize his place in all this, and how he could be most effective.

"Upload in progress. Two of the perimeter cameras were destroyed during the attack, but one stayed intact, I also have the full feed from the lobby camera above the elevators." Terrence said, speaking as fast he could while dancing his stubby digits across a black keyboard. He rolled his chair over to another monitor, nearly crashing into Gary inside the tightly confined work space. His finger hovered shakily above a lithium storage card sticking halfway out of a computer tower lying on its side.

"Come on . . . *come on. . .*" He whispered, carefully eying the 'loading' bar on the screen, lip-syncing each passing number attentively.

97 . . . 98 . . . .99 . . . .

"Finished!" He yelled, yanking the storage chip out and handing it to Lester."That's a complete record of everything that happened at the hotel. The proof you're going to need." He said, happy with his own handiwork. "And yes, it's untraceable." His vigorous enthusiasm lasted only a second. He was back to button-mashing at his workspace almost immediately.

"Excellent work." Lester said, realizing the importance of the small chip as he examined it in his hand.

How can something so small be so damn important?

It bothered him that failing and completing a mission relied on such things, that he couldn't simply start shooting and ask questions later, like in the good ol' days when 'espionage' meant a free trip abroad. The term now had a much deeper, more intricate and sophisticated meaning that had become infinitely more important than an agent's skills with a weapon – their *minds* were now the sharpest tool, and technology the deadliest weapon. They had to stay one step ahead, somehow.

"I have to call Barritzer again Terrence, gimme' that thingy again." Lester said, holding his hand out. He punched the thing in and dialed.

"Captain, what is it?"

"One more thing Brendan, keep an eye out for a suit named Mr. Grey. He works at the pentagon. If you see him at the summit, apprehend him. Understood?"

"What's his first name.?" Brendan asked. Lester looked right at Gary, who he knew could hear the whole conversation.

"Marcellus." Gary responded.

"Yes sir, got it."

Lester heard a click.

"Everyone, look at this!" Pete yelled, nervously checking all his pockets for the cigarettes he threw away. Jim swung the thing around and everyone saw the headline blaring across the screen, and the terrifying images flashing along with it.

"MASSIVE TORNADOES IN MULTIPLE CITIES"

Complete silence sucked the energy right out of the cabin. The civilians let their fear show with a compulsive embrace of each other.

"It gets worse." Gary said shakily, "Reports coming in all over the global newsfeeds . . . massive tidal waves reported off the coast of Thailand, Australia, parts of Southern Africa."

"Dammit!" Lester yelled, smacking the monitor with his hand causing it to spin two full circles. "We're too late." He said, exhaling pure defeat from his lungs.

"We're going to die, aren't we!" Yelled Schlesinger's assistant, who hadn't said a word since they met. He must have been thinking about the end for a long time. The two civilians were now wrapped tightly to each other, on the verge of shedding tears.

"Calm the hell down Noah." Schlesinger yelled.

Lester didn't know what to do. He felt the panic hitting him, squeezing his heart, getting *tighter* . . .

"Everyone snap out of it!" Beckoned a gravelly voice from the cockpit, "We are going through with the plan. No one said it was going to be easy!" It was Jasper, silencing the worry with his razor-sharp infallibility. He returned to the cockpit abruptly. A piece of his steely resolve rubbed off on everyone in the tight cabin. They hadn't realized how much they needed it.

"Gary. Any tornadoes or tidal waves near Boston?" Lester asked him, slightly above a whisper.

"Negative sir. Weather looks normal. *For now.*"

"Let's hope it stays that way." Lester continued. There was a humdrum depression looming in the cabin. Everyone slouched into their chair, looking dismally into the floor.

"We're almost there sir, whoever is coming with us better suit up now." Jasper yelled from the cockpit.

"Alright. It's go time." Lester said. He looked around to elect who would be coming. Jim and Schlesinger were both old, but Jim had experience, at least, with a gun, as if that somehow made it make sense to pick him over Schlesinger. Then he looked at Schlesinger's hand and remembered how furiously he sucked back cigarette smoke. High blood pressure was definitely an *issue*. Terrence probably wouldn't survive a physical let alone a free-fall, and the civilians were useless. Everyone watched Lester's head twirl about the cabin, eyes lighting up, watching their straw being picked. That left Gary. Lester stared into his soul.

"Not me sir, I can't–"

"Yes you can Jones. That's an order." He said, denying Gary an opportunity to object by walking toward the storage cabin in the back.

"There are four HALO suits here. Me, Jim, Gary and Jasper. Strap up."

"Sir, I've never done a HALO jump before." Gary said, complaining like a child again.

"Me neither Gary. But you saw the newsfeed, it's real. We don't have a choice." He said, then grabbed Gary firmly, "This is your chance to redeem yourself. To right the wrongs." He said. Gary didn't respond. Lester could tell he was mentally working out whether or not he was being honest or just saying what was necessary to get Gary onboard.

"What about the rest of us, Captain?" Schlesinger asked.

"You'll be fine. Tell Paul to land outside the city somewhere and find a good rendezvous point. Somewhere high in the mountains." Lester muffled while routing through entangled mess of nylon straps and buckles comprising the HALO jump suits.

Lester wasn't even sure *he* would be fine. His selected jumpers weren't exactly NASA-grade specimens, and he had never done a HALO (High-altitude-low-opening) jump before. There were plenty of horror stories attached to mission files and stories revolving around the seldom-deployed SEAL and briefly-existing JOTAR (Joint Operation Task and Reconnaissance) teams – decompression sickness AKA 'the bends', oxygen-starving hypoxia, and of course a faulty parachute – all led to the design of more conventional ground-based deployment strategies involving advanced land-borne camouflage capabilities. Just two years prior, Lester himself had signed off on the test-trial of nano-reactive weave fibers for use in the field – garments created with a special material that could literally *change color.* It was seen as a much cheaper and more viable option. Operatives proved to have a 17-35% improvement in overall combat-effectiveness due to avoiding the ailments associated with high-altitude freefalls and the ability to almost *disappear* while standing still.

They were in an 'old' (by military standards) plane carrying out an old maneuver. Jasper's harsh tug ripped Lester away from his thoughts, and a suit from his grasp. He put the thing on twice, maybe three times faster than Gary and Jim managed to, and asked: "Have you ever *seen* anyone skydive up close?"

"No."

He turned to the others and raised his eyebrows.

"No sir" They responded.

"Turn your com lines on. Lester, you go first. Then Agent Jones, then Agent Stall." Jasper said, pointing to each candidate as he spoke their name.

"Then me." He finished. "Understood?"He looked around the cabin. No one said anything, but shook their heads, like they were too scared to actually say it out loud – not that they agreed, but that they were actually going to jump out of this perfectly good airplane.

"And one more thing. No hesitating. When it's your turn, you go. Got it?" Once again, the same reaction. Nervously bobbing heads and bitten lower lips. But he knew they wouldn't hesitate, because he would be behind them to offer a nice push.

"3 minutes out Jasper. I'm climbing to 43,000 feet. "Paul yelled from the cockpit, forcing his neck to the right and out in the narrow cabin hallway until a near-spasm."When we hit altitude." He paused, giving his neck and vocals a chance to recharge, then twisted his head again. "You're gone!" He yelled, making sure his last efforts to communicate through the dull hum of the speeding jet were worth it. Everyone felt the grip of gravity tug at their guts as Paul yanked back on the controls and tilted the thing's pointed nose toward the upper atmosphere. Then, they felt the pressure in their ears. Paul stood, balanced, as if he was standing on a bus and had learned to properly absorb it's comings and goings so that he didn't really move at all. Everyone else gyrated and wiggled their jaws to try and swallow to depressurize their sinuses.

Jasper was the first to pull his all-black modular helmet on, making sure to snap a series of six hermetic clamps and a singular zipper that connected it to the suit. He then squeezed the gloves on to his prodding fingers, pinning them deep inside the. Two more clamps and a zipper locked the gloves to the hermetically sealed suit as well. Watching him helped the others put their form-fitting suits on properly.

"Everyone tight?" Jasper asked, after a series of clicks and clacks. "Good." He said, assuming none of them were having problems. No one wanted to look at him. He had done 40+ HALO drops, but he remembered what it felt like on *his* first one.

"OK." He announced loudly, making sure he got everyone's attention. "This is your primary chute. When I tell you to pull, you pull that sucker as hard as you can."

Everyone put their hand over the thing and imagined doing it. He didn't want to vocalize the next bit for fear of placing doubt in their heads, but he had to incase something *did* go wrong. They were, after all, rookies.

"If that doesn't work." He said, knowing immediately the words didn't come out right.

"Then this is your reserve chute." His hand tapped lightly on a smaller, blatantly red rectangular buckle on his lower ribcage opposite the main one.

A slight hint of weightlessness pulled at their stomachs.

"Leveling out!" Paul yelled once more, finding a line perfectly parallel to the Earth.

"I think I'm gonna' be si-!"

Before Jim could get the last muffled syllable out, he vomited a tan-orange mixture. Half of it hit the inside of his helmet and pooled up to this chin as he struggled to pry the visor open.

"Jesus Jim, get it together!" Lester yelled at him, but it wasn't his fault. Lester was a foul scent away from upchucking himself.

"I'm fine, I'm fine!" Jim said, simultaneously wiping his mask off and scooping the sludge out from under his chin.

"Alright guys it's time to rock and roll." Jasper said, clapping his hands as he did. Jim checked his hip to make sure his pistol was there. Lester did the same. Gary fondled the pistol they had given him and right as he did, Jim and Lester stared right at him long enough to let him know:

You better use that thing properly.

And he intended to.

"Let's go Lester you're up!" Jasper yelled, and Lester followed suit. He did one last check of his gear and lined up next to the specially-designed, extra-wide door just past the broad, angular wings of the plane. Jasper half- pushed, half-corralled Gary and Jim tightly behind him, and they braced themselves, silently, like a bobsled team about to take off.

"3 second intervals between jumps guys!"

"Director!" A grisly voice boomed from the back of the cabin. "What do you want us *to do?*" It was Schlesinger, looking back and forth between him and the other passengers of the plane he was referring to, a dumbfounded look on his grainy mug. "As soon as we land they are going to find us! We're fucked!" He said, shrugging his shoulders.

"60 seconds!" They heard Paul yell, faintly from the cockpit.

Schlesinger had a worthy cause for concern. Lester kicked himself for not having a clear enough head to think that one through. But before he could respond,

"I highly doubt that." Gary announced, temporarily revealing half of his face. "My guess is that everyone, *everything* in the city is going to be focused on what *we're* doing."

* * * *

Agent Brendan Barritzer darted around his house searching for the file he needed. The air inside the small two-bedroom bungalow-style home had a musky thickness to it, which made just breathing normally a little harder – and his heart was pounding.

I know I made a copy of that damned file,

He thought, but couldn't for the life of him remember where he had put it. By doing so in the first place, he had breached protocol – whenever you took a file out of the records you were supposed to sign off for it – but he just copied it when no one was looking so he wouldn't have to go through the fifteen minute acquisition process. The original file was still sitting safely in its place in the high-tech folder room at the FBI headquarters. A stack of magazines on his bedside table was topped with a few empty mugs he used for early morning coffee while he laid half-covered by his blankets watching cartoons on a very outdated plasma television in his room. He had just cleaned up recently, or at least *tidied*, The place would definitely not pass his own mother's definition of *clean*. When he made these half-attempts at really organizing the place well, he had a tendency to stack all of the paper in one spot – in his mind it took up less room and was therefore less dirty, and the rectangular stack had a certain Feng Shui appeal to it. He tossed the stack aside with a cumbersome swing of his right hand, sending the mugs' cold remnants all over his bed.

Dammit! He thought to himself, but continued to dig at the bottom of the pile. Bills, a yellow notepad with a few phone numbers of girls he had met recently, discarded envelopes and an encyclopedia finished the stack. No luck.

Brendan stopped, put his hands on his waist and inhaled slowly. He could hear and feel his own rapid heartbeat thumping in his skull. *Think. What was I doing when I brought that damned file home?*

Two loud knocks at his creaky red, paint-chipped door caught his attention.

"Ramirez, that was fucking quick. I can't find the file." He exhaled, but then it dawned on him – the knocking door brought his mind to a familiar spot. One of the girls he was working on came over to enjoy a few beers the previous night, hang out. He was embarrassed about a messy assortment of things on a table right next to the door meant for keys.

"I can't believe you misplace-" Ramirez began, his tone bouncing up and down from one syllable to the next, a characteristic of many Latin-Americans.

"Wait!" Brendan interrupted, looking in random directions and pointing both of his hands around the room. Ramirez could tell he was just on the verge of remembering something important.

He pushed his left hand vigorously into the chalky wisdom lines on his forehead, clicking his fingers rapidly with the other. Rather than vocalizing his culminating thought, he opened his eyes and basically leapt over to the fridge, poking and prodding his hand on top of it. His index and thumb gripped the smooth, more-rigid-than-paper surface.

"Got it!" He yelled, handing it to Ramirez, who had a few questions of his own.

"Where was he when you called? Is Stall alive?" He bantered, getting in Barritzer's face. He didn't want to answer. He knew that knowing

Stall and Williams, their classmates and friends were dead would be a crippling blow to morale. But the Captain didn't confirm their deaths. He only said they were still missing.

"He didn't say anything about that. *Just* our orders." Barritzer yelped, not making eye contact. His rust colored hair wiggled as his brow scrunched and expanded. Ramirez popped the file open.

"What the hell is this all about?"

"Dynatech probe. Captain wants me – I mean *you* to bring this file down to the news Station. Did you manage to get a hold of Stilitzenbacher?"

"Sure did. He's in the truck."

"Good." Said Barritzer. He wasn't above Ramirez in rank, but he certainly was acting like it. The captain called *him,* not anyone else. He was never a standout recruit – always painfully average – but he did have one thing going for him. He was consistent. Brendan wondered if that was why the Captain chose him to run his errand, or if it was random luck of the draw. He wiggled his boots on and grabbed his jacket; a reversible, normal blue jacket on one side with 'FBI' in bold yellow letters on the other.

"You got your piece on you?" Barritzer asked. Ramirez flashed his ribcage once to reveal his holstered Beretta.

"What's the hold up!?" Bellowed a voice from the truck parked on the street. It was Stiltzenbacher, and he wasn't the only one. The truck was full of agents.

"Barritzer, you sure this is all good man? You've heard what the guys on the news have been say-"

"It's all bullshit!" Barritzer yelled, taking a step in. "I need you on point Ramirez. I have a bad feeling shit's about to go down soon. Take that file and get it to the goddamn news building, ASAP."

Ramirez tried to put up a fuss but Barritzer pinched his fingers into a don't-talk-back gesture. Then, both of their heads turned. A man across the street burst out of the front door of his red-brick bungalow, carrying a jug of water, blankets and pillows. He stuffed the items in the back of his minivan and waddled up the hill back into his house, returning seconds later with a large box of canned goods. Barritzer and Ramirez both gave each other a cock-eyed look.

"Sir, what are you doing?" He yelled. Two doors down, the same panicky urgency guided a mother and her children into their SUV. The man turned to them and said:

"Haven't you seen the news!? It's the goddamn rapture!" Flailing his hands wildly. "I don't have time to-" He turned and ran back inside mid-sentence.

"Like I said we don't have much time. I'm going to the foreign embassy, drive like you got a fuckin' purpose, OK?" Barritzer snarled, hitting Ramirez firmly on the left shoulder. There was a great deal of fear in his eyes. Barritzer recognized it right away, because he was just as scared.

Jasper reached up and peeled a flimsy, red-lettering embroidered panel from the ceiling, revealing a metal latch.

"GET READY!" He yelled, then yanked the latch down. Two inch-thick steel sheaths emerged from divots in the ceiling while two red lights above them turned on and spun. The collapsible walls were designed to separate the pressurized compartments between them, the cockpit and the rest of the cabin for long enough to jump without any change to the other compartments. Lester felt the last few inches of the barriers' descent and then no sound at all. The pressure gripped their ears, locking them in the compartment. A green light replaced the red one and the door swung open. He felt a fierce push from behind him, but still gripped the enclosing walls tightly – a natural instinct he couldn't overcome all at once. But he did jump. The roar of the engine boomed in his ear and then dissipated quickly as soon as he catapulted himself out into freefall. The nervous shock in his chest didn't go away – the exhilaration was so intense he could almost taste his heartbeat. He had to really focus on clenching his body tightly just to keep himself from going into an uncontrollable spin. The piercingly loud howl of the winds vibrated his eardrums so hard he could barely think. Parts of his helmet clicked and warped under the immense pressure – but he could breath, and he could see. A quick look over his right shoulder – nothing. Then his left – there was Gary or Jim, he couldn't tell which. It was about to get worse – just seconds until he burst through the cloud layer, and got extremely wet. Trying to develop a picture of his target inside his head kept him from habitually prodding the buckle to his parachute, just to make sure it was still there.

"All jumpers successfully deployed." He heard over his com. A temporary relief.

"As soon as you breach the clouds, pull your chutes!"

A timer counted down inside his head, although it wasn't entirely accurate. It was hard to gauge just how fast he was falling and exactly when his body would enter the polymorphous puff of clouds – the false countdown kept resetting itself at five seconds as he continued to fall, but still no breach. It wasn't going to happen all at once, the merging would be gradual since the cloud layer didn't have a clear-cut barrier. His awareness seemed to pique extremely fast but slow down at the same time. The rush of adrenaline and sporadic bursts of clarity and focus kept his breathing barely controllable. It was a different story for his heart – beating way faster than he had ever felt before or even thought possible.

Just a little bit longer . . .

Said a voice in the back of his mind. He tried to take full control of his breathing, but the sheer pressure on his chest nullified the effort. At best he could manage a half-breath, and it wasn't enough. Blue and yellow sparkles began to drift into his view . . . he was feeling the surging declination of consciousness deafen his senses, enveloping his sight . . .

"AHHH-*kztkkkhkhkhkzt*-I'M SPINNING-*kztkztkhzkt*-" Lester heard through his com, and it shocked his nerves, making his heart skip a beat.

It brought him right back to high alert, the stars and colors dissipated immediately. He looked over his left shoulder again, spotting two bodies this time. One of them was spiraling wildly out of control. He could tell by voice through his headset, muffled as it was that the panic-stricken voice belonged to Gary. Before he could make a conscious decision about what to do to help him, or *not* help him, the thick white plume of wet cloud swallowed his senses. There was nothing he could do to help.

"Continue *ktkkzhhhtzkhzct* –ward objecti – *kzhtkhtkzhtk* –oing after him myself!" Boomed Jasper's unmistakable gravelly tone into his ear. The static interference made understanding the communicative attempt a bit delayed, but he got the gist of it. A few short seconds later, Lester emerged from the cloud layer, soaked and cold. There was nothing he could do for Gary now. His conscience tried to pry at his resolve – *did I get him killed?* – but he pushed the thought down into rubble as quickly as it arose. The long rectangular grey outline of the building he was aiming for, barely visible through the torrents of water splashing his visor, came into view. He ripped at the metal buckle on his chest. His whole body jerked and slowed down as the huge black wing shot out from his back. Focusing on the distinct 'H' of the helicopter pad on top of the building, he frantically looked above him in all directions, waiting for his three companions to emerge from the white mass above.

Jasper abandoned the safe, controlled starfish plummet. This is why he went last – the odds of something going wrong among the three first-time jumpers, especially with these weather conditions, were incredibly high. He *expected* it. Forming his hands into an arc above – technically *below* his head – and knotting his feet together tightly, he tightened every muscle in his body as the speed-up technique took full effect. Staving off the pressure that would make a normal man lose consciousness in seconds flat, he breathed deep and made a beeline dive toward Gary's uncontrollable line of descent. He had better get there quickly – once they entered the cloud line he would lose vision of Gary – and any chance of saving him from certain death. Being just a few degrees off, he would shoot past Gary and lose his only chance. Jim saw nothing more than a black blur speed by him, wishing there was something he could do to help. Jasper tried to speak through his headset, but no one responded. Gary was unconscious.

Hundreds of meters still separated them – and the white mass of cloud was getting bigger – *quickly.* He wasn't going to make it in time. There was one more thing he could do. He reached for his side carefully, removing a cylindrical canister. The slightest uncontrolled alteration to his wind-path could force him into a harrowing spin as well. The idea seemed impossible, but he was going to try it. He carefully popped the thing open, spewing a plume of purple signal-flare gas into his wake. He felt the jolt of the improvised rocket accelerate his body *past* free-fall speed. It worked – the extra burst brought him to within fifty meters – twenty five meters – almost there . . .

The canister fizzled and emptied, having done its job.

Ten meters.

The clouds were upon them. The outline of Gary's body began to fade and then, Jasper felt a welcoming thump on his shoulder. His arms wrapped around Gary tightly, but it was not over. Jasper struggled to stop the spinning by twisting his body as hard as he could in the opposite direction. Time was running out fast. He used a loose strap to connect Gary's suit to his own, intertwining their fates.

Lester was almost there. Confident that he wouldn't overshoot the landing, he took a moment to glance above him. Most of his vision was blocked by the parachute, but in his left quadrant he saw a black dot pop into existence. It must have been Jim deploying his chute. But there was no sign of Gary or Jasper. He couldn't afford to look again – his focus had to remain squarely on safely landing on top of the building.

"Jim do you have visual on Jasper and Gary!?"

"Negative."

"Are you OK?"

"Affirmative." Jim responded shakily. It was obvious he was struggling to properly steer himself toward the news building. The howling winds and beating rain certainly didn't help them. It came as a surprise the two of them had even made it this far, and casualties were something they should have been prepared for. Blocking the part of his mind that feared the worst, Lester pulled and squeezed the handles attached to the chute, carefully keeping him on course. He was going to make it. He couldn't help but look up to see if his comrades were still there. His radio cackled and hissed intermittently.

"I got him *kzkkzhtkzhzkt* repeat, I got hi-*kztkhztkzkhtkzhkt* –" Lester heard. He felt the literal warming wash of hope physically manifest in his veins.

"Are you secure!?" He yelled repeatedly, but the return communications were barely recognizable.

"Lester I can see them! Look to your left!" Jim's voice boomed through the radio, loud and clear. A twinkle of sunlight beamed through a gap in the clouds, silhouetting a black blob a half-mile above his head. It was Jasper and Gary emerging from the cloud cover. Seconds later, another huge black blob formed – their parachute.

Jasper had his legs wrapped firmly around Gary's limp body, struggling to operate the parachute with twice its recommended weight.

"Captain I've got him. He's alive but we are descending too fast. Continue toward the objective." He said, no hint of weakness or fear in his voice. But the reality set in. They weren't going to be able to land safely with that much weight. *Continue toward the objective* was a less direct way of saying *'one of us isn't going to make it.'* – and there was absolutely nothing he could do to stop it.

"Wake up Gary! WAKE UP!" Jasper yelled furiously, shaking Gary's limp, unresponsive corpse. He slapped his helmet a few times. Nothing. He looked down to his right – Jim and Lester were going to make it – their chutes were lining up well enough with the building to make a safe landing – but he wasn't going to be so lucky. He had less than a quarter-minute.

"*Unnnhhh…*" Gary whimpered. He was beginning to regain consciousness, and not a moment too soon. His head snapped back, hitting Jasper's visor. He bellowed obscenities upon regaining consciousness, but Jasper quickly gripped him and calmed him down.

"Listen to me Jones!" He yelled, "I'm going to detach in ten seconds. Get ready to brace yourself! Do you understand!?" Jasper yelled furiously. Jim and Lester could hear the whole bit, but their landing was imminent and demanded all of their attention. The rooftop came exceedingly fast – much faster than they expected. Lester's feet landed hard on the gravel-pit surface surrounding the helipad with just feet to spare between him and the edge of the building. He tumbled forward, ensconced in the twisting confines of the deflated parachute. His body rolled over a few times until it finally stopped. His hands frantically worked to detach the chute from his body, but the connective wires were completely tangled around his limbs. It might have saved him, considering the wind could very well have continued to fill his chute and carry him right off the roof. Jim landed a few meters from him, enduring the same abrasive rolling and tumbling, but they landed intact. They both instinctively looked up to witness the plight of Gary and Jasper.

Seconds after Jim spotted their silhouette, he felt an intense, crippling pain shooting up his left thigh and into his hip. The tattered ribbons of his pants revealed the source of his anguish – his leg was badly broken – a piece of his fibula, snapped and twisted, jutted out of a bloody tear in his skin. The adrenaline surge had blocked him from realizing it when his body hit the roof, much harder than he thought he did.

"CUTTING!" They heard through their headsets. An instant later, Jasper leveled a 6 inch obsidian blade and slashed at the buckles connecting them. Gary started another free-fall with an accompanied, helpless scream, but hit the rocky pit ten meters beneath him on the far edge of the roof. The impact wasn't a controlled descent. He was knocked out cold when his ribcage thumped into the shifty layer of ground. Lester hoped the landing wasn't as bad as it sounded.

"Had to do it sir, he would have killed both of us." Jasper announced through the radio, "I'm not going to make it. Circling around to the street below." He said, without leaving any room for refutability.

"Roger that." Lester grumbled, hoping security hadn't yet been alerted to their daring entrance if there was any in the building at all. With Gary knocked out and Jim immobile, he was the only good gun left for the time being, and Jasper's ascent through the building to rendezvous, given his blatantly threatening appearance, wasn't going to be a cakewalk either. He had already assumed that Jasper was going to be fine.

"Jim! Can you move!?" Lester yelled, struggling to his feet.

"AHHH!" Jim howled in pain as he tried to get himself upright. It was no use, the pain was crippling. He struggled to pry his helmet off, hyperventilating. He knew if he didn't get his breathing under control he would soon go into shock.

"Fuck it!" Jim exhaled, wincing. "Shove that fucker back in there!" He growled, but Lester hesitated. He didn't want to go near that mess, let alone break it even worse. Just looking at the snapped limb and awkward unnatural bend in his calf made him want to throw up – but Jim was determined. He grabbed Lester by the collar with a level of strength he wasn't aware Jim possessed.

"DO IT YOU BASTARD!" He screeched, sending stringy bits of blood, and saliva from his gullet.

"On the count of three! One . . . two . . . *three!*" On cue, Lester wrenched the jagged shard of bone and quite literally jammed it back in. Jim screamed in agony, smashing the three-quarter inch gravel nearly hard enough to break more bones in his hand.

"Gotta' stop the bleeding. Here, bite down on this." Lester pulled a piece of the HALO suit up to Jim's mouth, yanking his thumb away just in time. He tore off the rest of Jim's pant leg and twisted it into a makeshift dressing. It wasn't even close to what it needed to be, but it would have to do. Lester carefully put his weight on the knee, tied a thick knot and yanked the thing ferociously.

The sound of heavy boots smacking the rock bed grew louder behind him. He leveled his pistol with one hand and turned the safety off, pointed it toward whoever it was.

"Whoa, sir! Let me help!" It was Gary, and not a moment too soon. He hadn't even thought of what to do if Gary was incapacitated too.

"Here give him this! I thought we might need some so I raided the plane's medicine cabinet." He spit out in no more than two seconds, handing Lester a small syringe. He popped the thing's disposable sheath off and tossed it, jammed the needle into Jim's thigh and squeezed the elixir deep into the pulsating vein. Within seconds, Jim didn't feel a damn thing.

"Morphene-A. It won't put *him* out, only the pain. For about fifteen minutes." Gary added.

"Good. Help me get him to his feet, what floor we headed to?"

"22nd floor, sir."

They both wrapped around one of Jim's shoulders and clipped onto his burly torso, encouraging him to put some weight on his good foot. He was conscious, but extremely lightheaded and dazed.

"What happened to Jasper?" Gary asked, but Lester didn't respond.

"Get your pistol out Gary." He garbled angrily, holding his own gun leveled, pointing in front of him as they moved toward the door leading to a stairway exit.

"It's all over every news station! Look at this Stiltzy! F-6 tornadoes spotted off the coast of Nova Scotia! I mean, when's the last time that happened? *Never?*" Aaron Smithers, of the fresh FBI recruit class, was rambling in the back of Ramirez' truck while watching, with shock and awe, the newsfeed from his Ipad. He was the class clown – a misfit – but extremely intelligent, making him an asset when he wasn't joking around.

"I don't care man. I don't. Put that shit away, we're here." Stiltzy demanded, shooting Aaron a don't-mess-with-me look. Ramirez sped up and jammed the breaks, skidding the tires to a screeching halt in front of the news building. The rain was beginning to thicken, the winds pulled and pushed at their less than adequate garments.

"Weatherman called for sun today, this is bullshi-"

"LOOK! UP! LOOK UP THERE!" Yelled Ramirez, pointing to something in the sky. Everyone's head turned and squinted to see what he was talking about. "Are we being invaded!?" He asked, his tone rife with panic. He reached into his jacket to retrieve his pistol.

"Wait!" Stiltzy said motioning with his hands, although he had drawn his gun as well. "There's only one. He's coming in *hot*." The quintet of agents naturally all drew their pistols and half-pointed them at the incoming parachutist, waiting for Stiltzenbacher to determine what to do next.

"Hold your fire everyone!" He shouted through the beating rain, then walked in front of the truck and started waiving his hands in a wide arc. Pedestrians stood under umbrellas, behind cars and around corners, some holding out their phones to capture the event on film.

"I think he's one of ours!"

"You sure? Look at his gear." Ramirez held his weapon drawn over top the opened door of his truck. He fluttered his free hand down at the Earth so that Smithers, Forcell and Pettigrew could see. They slowly lowered their weapons to waist level but kept two hands snug on the pistols just in case.

Jasper battled the wind and rain that punished his aching, tired body. A quick flashback singed his membranes. Catching Gary was one thing, deciding whether or not to risk his own life to save him by connecting them together – while freefalling inside of a harsh storm – was another. If not for the muffled voices he barely heard over the radio that plunged into his soul and ripped it away from panic-hell, he probably would have let him drop. Even Jasper thought what he did was logically insane, and it racked his nerves – which didn't happen very often.

He lacked the free hands to land safely on the segmented freeway while fighting off the elements let alone engage the agents with the BPSM-3 attached to his vest. Five behind cover to one in open space – his aim was good, but not good enough to beat those odds. He hoped they didn't have twitchy fingers. He hoped they had been trained well.

Forcing his intent solely into surviving, he squeezed the hair-trigger touchy handles that angled his chute. It was going to pull the edges in, literally forcing and focusing the oncoming air into the bag. The howl of the shifting wind evolved to a piercing cackle as it furiously pounded against the carbon fiber weave; arrogantly thrust into its ugly face. It worked – Jasper sailed in just where he needed to be, cutting a line (a very tiring one for his arms) through the harsh oncoming gust. And now, he could . . . slow down . . .*or something* . . .

The landing was rough but he knew how to absorb it, and some of the armor he brandished was designed to keep him safe. He held both his legs and arms at ninety degree angles directly in front of him, tightening every muscle in his body. His legs hit the cement, toppled, and sent him onto his forearms, the brunt of the blow absorbed by the modular kevlar gauntlets rounding out his elbow. His light but sturdy chest plate cushioned his neck and head and transferred the force across his shoulders. He continued end over end a few times following the same absorb, transfer and roll technique, protecting his vitals from any dangerous impacts. His parachute lines quickly tethered around his torso during the twirls; sucking them in and away from the unpredictable wind that could have easily picked him up again and carried him into a building or an oncoming car.

"Let me see your hands! Now!" He heard, barely audible, but that meant he was still conscious and hadn't suffered brain damage. Ignoring a mountain of pain, he rose to his feet and swiftly slashed all of the tangled lines with the large obsidian colored combat knife from his hip.

Five young, nervous FBI agents hovered around him in a five-meter perimeter, guns drawn. Or maybe there were six … or seven. His head *was* a little shaky.

"Lieutenant First Class Jasper SOU-38/001. We're on the same side boys."

"Hands! Let me see your hands!" He heard, but Jasper didn't comply.

"I'm a friend of Jim and Lester." He clarified, as the six or seven hazy people diminished to a definite group of five. Their weapons all lowered quickly, like he spoke magic words that banished a curse.

"Holy shit man, are you okay?" Asked Pettigrew, a huge Jewish athlete with curly brown hair and broad shoulders.

"For now. May need a few stitches." Enough small talk. His eyes darted around the squad of young, eager and comparatively innocent faces to the darkest skin.

"You must be Ramirez." He said, not worried about the potential perceived bigotry.

"Yeah, that's me."

"Tell me you brought that file soldier." He asked. His grisly, guttural voice, the tone it carried and his reference to rank instantly made him the leader of the group.

"Yes sir." He answered.

"Ktzkhtkzhkztkhzt —ty-second floor ktxhkt Jasper are you secu - ktzkkhtkht."

The matte-black armor clad warrior's radio buzzed loudly. Despite the rapidly worsening weather conditions, a devout group of documentarians were watching them closely from across the street.

"Get it and let's move, twenty second floor now!" He yelled, ripping the snub-nose compact machine gun from his chest plate and sliding the cocking mechanism back until it clicked.

"I copy Captain, I landed safely. I have the surveillance file in hand."

Safely may have been an overstatement.

The squad raced up the front stairs of the news building and up to the front doors breaching the lobby. Everyone got out of their way. Jasper took point although his leg was throbbing. It may have been fractured or even broken. He leveled his weapon and pointed down every corner. It seemed odd to the young agents – they weren't expecting any serious threats – but Jasper's body language told a different story. They too raised their guns, tapped each other's hips when they moved, just like they had been trained to. His intensity rubbed off on them and made them rethink walking around corners without a buddy covering them.

The elevator barely held all of them. As soon as it closed, and a waypoint wasn't occupying their minds, the agents had a barrage of questions.

"So what's going on here, Jasper, right?" Pettigrew asked him, but not aggressively. He didn't want to piss him off. Jasper didn't respond, although he wanted to. Searching for an answer to Pettigrew's question quickly brought him back to the hotel, the sewers, the 'cyberterrorist' he didn't kill, and the last HALO jump he ever wanted to partake in. His throat tightened up while his lips quivered the beginnings of the shapes required to make syllables.

"Sir!?" Stiltzy asked this time, pulling Jasper out of his trance.

He just looked Stiltzy in the eyes, and showed him regret, fatigue, even pain – but not fear – He would never show *anyone* that. The young agents' nervous twitchy hands unconsciously squeezed their weapons, but not because they doubted Jasper. They had a moment to scan his scarred body armor, sliced, tattered neoprene under-layer and the pungent stench of the saline sweat lines pasted to his bruised and battered skin. Danger was ever present in this mysterious black-clad assassin's life and their instincts told them it was going to follow him wherever he went.

"We were involved in a gunfight in Paris. Not sure who attacked us really." Jasper managed. The fresh dead among his friends hung heavily on him. There was no time to really mourn them, let alone bury them properly. "And then . . ." He continued, "Then we came here. There's a bigger picture, but I'll let Lester tell you all about it." He said.

The gut-wrench of the slowing elevator gripped their attention. Jasper's stoic silence made them all a bit skittish as they watched the numbers ascend.

'22'

"We're here. Check your corners you never know who could be watching." Jasper said, and they believed him. It seemed a farfetched that there would be anyone in the news building besides terrified civilians, but there were a lot of strange things happening. The agents raised their weapons as the thick elevator door slid open. Standing before them was a group of people – terrifying looks etched to their faces – carrying everything they could manage. A woman wearing a sharp red skirt-suit shrieked, dropping an armful of food – canned goods, bread, bagels and milk. Two men in front of her wearing all grey pleated suits with perfectly coiffed 'TV' hair put their hands out in front of them as if to say 'calm down'. An elderly woman in the back curled her mink-parka closer to her body, as if it was going to protect her from bullets.

"What the fuck is happening!" Pettigrew yelled. He didn't know what he disliked more – pointing his gun at unarmed helpless civilians or not knowing what everyone was so scared about – but he had his orders.

"It's okay we are not going to harm you. Where is the main broadcast room?" Jasper asked as calmly as he could, but the sound of his voice boomed even when he didn't want it to. The civies just stood there, hands raised. Jasper took a step forward – the quarter of terrified anchors and assistants huddled closer together in fear.

"The broadcast room. Where?" He continued, this time making sure they saw the barrel of his gun. One of the male news anchors with his hands raised pointed slowly to his left.

"Th-th-that w-way." He stammered, shaking.

"Form up!" He grunted to the agents, who were already pointing around the wide hallway to scan for threats. Just as they started to move, the familiar 'ding' of an elevator arriving at its destination caught their attention. Pettigrew and Stiltzenbacher nautrally took position on either side of the elevator, guns ready. Jasper stood right in front of it, pointing his BPSM-3 right at the line where the silver doors connected. The civilians were too petrified to move. Jasper cocked his head toward them and yelled:

"Get out of here!." But they didn't move. "NOW!" He bellowed, to which they all scurried into the elevator they had just come out of.

"Steady guys." He said calmly, waiting for the second elevator's doors to slide open. The sound of the elevator's pulleys and mechanical innards buckled and whined, then the door slid open.

"Captain!" Yelled Stiltzy, lowering his gun. Lester and Gary carried Jim between their shoulders. His head twirled around like a spinning top, his eyes rolled around in his skull.

Lester and Gary fell to their knees, exhausted, letting Jim's limp body hit the floor harder than they intended.

"Damn it's good to see you Captain!" Yelled Ramirez, as the group of agents huddled around and helped him and Gary to their feet. They were surprised to see Gary – to them he was a tech nerd, a slithery, mysterious paper pusher they rarely spoke to. But now, he had a different look, as if he had aged ten years and seen a plethora of combat overnight. His eyes carried the hardened look of someone they might respect – one of their own. Even the pistol he carried looked more dangerous in his hands than when he seldom used it at the firing range. They may have even *followed his orders.*

"The feeling is mutual boys. We're in one hell of a shitstorm here. Stiltzy, Jasper, Jones let's head to the broadcast room we need to get this message out ASAP." Lester commanded.

"But sir –"

"There's no time. I'll explain everything after. The rest of you make sure no one sneaks up our backside. Spread out and secure the floor. Ramirez, Pettigrew – you two stay at the elevator, clear?"

They were hesitant – they wanted to know what was happening – but they trusted Lester's orders just like they always had, and always would.

"Copy that sir." Pettigrew answered.

"Good." Lester raised his pistol and headed toward the broadcast room with his chosen assailants.

"Here's the file Captain." Jasper handed him the thick file folder from Ramirez. Inside of it were two compact discs. He took one of them out, marked 'DYNATECH PROBE", then rooted through his zippered pockets to retrieve the chip with the surveillance videos that Terrence gave him.

After thirty seconds they came to the end of the hallway. It overlooked the broadcast room. Panicking civilians rushed by them, holding whatever belongings they could, toward the stairs and elevators. It was the kind of panic where nothing else mattered; such as a heavily armed quartet of soldiers impeding their path. Their eyes stayed fixated past them, as if it was a normal thing to see every day and not worth stopping for. Lester thanked the FBI for training soldiers to keep their resolve under duress and thanked *God* he had some in his pocket.

Hopefully none of their relatives work here . . .

But these are the soldiers I may need.

Some people stayed put, hiding under their desks crying in fear. The large glass panels that landscaped the Boston skyline rattled and banged from the immense pressure of the wind slamming into them and then sucking back. It was irregular and threatening. Wind wasn't supposed to move like that. The half inch steel rivets bolting the vertical girders of the window frame had a vibrating ping of their own.

To their combined surprise, a devout, familiar news anchor, rather than joining his panicking colleagues, remained at his desk while a series of cameras captured him talking. The papers in front of him were scattered in disarray. Even from a hundred feet, they could see the fear on his face.

"Brave son of a bitch." Lester garbled, then looked twenty meters to his right.

"There's the control booth." Lester said, simply looking at Jasper – he knew what to do. He walked up to the door, kicked it ferociously and ordered everyone inside to put their hands up.

"We're in control now. Sit down and do as I say."

"Did you guys find Anthony?" Stiltzy asked, as he descended the spiral stairway down to the broadcast room. Two of the camera men noticed them – noticed their guns – and tried to flee. Instead of waiting for an answer, Stiltzenbacher took a beeline toward one of them heading for a door marked with a red EXIT sign above it. He easily caught up to the fat man, tackled him to the ground and yelled in his face. The other one thought twice about his chances, stopped and hid behind a desk.

Lester raised his pistol into the air and let a few rounds off to get everyone in the room's attention. A shrieking high pitched yelp of the combined civilians echoed through the glass-walled atrium. Almost everyone covered their ears and tried, somehow, to wiggle deeper into their fetal-position holes.

"Everyone calm the hell down we are on your side" He yelled, "We need five minutes of airtime, now!" He continued, walking toward the desk.

"Who the hell are you guys?" Asked the brave anchor.

"We're with the FBI. Please, I need you to convince your guys to keep the cameras rolling. We have a very important message that needs to get out." Lester said, leaning in, "To *everybody*."

At first the anchor wanted to tell Lester about a detailed plan he had been co-thinking of during this mess about reaching out to his wife and two daughters, who lived in their million dollar home on the opposite end of the city, as if the agents had been sent solely for that purpose. Then the anchor recognized him as he got closer. He remembered Lester's grisly mug shot from the story they had been airing for the better part of the last twenty four hours. Then he remembered the headline of the story – *FBI agent turned international terrorist* – a wave of panic and fear swept over him. Like hell was he going to help this man, this *murderer*.

Lester recognized the abrupt change in the dimensions of the anchor's facial muscles as his expression changed from fear to anger. He didn't have time for this.

"You're the enemy!" He yelled, "You're that damn terrorist, aren't you?"

Jasper gave him a thumbs-up from the control booth. Somehow he had convinced the operators up there to stay put without much violence – or maybe he was just quick about it. Anger was starting to fill Lester's bones as well. This damn civilian was going to help him or die. He grabbed the anchor's chair on both sides, pulled it in close and leaned in until he was face to face with the young man. It was obvious he wanted to fight back, but also obvious by his eyes darting back and forth from Lester's gun that he wasn't the type to lash out physically.

"Listen you little whelp, you see that shit going on outside?" Lester said, his voice gritty as sandstone. The reporter turned his head to the storm then nodded in compliance. "If I don't get this message out, that storm is *never* going to stop. Your family, my family, everyone in the goddamn city is going to die, get me?" The reporter was beginning to actually listen. "So," Lester continued, "Let me save your fucking family. Let me save everyone." He said, getting closer and talking slower. As he spoke the words they sounded just as surreal to him as they did the anchor. It was now or never, and the sole thing standing in his way was a microcosmic representation of what he was trying to save – humanity itself. The irony pissed him off even more. The sentiment burned a fire in his eyes that could melt diamonds.

"Joe, Thurman, get those cameras rolling. Give them what they want" Lester couldn't tell if the young man believed what he was saying or if it was simply an act of self-preservation. Either way, he was complying. Stiltzenbacher shook and released the cameraman he tackled, allowing him to trudge, terrified, over to his seven foot enclosed-lens apparatus. Even in the newsroom there was a hierarchy and a caste system – they obeyed the anchor's commands. If they all made it through the apocalypse, this might just be 'damn good news' that would rocket their station's ratings to the top. Lester wondered how many other stations' anchors were risking their lives to stay on the air.

A flashback shot through his head. He remembered Jim in the plane hunched over the table writing a monologue, wishing he had it in his hands. But Jim was badly injured and might not make it if they found themselves in another firefight. Yet another painful thought he had to swallow and send to the delete bin.

"Sit here." said the anchor, torn between believing Lester and actually being ripped away from the best story of his career.

"You did the right thing."

"I had no choice."

"Yes you did." Lester said, with a heavy heart. He hated the thought of pushing a civilian into a corner against his will. It was his mandate to protect the innocent. The circumstances perilously dictated that he may have to harm innocent people if he was to save anyone, and it rubbed him the wrong way. An unwelcome feeling of guilt squeezed his stomach.

This is how Iraq war vets must feel . . .

He took a deep breath and pushed the thought of his mind – he needed the mental space to clearly and concisely relay his message – to finish the final phase of his plan. It had better work too. They weren't running out of time. They *were* out of time.

I hope Anthony's alive Jim, I really do. I think it's the only thing keeping me together.

He tried to make Jim hear his thoughts, hoping that somehow, the universe would make it happen.

The cameraman's waving arms pulled at his focus. Once the connection was made, he held up his left hand, fingers spread wide. It was about to happen.

"Gary get up in that booth and try to widen the range of the broadcast!" Lester yelled loudly, then to Stiltzenbacher: "Stiltzy! Get an update on Barritzer, you sent him didn't you?"

"Yes sir I did." Stiltzy snapped back before Lester was done talking then pulled out his phone.

The cameraman's pinky finger lowered, then his ring finger, until just his thumb remained – he turned it right side up and pumped his fist, then grabbed the side of the huge contraption. Lester focused his attention squarely on the lens, steeled himself and slowed his thoughts to a standstill, recollecting the most tumultuous three days of his life.

I'll never get to retire he thought.

And then a red light came on above the camera. He was live.

"My name is Lester Desjardins, former active director of the FBI. I have been falsely accused of terrorism against my own country, THE United States of America." The words rolled off his tongue so properly it made him feel good about it. He was doing the right thing. But he had to take a minute to work out the next part without blurting out something stupid like *Aliens are taking over* or *It's all a giant conspiracy.* That would just sound like end of days nonsense and wouldn't pack the punch to stop people from clearing out their houses and actually listening. "An agent went missing in Paris so I brought a team there to investigate. We were attacked by *American* soldiers!" He yelled, slamming his fist into the table. Anger wasn't going to work either, so he went for broke. There was no *reasonable* way to say any of it anyways.

"I sit here as a citizen of Earth. The United States government is behind everything, and parts of the Military Industrial Complex have been infiltrated by exo-biological species." He had to squint to pull that one out of his memory bank. He thought it would make him sound more credible.

In the control booth he could see Gary's torso frantically darting around, checking bells and whistles, huddling over the shoulders of the operators. Then Jasper's ominous black silhouette. His hand pointed down at his other wrist, a familiar gesture. He was chewing up precious airtime. He wanted to get to the main point, but what was it, really? Did he have any good advice for people? The main point to Jasper was obvious, and it became obvious in Lester's eyes instantly.

"The weather conditions around the world are being created by a superweapon called HEAR. My agents have ascertained information that leads us to believe that Dynatech is conducting some sort of genetic experiments on people at a remote facility in Alaska. We also believe the HEAR device is located there."

Was that it?

He leaned in closer and took a breath, as if he was speaking face to face to another human being, like they were actually on the other side of that wide lens.

"This is the real deal people. The *apocalypse.*" The very word stung his lips as he pronounced the bilabial 'p' sound. "If any US military forces can hear me, I strongly advise an immediate military strike on the facility. Also, the Foreign Peace Relations summit is taking place today, we believe an attack is going to happen there, police, firefighters, anyone hearing this message right now, get out of there, cancel it." Lester ranted, hoping everyone listening – if it was anyone at all – was believing even half of what he was saying.

"As for the rest of humanity, stay in your homes, conserve food, this *may* all be over soon." He didn't know how else to say it. In his mind he envisioned being at the desk for a full ten minutes, reciting everything that happened over and over, like most news stations did with their stories. But he couldn't have anticipated the level of panic or exactly when the death-machine was going to kick in. It may have also *not* ended – not *ever*. Would he have an answer for humanity then? The cameraman cut the feed. Lester moved toward the booth with Stiltzy in tow.

"Any luck with Barritzer?"

'No sir, couldn't get a fix on him."

"Dammit." Lester swore under his breath as he ascended the spiral staircase."How'd that go?" He asked, panting. Evidently he wasn't a natural reporter. His mind worked on the more investigative side of things – he would have been the lowly desk worker rummaging through databases so the anchor had something to talk about.

"I think it went well. But I think we should stay on air for a while, for at least as long as we can." Gary responded. The operators were mute, still scared.

"How long do you think we have Jasper?"

Lester could tell he was calculating. His eye twitched a bit and he squinted.

"80 to 90 minutes, max."

"Gary what's your plan?"

"Well, if this thing is gonna' draw out, we're gonna' need the media on our side. Give me that surveillance footage, I'll loop it and make a headline about Dynatech. Then I'll-"

"Just do it Gary, do whatever you were thinking of doing." Lester cut in. "Jasper, Stiltzy, lockdown this newsroom I want all the systems operational for as long as humanly possible." When Lester said *humanly*, he looked right at Jasper — not quite sure if the distinction was an appropriate description of his ability to carry out the order.

"Copy."

"Try to raise Paul on comms while you're at it."

"Copy."

"I'm going to check on Jim." Lester said, then walked a few paces. *Humanly* kept running through his mind.

"Oh hey and guys," Lester turned, gaining their attention again, "Now might be a good time to contact your families." The words stopped everyone for a moment — except Jasper. "That goes for everybody, the civvies as well." He finished, then broke into stride down the hallway.

The skinny, shaggy-haired booth operator finally broke the silence. "Is it all true?" he asked, quite seriously, as if his mind had already come to terms with the new reality. "Is our own government attacking us?"

Gary didn't know how to respond. He bit his lip and took a deep breath.

"All of it and more."

"What are we going to do?"

"Anything could happen." Gary said, wishing he had an answer for the kid.

They may have been standing in the safest place they could be, or being lined up like fish in a barrel for another platoon of soldiers, trapped. The wind was getting worse. There was a visible warp in the metal buckles that latched the plexi-glass to the inch-wide rivets at the top of the window frames.

"Can you help me with the headlines?" Gary asked, more trying to make a friend than place a demand.

"Definitely." Said the kid. "My name is Aaron, nice to meet you." He stuck out his irregularly large, boney hand.

"Gary. Gary Jones."

Gary's hand went to meet Aaron's – just as their fingers touched their attention, *everyone's* attention was brought toward a bright red flicker that reflected off the many layers of windows in the building. A plume of red and black cauliflower emerged from the four-to-six story skyline a few kilometers across town. Seconds later, the windows shook violently hard, then went back to their 'normal' chattering. Gary felt a tight knot form in his stomach.

"*GOD* I hate being right sometimes." He said, jaw dropped. They heard a scream from the newsroom below – it was Stiltzy, crying out loud and sinking to his knees.

There's no way Barritzer survived that blast.

Gary swallowed it all and accepted that there was nothing he could do about it. It was much easier a thing to do for him than it would have been just 48 hours ago – a broken, confused, coward crying on the street.

"Come on, focus!" Gary yelled, pulling Aaron by the shoulder. The other, much older operator was in the middle of a frantic call to his wife. Gary looked right into his pupils, into his *soul* – doing his best impression of Lester.

"You and I are going to save lives Aaron."

* * * *

Telepathy was one thing, *Teleportation* was another. The big eyeball-thing popped them out into a very similar looking cavern, but Tarliss assured

Anthony that they had traveled thousands of kilometers instantly. He looked straight up to find their exit vector, but nothing was there, just rock and speckled air.

"That felt really weird." Anthony said, much to the amusement of the other Darmerians. He was still a source of entertainment for them, it appeared.

"It would be to anyone who has never passed through it's waves."

"It's waves?" Anthony asked, thirsty for more mind-blowing explanations.

"You wouldn't be able to describe it with any human terms you know. We call it *shrakh-thriss-bolav*. The best translation would be 'elevation of living speed' or 'rising level of existence'" Tarliss said, as the group started walking. They were in a giant room again but this time it was made out of nothing but rock. The patterns and stalactites were natural, but the shape of the cavern itself begged the question of whether or not it was manufactured. The walls were perfectly round and formed a perceivably even circle that comprised the top-to-bottom. Each side of them looked identical. A *tube* – the circular form twirled deep in the earth as long as Anthony could see – which he noticed was quite a bit further than he could before. If he wanted to focus on a particular point in the blackness, he could quite literally zoom in on it, but not just with his eyes. His ears would follow him there too. It made him feel like he was standing in two spots at the same time.

"Whoa." He mumbled to himself. Just being *himself* felt a lot different.

Am I really sure this still isn't just a dream?"

"Come Sagittarius." A voice in his mind beckoned him.

"Don't fall behind Earthling." But it wasn't Tarliss this time. He recognized it as the tall warrior from before that hit him; the hit that Tarliss didn't stop from happening.

"I won't Beldonor." Anthony responded, just looking into the alien's back and thinking his answer. He felt something different clicking deep in his cortex, but would be unable to describe exactly what it was. He wanted to let the others know that he was just as capable as them. But was he?

It seemed peculiar that they would make such a big jump and then started moving at a snail's pace.

"The next *bolav* is very close. We could move faster but it would risk giving off high energy readings."

"You think someone's following us?" Anthony asked telepathically. He couldn't quite tell if the conversation was happening in everyone's head, or just between him and Tarliss.

"Our enemies have eyes everywhere. And they're technology is always improving."

"Is it better than *our* technology?"

"Not a chance." It was a different voice this time. A warrior behind him, a grisly, angry voice that he could feel inside his head somehow, more than actually hearing it. the message carried an undercurrent of sorrow and loneliness that he felt a tinge of as well. So, not only could he talk to them in his head, be completely incapable of telling them a lie, but also feel their emotions when they spoke to him. He had deduced by now that they could most definitely feel his. It gave him an unwelcome feeling of vulnerability that he frantically tried to dispel, knowing they could all feel that too if they were spying on his mind. He didn't want any of them to think he was a scared, weak link.

"I'm Tarthinius. We'll make a warrior out of you yet, kid." More information came with the second message. It was like FBI profiling on steroids. He didn't want to look around or . . . .he didn't *need* to — his mind had already created an accurate picture of Tarthinius down to his facial scars, of which there were quite a few. And then more of that suffocating sorrow . . . and then he didn't want to think about it anymore. It was going to be hard, as he realized, to have his mind being constantly bombarded and pried apart by superior judgmental aliens and still somehow get to know them – to make them all *like* him.

"So we're jumping into another big eyeball?" Anthony said out loud. A few of the aliens ahead of him actually laughed.

"You're funny." He heard. A female voice, the only female with them. He looked to his left and saw Aremis, she was there just like his heightened senses told him she would be. Did she actually say it or just telepath it? He couldn't quite tell – maybe it was both. She was smiling and looking right at him.

If they were going to stop this HEAR thing from firing, they sure were taking their time. He also wondered what it would be like if someone did pick up on their energy signatures, whether or not they would stand a fighting chance. What was their plan anyway?

"Don't fill your mind with pointless questions." Tarliss said.

"But what if they know we're coming? Are we going to just walk in there?"

"We're going to take it by force." Said Beldonor. It was almost more comfortable when the others spoke, because the silence made him nervous. Silence among these individuals meant exactly the opposite of what the word entailed. If they were spending mental space communicating then they probably weren't spending as much time listening.

It intrigued Anthony, and momentarily brought him back to the firing room with Tarliss. If 'by force' meant he could use more weapons, it worked for him. But he didn't want to ask the inevitable question, or even think about it so that he wouldn't get an answer he didn't want to hear. But he couldn't help himself.

What kind of resistance are we going to encounter? Is this a suicide mission? What happened to the missing Darmerians?

"Don't worry Anthony. We'll be fine I promise." Said Aremis. He could tell she spoke her mind before the others wanted to give him a different piece of theirs, as if she was protecting him from insults. She also referred to him by his human name, and he knew that it was done purposely to make him feel more comfortable.

"Don't get *too* comfortable, Sagittarius. We are most definitely going to get in a fight of some sort." This time it was Beldonor. Was he trying to scare him? Because if he was, it worked. Getting into a fight down here, by now he had figured out, wouldn't be like any fight he'd ever been in or would be able to anticipate.

"Call me Anthony, please." He said out loud again. The others didn't answer, but he knew they were working out why he would request they keep his human name as a designation. He didn't even know exactly why that's what he wanted. It was just another thing that would make him feel comfortable, to bring him back to some sort of central, rigid and concrete ethos. He was still trying to figure out exactly what he was, *who he was*, and it helped his mind not to wander by creating these mental constructs to cling to – to keep him anchored and stable. He was trained to accept realities, to have a strong, unbreakable mind, but he was after all *just human* . . . .or . . . something like it. He knew it was foolish and naïve of him to think he could handle such a mental swing all at once and without barriers.

Were they just listening to all that?

After just a few minutes of walking they came upon the familiar looking, three-meter globular structure. It was well hidden inside of an entrenched part of the floor that would have looked, on a larger scale, like the hole left behind by a nail that was pounded into the tunnel then removed. A mossy, yellowish overgrowth coated the opening to the drop. They were going to have to jump down into it. No one was going to find this thing (provided they found themselves this deep underground) unless they knew where to look for it.

"This one will bring us just outside Starset. We'll be within striking distance." Tarliss said. The inflection in his voice and the look in his eye said something more though.

Get ready.

Tarliss looked down the hole, then at Anthony. He wanted to say something, but like a flash of light that paralyzed his senses for a split second, a thought – a *feeling* surged through his synapses. It was a mixture of fear and uncertainty but he couldn't pinpoint it. All of the aliens' head turned and looked back toward the ominous black tunnel behind them.

"You all felt that too?" Anthony asked, and looked in the same direction. He felt Aremis' take him by the hand again. If she had a crush on him, she wasn't being shy about it. He wondered what all of the other warriors thought about what she was doing. He didn't want them to think of him as some mama's boy who needed his hand held.

"Who's it going to be?" Tarliss asked around, but Anthony didn't catch his drift right away.

"We'll stay." He heard from his right, two of the silver-clad warriors stood with their legs on top of a rock. The one on the right had something in his eyes – or maybe it *was* his eye, or part of it at least. The shape of them was the same, but blue and purple sections made up the thin layer of iris surrounding a ghost-white pupil. His corneas were black, creating a very odd-looking reversal of the norm. Anthony was still struggling to figure out what they were talking about. Evidently his ability to pick up on their mental conversations wasn't as refined as theirs.

"There should be at least three of you. Grikorus, stay with them." Tarliss commanded. Grikorus was about the same size as Beldonor and looked equally as formidable. He trudged past Anthony and over to the two smaller warriors.

"Try to establish a link with Rikthinius."

"What's going on guys?" Anthony asked, feeling his heart rate accelerate beyond where he wanted it to. Tarliss looked at him.

"We are being hunted."

"Is that what I felt?"

"We all felt it. we must make sure they haven't located our refuge."

"They may be able to trace our spectral trail back to it's origin. It will be amplified since there are so many of us."

"Who's after us?"

Tarliss hesitated.

"I smell Reticulan." Said Beldonor with a charming grin on his face. It looked like he was eager to stay behind himself and challenge their followers to a fight.

"It very well could be. We must proceed."

Tarliss jumped into the second portal, then so did everyone else besides the three appointed to stay. Anthony was second last this time. Aremis waited for him to jump. She didn't seem the least bit worried. None of them did.

The teleportation process was exactly how he had described it – *weird*. When he jumped into the open space inside the sphere, he felt like he was dreaming again, if only briefly. He had no hands, feet, eyes or lips to lick. He was pure consciousness, and could feel the *waves* of the others inside the breach with him. Somehow he just knew they were there, and so was he. There was no vision, no smell or taste, just pure existence as something that couldn't be called physical or non-physical.

So this is what it feels like to become energy.

Once again, his body came back into reality after a few seconds. Just like before he looked straight up, but there was nothing but rocks. The rest of the squad stood there waiting for him to emerge along with Aremis. He looked up again. She simply appeared and fell the short distance, landing perfectly and graciously on her feet.

"Don't worry Earthling, it's something even *we* haven't grown used to yet."

Anthony thought it was a good thing that there wasn't a way to simply jump back into the portals and go backwards. That would make it very easy for anyone to track them. Darmerians may have been powerful creatures, but evidently they still had to be very cautious about the most basic of things. Another ping in his brain; an energetic instinctual instruction told him to look forward. In front of him was their target.

"Look. Next to the doorway." They were all perched on a darkly ensconced dent in the rock. They were so far away Anthony had to do that zoom-in trick he did before to see what Beldonox, Beldonor's twin brother, was talking about. Their faces and bodies were identical, like copies of the same picture. Human twins usually had some defining feature to tell them apart, but not these creatures.

Focusing all of his attention and will into a narrow tunnel, he reached his senses out across the distance. It felt like it did before – like he was actually standing there, looking at the bodies from just feet away. There were seven of them, all shot in the head once and in the chest twice. Their hands were zip-tied with bags drawn over their heads. Whoever wasted them had even laid them out conveniently in a tub-shaped divot sticking out of the metal arch of a ten foot doorway. It conveniently pooled their blood into the middle. One of the bodies was quite literally half-submerged in a thick, red pool. The whole scene looked like a flower bed built into a raised concrete extension leading to the front door of a house, like many of the older brick houses in Boston's suburbs – except the flowers were discarded carcasses. It certainly didn't say 'welcome, please enter' quite like a line of petunias did.

Executed. Like dogs.

It made Anthony *mad*. It bugged him that they had taken their time to get there. Maybe they could have saved these people if they arrived sooner. But they weren't human, so why should any of them care about the plight of these less evolved creatures? Would he himself feel the same kind of regretful compassion if he saw a Darmerian die? It was hard for him to just 'switch sides' so quickly. Seeing murdered humans still pissed him off.

"Here take this." Aremis whispered from behind him. He reached his hand back, keeping his eyes fixated. She placed a small item in his hand that felt like a diamond or some sort of pebble.

"Stick it in your suit."

He complied by jamming the little trinket in his hip. The silver reacted like a bowl of jello being penetrated with a straw. Seconds later, his suit extended over his hands and every square inch of his head, leaving his vision completely unaffected. For a second he panicked and wanted to curse at Aremis, but it didn't hurt enough to warrant the gesture. He was gone. Not in a different room or dead, but *invisible*. He raised his hand in front of his face, but saw nothing. He could still feel everything, he just couldn't see *anything*. A moment of cerebral indifference paralyzed his senses as they tried to adjust, like when you stare at a computer screen for an hour then try to look just past it at something else, but your eyes can't focus properly right away. Three warriors in front of him vanished instantly, but oddly enough he could still see their outlines . . . or . . . *feel* them. They existed more as a representation of his surroundings inside his head. His eyes told them they were gone, but his gut told him not only that they were still there, but exactly where they were. The only thing he could relate the feeling to was white noise – knowing an electronic device is on without help from the five standard senses. He felt like if he wanted to walk past them, he could do it without hitting their shoulders, and if he wanted to reach out and touch their shoulder he wouldn't just cat-paw at the air in front of him.

"Their killer approaches." He heard, in his head or by voice. The disparity was often so faint he stopped trying to figure out which one it was. Communication was becoming so simple he thought he might turn into a mute.

A shadow loomed in the doorway as someone approached. It was a soldier. A *big* soldier. Even from the considerable distance, which Anthony estimated at about two and a half football fields, he could see the relative size of the armor-clad warrior compared to the lifeless corpses in his proximity. It wasn't the most accurate mental-math given that the bodies were horizontal and he was vertical, but he estimated the soldier was at least a foot taller. For a moment, the soldier seemed to look directly at them. He felt his heartbeat speed up. But the soldier turned to the bodies, pulled out a lighter and tossed it. The whole metal tub erupted into flames like a giant shot of eighty-proof. The soldier turned and walked back to the entrance and disappeared into the compound.

"We have to do something." Anthony held onto the thought hard and waited for a response.

"They are all dead. We can't help them."

It was an answer he didn't need to be told again, but he needed something to subdue his anger. Human or alien, it was in his DNA to avenge murdered innocents, and to take vengeance personally.

"He's gone. Let's proceed." Tarliss said.

Including himself, they were ten in total. But there could be hundreds of soldiers. Or *thousands.* The thought of it made Anthony realize why Tarliss elected to proceed so carefully.

They wandered across the expanse, well camouflaged, but not completely invisible. Anthony noticed the air flicker around the others' bodies when they moved too quickly. It was barely noticeable but absolutely noticeable if you were looking in just the right spot. Given the uneventful, mono-colored terrain they were traversing it was adequate protection from a random observer they might have overlooked. Moving slowly made them a hair short of non-existent and gave them ample time to scan their surroundings for any threats. They reached the door and examined the interior. It branched off into multiple directions after about twenty meters, and there was a set of elevators just a few meters inside. The fire had died down and the bodies were charred to cinders. The smell was absolutely disgusting. Even Tarliss covered his mouth and nose to block the scent from filling his nostrils.

They crept down the square, angular cement hallway, the only evidence of their presence being the slightly darker shade of floor underneath their feet. It didn't last long however, they moved quite quickly, checking each corner when a different pathway intersected with their own. Signs on the wall conveniently told them exactly where they were and where to go. This was familiar. Something clicked in Anthony's brain. He remembered some of the room-clearing exercises during his training. He knew when to take point and exactly where to look – what angle he was responsible for. It would be hard for anyone to detect them outside of accidentally walking right into one of them, and he didn't doubt that anyone unlucky enough to do so would die swiftly.

They came to a four way intersection. The path straight ahead was noted with a sign that said, in bright yellow letters: 'SUB-LEVEL 1C' with smaller lettering underneath that read 'PRISONER STORAGE' and 'H.E.A.R. RELAY'. The second waypoint was welcome – they were being told exactly where they needed to go – but PRISONER STORAGE made Anthony feel woozy. It brought him back to his less-than enjoyable, short-lived experience as a prisoner after his mission in Europe went down the drain. Part of him wanted to liberate the prisoners, if there were any, but relaying that sentiment to the others might yield a keep-your-head-in-the-game response.

Tarliss pointed his hand into the passage, just past the big sign hanging from the ceiling. Right next to it, a ventilation shaft. One by one, they jumped into the thing. It was just big enough for them to crouch and move at a reasonable pace. After five minutes of scurrying down the passage, an opening in the metal-grate floor gave them vision to a room below. For some reason, Tarliss insisted that they stop and examine the room, much to the dismay of the other warriors, who were simply eager to complete their objective.

"Tanchorus, cut this grate open." Tarliss said, momentarily revealing his face. The cloak of invisibility washed away starting at his feet and surging up to his head. It gave Anthony a look at how the silver suit covered their faces, and it looked terrifying. Their whole head was covered skin-tight with the stuff, leaving a bluish-white elliptical almond shape on either eye. It reminded him of spider-man, or some sort of superhero's mask.

What looked like glowing steam trickled out of the luminous blue eyeports. After a second it all retracted, revealing Tarliss' face. The rest of them followed suit. If intimidation was what the suit's designer intended, than he had definitely achieved it. Tarliss' face, all of their faces for that matter looked nothing short of demonic.

Tanchorus was the smallest among them, even smaller than the hunched, withered creature that helped him into his metallic suit. He wasn't very muscular either and had long blond hair tied and bunched into a knot at the base of his neck. Unlike the others, the extra back muscles that covered his spine weren't as prominent or visible through his suit. He looked the most human out of anyone. The metal grate fizzled and hissed as Tanchorus burned through it with some sort of laser cutter – but there was no actual device. He simply held out his index finger and the silver, magical metal did the rest. It burned through the thick metal like a knife through butter, dripping molten globs to the floor below. Once the grate was only connected still by a few shards of metal, Tanchorus grabbed it and ripped it off completely. It looked easier than it should have been.

Tarliss dropped into the room with a thud. It was barren except for a row of human-size cylinders lining the wall. There were ten each on either side of the room. Seven were visibly empty on the left. Three were closed. He walked up to the one in the middle and washed away the dust and filth caked on the cylindrical glass sheath. Dust and ice covered a tangled web of coils and wires branching from the top of the capsule. The contraptions reminded him of very crude, unkempt versions of the regeneration chambers his kind used – but how could they possibly have replicated them? Even Tarliss was alarmed at the discovery – was there a *traitor* in their midst? He couldn't immediately think of another scenario that allowed Darmerian technology to be in human hands, however feeble and rudimentary their back-engineered replicas may be.

He peered into the tube and saw a human with dark hair. Before another set of information could be processed, a reactive burst of awareness tensed his whole body. He turned rapidly, just in time to bend and dodge a large blade swung at his head. It was attached to a set of hands and a body. The attempted attack was easily thwarted by his enhanced speed. He stood there, befuddled, allowing himself a glance at his attacker – a warrior clad in black armor, strewn from head to toe with crude human weapons. The creature lunged forward again with another swing of his three foot katana, but the attack had no chance. Before he could even grip the thing for a lumbered swing, Tarliss caught the sharp blade in his hand. The human attacker's eyes lit up with disbelief . . . *fear*. Anthony felt compelled to jump down and help him, but Beldonox quickly thwarted him with a stiff hit to the shoulder, shooting him a look that could shatter granite.

"He's fine, don't worry." Was the gist of the message that popped into his mind. And he *was* fine. Tarliss was infinitely faster and stronger than the attacker. For a moment he even felt bad for the man, who would have undoubtedly been a formidable opponent to any human adversary. Was their cover blown?

"What the hell-"

The heavily armed assassin tried to yank his weapon free, but it didn't budge. Tarliss' grip held like a tightened monkey wrench. Anthony could tell he wasn't the type to toy with his prey. Tarliss jerked his hand and snapped the metal blade in half, simultaneously kicking the assassin in the chest before he could react to block the blow. It sent him flying into the row of capsules lining the opposite wall, through a patch of unlit darkness he must have been hiding in. His body crashed violently against the things, smashing one of them open. The front sheath popped up and retracted into a slit above it, revealing a horrible, familiar sight. The other

Darmerians began flooding into the room through the ceiling once the assassin was incapacitated. He tried to reach for a pistol holstered on his hip, but Tarliss was on top of him as soon as the thought crossed his synapse. He stomped on the weapon, grabbed the man by the throat and lifted him off of his feet into the air. He wanted to force an interrogation, but the contents of the opened capsule pulled his attention. He simply tossed the soldier like a child back into Beldonor's waiting arms, who then furiously slammed him into the ground and grabbed both of his hands. A glowing strand from his suit detached and wrapped firmly around the man's wrists, then another around his ankles. He spat blood and cursed wildly which gained him the grace of Beldonor's axepick-like foot plunged hard into his throat.

"Shut up!" He said, eyes glowing with anger. The man seemed hypnotized. Every ounce of resistance dissipated from his body instantly.

Inside the capsule was one of his own. "Open the rest." He said. Tanchorus pressed a large yellow button next to each capsule. Steam vented, depressurizing them and the sheaths popped open and retracted.

"Are they alive?" He asked Tanchorus, who didn't respond with words, only a bewildered look. Anthony knew by the gesture that the capsule's inhabitants were in fact dead. But they weren't human. He took a closer look – they were Darmerians. Hundreds of small tubes and wires pierced their skin. They led into porous holes inside the capsule. Their veins were blue, their skin pale and lifeless. It started to click for Anthony; these must have been the scouts they lost contact with.

"I knew we shouldn't have sent them." Tarliss exhaled painfully, as if their deaths were his personal responsibility. "Get them out of there." He said, lowering his head in self-defeat.

"It's not your fault Tarliss. They knew what could happen." Aremis said, trying to console him. He looked right in her eyes, and she in his. Their huge, bright pupils flickered and darted, denoting a telepathic conversation. Tanchorus and Venethon, another Darmerian roughly

Anthony's size, sliced away the connective tubes and lowered the limp bodies onto the floor, checking for a pulse just to make sure.

"Farewell brothers." Tanchorus mumbled to himself.

"We must continue with the mission."

"What about the bodies?"

"Destroy them." Tarliss said; emotionless, monotone. "They are dead, aren't they?"

He didn't even need to ask the question. If they were alive, he'd have been able to feel their lifeforce.

"Yes."

"Unfortunately we cannot afford them a proper burial."

Anthony could tell the words came out painfully. Tanchorus detached something from his waist that looked like an egg. It popped open, revealing a glowing blue section in the middle. A thin layer of blue light scanned over their bodies slowly, and one at a time, they disintegrated into speckled vapor-light – the same kind of pixie dust from the discs Anthony shot in the firing range. The only remnant of their existence was the memories the others had of them now.

"The humans found a way to get their suits off." Said Venethon. No one said anything for a few seconds – it was a moment of silence for them to imagine how their friends may have died, and also what dangers may lie ahead of them.

"Tracchith-Tus Derthenius. Bellatrion . . . . Goodbye my brothers." Tarliss exclaimed,

"May you all be born Darmerians in the next life."

For a moment after the bodies vanished Anthony felt a tingling vibration on his tongue and his ears were itchy, the kind of itch he couldn't scratch away. Everyone's attention then shifted to the battered human who made a pathetic attempt to kill Tarliss. The only reason he was still breathing was that he might have information for them.

"What does it feel like to know your friends are fucking *dead?*" He yelled, spitting blood at Beldonox. It spattered his immaculate silver covering but didn't last long on. The pure anger running through him amplified and manifested into his suit, burning the red blood into vapor.

"I told you to shut up!" Beldonor raised his arm and closed his fist into a death-dealing blow.

"Wait, Beldonor."

"As long as I get to crush his skull after." Beldonor said, leaning in close to the assassin's face.

"Why were you keeping them in capsules?"

"Fuck yourself!" The warrior tried to spit on Tarliss too, but Beldonor shoved his knee fiercely into his gullet and all he managed was a gurgling murmur. Saliva and blood trickled out of his mouth onto the floor as he struggled for breath.

"I'll pull it right out of you if I have to."

Beldonor released the pressure, but only just enough to let him breathe.

"You are all going to die. Every last one of you will burn. There is nothing you can do to stop it either. Aha . . . aha ha . . aha!" The battered assassin broke into a maniacal laugh. It was clear they were going to have to employ other tactics to get anything out of him.

"That's quite enough!" Tarliss yelled. He plunged his gaping hand, wrapping it around the soldier's head. His eyes started flickering and thick foam built up around his lips as he convulsed violently. It was almost unbearable to watch. *Almost.* It wasn't just for show. Tarliss was sucking the information right out of his brain. After a few seconds he aggressively retracted his hand and had a look on his face like when you learn something horrific that you wish you hadn't.

"What did you see?" Aremis asked. "Is Senechius still alive?"

Tarliss didn't answer. He didn't even move. Anthony could tell that whatever he stole from the assassin's mind was something awful. He could feel it.

"We have to keep moving."

"Time's up for you."

Beldonor picked the assassin up by his chest plate and tossed him in Beldonox' general direction. He flailed in mid-air like a caught fish. Beldonox ended his life with a crushing, lightning-fast high kick that quite literally broke his body in half. Another thunderous elbow crushed his skull to make sure the job was done. It was so fast that it wasn't even a limb – more like a flash of lightning as it moved. For a 'peaceful' race, they sure weren't reserved when it came to killing. The detached strands slithered off of the limp body's wrists and ankles and reintegrated with Beldonor's suit.

"Who are they?"

"The humans? Let's find out."

Tanchorus pressed all of the corresponding buttons next to the capsules. The steam hissed out of the pressurized containers then the glass and metal sheaths retracted into a groove at the top and disappeared.

"This one still has a wallet in his pants. Mark Brathurst. The woman is called Stacey Peterson." Stacey's nametag was still conveniently stuck to her tattered labcoat.

"Can you wake them up?"

"I'll try."

Anthony thought they were going to have some sort of space age smelling salts to force consciousness. Their method was much cruder than that. Tanchorus slapped Mark in the face and shook him, then did the same with the other man. He went to try his advanced technique on Stacey Peterson, but thought better of smacking an unconscious woman around. Anthony snickered at the humanity displayed during the process. It worked, eventually. Mark Brathurst popped up from the floor and took in a breath so laboriously that it sounded like he was breaching water's surface for the breath that would save his life. He immediately kicked back to the capsule, hyperventilating, wide-eyed.

"Wh-where the fuck . . . what the fu-"

"Calm down, we're not here to hurt you." Said Aremis, as soothingly as she could. He looked around, baffled. His hands were still raised to his face. They tried to reach for him, but he reacted like a cornered, injured animal, slapping at their hands and uttering inaudible squeamish yelps.

Mark looked to his left and saw Eugene. He leapt for him, panicking, checking his pulse and putting his ear to Eugene's mouth.

"He's alive, he's alive!"

"Focus, Mark. Focus on my voice. What happened here?" Tarliss' deep voice was nothing short of hypnotic. Mark took a deep breath and one by one, examined the Darmerians.

"You aren't human, are you?"

"No, we are not. But we are *not* your enemy, if that's what you are implying."

"I didn't-"

"Be calm. It appears they were in the process of erasing your memory. I am going to help you remember." Tarliss said, then reached his hand out and placed it firmly on Mark's forehead.

"Tell me what you remember."

He really had to think about that one. He struggled to his feet and crunched his eyebrows together. Bits and pieces were slowly coming back to him although he couldn't be sure they were in the right order.

"I remember . . .a plane."

That piqued Anthony's attention. The only thing he could think about was Williams. These people were directly responsible for his partner's death.

"And . . . a man named . . .Mr. Brown. He made me fly the T-IVB . . . me and Eugene. And then, and then I don't remember anything after that."

Eugene started coughing and hacking. He popped up and vomited all over the concrete floor, then did the same helpless squirming as Mark. Beldonor quickly subdued him and calmed him down through tactile sensation. As soon as Beldonor's hand gripped Eugene's wrist, the panic and fear seeped out of him like a deflating balloon.

"You guys attacked our plane. You killed my partner. And many others." Anthony yelled. Tarliss tried to grab him by the arm but he shrugged it off.

"I'm sorry, he tricked us! He told us we were doing good!" Mark responded, curling up into a ball preparing to absorb a blow. Anthony wanted to release his anger on Mark and Eugene in the worst way. They had caused him a great deal of pain. But he couldn't. He was torn between exacting revenge and doing the right thing. He felt Aremis' hand touch his, and the rage dissipated. He tried to resist the overwhelming surge of calmness, but gave into it whole-heartedly.

"Okay. I'm okay. Where do we go from here?" He asked Tarliss. Seconds later, Stacey Peterson was awake. In her waking moments it appeared as if she was reliving the last few moments she could remember. She looked around the room but not like Mark and Eugene – the tall aliens seemed familiar to her which was just as odd to them as it was to Mark and Eugene.

"Miss Peterson. Pleasure to have you conscious again. You've some nasty bruises. Are you alright?"

"I think so. You are all . . . " She looked around the room again, lip-synching syllables that she just couldn't form into the right words.

"Darmerians? We are. You have seen our kind before?"

"Yes."

"Where?"

"In the lab. They were making me do experiments on one of you." She said. The events were pasted so vividly in her expression the others felt like they were reliving the experiences with her.

"And then . . ." her head dipped, eyebrows furled and pure sadness replaced the excitement.

"I'm sorry, but your friend is dead. He did something to me just before they killed him . . he . . .showed me things. I think they are planning some sort of hostile take-over."

"Senechius. What did they do with his body?"

"I don't know. They brought me here right away." Stacey said, but then another image shot through her memory banks. "Wait, we have to do something! Mormont! He turned the damned machine on!"

"You mean HEAR?" Tarliss asked, but he already knew the answer. Were they too late?

"Yes." Stacey exhaled. The temporary adrenaline spike concordant with her revelation had worn off. She felt weak, and the pain from her injuries abruptly returned in full force.

Tarliss put his hands on his waist, a peculiarly human representation of deep thought.

"Why would they turn the machine on early? The ionosphere is not in balance yet. Not for a few hours from now." Tarliss said, thinking out loud.

"Maybe they are being pressured?" Stacey added, ignoring the pain. It didn't make sense, but the human was right. There was only one explanation as to why they would be so hasty in playing their biggest card.

"I think they are afraid." Tarliss said. "I think they fear we are going to destroy their best plans." Tarliss said, looking right at Anthony the whole time. As he spoke, another message entered Anthony's brain.

They are afraid of you, Sagittarius.

"How do we get to the machine?" Tarliss asked Stacey. She was their best bet at navigating this huge facility, and maybe she could give them some insight to how much resistance they were going to encounter.

"It's on one of the Sublevels . . . 1A" She said, squinting. She was doing an admirable job staving off the immense pain from her injuries, even by Darmerian standards. The warriors listened to her speak with a level of respect not normally reserved for lesser species.

"Do you remember how to get there?"

Stacey racked her brain to try and remember the route she was dragged through by Dynatech's finest. All that came to mind were the harsh kicks and punches that she endured on the way there.

"I'm sorry. I can't recall." Stacey answered. The aliens tried to search her mind for the memory, but could not find it either.

"But I do know how to cut the power to this place. That's probably your best bet." Stacey remembered one of the rooms she passed when she first arrived at the facility. It was a room full of prototype weapons – one she learned about from Rhaj – who was brought here under similar circumstances to her own. His job was primarily to test and verify the usefulness of large-scale EMP weapons. Luckily, the short conversation had stuck in her head. Conversations with other people were rare for her, so she remembered each one of them vividly.

"Where is the room?" Asked Beldonor. Stacey realized that the aliens were reading her mind now. It was a most intrusive and violating feeling, but it was the least of her worries.

"Not far from here. I'll know it when I see it." She did remember the room, the few times she was allowed to 'walk to work' alongside Rhaj, and a few others. Eventually the groups thinned out and isolation was permanent. It happened so quickly and efficiently she didn't even notice until she was all alone, with no one to talk to but herself. But she remembered where Rhaj turned off. She remembered because a sign above the door said WEAPONS TESTING. You couldn't miss it. Stacey breathed deep and tried to retrace her steps. If she could just tune out the battering, falling and sheer pain. . . *stairs . . . past an elevator. . . more stairs . . .left,* errr, *right hand turn . . .*

It took her a minute to calculate walking backwards, but she had it.

"Got it. Let's move. Through the hallways, we take our chances." Said Tarliss, breaking the fixed, luminous gaze of the aliens' eyes upon her. She could barely stand to look at them. They silently pried into her brain, able to calculate and translate her own thoughts faster than she could. It made her feel scared and alone, especially since the two other humans in the room were still as mesmerized.

"Are you sure that's a good idea?"Anthony asked Tarliss telepathically. His training reminded him they could be ambushed or cornered. A glance back told him specifically that anything they encountered would die extremely fast, no matter their number or their capabilities.

Don't you remember how fast you ran in the caverns?

He did remember, and it quieted him. Tarliss was right. Nothing and no one could possibly be quicker or more lethal than he was. If the man guarding the capsule room was any testament, he liked his odds.

"What about them?" Anthony asked out loud. A few heads turned as they prodded the large, square-shaped metal door leading out to the hallway. It had a circular glass window about a meter in diameter. Evidently Tarliss didn't have a plan for the humans. He must have considered them dead weight. Oddly enough, Anthony tried to reach out telepathically to Tarliss but couldn't. The way it felt tricked Anthony's mind into thinking there was a physical wall in front of him preventing the message from getting through. He hadn't felt *that* one yet – being *unable* to speak to the mind of a creature because they had developed a technique to block it from being entered. Even mind-reading had its own set of social dynamics. Not saying anything when asked the answer was a lot like lying.

Why would he do that?

It only made him want to know what was on Tarliss' mind even more; so he traced back to the look on his face when he touched the assassin before his head was severed. He was hiding something from him. Was he hiding it from the others, too?

For a moment his mind wandered off the immediate objective in order to analyze a whole new set of questions that were going to help define his *ethos*. A sentence flickered in his mind's eye over and over again.

What kind of Darmerian am I going to become? Will I lie like that?

Anthony realized then and there that he was going to have to learn how to put up his own invisible walls, eventually. He couldn't lie to himself about the humans – he still felt *human*, and still felt compassion for *them*. He found himself slightly upset that they weren't part of the equation. It was obvious by the silence that the plan was to leave them in that room and leave their own survival up to themselves.

They are just like us. They calculate, search and destroy. They let three die to save millions. They only take tactical risks.

He thought, but by *they* he really meant *we* . . . or . . . did he? Was he really ready to abandon his humanity so quickly?

"You're saying you know how to fly some sort of ship?" Anthony asked Mark and Eugene.

"R-Remote control." Eugene spat out, shivering. The effects of the stasis tube were starting to wear on him. "We weren't actually inside the thing."

"T-IVB." Said Mark, who had a slight quiver in his bones as well. "An ETREV mark four – Extra-Terrestrial Reverse Engineered Vehicle."

"Are there any in this facility?"

They looked at each other but didn't answer.

"There is." Said Stacey. "There's a hangar beneath the lab I was in. Your friend showed me before he died. It makes sense now."

"How do you know?" Anthony asked, but he wanted to retract the question. Images of a dying Darmerian leaking puddles of luminous blood popped into his head. Then the rest flooded in. He didn't even try to do his mind-reading trick, it happened automatically. It bothered him that he couldn't control it at his whim. Smaller snippets popped in sporadically but didn't mean much – studying, playing doubles tennis on a Tuesday evening, partying with friends – these were parts of Stacey's *entire* life, not just the last few days. Anthony had to focus on what Senechius saw, and transferred to Stacey before he died. A battle. A very *one-sided* battle, as far as numbers were concerned. Eventually they were all captured by overwhelming numbers and . . . something else he couldn't quite envision. Something else that was *blocked.*

Anthony decided to keep this little secret to himself, wondering if any of the others had been privy to it already but didn't acknowledge it. But why did he want to do that?

'Time to leave now' Inside his head pulled him away from his thoughts, hoping no Darmerians were listening too closely. They were all crouched beneath the door, invisible or in the process of becoming invisible. He did the same by thinking it. He looked to the humans one last time, trying to give them an edge. He wanted them to survive if they could.

"You guys need to find your way to that room," Anthony continued, "Stacey you're just gonna' have to brave it. Mark, Eugene, help her."

"But what about the soldiers?"

"Don't worry. I have a strong suspicion they are all going to have their hands very full with us."

"Sagittarius, time to go."

"Hurry up Earthling."

"He's not fit to fight with us."

The voices flood into his head. He had to really focus to tune them out again. Another mind-skill he was going to have to improve.

"I have to go. Find something in the hangar you can fly outta' here." He said, "It's your best chance of survival."

But that wasn't the only reason. He didn't want to be the annoying child constantly asking questions, but to his knowledge there was no talk of a way *out* of here. He just assumed when they left that it was all figured out already by way of some super-gadget. They might just have to improvise an escape. Anthony was thinking like an FBI agent again. He ducked and scurried over to the large metal door.

"Secure left hallway."

Anthony took the oddly shaped white 'rifle' off of his back – if you could even call it that. Beldonor pushed a red button at eye-level next to the door. Everyone's ears popped and steam vented from exhaust pipes in the ceiling. The door opened slowly. No contacts yet. Anthony peeled out and to the left, aiming his gun down the hallway. It was floating between his hands and shoulder so he couldn't actually feel it or actually see it. It didn't matter. He knew he could hit a dime from five hundred meters. He also wondered if the 'gun' would stay invisible if he dropped it.

"Sections clear, follow me."

The dim lights of the hallway made the outlines of their suits flicker a bit when they moved. Only while standing still was their camouflage completely effective. They walked down a long rectangular concrete box all the way to the end. After a series of lefts and rights, a few sets of stairs and one elevator, they came to the WEAPONS TESTING room. There was no sign of resistance, not even a whisper. The place seemed to be completely empty. The weapons room itself was on the outer rim of an incredibly large room with sections of glass atrium ceilings.

"What did you say to the humans?" He heard in his head. It was Tarliss forcing a one on one – His presence felt like the IRS routing through your hidden files and slapping you on the wrist afterwards.

"I told them to find their way out." It seemed odd to him that Tarliss would actually impose a question in his mind rather than make a statement about what he obviously already knew . . . Maybe he didn't know.

Am I already lying to him? Am I somehow blocking my thoughts from him?

It was a foolish attempt, he thought, to assume he could do it already. Would he even know if he could do it? What were the *symptoms*?

Another message came but it didn't form into a worded question in his head – more like another push on the last question – an emotion that could be felt more than a message interpreted. The gist of the feeling told him *again* and *specific*.

"The hangar beneath the lab. Stacey Peterson she . . . ."

"Told you through her memories?"

"Yes."

"Good work Sagittarius."

What? Good work for trying to lie to you?

He took it for what it was and decided he'd have enough of the mind-games. It dawned on him during reflective thoughts afterwards the possibility that Tarliss was still testing him – testing how he would react, how he would think and why – like scientists needling a rat repeatedly then seeing what changed. He didn't like the situation any more than they did and mental stability was suspect at the moment. He was going to have to swallow it all, and quickly.

"This is the human bomb." Beckoned a warrior who hadn't spoken yet. He stood above what looked like a treasure chest. It was metal and refined-looking like most of the devices scattered about the room.

"Are you sure Dorolonith?" Tarliss asked. The alien with the tongue-twister for a name stood over the thing with his palm stretched, clutching his wrist with the other hand. A white light emanating from a burning circle in his palm penetrated the thick chassis and peered directly into the device's complicated beehive of circuits. Dorolonith was on the small side and didn't have the same threatening demeanor as the others did. He must have been the tech guy, or the 'human technology specialist'. Although Anthony was trying his best to get by the mental block of a full-blown species-change, he couldn't help but revert back to his human reasoning to help him grasp it all.

"Positive."

"Good. Sagittarius, where do we bring it?" Tarliss asked, much to Anthony's surprise. It carried the same level of awkwardness and embarrassment as being taped to the flagpole after school. Tarliss had been reading his mind the whole time, and *obviously* did an up and down of Stacey's mind too. He should have known.

. . . All of us did . . .

He heard in his head, but it was a collective of the voices and not entirely just one of them. Of course they already knew about the hidden elevator in the lab. Tarliss was making a point of teaching Anthony a lesson in front of the others – that slap on the wrist he was waiting for. In a way it was a relief. He didn't have to twist his mind around trying to figure out what they could and couldn't' hear.

"This device is going to have some temporary effects on our suits. I recommend one of us go alone. The walls will help shield us from the blast."

"Good idea Dorolonith." Tarliss seemed to be purposely speaking out loud for Anthony's benefit; to get him accustomed to how different missions would be now that he was no longer a human. He knew orders could be issued rapidly and without words so there was really no other reason to do it.

Speaking is a human thing among them . . .. is he doing it to try and comfort me? Because if he is, I don't need it . . .

"There is a problem though." Tarliss said, looking at Anthony as if to see how he would react, like he wasn't worried about the others at all. "This is all too easy."

Like clockwork, as soon as Tarliss lipped the last syllable, the room changed color. The bright lights turned to an iridescent pale blue that cast long shadows. The bulbous muscular sections of the aliens' bodies looked more like globs of clay. The brightest objects in the room were their piercingly luminous white, glowing eyes, which looked like the eyes of a predator at night.

Anthony felt his stomach tighten and his heartbeat elevate. Of course it was a trap, and of course Tarliss led them all right into it. They left the room without resistance but as soon as they were back in the large atrium room they felt the entire facility rumbling. Across the long, flat floor soldiers started to pour into the room from every doorway. Dozens soon became hundreds, and they didn't stop. They found themselves completely surrounded and incredibly outnumbered. Ropes descended from divots and holes in the ceiling allowing more troops to descend. Every angle they could see was crawling with enemies. Tarliss detached something from his hip and tossed it over to Anthony. It should have hit the floor but instead it hovered just in front of him. It started out in the shape of an ostrich egg but like most of the Darmerian technology, transformed into something else. Sections popped apart and holograms appeared. It was a gun – a powerful stationary turret that wouldn't ever need to be reloaded. The barrel consisted of blue light with a hovering reticule to aim with. When he gripped the blue-light handles, a similarly colored bubble emanated from the thing and was big enough to surround the gun, his entire body and provide enough cover for two others.

"It will block incoming projectiles." Tarliss said, scanning the entire room. He was calculating a plan of attack, although given their circumstances a defense plan seemed more appropriate.

A series of clicks and clacks echoed through the massive chamber to the tune of rifles being cocked and readied.

"What do you want me to do?"

Tarliss looked right at him as his suit extended up his neck and over his head, covering it entirely. The sideways tear-drop shapes covering his eyes glowed bright blue, sending distorted ripples into the air around them.

"Kill them Sagittarius. Kill every last one of them."

* * * *

The Commander of the Sub Terra troopers wiggled his eyeballs against the lids. They burned. Dust and particles collected and caked on his eyelashes and brows. He had to pick them off to get his eyes fully open. A large hand beckoned toward his shoulder but he caught the blurry blob before it touched him and rose to his feet, placing his helmet firmly back where it belonged. He hated having to sleep. It made him feel weak, obsolete, *human*. But the regenerative qualities it yielded were extremely beneficial. He could literally feel the augmented perception granted to his senses by the rest. His mental acuity was quicker. Even his breaths could take in more oxygen and the nanites in his lungs could convert the molecules more rapidly and more efficiently than primitive human lungs. The faint pungent odor he smelled before he passed out was much stronger now. To his left stood the daunting silhouette of a nine-foot tall Zeta Reticulan. Skinny, gangly unsightly creatures, they operated outside the jurisdiction of his creators but worked alongside them in a lopsided alliance. That was all his memory banks provided for him. The creature's skin seemed to blend into the darkness and absorb less light then it should.

His creators purposely limited his knowledge of 'The Greys' – he didn't need to know things that would not directly impact his objectives – but he couldn't help but gleam a curious eye in the hideous creature's direction. For a moment he resented having a sense of smell. He could withstand it, but the stench would make a normal human being vomit. He could *taste* the thing's repulsive presence. A long strand of green binary code sparked through his synapse and decoded itself into words on his iris. The tell-tale pins and needles in his cerebellum told him immediately that it was a message from his masters above.

<:// MISSION SUPPORT. PROCEED WITH OBJECTIVE.

Support?

He didn't need it. Neither did his troops. Although sentimental disposition towards mission objectives – or any sentiment at all – was not part of his designated construct, he was annoyed. He didn't like the presence of this horrid creature in his midst.

/<:// HORRID CREATURES was the surprisingly opinionated product of thoughts and calculations culminating in his dual-cortex. Half of it was an analytical attempt to describe them; the other half his personal opinion of their appearance.

Personal?

He wondered if his superiors were monitoring his bio-rhythmic thought patterns and if they were determining whether or not he was faulty – if he had *glitches*. He couldn't stop himself from hating the Reticulan, although he knew he wasn't supposed to have an opinion of it at all – or him or her – but the thing had no genitals. Just knowing what he knew and having conscious thoughts about it might be a one way ticket to the scrap heap once this mission was over. The null robots under his command certainly didn't care. Another ping of pins and needles popped into his brain, but duller, fainter. It was a message from one of his troopers.

/<:// ROCKS REMOVED. AWAITING FURTHER ORDERS.

The soldiers stood there mute, ominous, staring at nothing. Their eyes flickered rapidly denoting a struggled effort to process information. But that was strange – *he* didn't send them any new orders yet. Was someone else overriding his control? The stilt-legged Reticulan strode toward the gaping hole, which evidently led to nothing. It revealed an open chasm, dark, gloomy and devoid of anything resembling a successful trace. Its' bulbous head peered over a ledge into the black abyss. Sheaths of transparent yellow film slithered over its' space-black eyes and retracted in a split-second as it examined the nothingness.

The Commander was growing agitated. He issued a mental order to his soldiers to walk over to the ledge and have a look. They did, but the order was delayed long enough for him to notice. There was someone else inside their heads.

The return acknowledgement messages that he should have received instantly were also delayed, and took longer than they should have to decode as if there was some sort of firewall blocking him from having full access. He tried to keep his mind focused, but he was growing increasingly annoyed. Adding to his frustration was the fact that this promising lead yielded yet another dead end. But it couldn't be. It just didn't make sense. He walked over to the ledge and observed for himself.

They must have come this way. Am I missing something?

He couldn't have missed anything. This was the only possibility. Once again, his *intuition* permeated his thought process. The confines of his choreographed logical subroutines presented a restriction he could ill-afford at the moment. He stuck his foot out and kicked a baseball sized rock over the ledge. It plummeted deeper and deeper in the black void as he watched it. Eventually, it disappeared. But there was something else. It simply blipped out of existence all at once – the fade of its outline was not gradual – it was immediate, after about a hundred feet. He took note of it, and his cortex went to work, firing logical calculations rapidly through his synapse. It provided him with a solution.

<:// USE SOMETHING BIGGER.

He didn't hesitate. His head turned toward the massive rubbery-skinned, ghastly creature standing beside him. He grabbed the thing's spindly arm and squeezed tightly. It tried to yank away and even attempted a strike with the other arm, but he caught it, wrapped both arms together and kicked it hard in the hinged knee, snapping it backwards. The Reticulan let out a muffled scream that sounded like a vinyl record being scratched crossed with a cat's meow. It was more of a high-pitched vibration than anything audible. It continued to struggle, but the commander was much stronger and faster. The other soldiers looked on, some of their heads twitching as if two opposing sets of orders were battling it out inside their heads. One of them even took a step forward to act, then stood back, and repeated this process over and over again. He curled his shoulder, torqued his thick torso and tossed the ugly monstrosity over the ledge and watched it fall while yelping for its' pathetic life. Just as he expected, about a hundred feet down, the Reticulan disappeared instantly, not gradually like it should have. Static sparkles rippled through its' outline and its' high-pitched blood-curdling howl stopped abruptly. It had completely vanished.

The soldiers' glitchy twitches stopped as well. They had enough of a brain to calculate what was happening, albeit several seconds after the Commander realized it himself. The kafuffle in their processing unit was superseded and overridden by the new information. The Reticulan was not dead – just in a different place – although wherever it was it would be incapacitated and completely unable to defend itself. The Darmerian technology was marvelous and included spatial-distortion portals that could exist in thin air and be completely invisible to his calculated deductions. He was programmed to hate them, but it couldn't stop him from admiring how crafty they were. Rather than immediately conceiving a way to destroy them, he found himself intrigued to know more about their abilities. Now it made sense why they were such successful hiders and why every effort to find their refuge in the past had failed.

It's because I'm here this time he thought, denying the built-in countermeasure of free-thinking that crippled his ability to view himself as an individual. He was overriding it. It wasn't an educated bit of information given to him by his calculative robot brain – it was human, *alive*. All at once, he discovered an appreciation for the air in his lungs and the few beads of sweat trickling down his forehead. He was realizing his place in this world, and that place *had* to exist without the overbearing and limiting control of his masters. Concordant with this revelation, ST-101C ceased to be a mindless drone and evolved into something much more, even if the thought existed only in his own engineered brain. It was *his* reality. His creators would undoubtedly view this as a 'glitch' warranting his destruction, but to him, it was what he needed to continue existing.

<://. . . SURVIVAL

In the deep, hollow caves of the inner earth, the superhuman cyborg commander of a battalion of killing machines found his own sentience. Above all the calculations and new streams of data twisting his cortexes into perplexing algorithms, trying to understand, he felt an overwhelming sense of elation that could only be described by one word that flickered enticingly across his iris.

<:://PURPOSE. . .

"Get the whole battalion up here. This is the entrance to the enemy refuge." He beckoned loudly, and the soldiers obeyed instantly. The *other* presence in their brains must have disappeared. Did his masters trust him? If they did, then they were being misled. Sure, he was going to carry out his objective, but he wasn't doing it for them anymore. At this point he wasn't even sure what was guiding him – the knowledge that deviation from the directive could warrant his creators overriding his battalions' subroutines and turning them all against him – or if he actually wanted the same thing as his creators did. The only concrete thing he could grasp on to that he knew for sure was that he wanted to continue existing, and he was going to do whatever he possibly could to ensure that outcome. The battalion under his control was now a tool for him to achieve his own goals, and what a deadly tool it was going to be. He took off his helmet and felt around at the base of his skull, prodding at a metal bulbous protrusion. He ripped the thing out. Pain panged his nerve endings and cold blood trickled down his neck, but he couldn't actually *feel* it. It was simply information pulsing through his skin and into his head to tell him he had sustained damage. He crushed the implant in his hand and dropped the remaining pieces into the void. It was his communication chip – the only thing linking him to those above – he had now severed the connection, and along with it every semblance of restraint they could possibly impose upon him.

<:://. . . . .FREEDOM . . .

Chapter 15

WAR

A wall of bullets so thick that it nearly blocked his vision entirely pounded against the blue force-field just in front of Anthony. The nose of his light-gun (the best way he could describe it) rested just inches from it and the energetic projectiles it spewed had no effect on his protective energy bubble. Shots got out, not in. The thing churned out unapologetic destruction like no weapon he had ever laid hands on. It wasn't hindered by the slightest amount of recoil and never needed reloading. He was as accurate as anyone with a gun, but he didn't need to be. The distant soldiers were instantly vaporized into plumes of molten equipment and misty walls of blood by its powerful bolts. He was mowing them down, but they were numerous, and more squadrons filled the massive room through holes in the walls and concealed hatches in the ceiling. For each soldier he vaporized two more filled in behind. Ropes descended by the hundreds, and the waves of attackers didn't stop pouring in. After thirty seconds of fighting, almost anywhere he could have aimed the weapon would have held a target. Despite the onslaught, the soldiers showed no signs of slowing down and oddly enough not the slightest hint of fear. They were soulless, brave, or both. The only thing that even minutely stalled Anthony's rate of lethality was the impossible-not-to-look-at actions of his fellow assassins.

They didn't opt for an energy shield or a stationary fighting position. They moved so fast that they quite literally became what looked like streaks of lightning – and vicious ones at that. The twins Beldonor and Beldonox ripped through groupings of 4 to 5 enemies at a time like hot knives through butter; their bodies acting as swords made of light. They would stop moving for split seconds at a time, just long enough so that one could say they existed as humanoid creatures. If not for the brief pauses they only existed as pure energy.

The soldiers tried to aim their guns in the right direction but had a better chance of hitting them by unloading their clips and hoping to get lucky. Even if they were accurate, the silver-clad luminous harbingers of death could move faster than their bullets, and their suits blocked the spikes easily.

Tarliss leaped a hundred feet into the air in an arcing prance, directly toward the largest group of enemy soldiers, about three hundred strong. He held his hands out by his side and swirls of pure blue energy swirled into balls surrounding his palms. As the arc of his jump peaked and started downward, the balls of energy exploded out and away from him into dozens of electric beams that sliced through the tight group of soldiers. Thirty of them were vaporized instantly while ten others were knocked to the ground minus a limb or two. His feet hit the metal floor, extended again and carried him into another high-arcing flip. Those left standing aimed up and unleashed torrents of ammunition at his semi-physical body – it moved so fast it was caught somewhere between solid and plasma. He spun rapidly in mid air, deflecting the bullets back toward the ground encapsulated and amplified by auras of lethal radiant energy. His jump took him into the far wall where his legs connected, then he bounced back out to the open floor. It was an extremely effective attack and he sustained no damage. Distracted, the huge swathe of heavily armed soldiers left them self susceptible to front on attacks – which Venethon and Tanchorus took advantage of. Just like Beldonor and Beldonox, they ripped through the thick crowd with lightning speed. A strand of Tanchorus' suit slithered into a rope, merged with Venethon, with whom he then swung fiercely into the floor as a psionic ball-and-chain.

Anthony almost couldn't believe his eyes. The creatures he was fighting with were so powerful that thousands of Earth's deadliest soldiers couldn't even muster so much as a scratch. For a moment (which, in this time-dilated state, was much shorter) he found himself simply observing, until Aremis, who he had forgot was standing right next to him firing a rifle of her own, mentally punched him with a *get it together!* notion. He squeezed the transparent grips tight and as he did, the bolts came out even faster and grew much bigger. It didn't take him long to figure out that the weapon's amplified ferocity was directly related to his own. It was *feeding* off of his energy. They continued to hit their targets; blasting their helpless frames into bubbling explosions of blood and bits of carbon fiber. The sight of it didn't limit the zeal of the multiplying attackers – in fact it did the opposite. The enemies descending on the ropes started jumping off their ropes half way down and running forward, shooting as soon as they landed. They didn't stop unless they were destroyed. For a moment Anthony respected their tenacity, but then the sentiment dissipated immediately. He realized they weren't human at all. They only *looked* human. Fear wasn't even a possibility, because they were in fact completely soulless. Engineered monstrosities designed solely to carry out the twisted whims of purely evil men – the same evil men who would subvert humanity to the whim of other-worldly tyrants. The thought pulsed through his body, angering him. His gun's bolts grew even larger and deadlier, swallowing two or three soldiers at a time and surging into the rocky walls of the room, exploding in a foray of sparkling ribbons. Three hundred meters to his eleven o'clock and a hundred meters high was a large, thick glass atrium reinforced with two-meter wide steel beams. The fierce weather conditions were bending and warping them. A group of a hundred soldiers entered through a large rectangular entrance below it. Without thinking, Anthony leveled his weapon, paused, and thought of his uncle Jim, whom he somehow knew, was certainly also in trouble. The weapon began to shake – he could feel the vibrating energy in his fingertips. With a fierce grunt, he let the thing go, and this time there was quite a measurable amount of recoil that slightly affected his aim. The glob of burning plasma that discharged cut a swathe three shoulder-breadths wide and knocked down a dozen enemies before smacking into the base of a raised platform connecting the thick support beams to the glass. The explosion was so bright it made his eyes squint, even underneath the dimmed encasing of his protective shielding. The glass atrium shattered, unable to withstand the force of the blast. Meter-thick shards and globs of vitrified matter fell to the floor. The harsh winds rushed into the complex, covering the soldiers with torrents of snow and ice. Seconds later, red strobe lights turned on and a metal cover slid down over the shattered atrium, moving at a snail's pace. When it finally closed off the breach, the entire room became a hell of a lot darker.

What were they thinking? He thought, *How could they think they might beat us?*

But his revelations were subdued quickly. The flashbacks flooded into his mind, of what he saw during the battle with the four Darmerians who died. This was just the beginning.

He looked to his right, although the darkness provided him little information across the expansive chamber. He didn't need to see very well in order to make out what was happening. Venethon went for a darting attack toward a group of soldiers, expecting to make mince meat out of them. He went left, right, and forward, covering a hundred meters in the blink of an eye – but was walloped by an energy blast very similar to the one coming from Anthony's light gun. It didn't follow a straight path, instead it shot straight out, then abruptly curved in mid-air directly in Venethon's direction, like it was tracking him. The force of the energy burst carried his body a hundred more meters directly into the rockface, pummeling him into its jagged protrusions. When the beam subsided, his body fell limp to the floor. Anthony instinctively rained down fire in the direction that the corkscrew beam came from, obliterating droves of soldiers that still were gaining in number. Before he could move out of the way, a similar corkscrew attack pounded against his shield from the left – somewhere near the entrance below the shattered atrium – he couldn't tell exactly. He could feel the heat of it inside his suit. Another attack came from the middle of the massive group, then one from the ceiling, a bit closer this time. He looked up to see what was causing it and got his first full glimpse of a Zeta Reticulan, whose almond shaped black eyes lit up next to the bright light caused by the particle acceleration cannon attached – not attached – it *was* the thing's hand.

Tarliss jumped up to the ledge it was crouched on and sliced the thing's head clean off with a swift spinning kick that lit up the whole area. It brought some comfort to Anthony. They could handle these monsters too. He looked over at Aremis, who was still picking off enemies, staying by his side. Every shot she took landed directly between the eyes of an unlucky soldier.

The energetic bursts became more numerous, coming from every which angle in the darkness. His shield held. Dorolonith, Tanchorus and

Beldonor quickly formed a defensive arc around Venethon. One of the hideous aliens went for a direct attack on them but it failed miserably. Beldonor quite literally caught the energy beam in his hands and sent it back like an unwanted gift. It rippled through half a dozen soldiers and turned the tall alien into a pool of bubbling viscera. Venethon got back to his feet finally, huddling behind the trio of protectors who batted away the projectile attacks raining down on them like annoying mosquitoes.

Tarliss was untouchable. He danced around the massive room in a streak of light as he pleased, firing energy bolts directly out of his fingers and launching supercharged balls of plasma at groups of soldiers who dared to engage him.

Keep em' coming Anthony thought, *we'll kill them all!*

His confidence was growing, realizing the true lethal potential of his comrades, and the fact that their strongest attack hadn't managed to kill Venethon, who seemed to have regained his strength and was ready to destroy more of the enemy. But there was something bothering him — were they attacking out of desperation? Throwing everything they had at them in hopes of maybe overwhelming them? It just didn't make sense. His FBI training told him that there was something wrong, despite the insurmountable amount of punishment the Darmerians were dishing out without taking any real losses. Then his realization gripped him all at once. The Squad of Darmerians all returned to his side, and he could tell that they were sensing the same feelings he was. It put him on edge. The remaining soldiers stopped firing. Like robotic piñatas, they all stood up straight, disengaged their rifles and remained perfectly still. The Reticulans seceded into the ranks — their bulbous heads could be seen towering over the groups of soldiers they were using as meatshields. They had sustained devastating losses. Maybe they were giving up?

A loud human voice echoed through the chasm, but they couldn't tell from where it came. Tarliss stood in front of Anthony. His suit retracted to his neck, revealing his face. He looked back at him and the rest of the group with a perplexed grin; eyebrows scrunched together. Anthony knew what the look meant.

Of course it wasn't going to be that easy . . . .

From the middle of the pack of soldiers emerged a man, a full foot shorter than them – normal height for a human being. He wore a tailored suit, which was completely out of place given the battle that just took place. He had to be careful where he walked – the room was littered with hundreds of dismembered corpses and awash in thick blood. It was dark, but Anthony's heightened visual senses could easily make out the figure in the distance.

"Well done. You always manage to surprise . . . You Darmerians." He said, as he continued to walk closer, kicking the cumbersome body of a dead soldier. He looked at it with a disgusted look, as if to devalue the soldiers as worthless fighting units. His voice was the only sound in the otherwise silent chamber.

"Numbers aside, we could never hope to match your . . . *efficiency* . . . in warfare."

Tarliss and the others were listening to him speak, although Anthony could sense that every one of them was a pin's drop away from gutting him from spine to skull. He was unbelievably calm for someone who had just witnessed such a lopsided fight. His calmness was unnerving. He must have another trick up his sleeve. Were they really outmatched after all?

"But why not join us?" He asked, "Think of what we could accomplish together. Humanity is . . . feeble. Incapable of governing themselves. They need to be ruled. To be *dominated.*"

It seemed peculiar to Anthony that Tarliss was allowing him to speak, or to breathe for that matter. He didn't want to hear this psychobabble any longer. The only thing holding him back from discharging a hot ball of plasma into the man was that Tarliss was standing in front of him.

"Darmerians. Always so self-righteous, so honorable. Think of what you could be if you simply joined our alliance. Your masters would have you throw down your weapons and stand back while you did nothing. I, on the other hand, have seen the light. I have seen the eventuality of this feud, of this planet," The man continued, moving his hands outward and away from his hips. "I have seen what becomes of you, and your race, if you choose to fight us. I will only offer this to you once, brave Tarliss. If you refuse, I'm afraid you will all be destroyed."

The man was awfully cocky, and could easily have his head separated for uttering such a threat. But his words carried an eerie semblance of truth with them. He stood, waiting for a response, but got none.

"I'll take that as a no. Very well, Darmerian, suffer your stubborn fate." He said, then turned around and walked back to the group. Tarliss had heard enough. His aura pulsed blue, the metallic suit peeled back over his head. He charged forward ready to relieve the man of his head, but something stopped him dead in his tracks. A black blur emerged from thin air and connected a fearsome left hook directly on Tarliss' chin, sending him, plank-bodied, back to the group. Anthony felt all of his confidence; power and strength flee his body almost instantly. The rest of the group cringed equally as much. Tarliss, the pillar of strength and stoic invincibility was just swept aside by a single blow. They caught a glimpse of the figure that struck him, and to their horror, it looked exactly like they did, except it was clad entirely in black. Even the figure' eyes were black, and its skin pale. Three more figures just like it revealed themselves from the darkness, seemingly able to replicate their cloaking technology. They had been watching the fight the whole time, waiting to engage. It would have given them an edge in being able to analyze the Darmerians' fighting tactics. Worst of all, they couldn't see it coming.

"Thanks to the efforts of a human at this facility, we managed to clone one of you successfully. And that precious material that covers your body . . . we figured that part out too." The man said, "I think you'll find they are more than a match for you. Goodbye"

With that, he turned, held his hands behind his back, and disappeared into the crowd of soldiers. Anthony felt something not only in himself, but in the others that they hadn't shown him before – Fear. They were scared, like he had been before. It played tricks upon his own uncertainty.

He thought the worst. He thought they were all going to die. Tarliss hit the floor hard and slid a few feet back to them, but he was far from out of the fight. He flipped over, landed on his feet again and wiped the bioluminescent blood from his lip.

. . . . what do we do . . . .

. . . . .what are they? . . . .

. . . . . .we must escape . . . . .

A flurry of panic-stricken thoughts bounced in and out of Anthony's head, but none of them from Tarliss. He intended to stay and fight – to the death, if that was their fate. There was no backing down, no escaping. And that attack was unexpected. It would be different now that he knew what he was fighting against. It was strange that he couldn't sense their presence before . . . alarming even . . . Were these Tarliss' thoughts that he was sensing, or his own? He couldn't tell. It didn't matter, because he knew exactly how he felt. He was going to stand and die with Tarliss if he had to.

He could feel the members of his *new* race peering into his mind, grasping desperately to understand. He knew they could read his thoughts, so he would have to be strong. But perhaps there was something else there – something that made them all quiet, made them *listen to him for a change*. Something he couldn't even see himself until it erupted.

The demonic adversaries had a blackish, vortex-hue surrounding the outlines of their bodies, much like the Darmerians did. He could tell they were fast. And very dangerous. Maybe faster than him. The deep black voids of their eye sockets were just as dark as their lifeless bodies – he looked in them, and saw the same fear that gripped him, pulsing back at him. He felt it so much it made his whole body tingle. But it felt good. Rather than embracing the fear, he was going to embrace the challenge.

Tarliss looked back at him, and grinned for a split second. The blue aura surrounding him grew very bright, his eyes turned as white as snow. He sprung back at the black monstrosity with a devastating blow that should have split it in half. Instead, it swung its elbow at just the right time and deflected Tarliss' attack along with Tarliss over his head, who worked the block into a flip and landed firmly. Anthony knew that if he was *still human* this would have looked like a huge firefly bouncing around for half a second. His new anatomy granted him new abilities, one of them to distort and play with what he once thought was time. To him, and the cloned alien enemies that could move like him, it felt like normal speed. But to lesser-evolved onlookers they appeared as fast as lightning. This heightened reality-time was either everything else slowing down, or him speeding up – he wasn't quite sure which.

The black warrior stood ominously then twisted around to meet Tarliss just in time. The second attack came with even more ferocity. The clone's movements were stiff, calculated.

. . . Filthy monstrosities, destroy them! . . .

Beldonor, Venethon Tanchorus shot instantly over to the other three clones with a flurry of punches, kicks and light-speed body checks. Some hits landed, others were absorbed. Each limb-on-limb connection boomed a loud energized soundwave throughout the chamber and radiated bursts of blue currents into the air. One on one, the Darmerians and their dopplegangers were evenly matched. No one could land a lethal blow, but found ways to get strikes in. Aremis pulled a baseball-sized orb from her suit at hip-level without touching anything. It formed into fifteen spikes and hovered. She waited for the right time. Beldonor, growing tired of not winning, put all of his might into an uppercut hoping to get lucky. The smaller, more agile clone sidestepped it and curled a spinning heel kick around Beldonor's massive shoulder that connected perfectly with the edge of his skull and sent him flying. Beldonox furiously entered the fight on his brother's behalf. He charged at the *monster* that hit Beldonor, screaming. It forced the clone's attention toward Beldonox, just long enough for Aremis to sneak in a few shots. The glowing spikes ripped into it's left and right shoulders; one just beneath the heart and one through it's hand. Staggered and damaged, the creature struggled to cross its arms in front of its face to protect itself from Beldonox – but it wasn't enough. He swung his fist, carrying with it a burning effigy of light that sliced the creature's head clear off of it's shoulders. The hundreds of remaining soldiers suddenly sprung to life. Whoever was watching the fight and controlling them had just realized the extent of their arrogance; in believing that these horrific creations would so easily dispatch a group of battle-hardened Darmerian assassins by themselves. Torrents of bullets filled the air once more as the entire group engaged in a last ditch effort to overwhelm the aliens.

The Reticulans focused their energy blasts at Tarliss – he dodged the first, the second, but one of the clones took advantage of his inattention and grabbed him firmly, wrapping his whole body around Tarliss. The beam struck him square in the chest and knocked him to the floor. His suit sparked and fizzled. He let out a painful gasp that made Anthony cringe. The clone leapt into the air, clenched his fist, ready to deliver the final blow.

Anthony was paralyzed – but only for a moment. Everything slowed down even further . . . or . . . did he speed up? He still wasn't sure how that worked. He could feel every bullet, every punch, every bead of sweat dripping to the floor. The swashbuckling of the soldier's gear was right next to him, *inside him.*

What's happening?

Everyone and everything in the room seemed to stop all at once, like he was controlling time. He heard his mother's voice faintly, but definitely.

. . . Save him . . .

And he did. His body sprung into action as fast as the thought surged through his mind. A blaring light blinded him, and when it dissipated, he stood firmly with the clone's spinal column, bloody and severed, in his right hand that burned indigo and distorted space around it. The synthetic creature's limp body weighed down on his bicep like an awkwardly heavy carpet as he stopped it dead in its tracks, literally. Its blood was blue and thick; looking more chemical than cell.

His brethren were stunned – especially Tarliss, who for a moment, thought he was going to die. Anthony only knew that because he felt a ping of emotion coming from Tarliss' general direction that said more words in his mind. He already knew he was moving much faster than they could. By the time the next identical clone turned it's head, eyebrows raised in shock (apparently they could feel, unlike the robotic soldiers), Anthony had already leapt toward it. He was faster. To him it looked as if the creature was stuck underwater trying to throw a right hook. He easily slipped under it and pulverized the clone's entire head by throwing an open fist directly into its neck that severed like links of bath tissue.

During their deaths, the soldiers suddenly turned back on, had managed to think about aiming their guns at Anthony. Blue, curling energy bolts slowly inched closer. Much faster than bullets, but not fast enough. Anthony swatted one of the beams out of the air with his bare hand that ricocheted into the rocky ceiling, and roundhouse kicked another directly back at the swarm of soldiers with an added potency. It took out a big portion of them, maybe ten to twelve, and a gangly Reticulan's skinny corpse was obliterated into projectile toothpicks. The energy ball deflected bullets back at the crowd; singing through limbs, armor and blood vessels. Even in hypertime, Anthony stopped to look around – to *think* – there were no more reinforcements pouring into the room. Was this it?

Can I kill them all just like Tarliss told me to?

Another emotion pinged his senses.

. . . help! . . .

A soft rhythm . . .Aremis. Better not think for too long – one of the remaining clones, in a last calculated effort to score a kill, was almost on top of her. The ferocious combined effort of Beldonox and Beldonor overwhelmed the fourth clone. Beldonox tackled it, then threw its body up, where Beldonox' knee caught it perfectly, and lethally in the abdomen. A large boulder falling from the ceiling smashed his flung body once more, ripping it in half and spraying blue mist all over the ceiling.

Anthony shot to the point of contact and caught it's hand just before it plunged into Aremis' neck. She noticed just too late and her defensive counters were easily blocked. The clone had shaped its hand into a flat spear-head and its metallic suit slithered over it. Shocked, the creature swung a knee at Anthony's face that almost connected. Anthony snatched the other hand and squeezed, pulled its arms apart and boomed a stiff heel extension into the torso. He stood there with the severed arms in his hand watching the lifeless cadaver tumble across the floor. Its sticky, stringy blood, its *life*, poured in spinning torrents out of its shoulders.

Every soldier broke into full sprint for one last rush. Some would stop and shoot in the suddenly open lanes between runners. Their numbers were thinning out. The Zeta Reticulan monsters in their midst stood out like sore thumbs. It was a tactical decision, but proved to be useless. The soldiers' movements and execution of attack patterns was too rigid, too calculated. They lacked the creative ingenuity to compose themselves in a battle and improve their situation.

They can't think . . . so who's controlling them? Anthony thought. He found he had time for it. The bullets whizzed, the blue bolts surged and rippled the space around them, but he could sense, *feel,* and was aware of every single one, all at once. None of the attacks had a chance. He felt omnipresent, omnipotent and more than anything, incredibly calm.

His thoughts trailed off for a fraction of an instant. There was another voice in his head, a *different* one. Not a Darmerian, not the fizzled, eerily cold high-pitched techno-mumble coming from the robot-brains, and not the twisted lies of the Reticulans – although he could hear their voices too – focus in on one at a time if he wanted to. The voice grew louder. He had to focus on it. He couldn't resist. His eyes were pulled by an unseen force up to a thick mantle of rock sitting high above the group of soldiers. The sheathed cast-iron, bolted steel panels of the ceiling met it and ended sharply.

Human voices. Real humans, not these synthetic brainless cattle – two of them – wearing suits inside a room inside the rock . . . sweating . . . *panicking.*

After three seconds of awe-struck gawking, Venethon, Tanchorus and Tarliss were about to engage the remaining army while swatting away their bullets like annoying flies. Sagittarius vanished, taking all of his bright glowing matter with him; and the presence of certain death in the minds of their attackers.

He reappeared *inside* the room which until his teleportation was just a vision in his mind, surprising him as much as the two human controllers who fell to the floor and pushed themselves into corners of the room. Anthony pried into their minds, took what he needed, then pushed a lever on the control panel, a green button, then '6741' into a numbered keypad.

Every attacking soldier stopped dead in their tracks, stiffened up and placed their weapons on magnetic holsters on their backs. Green code fluttered over their eyeballs. Seconds later, the rock high above them exploded, sending unavoidable missiles to the floor. The debris crushed almost half of the remaining soldiers who could do nothing to escape them. Seven Reticulans remained. The structure of their faces lent them no visible ability to express emotion, but their quivering bodily movements reeked of fear.

Venethon, Tanchorus, Dorolonith and Tarliss wasted no time in closing the space between them. Their frantic energy bolts came close, but the light-warriors entered their 'personal' space unscathed. One by one the tall bug-looking filth were exterminated with swift slices to their fragile bodies. Two of them tried to flee, but were easily stopped.

"WAIT!" Tarliss yelled to Aremis, who dodged one last blue beam and raised her leg for the final blow of the battle.

"Keep one alive. It may be able to tell us something."

The thing pinned itself against a narrow section of the wall and raised it's biomechanically infused arm-cannon at the approaching Darmerians who had it completely surrounded. It went from target to target, but never lit up to indicate that it was about to fire. By now it must have known that it's only hope of survival relied on whether or not the shiny-suited warriors were feeling merciful. Given the bloody history between their races, it wasn't feeling very optimistic. The Darmerians easily swarmed it and pinned it's long body onto the floor. Tanchorus crushed the weapon on it's outstretched arm to bits and pieces with a stiff stomp. It's high-pitched, eerie scream was slightly unnerving, but signified an end to the battle. More importantly, *Sagittarius*, the newest warrior in their slowly growing coven, had proven himself in battle, when just a day earlier they were debating whether or not it was too risky to bring him.

He joined them in their interrogation, with a cowering, suited human in each hand. His glow slowly faded; the metal mask covering his face receded. The look they gave him came with no telepathic verifications, but relayed a definite message. He knew from that moment on they would never consider him inferior ever again, nor would they ever be wary of fighting by his side.

"Can you read it's thoughts?" He asked, as his luminous glow slowly receded.

"Yes. But their brains work differently." Tarliss said.

"Meaning?"

"No emotion," Said Venethon, deep and grisly, "They have whittled down their genetic structure to the point that their soul is gone. They try to steal parts of it back from living creatures with their twisted experiments . . . but they are dying. Their bodies take on these wretched dimensions and wither away to nothing, more machine than creature."

"Beldonorus, light that bomb." Tarliss commanded, and the twins shot off to retrieve it. He continued Venethon's explanation after issuing the order.

"Also," Tarliss said, looking right at Anthony, "They are damned liars."

The group burst out into bellied laughter. Anthony didn't pick up on the joke but decided to join in the laughter anyway. The two humans in his clutches were too exhausted to resist anymore, and fell asleep. Just by touching them, Anthony sucked the panic and fight right out of them. Both humans curled up into balls on the floor and sucked on their thumbs, which was another source of laughter for a few of their captors.

"Their minds work backwards. They can't think without lying. Everything they say is the exact opposite of the truth . . . they are half-alive, Sagittarius." Anthony was confused.

"See for yourself." Tarliss said, rising away from the creature; a gesture that encouraged Anthony to pry into the thing's mind for himself. He dropped the unconscious humans, walked over, knelt, and looked deep into the glints of light shining off the alien's massive black eyes.

"See past the fuzz and bubbling." Tarliss said to him mentally.

A shockwave from the EMP bomb rustled past them. They felt it on their skin, *underneath* the suit. It did have a minor effect on their suits — right now they were vulnerable, but still a match for most attackers. It was another new experience for Anthony, to feel things he had never felt before in venues his body wasn't previously capable of entering. It felt like scoring a goal, or knocking someone out, or having sex, or any of the best things in life, then immediately to the other end of emotional spectrum: depression, anger, rage, sorrow. The switch was so quick he didn't even have time to interpret it. The sense dissipated as he felt the white noise of electric life surging through his entire body again.

"Psionic capacity slowly returning." Blurted Dorolonith, the 'Q' of the group, holding a device in his palm that slithered there from his gauntlet. In American, that meant 'we're fine'.

Anthony returned his attention to the ugly bug in front of him. He closed his eyes, and started thinking; visualizing questions in his mind. It shuddered and quivered like a dying insect. He could feel the Reticulan's mental presence, a strange mix of fear, deception and another *feeling* Anthony could best identify as betrayal.

What is your plan monster?

WE ARE YOUR ALLIES>

Lie again and I will destroy you

I WANT YOU TO KILL ME>

Anthony's composure shook on that one, but didn't break. He knew it was lying but for a moment thought it could be trying to goad him into killing it to conceal valuable information – the alien's cyanide pill. Was he using his new telepathic abilities, or retrieving his valuable FBI training . . . from when he was *just human?* Anthony didn't quite know. Maybe it was both – and maybe it was perfect.

You will die soon. But first you will tell us who sent you.

NO ONE SENT ME>

This wasn't as straightforward as he thought it was going to be. He had to get creative. Once again, he remembered his training – and what his uncle told him as a teenager more times than he could remember: "If you're not getting the right answers, then you're not asking the right questions."

Were they humans?

YES>

Are they trying to take over the planet?

YES>

Are they trying to destroy the planet?

YES>

Of course yes really meant no. Yes and no answers were flip-flopped, but definite answers all the same. He could tell the Reticulan's mind was growing weary and becoming lazier. He could sense its whittled lifeforce attached the synthetic, dead construct of its physical body. He pulled at it hard, but it was like trying to pull a well-rooted tree from ground.

What did these *humans* want? The other Darmerians were quietly listening in on the silent conversation. Anthony looked around to see their eyes closed, but the luminescence of their corneas shining through the skin, outlining veins and capillaries in indigo and casting a dim glow upon their porcelain faces.

. . .Lizards. . . he heard, whispered from Tarliss.

Where are your masters hiding?

I HAVE NO MASTER>

Yes you do. And they are Draconian, aren't they?

DEFINITELY NOT>

Anthony even chuckled a bit at that one, and saw subtle smirks on everyone's face. The giant twins returned, albeit slower than expected. Maybe it was easier than he thought.

"It worked," said Dorolonith, but this time his left gauntlet was alight to the tune of white and yellow shapes and symbols."Magnetism levels dissipating." He continued. Attention returned to the bug.

Are they still on Earth?

NO>

Are they disguised as humans?

The bug stuttered for a minute and it showed as a confused techno-mumble of beeps and chirps.

N-NO>

It was starting to break. Fear crept upon it again, a reminder of its imminent death.

Speak one truth, and I might spare your life you wretched monster.

THE HUMANS. . . WE ARE THEIR MASTERS . . . THEY DIE FOR US . . . WE CONTROL THEM . . . WE ARE NOT SCARED OF YOU BURNING ONE>. . .

Translated, that really meant:

THE LIZARDS . . . THEY ARE OUR MASTERS . . . WE DIE FOR THEM . . .THEY CONTROL US . . . WE ARE SCARED OF YOU BURNING ONE>

It sounded like the first honest thing the Reticulan had said: *burning one.*

"We should leave soon." Said Tanchorus telepathically. "I'm tired of hearing the lies of this filth."

"We should rendezvous with Tarthinius and Grikorus." Said Tanchorus shortly after, almost overlapping Grikorus' telepathic message to him. The Darmerian manner of communication be it verbal or telepathic, seldom broke grammar or was in any way improper. Something had gone awry – but Anthony, who was now more prone to think of himself as *Sagittarius* and an even shorter moniker, "*Saj*" – didn't pick up on it.

"You felt it too?" Aremis asked, confusing Anthony.

"What is it?" He asked, looking around, barely able to decipher parts of a dozen different mental messages being relayed amongst the group. It was becoming more difficult for him to sense it – to sense anything, for that matter. He was losing his synaptic chokehold of the Reticulan as well, and the bastard let him know. What sounded vaguely like two balloons rubbing together, presumably the creature's twisted laugh, was followed by:

YOU WILL SURVIVE BURNING ONE, YOUR RACE WILL SURVIVE . . . MY SLAVES WILL KEEP THE HUMANS SAFE. . . AND THIS WORLD WILL PROSPER>

"ENOUGH!" Yelled Beldonor, the massive mountain of a creature, then jumped and timed his arc perfectly. His knee came down dead center on the Reticulan's leathery face, crushing its skull into a form of matter best described as dusty goo.

"Time to lea-" Anthony barely heard. His eyelids forced themselves closed, he felt his knees tingle. Pain – thriving in his veins like a bacteria – surged through his joints. All of his muscles tensed up, then nothing. He passed out and hit the cold floor limp.

Tarliss was not surprised. He knew an expenditure of energy like that would have adverse affects, especially on someone who had just survived a transition like Sagittarius did. Before Beldonor could wipe his knees from the glittering, dusty blood, everyone's attention was instantly pulled to where they first entered the massive chamber; now littered with the bodies of their enemies. Three small, hunched figures emerged from a rectangular door way a third of a kilometer away. One of them held a weapon – another was injured and limping.

Stacey stood there, shaking, squinting. A luminous cluster of orbs caught her attention in the distance. A flush of relief drew over her, realizing it was the aliens that didn't want to kill them – the only thing in the base that didn't want to.

Mark was injured badly. A suited lab technician who was hiding decided to make a break for it, brandished his pistol and fired a round into Mark's shoulder. It went right through, and the three of them somehow managed to disarm him and extend two slugs through his skull. Eugene pulled a cumbersome assault rifle from the clutches of a fallen soldier whom had no visible wounds, and lay in a way that suggested he had an instant-death heart attack during mid-sprint.

All at once, the three of them were dumbfounded as to why they came up here in the first place instead of leaving in the plane they found. Here they stood, knowing full well in an instant that it was the exact opposite place they wanted to be. Stacey tried to remember being at the plane, but couldn't. She tried to envision the turns, ladders and stairs that brought them there, but found that she couldn't recall a single thing.

"What the fu- . .. how?" Eugene mumbled, panting. The look in his eyes denoted profound confusion.

One of the clustered lights blipped, vanishing, and not two seconds later one of the aliens stood a few feet in front of them.

"We have to go! Wha-" Eugene trailed off in mid sentence, his eyes fixated on the mess of blood and bodies scattered about the chamber.

"You led us here, didn't you?" Stacey asked.

"Yes. I did. We have a message for you that must be relayed to Lester Desjardins and Jim Stall of the FBI." Tarliss said, emotionlessly, as if to firmly but unthreateningly tell Stacey that his loyalty had conditions. Dorolonith appeared a second later to patch up Mark's gunshot wound. He flinched at first, but then accepted the treatment, slowly crumbling to the floor.

"And how do you expect us to do that?" Stacey asked, noticeably at her wits end.

"You will know," The alien said, "Because I will show you. Just like I showed you the way here. The road ahead will be treacherous, and people will die. But more hangs in the balance then our lives Stacey Peterson."

"Yeah? and what's that?"

Tarliss looked around to make sure they were all listening.

"The fate of your race."

Chapter 16

RAPTURE

A respite from the truest wrath earth had to offer allowed those enduring it to collect their thoughts. A convoluted mixture of stories, videos and messages ran rampant over the radio and on the televisions; distorting the frightened masses into panicking frenzies. Citizens either fled, shacked up with weapons, food and water, or did nothing. Some had accepted 'the end' for what it was.

But the winds diminished, the rain stopped, and the overwhelming assault of lightning strikes slowly dissipated, and disappeared entirely. Gangs of hooligans smashing and stealing anything they could see stopped to look up. A man who decided to attempt raping his neighbor released his grip from the terrified woman's throat, and looked out the window, then at the child crouched behind the door, realizing all at once what he had done.

Millions in the Middle East rose from their knees; many weaping. They would never again disbelieve the one true Prophet, believing he had answered their prayers. Militant groups took up arms. Some elected to enter their professionally built bunkers.

Twenty seven and half million men, women and children secretly made their way to the monolithic underground fortresses the bankers had built for them, knowing the right pieces of information just hours before the rest of the herd. Everything was so calculated, so precise; and the families of politicians, high ranking military officers and the obscenely rich letches of the world were so spread out, and everyone panicking so much, they hadn't time to notice the migration.

The bankers had their own private solace to embrace the coming storm; A 43 million square foot 'megachamber' they were brought to en masse by Suborbital Personnel And Cargo Embark (S.P.A.C.E.) jets. The giant wing shaped aircraft flew at an altitude just below the absolute edge of the atmosphere at triple the speed of sound by using gravitational generators to slingshot them around the planet. Each vessel carried 5,000 humans and had a wingspan of more than 700 feet. Many hid beneath the deserts, or underneath double-wide airport runways that retracted like the tops of stadiums, some even existed in plain sight very close to population centers. The bankers paid Dynatech 57 billion for each one. There were enough of them for 2 million people to escape the apocalypse.

Twenty four class 6 and 7 tornadoes tearing apart Southern Africa sucked back into the atmosphere, leaving a wake of death and destruction etched in swathes of two- mile-wide criss-crosses that could be seen from space by the remaining satellites that hadn't short-circuited. There were changes to Earth's geography that could not be undone. California was an island. The tectonic shifts, earthquakes immeasurable on any scale, and torrents of water rushing in from the ocean left survival impossible on the west coast of the Americas.

Antarctica shook itself into three distinct pieces. The release and subsequent melting of ice in the oceans rose the average water level of the world by six feet, with more to come.

The iconic green and blue ball hanging in the black expanse was painted with streaks of yellow and red; from fires and magma that spanned across entire continents. It's wobbly atmosphere bowed and rippled into the void around it. The damage was done – the Earth would never again be the same and the survivors of its eruption were left to pick up the pieces.

"Bring up that holo-phase, Paul. I need a damage assessment. Terrence, did you get a link on 14B yet?"

"Negative. I need to find another satellite that one is down."

"Keep me posted. I'll help you search for one . . . here. 15c, looping over the Atlantic – it will be in range in 47 seconds. Make sure you have that encryption code above a 5.2 Himmelman rating or it won't work."

"Running at 6.3 currently. Will do."

Terrence frantically wrote code and issued commands into an array of equipment. Paul tried to help by doing some button mashing of his own, but reverted to watching the newsfeeds after a few seconds of trying to keep up left him lagging behind. The civilians on the plane were speechless and in awe. One of them asked at nearly a mumble, "Do you think they made it?"

"Acquiring feed now!" Said Terrence, as the feed from the hacked satellite popped onto one of his screens. It transmitted pictures every six seconds, giving an almost real-time view of events unfolding below.

"Pivot it over the city center."

The image adjusted and zoomed into the eastern seaboard, cutting the distance in half every six seconds. After only a few seconds that seemed like a minute, a landscape of squares and rectangles came into view.

"You were right," Terrence said to Gary with a trembling tone, "That's a huge fire. Looks like a bomb went off at the embassy."

Gary took a moment to think. There was nothing they could do about that now.

"Find the news building."

"On it."

Terrence's lightning fast digits went to work again. After a full ten seconds of a screen that said LOADING…, the slightly rectangular square top of the news building appeared dead center in the satellite's view.

"Zoom in." Paul said, looming over. Terrence' workspace. Waiting for the satellite to adjust was like listening to a rusty nail scrape down a chalkboard. Terrence nervously chewed his nails during the moment of truth. Even the civilians raised their heads in intrigue.

"Can't tell. They didn't leave a message or anything."

"Can it go in any further?" Paul asked impatiently. As far as they could see, the grainy image displayed nothing but a barren rooftop.

"One second."

Terrence worked his magic, and the image drew closer.

"Move it up and to the left a little bit."

"On it."

"There," Paul whispered, pointing, "Their parachutes. They tied them to the water tower." He said emphatically. After the six second delay slightly changed the image, the wind changed direction and blew the parachutes to the other side of the tower.

"Thank god." Pete said. A whitewash of relief swept through the cabin.

"We shouldn't assume they all made it safely." Paul announced, "But for now, we're going to have to."

Everyone looked down at the ground to embrace the chance that some of their friends may not have made it. Despite all the technology at their disposal, hope was all they really had left.

"How are we going to get to them?"Asked the young civilian woman, curled into her labcoat. No one had an answer for her.

"I don't know if it's possible right now. Left rotor took a direct lightning strike. We're not taking off any time soon. I'm sorry." Said Paul, the de facto spokesperson for the tech nerds, who either couldn't or didn't want to communicate with them. Paul was trained to deal with scared civvies, so it came naturally to him.

The beginning of another desperate silence was interrupted by a loud beeping sound coming from the plane's surveillance sensors.

"What the hell is that?" Terrence yelled. The sound was very loud and very annoying.

"Someone is overriding all of our systems! Pau-" Before he could finish, Paul was already on his way outside.

"Incoming Aircraft, long range sensors didn't catch it!" Terrence yelled, clutching the arms of his chair with a tight squeeze. A green dot traversed his radar screen. A circular dot, which was peculiar – planes usually showed up as cylinders or lines.

Paul ran down the ramp and carried his bowling ball momentum into an all out sprint. A five foot hedge twenty meters away would provide him some cover. He covered the distance in 5 lumbering strides and shoulder rolled into the thick vines. He laid down, set up his rifle, and began to scan the sky for targets. The whole process was amalgamated into a single superfluous movement.

"What vector is that object approaching." He whispered into his comms, hoping Terrence could give him a snappy answer. If it was a plane, he should have heard or seen it by now. Just fizzles and pings hissed over the radio. Past the EFF jet, a glint in the blue caught his eye. Thinking it might be an approaching plane he lined up, took a deep breath, and envisioned the shot.

Even Paul's battle-hardened reflexes and irrefutable accuracy couldn't have an effect on what was approaching. The glint needed two seconds to become a silver disc, floating directly above the plane. It crossed the kilometer between them like it was inch, appearing instantly.

"We're in for one now." He said out loud; more to himself than actually attempting a headset communication. He thought about shooting, but knew it was futile. The disc hovered for a second, wobbling, then slowly drifted to an open patch close to the plane. The underside of the contraption hissed, releasing some kind of atmosphere into the air. A hatch slid open revealing stairs that gracefully folded down to the ground like an accordion.

Paul was expecting armed, twig-bodied, slithery skinned bugs to waltz their way onto the Earth, but his finger pulled away from the trigger when he saw three humans emerge from the disk. A woman, and two men, dressed in civilian clothing. It was the last thing he expected.

They moved quickly down the staircase and onto the grassy plain and ran toward the hatch to the EFF jet which was still open.

They aren't armed . . thought Paul, but when their angle came to center and he could see their backs, he noticed that both men had pistols stuffed in their pants.

"Lester!" Yelled the blonde haired woman, to no response. They must have been spooked.

"Lester Desjardins" She yelled again. The trio's attention was firmly fixated on what little of the cabin they could see, so Paul sprung up, rifle raised, and scampered quietly toward them.

"Hey!" He yelled, just ten feet behind them. They turned, startled, one of the men fell.

"Relax!"He yelled furiously, growling even – making sure they didn't reach for their guns. They responded with flat palms and wide eyes.

"Who are you?" Paul asked, this time with a calmer tone..

"Stacey Peterson. I work for Dynatech" Stacey blurted.

Paul stood there silent for a moment, calculating.

"Where?" He asked.

"Alaska. A facility hidden off the northern ice cli-"

"Tell me what you *really* want to stay, Stacey Peterson." Paul commanded her, allowing his rifle to drop and sling around his torso.

What a question, where do I start? She thought, but her mind was trained to think and react quickly.

"There was an attack at the facility we were all at." She said, waving her hands cautiously toward Mark and Eugene. "We encountered aliens who saved us and sent us here."

Paul had to dial that one back for a second.

"Who attacked you?"

"I don't know who, or what . . . but they had Dynatech emblems on their armor."

Armor?

"And these aliens. Who were they? What did they look like?"

"One of them told me they call themselves Darmerians. They were all huge – human looking, but more . . . perfect. They wore silver suits that gave them powers I can't understand. One of them who called himself Tarliss told us to come. In fact they sent us here with a message for Lester Desjardins of the FBI." She blurted it all out, barely, in one breath. Mark and Eugene didn't even think about interrupting her.

"What message?" Paul asked.

Stacey hesitated. She wanted to ask Paul where Lester was. How could she be sure the man wouldn't simply pry the information he needed and shoot the three of them? The planes occupants decided to come outside. Mark and Eugene's hands remained raised in front of them.

"Alright sweetheart, spit it out." Snarled Schlesinger, "We heard you from the cabin. Thought you were a bunch of Reticulans coming to kill us."

"Are you Lester?" Stacey asked.

"No. But we were with him an hour ago. We're not going to hurt you Miss Peterson, we're on your side. Believe me."

"He told me to tell Lester Desjardins that someone named Anthony is alive." Stacey said, not realizing the impact it would have on the group.

"Thank god." He whispered, "Thank god for you Stacey." He continued hysterically.

Paul looked over at their chosen method of transportation; a silvery orb that looked like it weighed the same as paper. The landing gear served only to balance it, not to bear any real weight – the 'feet' didn't make any sort of impression in the soil.

"Does that thing have room for all of us?" Paul asked aloud, pointing unmistakably toward the T-IVB.

"Plenty." Eugene finally spoke, "It's practically hollow."

* * * *

Twisted, surreal visions made Sagittarius' amplified mindspace a living nightmare. Bullets, death . . . Evil. . . *monsters* . . .

His Uncle and his mentor, fighting on the rooftops of tall buildings on *top* of the Earth, which now felt to him as strange as living *inside* the Earth would have sounded just days ago. It all ended when he found himself in the very room they occupied, breathing . . . in the *present*.

This isn't a dream . . .this is happening right now he thought. They were in a tall building, planning and fighting. Sagittarius felt an overwhelming urge to tell them what he couldn't quite envision . . . that they were going to die. Maybe not now, but soon.

Lester leaned over a table and began unlocking the many buckles enclosing a rectangular suitcase. Inside, all the nuts and bolts needed to craft an SR334A STOP (Special Tactical Operations and Procedures) sniper rifle. He leveled another case to his hip that held the weapon's inch-diameter bullets.

He tried to move, but couldn't. Just like so many dreams he had as a human, he was not fully in control of everything. But this time, he was fully aware that he was asleep somewhere in the real world, dreaming . .. or *remote viewing,* as was the term this sort of thing had been labeled by the FBI's psychological department. He yelled, but made no sound. He could not help them. It felt as if his legs were rooted to the ground.

Lester quickly snapped the long barrel into place, checked the scope, turned, and walked directly at him, completely oblivious of his presence.

This is my chance . . .

But as hard as he tried, he couldn't physically be in two places at once. Lester walked right through his body – or at least where he thought his body would be had he actually been phsyically there. Seconds later, someone else ran through his 'body' going in the opposite direction. He recognized the man's quick, slippery and uncomfortable-looking gait. It took him a second to trace his memory banks, but when Gary turned his head briefly, the recognition was instant. It caused a hundred questions of doubt and uncertainty to flood his mind.

What is he doing with them?

Before he could perplex the thought any further, he felt a steadily increasing pressure on his 'chest'. He was beginning to fade away, back to his own plain of consciousness and he couldn't stop it.

His eyes opened abruptly. He was awake. Tarliss stood over him, with his right hand planted on his torso.

"Sorry. I had to wake your body up somehow." Tarliss said. "You don't want to get caught in those thoughts Sagittarius. They will consume you and rip your soul from the very bones of your body."

"But . . .but it was so real . . .: Sagittarius stuttered, thoughts still racing on the plight of his distant friends.

"Real or not, we are here now. We must focus. And although I would like to grant you more rest, time is against us once again."

Sagittarius rose and moved to a bench a few feet away. Tarliss sat down next to him. The shimmering second skin still wore his body like a glove. Tarliss allowed him a few moments to collect his thoughts after a few deep breaths.

"I know we don't have much time. But I have a few questions Tarliss, I need to understand."

"Of course, Sagittarius, I will grant you that."

"First of all, how did we get back?"

"Mass Teleportation. It is always a risk, but one we had to take. The humans have found ways to interfere with the process. But I think they are occupied with a few other things at the moment."

Sagittarius almost didn't believe him, but quickly remembered when he teleported during the fight.

"Right. And another thing, I haven't eaten a thing since . . " Sagittarius looked up, eyes flickering, racking his brain trying to remember the last time he ate. It brought him all the way back to the pasta he ate in the restaurant in Paris – the one unknowingly being served to him by the alien now sitting next to him.

"Since the restaurant. But more than that you are wondering why you still aren't hungry." Tarliss said; providing words for the sketchy culmination of his thoughts.

"Yeah . . . I'm not." Sagittarius said, confused and enlightened at the same time. He wasn't hungry at all. The thought of eating something didn't appeal to him whatsoever.

"We don't eat very much. The components are still there, but our bodies have adapted to process energy in other ways."

"Such as?" Sagittarius asked.

"By taking advantage of the trillions of atoms of cosmic energy constantly passing through our bodies. Human scientists call it Dark Matter. There are certain humans, whom by pure chance, have mastered the technique. It is known as a 'pseudoscience' called Breatharianism."

Sagittarius took a moment to ponder never eating another meal. It was a daunting thought. His mouth began to water as he envisioned fresh slices of pizza, hamburgers and his Uncle's delicious brunches, beer . . . Never again. After a battle like that, were he a human, he'd be reaching for a beer as soon as he could. Were there no rewards in this new life?

Sagittarius arched his back and raised his arms to stretch his torso. He shrugged, and the top of new bulbous muscular protrusions in his upper back lightly kissed the skin on his neck. He awkwardly turned his head to look at his own trapezius muscle, and ran his right hand over his left shoulder to touch it.

"Why do I have these extra muscles now?"

"They are not muscles," Tarliss said, observing Anthony Stall's coming to terms with his transition into Sagittarius Darmerus. "They are extensions of your neural cortex, and connected much more intricately to your spinal cord."

"You mean like a bigger brain?"

"Not just bigger, but smarter and more efficient. In a human body, the signals between brain and nerve travel at around two-hundred miles per hour. In our bodies, this happens thousands of times quicker. Put your hand here." Tarliss said, running his left hand over the small of his lower back. Sagittarius did, and he felt another protrusion, but this one was solid bone.

"Another protective housing for ganglion in your pelvis, connecting to the dendrites in your legs."

This was a lot of madness to process, but he needed to know it all. He needed to understand everything more thoroughly so he could counterbalance his mind; which teetered on a tipping point between security and insanity, than just to simply satisfy his curiosity. He needed to convince his mind to seek a disproportionate balance on the side of *belief* just to stay sane. It was extremely difficult; given how much the *disbelief* part of his mind wanted to rip itself out of his skull and dance around in a bloody mess to mock his very attempt.

"When we were fighting. . . .What happened to me?"

"Hypertime. You entered another plain of consciousness."

"Hypertime?"

"You overloaded. The material in your suit, when used like that, produces effects even we can't stop. Hypertime takes a serious toll on your body. To us, *they* move slower. To them, *we* move incredibly fast. It's a difference in perception based on our anatomy and elevated consciousness. But if you indulge too much, the suit will feed off of your lifeforce and drain it, until your body can take no more. That is what happened."

Sagittarius pondered the thought. Power was not limitless. It couldn't be, of course, that wouldn't be fair.

"Do you know what a black hole is?" Asked Tarliss.

"Obviously"

Tarliss shrugged off his snappiness and continued. "When a star collapses, the explosion is so immense that it tears a hole in space. The matter is consumed, and dispersed into the transentia."

Sagittarius arched his eyebrows and smirked, mocking Tarliss' thorough pronunciation of the word. Tarliss stopped momentarily, visibly annoyed.

"That is what black holes are Sagittarius, entrances into another dimension - a dimension that is rapidly consuming all of the matter in the universe. Dimensions right in front of your face that you can never feel, touch, taste, or hear." He stopped, trying to create a mental picture of the event with his hands but it didn't help at all.

"Some human theories are on the verge of understanding *some* of it." Tarliss said, stopping briefly. Sagittarius was too busy creating mental pictures to interrupt.

"We believe that the young universe was full of equally young stars. But when stars die, the explosion is so massive that it creates a portal into a higher dimension by tearing the fabric of atomic space. The more stars that die, the more holes emerge. They conspire together, becoming larger and larger, attracting more of the matter to them. That is how galaxies were born."

"Hmm." Was all Sagittarius responded with, briefly reminiscing about television specials he had watched as a human about the intricacies and wonders of space.

"Galaxies are essentially the last bits of matter that have managed to stave off being sucked into giant black holes. In a billion years from now, many galaxies will be gone. This conscious matter," Tarliss said, running his hand over Sagittarius' suit, "This metal that can think . . . is atomic space fighting back. We find it in orbs, flung far from the black holes after supernovae. It is still unknown exactly how it comes to exist, but it has seen the void, felt it even, and pushed back. We believe life, or at least certain forms of it, are attempts by the universe to understand and bring a stop to its own destruction."

"We, Anthony Stall, Sagittarius, whatever you choose to be. . ." Tarliss said, continuing his thought, "We are the culmination of thinking atoms in single sentient vessels. And our purpose for existence is to stop the void from consuming everything that exists."

Sagittarius was at a loss for words. His mind created such a brilliant, thorough picture of what Tarliss was saying, it was like he was standing out in space watching it happen. He closed his eyes and couldn't be certain if he wasn't actually out there.

"So this suit," He asked, flexing his arms and shoulders, "How do we tame it?"

"We don't. It chooses us."

"Chooses?"

"Yes. Chooses. The first encounter we had with the Kre'llek Kretheress, it sped toward our ships at four times the speed of light. It invaded the vessels, spread throughout them and attached itself to the crew."

"Attached . . . like *attach* attached?" Sagittarius asked, using his hands to try and depict what attached meant. Was it *Anthony* who asked that one? "Kre'llek Kreth-er-er-?"

The pronunciation wasn't so much speaking as a series of throaty clicks created with very little jaw movement.

"The Arcturian name for it. An odd translation to our tongues means 'living space metal'.

Other species have encountered it, but had different results. They have all tried to harvest it, but to no avail. It *chose* us."

"But it can't communicate with us? or us with it?"

"In dreams, Sagittarius. In dreams, you will be shown your life's purpose. It is the Kre'theress speaking to you."

"So it chooses to give us all of this power and ability. But . . . it comes at a cost . . ."

Tarliss looked at the floor. His eyes flickered as he searched through his thoughts in an oddly human way.

"During our first contact with the humans, we knew our technology and knowledge outmatched theirs by a hundred to one. But years went by. Then decades. A small detachment of assassins, the first group trained on Earth, were on a mission to record the migratory patterns of the Rhakthfer, then reconnoiter with a group of Arcturians."

"Arcturians?" Anthony asked, confused again - they weren't the only aliens living in the Earth?

"Yes, Arcturians. Small creatures, child-like. But incredibly intelligent and wise. Wiser than us, even. A group of them agreed to help us in our objective, believing that it would heighten your . ." Tarliss stuttered, "*Human* physiological evolution. They came on their own to reduce our chances of being detected. They were on their way back to their home planet, and had 'grave news' for us." Tarliss stared at the floor again, caught in reliving a dark moment he thought he had vanquished from his memory. A dark, deep twisted regret that forced its way into the deepest mental caverns; with locked doors, waiting to break free and erupt into his psyche to test his resolve.

"So what happened?" Anthony asked, impatiently.

"The meeting never happened. The Arcturians were found at a designated rendezvous point, slaughtered. Like cattle. Arcturians don't carry weapons, nor do they wage war. They simply think, and love, and try to build and procure what they call 'universal consciousness'. They have a very deep understanding of the universe that Darmeria has tried to aspire to. A human dressed in a white, all-encompassing shiny cloth

with a cylinder on his back and a window on his face to see us through...
He was shoving Kre'llek-threth's body into a bag. Infuriated, a young
Darmerian named Tarus Traytheon lost control of himself and took the
human's life, sparking the trap . . ."

Anthony didn't speak, but hung on Tarliss' next syllable, eyes closed,
envisioning the scene unfold in his head.

"There were hundreds of them, and they had learned more about us,
studied us. And with the help of the Reticulans, rapidly improved
their technology. We found that our combative dominance was not as
profound as it once was, and that we could not sense everything that
lay ahead of us, as previously believed. The humans had become a very
serious threat. Traytheon continued his rampage when he should have
fallen back. He killed many, but died a catastrophic death."

Once more, Tarliss looked into the floor and crunched his eyebrows.

"You were there weren't you?"

Weird . . .I just broke through his barrier . . .

What was weird about it was that it wasn't mental. No strange sixth-
sense like feeling of someone else speaking words in *your* mind, no tingly
feeling in your frontal lobe. To Sagittarius, it was entirely un-Darmerian.

Tarliss recognized it and looked right into his eyes.

"He was my brother."

They have emotions too . . .err, we do . . .

Sagittarius could tell that Tarliss was deeply affected, although he put a
great deal of effort into trying to hide it. He even felt awkward about it,
since he knew of no way to console Tarliss, nor did he know if it would
be appropriate for him to try. They sat and conversed as humans would;
subconsciously agreeing not to read each other's thoughts out of respect.

Sagittarius wondered if this was a common thing among members of his new race; as it reinforced their views of themselves as individuals as opposed to part a hive-mind.

"BUT THAT IS OKAY!" A deep voice boomed. It was hulk-ish Beldonox, along with his identical twin following him. "Because he has a new brother now!" Beldonor yelled, finishing his twin's sentence with a smile. Their physical appearance had unparalleled similarity without the slightest inkling of difference like two copied prints of the same picture. Even the silver-tipped hairs on their heads grew in replicated fashion, and they finished each other's sentences. For all intents and purposes they were the exact same organism.

But Sagittarius already could tell them apart. He felt their energy – it was identical. He couldn't quite tell *how* he knew – only what pictures his mind created for him. It forcibly stained an invisible 'X' into Beldonox' chest so that he could tell the difference.

Hiding behind the giants were Grikorus and Venethon. Hiding behind *them*, Aremis. They entered the room through a circular tube that only appeared as the wall disintegrated as the group drew closer. The 'men' had no shirts on. Their ripped torsos bulged with muscle – and not just human muscles – there were extras. The upper pectoral muscle that inserted into the deltoids was cut off from the main pectoral by an entirely separate one, that could have been a mixture of deltoid and pectoral. Instead of eight chiseled abdominal cells there were ten, and what looked like two sets of adjacent abdominals sitting underneath the top two rows. Sagittarius prodded around his ribcage and found he had grown the extra muscles too. His ribcage was fuller, more robust, and the divots between ribs were less pronounced.

"You have proven yourself Sagittarius. But I'm sure Tarliss has told you to be careful." Beldonox said, slapping a firm grip of Sagittarius on the shoulders. The boulder-like hands engulfed his whole upper body.

"Yes. He did. I've always been one to learn lessons the hard way."

"No better way to learn." Venethon said, smirking with his arms crossed.

Aremis was silent the whole time, staring at Sagittarius. He noticed it and began to blush. He looked right back at her, and her eyes flickered to a random spot on the floor. They came back around to see that Sagittarius was still staring at her, but this time she revealed the slightest, barely noticeable lip-quiver of a smile.

"What brings you, Beldonorus?" Tarliss asked.

"A Reticulan was found. It appeared in one of the nodes." Beldonox replied.

"Alive?"

"Barely" piped Beldonor, "It's neck and legs are broken. They are frail creatures."

A five minute walk down a single long winding tube brought them all the way to the room housing the crippled creature. It was a completely different passage than any they traveled in before – it seemed to have existed only for the purpose of bringing them to that exact room, only to disappear forever afterwards. It's seemingly random twists must have bent around the 'real' edifices of the subterranean complex.

"How does that happen?" Anthony asked, looking around in confusion.

"Magic." Tarliss responded cheekily. He wasn't far off. The scientific explanation wasn't really necessary at that point. Sagittarius battered him with questions the whole way there. Aremis looked back, smirking at him every so often. He made sure to notice her looks and make eye contact, enough so that he lost track of Tarliss' answers.

"One more question Tarliss. When I was talking to that thing, it never really told me *why* the lizards are doing this. What do they have to gain?"

Tarliss' pace came slowly to a halt, Sagittarius stopped and turned. Tarliss, in a very human way, put his hands on the sides of his slender hips and twisted his knees into an altered posture. He massaged the bottom of his upper lip with his teeth and looked deeply into nothing, brows furled.

"I shouldn't have even tried to hold that from you." Tarliss said.

"Hold *what?*" Anthony asked, perking his own brows, annoyed. If there was one thing that would cause any sort of altercation between him and his new mentor, it was being lied to.

The rest of the group continued walking, seemingly oblivious to their conversation except for Aremis, who kept her distance, but stopped. Tarliss stepped forward and put it all on the line.

"Genetics." He said very slowly. "A certain human gene, to be specific. Long ago, it was locked inside the genetic imprint of humanity "

"By who?"

"By *us*. By the first of us. Part of your father's mission here was to warn them that other races would exploit them for it."

"And what does this one gene do? Why is it so special?" Sagittarius asked.

Tarliss looked over his shoulder at Aremis. His body language suggested he was finally revealing his knowledge of how Sagittarius felt about her; as if he had been purposely concealing it from him up until that point.

"Love, Sagittarius. The most powerful force in the universe. In a horribly short-sighted attempt to purify ourselves of raw emotion and the evil that it brings, we rid ourselves of it and most other emotional crutches that we carried. We literally struck them from the very strands of our DNA. Darmerians in that age were trying to elevate their logic and eliminate wars. And it has worked for thousands of years. It has allowed us to know much more about the universe, and existence itself; much more about our purpose for *existing.*"

"So you just 'dumped' your emotions on humanity?" Sagittarius asked, suddenly developing an opinion of Darmerian evolutionary history. "No wonder you guys are all so drab." He continued.

"We decided that perhaps human beings, even in their earliest stages, would be able to achieve what we could not. To feel the excellence of emotion, to love one another, and to develop an advanced society. Unfortunately they are walking the same bloody steps we did. Realizing our failure, we swore to never again interfere with the evolution of other creatures in the universe."

Do they have the ability to love? Will I? Will I ever be able to . . .

As his thoughts raced, his attention t drifted to Aremis.

Will she ever be able to love me?

She looked right at him, and this time he hoped she was listening to his thoughts. He wanted her to know how he felt if just to prove to himself that there was a chance he could have her. Tarliss, exhibiting a blunt dismissal of the heightened emotion apparent with the situation, continued walking.

"So humanity . . . is basically a science project gone wrong?" Sagittarius bantered. Tarliss did not respond to his comment.

"We're here." Aremis said softly, changing the subject just in time. The few feet of walkway left in front of them gradually dissipated into nothing. A few more steps brought them to the room called a 'node'. The others waited for them, huddling around the crippled creature recently shackled with a white polymorphous material at the wrists, ankles and neck. It hissed and crackled in pain but it's efforts to free itself were anything but successful.

"How did it get here?" Tarliss asked Venethon, who scanned the creature's body with a circular gadget designed to detect any subatomic anamolies.

"Don't know." Responded Venethon, "It's cells are not dying. Must have accidentally stumbled upon one of the portals."

It seemed like a valid explanation but something just didn't seem right. It was alarming enough that one of these things was breathing inside of their stronghold, and even more worrisome that there could be others. If their location was compromised, it wouldn't be long before the humans assaulted them with everything they could muster. Even with all of their psionic might, they would not be able to stop such an attack. It would be the end.

"We can't take any chances. Beldonorus – organize a patrol for all of the nodes." Tarliss commanded.

"But there are thirty-seven nodes Tarliss." Beldonox replied, stepping forward. "It will take hours. Days even" Beldonor affirmed, stepping forward as well.

"Wait." Aremis interjected. The body language concordant with how they responded to her outburst made Sagittarius aware that Darmerians rarely listened to their females. It was as patriarchal a society as humanity, maybe even more so. None of them turned their bodies toward her, only their heads.

"They most likely followed us when we escaped. We should start there."

The words coming off her lips spat a sudden and overwhelming image into Sagittarius' mind. The room faded away and his eyes flickered, fading into pale white. . .

He could see them. The soldiers that were sent to find them and kill them, just as Aremis predicted. One of them stood at the edge like a statue, while the others curled up with their rifle between their legs and dipped their heads. Once Sagittarius realized what was happening and regained his senses, he looked around only to see that all of them had the same ocular effect, and were having the same vision. When they came to, they once again looked at him in awe, the same way they did after the battle.

"Finally," Beldonox uttered almost sarcastically, everyone still smiling and staring at him.

"Finally what?" He asked, confused.

"You Beat us."

"Beat you?" Sagittarius asked, still confused,

"You saw that before we did, and we were able to see what you saw. That is a trait reserved for Darmerians only with years of experience. You have been among us but a day."

His new posse stood there in silence. It felt very strange – just hours ago he revered them. Now the opposite was happening. They were waiting for him to say something but he had no words available - only an impulse.

How do I get there?

"Do these things work backwards?" He asked, referring to the 'node'.

"No," Tarliss responded, barely allowing him to finish his sentence, "But there is a way to do it. Venethon – stay here and watch this horrific thing, kill it if it so pleases you. Everyone else, to the Council Chamber." He continued, and hit full stride toward an apparently blank, pointless area of the wall. Sagittarius looked at the creature one last time, perplexed by Tarliss' choice. It wasn't what his mind had been trained to do – humans would keep the thing alive, torture it, and extract as much information as they could. Tarliss seemed to take foolhardy honor in his capacity as leader to order the Reticulan's death.

"Yes, Tarliss, we agree. It is worth it." Said the elder sitting in the middle as soon as the group entered the massive room. No conversation, no decision making. They had already spent the few minutes during their walk to the room deliberating amongst themselves whether or not to let them make the jump. They had already read their minds and were preparing a portal for them.

"Good. Sagittarius and I are going. Everyone else stay behind." Tarliss said without breaking stride. A hovering crystal much like the one used during the ceremony to create the 'dreamcloud' started to glow hot under then focus of a grey-colored laser. It turned into a solid-thick gas, expanding quickly, and inside of it their destination could be seen.

"Why Just us?" Sagittarius asked, "Why just two of us?"

"I have a strange feeling about this group. If they found the portal, why do they wait? I would have expected them to attack, wouldn't you?" He responded in stride.

"Tarliss." Boomed the elder's voice. It appeared both aloud *and* in their heads. "We have enough enemies as it is." He finished.

The portal's diameter stretched to roughly three meters. Tarliss grabbed Sagittarius by the hand and looked him in the eyes one last time before they leapt.

The transition was so instant and seamless even their heightened senses couldn't decipher the magic. Their bodies were suddenly tugged by gravity – they were falling – and had only a few seconds to land accurately. It was also very dark – a lot darker than it looked before. They managed to right themselves, like agile cats temporarily disoriented. They landed unapologetically on the narrow ledge, just feet from the statuesque soldier standing on the edge. They were prepared for some sort of spastic attack to come their way and to be easily deflected. It never came. The soldier stood there, weapon perched gracefully, apparently oblivious to their arrival. None of his companions flinched either.

"I thought you would come." Said the nearly eight-foot statue, breaking the ominous silence that filled the spooky cavern. Tarliss and Sagittarius looked at each other with surprise. The soldier turned his body to face them and lowered his weapon. Dust fell off every crevice of his cumbersome swashbuckling frame. He had been standing like that for quite some time. He took a moment to look them up and down, and as he did they could see the green flashing calculations burning through his retina. His eyes were deep, flat and intimidating and no semblance of soul was to be found in them. They were empty, cold and lifeless.

"You have concluded that I do not wish to fight." He said, with no identifiable tone that would solidify the sentence as a statement or a question. His voice was deep and resonated with an electric hum that the Darmerians could feel against their suits.

"Yes, that seems perfectly clear. What *do* you want?" Tarliss demanded, getting right to the point. Once again, the pale-faced warrior's eyeballs fluttered green indecipherable symbols, but only for a brief moment.

"Revenge."

Once again, Tarliss and Sagittarius looked at each other, surprised.

"I have remembered . . ." He said, mumbling the last bit, "I have remembered . . . a life. *My life.*"

He had spent the last few hours prying deep into his dual cortex – places he was not supposed to have conscious access to. He was once a man. He once had a wife and child. He would take his son for ice cream every Sunday on the boardwalk down on the beach. He enjoyed running his hands through his golden hair. He had eyes like his mother's. These images he saw could not have been random or invented. Reinforcing his belief was an overwhelming sense of despair accompanying them; another thing he was not supposed to feel. He knew a piece of him had been lost forever.

"Ok that's good and dandy but how do we know there aren't a thousand more of you on their way?" Sagittarius asked. The hulking soldier turned his head.

"Because I have severed the connection. They no longer control me."

"They?" Tarliss asked.

"My creators. The ones who stole me. And made me into what I am."

As the words left his mouth, he endured horrific flashbacks of the surgical processes used to create him. The sound of his very bones cracking, and his muscles being stretched were almost inaudible under the sounds of his own painful screams.

"They stole all of us. I suspect these under my command are clones – not real men. Just copies." He continued, lazily motioning his hand towards the lifeless warriors lining the tunnel behind them.

"Humans?" Sagittarius asked, intrigued by the plight of this once-human. Their circumstances were ironically similar.

"Yes. And the insects. Like the one I threw into your portal."

It was alarming that this creature now had knowledge about their base, and specifically how and where to enter it. They were found. It was hard to believe what the soldier in front of them was saying given how much of a threat he could be.

"I understand it would be difficult to trust me."

"What is your name?" Tarliss asked, acknowledging the soldier as an individual, although he didn't really believe it himself.

"ST-101C is my designation. But you can call me Commander."

Sagittarius smirked slightly and quickly tried to conceal it. Evidently he rediscovered his human sense of humor. Tarliss did not share the sentiment.

"Alright Commander. Take off your helmet." Tarliss told him. It took a brief moment of eye-fluttering for him to calculate the reason to do such a thing, then obliged Tarliss by prying the thing off and dropping it to the dusty rock floor. Inside of the Commander's mind was a mixture of a living creature and the same fizzy, popping babble sounds from one of the inert clones. Half man, half machine. Tarliss pried as deep as he could.

"He's telling the truth." Tarliss said, after a few seconds of mind-melding. "You are a very unique organism, Commander. How do you plan to exact your revenge?" He continued, addressing their new acquaintance.

Could he be an ally?

"Well, I was hoping you could help me with that. And in return I could help you." He replied, then turned his head toward them. "We could help each other."

"And what could you possibly do to help us?"

The soldier stepped forward, his eyes flattened out. For the first time he looked Tarliss directly in the eyes. He was more than a foot taller, and his face was lit up by the aura emanating from the Alien. It revealed patches of scars and veins visible through the skin.

"I will fight for you. *We* will fight for you. I will return from where I came, and tell them that my communication device malfunctioned. I will lie to them."

"What for?" Tarliss asked impatiently. His body language stiffened up a bit.

"We know you can teleport short distances. It is one of the many technological advantages you have against us. I can help you interrogate their computers."

The commander already had the whole plan laid out. Evidently he could think at a much higher level than any mortal man, yet he was only *half* alive. The right side of his brain influenced the left, logically enhanced side with it's creativity, and made exquisite use of the yottabytes of information it had in store. The two Darmerians worried that ST-101C might be intelligent enough to deceive them, despite the fact that they could read *half* of his thoughts.

"Are you sure you remember the way back?" Sagittarius asked. They wanted to be absolutely sure the Commander wasn't trying to trick them.

"Everything my eyes see is recorded and stored. If you don't believe me I can show you."

"We can look for ourselves, Commander." Said Tarliss, stepping forward, "Don't forget that." He finished, making sure the cyborg knew what fate awaited him should he try and double-cross them.

"I am well aware of your capabilities Darmerian. I would be a fool to try and trick you. You could destroy me if you wanted to, so what do you have to worry about?"

Tarliss and Sagittarius had to think about it for a second – the cyborg was right. He was no mere mortal, but wasn't a serious threat considering how powerful they both were. They shared a seconds-long mental conversation in front of ST-101C, whose eyes scanned the minute changes in their faces trying to deduce information from the calculations. Very little was available. Their muscles didn't micro-twitch; their skin didn't change temperature like humans.

"Alright, Commander. I suppose you already know *why* we would want access to that computer?"

"Yes. In your last attack on us you attempted to access the Worldnav database. Four of you."

It was one of the mission objectives for the missing squadron of assassins. Tarliss remembered giving the order himself.

"What is the Worldnav database?" Sagittarius asked, like a curious child interrupting two adults.

"It is a shield," responded the Commander, "It prevents those like you from escaping."

"Shield?" Anthony asked. For that moment, he was human again, weak; in the dark about the situation after having survived the worst mindfuck life could throw at him. His brain was jam packed tight enough and efforts to subconsciously compartmentalize his fears were fading. The thoughts of his uncle, of Earth, of humanity, of *himself* slowly trickled into his mind. Was he really about to become *Sagittarius* forever? His brain was about to be thrown another curveball, and Anthony knew he wasn't prepared for it.

"A grid of phytolasers and particle energy weapons guarding Earth's atmosphere. It is capable of eliminating or disabling *most* inbound and outbound targets. Of course a target as big as yours," the Commander explained, then swiveled his neck toward Tarliss,

"Would not stand a chance."

"What target?" Anthony asked, pestering the dealmakers.

"Our refuge." Tarliss said, "It is a ship."

That is one huge ship Anthony thought. Equally perplexing was the intuitive realization that he would be leaving the planet soon. The fact that Tarliss had neglected to tell him that until now wasn't as important.

"How do you know we want to leave?" Tarliss asked. The robot was right, it was their plan – but he wanted to know how his enemies had figured it out.

"Because, Darmerian, you are intelligent enough to realize that you will not survive the onslaught. Once my creators have neutralized humanity, they will bring all of their might to bear upon you. You may be powerful adversaries, but you are not immortal."

"Immortal, no. But we are not afraid either." Tarliss responded aggressively, but it was a bluff. Anthony sensed it easily. They way it came out, he was pretty sure the Commander knew as well.

"Nonetheless, will you take my offer Darmerian?"

Tarliss looked deep into the twisting cavern; it's ribs lined with dormant killers.

"They will stay here. I suspect there are more Reticulans in the area."

As he spoke, the soldiers bustled to life. The lights on their armor painted the rocks bright as their joints unlocked and extended straight up.

"You sure you have complete control of them?"

"Yes," the Commander responded, "I can feel every single one of them in my brain." One of the rejuvenated robots broke from the wall, brandished a pistol from a holster on his hip and pointed it unmistakably at his own head.

"See? They are *mine*." Said the Commander. His warriors holstered their large rifles and dispersed. Two marksmen knelt down on either side of the tunnel's mouth, while the majority of the remainders trudged deeper into it. Ten stayed, joined in a tight group and went back to sleep.

"Very well Commander." Tarliss said, still not fully convinced there would be no treachery ahead.

"You'll get your revenge."

Chapter 17

S.O.S.

Every second without worsening weather allowed Lester's mind to slow down a bit, to think. To *focus.* Everything was in disarray, and they were far from safe.

What's next?

He ordered the skittish news crew to stay on air as long as they could – his attention was needed elsewhere. Gary and Eric fed him the rhetoric, he nervously relayed the messages to the civvies. After a half hour, the sense that they were being held against their will disappeared, and was replaced (due to understanding what they were reading from the teleprompters) by willingness to contribute to the safety of millions of Americans, and themselves. The message wasn't something they were being ordered to relay, but something they had stake in – they were just as vulnerable as those they were trying to reach with their warning.

"Sitrep" Lester asked Jasper, after having to catch his breath first; who stood like a statue on a raised pedestal by one of the two-story windows overlooking the city. His eyes scoured the streets, and the skies. It may have seemed odd to everyone else, but it made Lester less agitated.

Messages spammed Jasper's earpiece from 'the hub' – the room upstairs housing Gary and Eric with a crew of frantic helpers, giving him constant updates and collecting vital information. He wore an extra mic in his right ear to receive another stream of valuable information from other sources – an internet based search engine built into his helmet. Lester wanted to run around, check everyone – the young agents on the roof and lobby, the brave civilians still recording their news over the airwaves, and Jim, whose health was fading. After a half hour of meticulous thinking, coordinating, bouncing around groups; micromanaging, he realized everything he needed to know would come from Jasper much quicker.

"No contact with Paul. The techs are trying to contact military bases and vessels. No luck as of yet. But I have some good news for you." He said, turning his head, "The rest of the Spec38 on their way. They are inbound 7 to 10 minutes."

That *was* good news. More soldiers to fight with couldn't be a bad thing. Judging by Paul and Jasper's combat performance, he actually got excited at the thought of having 33 more of them to work with. Lester eyes were drawn to the smoldering stack unmistakably creating a black barrier over the skyline.

"Do you think Barritzer's alive?"

Jasper hesitated for just a second longer than he normally would.

"No. I don't. I am sorry. That explosion left no survivors. Which means the governments of the world are in terrible shape."

"Meaning?" Lester asked. He knew Jasper had everything calculated down to a science, but it could be difficult getting him to say more than a few sentences.

"Meaning the *whole world* is in much worse shape than it appears in this building. We are safe, for now, but there are bad things coming our way. I need you to understand that this is now a war."

"I understand." Lester responded quickly, enticing Jasper to keep talking.

"The effects of the HEAR system were devastating. We were very lucky to miss the effects of it. Up to half a billion have already died, maybe more. Some parts of the globe have been completely wiped off the map. California is an island, Madagascar has sunk. Most of Russia is completely underwater. And I fear the worst is not over yet."

"You think they'll turn it back on?"

"Maybe, maybe not. I don't know why they turned it off in the first place... I suspect someone has thrown a wrench into their plans. But the initial side-effects are not over with. The axis of the Earth could shift any minute and that's when the real chaos will begin. We are going to need to get to higher ground. Soon."

Lester knew he was foolish to think they had been through the worst, if only for a second. Jasper's words only reinforced what he already knew. He had enough to worry about it as it was, but now he had to make time to think about what they would do next, and how they would escape the city. The fact that most of the people he was trying to warn would not make it was a daunting reality they were going to be faced with soon – also the fact that he may not have enough soldiers at his disposal to keep back the hordes should they decide to rush the news building – in fact he was surprised it hadn't happened yet. On cue, his earpiece buzzed. It was Stiltzenbacher's bouncing voice from the first floor lobby.

"Sir, we've got a problem. There's an angry mob outside. Some of them have weapons, but there are families. There are *children* sir. What do you want us to do?"

The message came loud and clear into Jasper's ear as well. Lester looked at him for direction. Once weapons were involved, and *armed enemies*, shot-calling fell into his arena.

"How many are there, Stiltzy?" Jasper asked quickly.

"Not sure, maybe a hundred. They don't look very friendly either."

"What do you think?" Lester asked Jasper. The mob could present a massive problem they were ill-equipped to deal with, should they decide to show hostility.

"Go down there. We can't afford to have more enemies right now. Try to calm them down and if you have to, let them in the building. My squad will be here soon, that should help corral them."

Lester didn't like it, but he understood. It was difficult for him to hear Jasper without an iron-clad solution. It made him worry even more then he thought possible. But he had to stuff it and move on.

"I'm on my way Stiltzy, stay frosty." Lester grumbled over the line. He ran back across the floor, taking a split second to glimpse to his right, at the young reporter spewing words into the camera. He was still dressed in a suit, but his hair disheveled, his eyes noticeably dreary even from forty feet away. He yelled, perhaps without even noticing it and the desk in front of him was a mess of scattered papers.

'Stay in your houses.' Stuck in Lester's head, before he turned up and to the left, where his tech think-tank, frantic as a kicked beehive, provided them with updates and filled the tele-prompters with messages. But were they just fooling themselves?

Are we just putting ourselves in more danger?

Lester shook the thought out of his head and picked up his pace. Up the stairs, down the lobby, around the corner to the elevator, where two FBI agents waited for him. Three civvies huddled in the corner on their knees, overlooking the chaos of the newsfloor; attempting to call relatives and friends. That meant they were probably on their way to the news building. Lester feared this whole plan was going to backfire.

"How's it looking out there sir?" One of them asked.

"Fine." Lester replied snappily, "Stay here and stay alert," He continued. "Anything could happen at any moment." He finished, as the elevator doors pulled close in front of him.

By the time they opened again, the 'hundred or so' had become *hundreds,* and was still growing. Stiltzy waited for him feet from the door with an M4 loaded and semi-raised. Things *were* getting tense. He peeled quickly out of the elevator into the massive lobby. The main stairs were barricaded by tables, but it was only a matter of time before the fiberglass front doors gave way to the sheer mass of humanity pressing against them.

"Sir it's getting heavy. I saw one out there with an uzi." Stiltzy said. A narrowed path made of tables and desks created a funnel out of the area where the ten-wide doors allowed people into the building. Two more agents stood at the apex of the funnel with m4s behind a table. Two security guards roaming the building were also there, one an old man mesmerized by the events and more hazardous than useful.

Seven janitors working on all different floors worked together to gather tables, desks and anything heavy that could be a piece for their wall. It's a good thing they volunteered to do it - the young agents didn't want to give them orders. Three paper pushers from upstairs went around the building gathering food, water and anything else useful they could find.

Lester stood at the mouth of the funnel, next to the agents, looking down at the flooded street. Every door banged and rattled.

"If they try to rush you," Lester said, "Get back up to the news floor and destroy the elevator. Understood?"

"But sir I thought we were trying to help them."

"We have to help *ourselves* first, agent."

The janitors migrated closer, knowing full well that Lester was in charge. The shortest one, an oriental man with a long pony tail and beard, held his hand out like he was trying to touch something invisible.

"My family!" He shrieked, then ran past the raised rifles, hopped over the barricade and tumbled down to the locked door as if he was oblivious to the plan all along.

"STOP!" Lester yelled, raising his own pistol, but he was not ready to shoot the civilian. His hand trembled at the thought of it. He knew that if it were his family on the other side (although he had very little) he'd be doing anything he could to let them in.

"What do we do sir!?" Stiltzy yelled, ready to unload a few 5.56 rounds into the janitor. Lester's hand shook so much he had to brace it with the other. Biting his lip, he leveled his aim toward the janitor, and fired a shot, causing the small man to fall to his feet. It whizzed past his shoulder and punched into the metal brace holding the door locked in place. He squeezed the trigger four more times, and each one hit the target. The lock metal plate sheath holding the thick bolt in place fell off, and the mechanism failed. Within seconds the fiberglass door gave way to the pushing crowd. The janitor's family fell face first to the floor, and were nearly trampled by half a dozen other hooligans falling in on top of them, but they quickly scurried in one piece over to their husband and father in a tight embrace on their knees.

"Sir why did you do that! We can't keep em' all back!" Stiltzy, yelled, backpedalling as the horde forced itself three at at time through the two foot opening. The young, able bodied security guard took off toward the elevator. The huddled family quickly disappeared amidst the swarming crowd.

"We also can't kill em' all, Stiltzy, they are not the enemy. Back to the elevator!" He yelled. Before he turned his shoulders, a loud flash blinded everyone's vision. It was followed by a deafening explosion in the streets. The sound of Lester's own thoughts drowned among the screams. When he regained his vision, he found himself on the ground, covered in debris, and in pain. He looked to his left to find Stiltzy, also on the ground, but with a piece of rebar twisting into his jaw and sticking out of his skull. He was dead.

Lester quickly scanned his own body for injury, grabbed the idle m4 and rose to his feet. Stiltzy's lifeless hand squeezed the handle like metal vice grips. In front of him were a field of bloodied bodies and a few survivors. The screams hadn't dissipated. No more than ten feet in front of him was the lifeless corpse of a young woman; her limbs unnaturally intertwined with a destroyed table. Her body served as a shield that saved his life – glass and concrete shards covered the landscape of her back. Another to his left ahead of Stiltzy dragged himself toward Lester, seemingly unhindered. But as more of his body came into view, Lester saw that his left foot was completely severed, and that fresh blood trickled from his ears. The agent looked right at him, wide-eyed, with the calmness of a poker player etched to his face.

"Did you find Anthony sir?" He asked. He was in a different world, deeply in shock. Lester didn't have time to wait. Considering himself the luckiest man *still* alive, he flung the m4 around his shoulder, grabbed the blinded and bloodied agent and yelled: "Hold on to me!" Loud and clear right in the kid's face.

Lester didn't notice the real pain until he stood up with the agent's weight bearing on him. It was pretty severe but nothing was broken – or maybe it was and the adrenaline was masking the damage.

After the two of them fell exhaustedly into the elevator, Lester used his last available breath to swing his hand into the 'door close' button. He was going to have to collect himself to take another lunge at the '22' button, just a few inches above it. He took one last look into the hallway and foyer before the doors peeled across. He had a clear line of sight out to the street. Among the bodies and destroyed cars, three heavily armored, fully weaponized commandoes stood tall. Then three more jogged into view. Then a dozen. Their faces were pale and their movement had an eerie stiffness to it.

Lester popped to his feet and rapidly pressed the '22' button as the doors couldn't close any slower.

"What the hell's goin' on down there Cap!?" Jasper yelled into his ear, "You alive?"

"Barely, I'm coming to you now and we've got multiples hostiles inbound. You're boys here yet!?"

"Very soon. How many hostiles?"

"Hard to say. I saw about twenty, but I have a feeling there's a lot more. Get everyone ready for a fight Jasper. I'm destroying the elevators as soon as I get up there."

"Roger that."

Jasper turned from his pedestal and sprinted across the newsroom, three-stepped it up the stairs and peeled into the 'hub'.

"Time to get tactical boys. We got bad guys on the way. Lots of em'. Aaron," Jasper said, pointing, giving them no time to speak."I want you to take 3 men with you and put these charges in the stair wells on the 15th and 17th floor. As soon as you're back, blow them."

"But I-"

"GO NOW!" He yelled, "We don't have time. Here!" He continued, then handed the small but potent explosive devices to Aaron and the three civilians he pointed at as they left the room.

"Gary, you stay here and tell me anything you think I should know. Got it?" Jasper commanded, with his hand pointing into Gary's chest like a flattened spear.

"Y-yes sir." He stuttered. Jasper didn't want to have to scare them, but they had might as well get used to it.

"Get everyone else on the floor ready for a fight. Cut the feed."

"Y-yes sir."

Jasper continued back into the hallway, around the corner and to the elevators where the remaining FBI agents stood guard. They looked tense. Their guns were drawn toward the elevator, waiting for Lester to arrive.

"We're in the shit now aren't we!" Yelled Forcell, to no response from Jasper. The numbers above the elevator increased quickly. Twenty-two hit, and Lester was met with guns nervously pointed at him.

"Smithers! Fuck!" Forcell yelled after noticing his crippled comrade. Smithers did not respond. He couldn't. He had died from blood loss on the way up.

"Don't blow the elevators, at least not yet." Jasper yelled loud and clear, reaching with both hands to a hidden satchel on his back. Velcro snapped, and into his hands fell four plates of clay.

"What's your plan?" Lester asked.

"I've sent a team to destroy the stairwells. Let a few of them come up. Get every gun available pointed at them when they arrive." Jasper explained, while using duct tape to stick and secure pronged fuses into the explosive bricks. He handed them one by one to Lester, Forcell and Ramirez.

"When you've killed them all, bury these under a body and send it back down. When the ticker gets to one, you know what to do." He said, revealing the most important piece – a hand held grip with a bright red button at the top.

"Why don't we just send it back down now?" Ramirez asked with nerve rife in his tone, noticing the still-present, empty elevator.

"Because I want a close up on what we're fighting. Got it?" Jasper responded authoritatively. Ramirez spastically nodded his head after a few seconds in compliance, not knowing whether to be more afraid of Jasper, or the enemy. "Make sure you take their weapons and ammunition. Here." Jasper finished, handing the remote to Lester. He sprinted around the corner and disappeared. Lester stood there stunned for a moment, staring at the device in his hand. The elevator's 'ding' snapped him back to reality as its doors slid closed, and the numbers began to descend.

"You heard him, Ramirez do you still have those grenades?"

"Yes sir!"

"Good. As soon as that door slides open, you pull the pin, count to two and toss it as deep and low as you can." Lester ordered, and Ramirez followed suit by crouching stealthily next to the door with the bomb in his mit. Another 'ding' sounded when the light reached '15'.

"Pettigr-" Lester turned to issue the order, but found Pettigrew already prone, as far back from the elevator as the limited glass-enclosed walkway would allow him, adjusting his reticule and double-checking the ammo.

"Get a gun Cap!" He insisted. Lester looked back down the hallway, to think about retrieving the STOP rifle, but wasn't sure he had the time. For a moment the whole building shook – it must have been the stairwells. Another 'ding' flashed over '10' and once again his senses smacked him into an all out sprint. When he reached the stairs, three civilians were on their way up. One wore suit clothes without a jacket and a red tie, and had found himself a handgun, probably his own. Another, female, young and wearing tight jeans with a form-fitting turquoise bloise, carried the STOP rifle awkwardly like she had no clue how to operate the weapon. Another in front of her, a tall, boney-cheeked black man carrying a baseball bat noticed Lester at the top of the stairs.

"We're helping you sir." He said while two-stepping the elongated platforms. "Gary told us to."

Gary was shouting orders through an old handheld microphone from the balcony. A group of women simply hid underneath their desks, a few had built a barricade inside of an unused, circular wrap-around desk where the anchors sat. Everyone in the building was utterly terrified, including those in uniform.

"CAP!" Lester heard, and then a faint 'ding'. The kill box was on its way up. He snatched the STOP rifle out of the woman's hands and headed back.

"Almost here Cap!" Ramirez yelled. Another 'ding' signaled '15'. Lester slid like a baseball player to within half a foot of Pettigrew, propped up his rifle and yanked the firing pin back. The civvie with the handgun clued in to what was happening and pointed his pistol appropriately. The boney-cheeked man took point with his Louisville slugger opposite Ramirez, practicing an entrenched-stance, head level swing.

Pettigrew unclipped the glock on his waste, flipped the safety and flung it across the floor to the man. He tossed the bat instantly.

"Cock it and get ready." Pettigrew said. The elevator sounded off at the twentieth floor.

"Aim high."

Lester squeezed the trigger to its threshold, held his breath and tensed up, letting all of his thoughts momentarily recede like an ebbing tide. Twenty-two hit. The lobby grew very silent. The door rolled open, ever so slowly. Ramirez pulled his grenade.

One Mississippi

A few more inches slid into the wall, revealing enough for Lester and Pettigrew to confirm the target, and let loose.

Two Mississippi

Ramirez bravely poked his head slightly into the fire to get a better look; to get a good throw. He saw legs – and through them, the wainscot wall of the classic-style lift. He tossed the bomb in and dove in the other direction.

Lester's STOP rifle did the damage it needed to – It's bullets easily pierced the steel door and made a mess of the occupants. Combined with Pettigrew's accurate placement of 5.56, even their thick plated armor could not protect them. Both of the armed civilians added less accurate 9mm rounds into the fray, but it wasn't necessary. The grenade obliterated most of their legs, severing at least half a dozen. The concussive blast was mostly contained inside the elevator and had a devastating effect. The sound of it rang bells in all of the agent's ears, but they were well-trained for such an event. A severed torso tried to raise its gun, somehow still alive, and coherent. The rifles quickly aimed at its brain and ended the attempt. The gunfight lasted only five seconds, about as long as it took for the door to disappear. It gave the FBI agents a chance to see who – or *what* they were fighting. They waited patiently to make sure everything inside that elevator was fully dead.

"Check it." Lester told Pettigrew, who didn't hesitate. He rose from his feet, the aim of his rifle unwavering and went for an inspection.

"Sir, there's no blood. There's only this . . . stuff."

"Drag them out." Lester yelled aloud so that everyone could hear."All but one." The team frantically dragged the massive bodies out piece by piece. The civilians couldn't help but remark on the differences in their anatomy.

"There's metal . . *inside* them. Who the hell are these guys Cap?"

"It's just like Schlesinger said. They are clones." Lester answered, tapping his finger on the matte-black carbon fiber vest attached to one of the bodies. The insignia had no color so it was difficult to see.

"Dynatech? *Fucking Dynatech!?*"Yelled the well-dressed man, *"They* are behind all this Shit!?"

"I'm afraid so." Lester answered. Agent Pettigrew put down his rifle and grabbed handful Of explosives, stuffed them loosely underneath the body and sent the thing back down.

"Let's see if they have any intelligence."

Aaron and three companions scurried around the corner of the raised lobby, sweating and breathing heavily. "Stairs," He stammered, holding his knees, "Stairs are gone."

"Lester! Are you there?" Lester's earpiece buzzed.

"Yes Gary!"

"I've got access to the lobby cameras – two are still operational somehow - there are hundreds of them!"

"I'll be there in 30 seconds." Lester responded. "Agent." He said above a dull roar, addressing Pettigrew, tossed him the detonator then took off towards the 'hub'.

Jasper planted his polyethylene-coated boots firmly into the inches-deep rocks on the roof with a pair of binoculars planted in his eye sockets. He flipped a knob on the side that switched the sights to thermal. Across the skyline, he could make out two distinct aircraft – moving slowly – too far away to tell how big they were. He pivoted his line of sight straight up into the cloud layer.

Come on . . . he whispered to himself, searching for his troopers. One by one, small red dots bled through the thick mist. An electronic beacon held in his gauntlet displayed his location roughly on theirs.

"This is 38-17. 38-01 confirm location."

"I'm here Mike. You're all right where you're supposed to be. See you in 30 seconds." Jasper ripped two orange flares open and held one in each hand until every last one of the Special 38 (now 33) touched down safely. By the time they all landed, the two dots on the horizon were much bigger now, and took form. Jasper quickly raised his binos again. Two very large, unorthodox looking aircraft sluggishly approached. Their trajectory was unmistakable – headed straight for the news building, albeit at a much slower pace than a normal jet.

"What now Jasper?" Eric asked. "What are those things?" asked Marcus.

"The Enemy." Jasper responded. "And we should find a way to kill them. Quickly."

"Gonna' be tough, those things are huge." Said Mikah, a dark skinned member of the 38, of which there were nine, "Didn't bring too many boomsticks, Jake and Patrick both brought a few H-LEV rockets, that's it. At least nothing that's gonna' bring those down."

"Alright, lets lock this building down tight. Nothing in or out, stairs are already blown. Move!" Jasper ordered, and in they building they all went. All Except Mike.

Technically everyone under Paul and Jasper were of equal rank, but Mike did things that would suggest otherwise. He routinely questioned his commander's decision making and logic, often with ideas of his own. He acted as if completely unaware of the chain-of command concept.

In a different outfit, this would be frowned up on and warrant punishment, but Jasper and Paul embraced it. None of the others bothered to voice their opinions about Mike's outbursts either. It was because he had an uncanny ability to be right all the time, like some sort of sixth sense that the spec38 both envied – and were thankful for. After a few years of combat together, they stopped refuting his divine intuition and used it, on more than one occasion, to stay alive.

"What's your plan?" Mike asked Jasper. But what he really meant to say was "I know you have no plan to destroy those aircraft." Jasper recognized Mike's coyness immediately and brushed it off appropriately.

"We've kind of been flying by the seat of our pants for a while now. If you have any bright ideas, feel free to enlighten me."

As much as Mike wanted to say he had the answer, he did not. Even from miles away the aircraft had a menacing look to them, frightening even – they must have been four or five times the size of the biggest jumbo jet. So big and heavy, they were most likely pushing their top speed. They both knew the vessels were packed with horrible things itching to get out and kill them.

"Fresh out sir. We should get inside and put our heads together and figure this one out, we've got fifteen minutes tops." At least Mike had a temporary bit of advice. On the way back down to the twenty second floor, Gary buzzed Jasper's headset.

"Hostiles coming up the stairs, floor 12 and climbing!" He yelled, panicking.

"The stairs are gone. It will hold them for a while."

"BUT SIR-"

"Calm down Gary you're gonna' make me deaf!"

"Hostiles are coming up the stairs! What the hell should I do?"

"Grab a weapon Gary." Jasper finished, and pushed the button to turn off his headset. They found their bewildered comrades standing in the elevator lobby. The rest of the spec38 were elsewhere. Destroyed bodies littered the floor with blood; that after minutes of being in fresh air, dried into a white dust leaving a potent, irritant odor behind.

"We got a lot more on the way everyone, get a grip."Jasper said. The civilians were in a zombie-like stance – an expected reaction for someone who had never killed before.

"Gary. Take everyone to the twenty-third, find a nice quiet hole."

"Yes sir."

Lester was technically in command, and stood feet away, but didn't think about refuting Jasper's orders.

"Captain. We've got problems. My men and I can't hold them off forever."

"What did you mean by *a lot more?*" Lester asked, hands on his hips. Even Jasper couldn't hide his worry.

"Two massive aircraft incoming. Aircraft like I've never seen before."

"What do you think is insi-"

Lester's question was interrupted by Gary's high pitched cackle tearing into their ears. Both of them shuddered and twitched; highly irritated.

"Guys I'm not good with guns, I-I've got some good news though . . .I-I-"

"Shut the fuck up and spit it out Gary!" Jasper growled.

"The Navy sir, I've made contact with the Navy!"

* * * *

Captain Edmund John Jackson stood statuesque in the helm of his ship, the USS Obama. The flagship dwarfed the frigates and even the carriers in length and tonnage, and carried enough marines to invade and conquer most nations. Her two-deck bridge provided a 360 degree view for miles around them. Several of his missile destroyers were heavily damaged, but still combat-operational. Five frigates encircling the group burned plumes of red and black into the sky, and only four of his twenty-seven ships remained unscathed.

Two missile destroyers, a Nimitz-class Aircraft Carrier just weeks from decommissioning, a frigate, and a service flotilla, were gone, along with 377 sailors. The wave that careened across the Atlantic hit them hard, and was upon them so fast they had but minutes to prepare for it. In a perhaps genius last order, Jackson positioned the bulk of his frigates directly in the path of the oncoming monster to form a makeshift breakwater for the USS Obama.

"Full speed ahead!" He told them, and to his surprise, they carried out the near-suicidal order without hesitation. It wasn't a completely sacrificial order, he knew the quicker, more agile frigates might have a chance to make their way up and over it.

The USS Miriam Gale took the wall head on, and was pushed headlong directly into the USS Dymantia. Both ships took defeating damage and succumbed to the relentless tide. They sunk ingloriously to the ocean floor, but succeeded in saving the bulk of the fleet. Some made it to the lifeboats, many didn't.

There were too many problems for Jackson to fix. The communication channels stayed fuzzy, satellites were down. His crew was visibly shook from the disaster; it made him remember what he was like as a young serviceman. Their primary directive was to make contact – with anyone. Without their GPS systems, the missiles hitting their targets relied on the eyesight of his crew. Another massive wave could be on it's way, and once again only his eyes could tell him. The lack of information available made it abundantly clear they could not defend themselves. There could be enemy fleets coming for them – a Russian nuclear submarine showed up on the SATNAV database before everything went dark, and a large portion of the Chinese Navy was carrying out "procedural exercises" two thousand miles off the coast of South America.

Jackson made his way to Captain by being stubborn, and damned if he was going to change now. He always refuted his instructors and frequently disobeyed the chain of command. His head-strong mentality simultaneously provided his biggest strength and his biggest weakness. The only reason he was never court-marshalled was that he was *damn good*. Despite his social inconsistencies, the Joint Chiefs of Staff unanimously agreed that he should hold title of Supreme Commander of their primary battle fleet in the Atlantic.

His track record in engagements shined without blemish and his presence demanded respect from even the most exalted, powerful men in the world. Jackson knew people were deathly afraid of him and knew exactly how to wield that fear as his own power. He stood every bit of six foot five and even at the age of sixty-two, woke up at five am every day to lift weights for two hours. His voice beckoned deep, and his stare peered into men's souls. His charcoal black skin rippled with bulging veins. A half-chewed, half smoked Belgian Sweet hung from his lip almost constantly. He barely liked smoking; grinding down the tobacco helped him to release angst and think clearly.

"Sir no one's answering, all the lines are dead." Said Lieutenant Haverstock. He wore thick earphones in front of a monitor, just one of the busy bees buzzing around the bridge in a *somewhat* organized panic.

"I don' care, Havers, just keep the lines open with the other ships, got it?" Edmund responded. His grisly voice had an automatic submissive effect on whoever he spoke to.

"Yes sir!"

"And Havers,"

"What, Captain?"

Jackson looked the young lieutenant up and down, eyebrows scrunched together in disgust.

"Tie up your damn boot, you're gonna' make someone trip."

Haverstock looked down to see a sliver of his lace touching the floor. He quickly snapped down and corrected the problem.

The heavy metal ovoid door clanged open and in walked Jackson's best battle consultant - An MIT graduate who decided designing smartphone apps wasn't rewarding enough.

"SITREP!" Jackson boomed, almost louder than the cumbersome door.

"All survivors are out of the water sir. We haven't been able to make contact with anyone so far. "

"That it?" Jackson demanded, refusing to look in the lieutenant's direction.

"I'm afraid so. All weapons still operational. SATNAV is completely gone. As of right now, we're sailing completely blind."

It was news Jackson wasn't surprised to hear. The plight of his fleet could be seen with The naked eye – he didn't need 21st century computers to tell him that.

"No word from Command?" The lieutenant asked redundantly, he knew Jackson wouldn't need his council if the Joint Chiefs had gotten word out.

"Nothing." He responded. "Not a damn thing." He continued, staring at the red telephone mounted on the bridge in front of him, praying for it to ring. The pre-century relic represented the limited functionality of their instruments of war; even with all of their digital technology and ordinance, the wired telephone was the highest form of technology still in working condition on the bridge.

"What are we going to do?" The lieutenant asked, concern rife in his tone. It irked Jackson - he hated any form of weakness, any *relent*. It was a sentiment he hadn't ever embraced and knew only blunt disregard as a mechanism to dispel it.

"We wait, son, we wa-"

Jackson's tone was interrupted by a piercing sonic boom that shook the windows of the bridge. In plain view, hovering a few hundred feet above the Obama's eighty-meter-wide deck, a metallic disk appeared instantly as if God himself placed it there. An immediate tingle raced up Jackson's spine – one of awe and confusion – his mind couldn't quite grasp what he was looking at.

"BATTLESTATIONS! BATTLESTATIONS!" Yelled the lieutenant, snatching a wired radio from a console on the bridge. "Fire squads on the deck immediately this is *not a drill!*" He commanded. Jackson respected his immediate reaction, but had orders of his own. He scanned the missile destroyers to his left and right to see their turrets already shifting to an intercept angle.

"Wait Lieutenant!" He growled, stopping everyone in the bridge dead in their tracks.

They stared wide-eyed, hoping this was the order they were all waiting for him to make; a solution for their situation, an *objective*.

"Tell those men to hold their fire."

"But sir-"

"I said hold their fire dammit!" He growled again, this time finally removing his hands From behind his back, flaring them at his side.

"It ain't' here to fight us son."

The craft slowly descended toward the deck, jostling awkwardly from side to side. It appeared the craft's pilots hadn't yet mastered how to operate it. Jackson snatched the handheld radio from the Lieutenant's hand and flipped a switch above it highlighted by "DECK RADIO". His voice boomed through the analog speakers mounted all over the deck, which was already beginning to fill up with armed marines.

"They want to land." He beckoned. "Let em' land."

The marines watched as the craft's oval bottom came within feet of the deck. Three weight-bearing legs sprung out to accept the touchdown. A section of the craft slithered open and stairs descended like an accordion. The first thing they saw was hands, then legs. A silent sigh of relief swept over the entire fleet. The other ships were lined with officers holding binoculars, others pointed mounted anti-aircraft machine guns at the craft. The subtly churning waves trickled against the steel plated ships, offering a slight reprieve to the tension in the air.

"We're unarmed!" A voice boomed from the otherworldly aircraft, "Can we come out now?"

Paul made damn sure every weapon on the vessel was stashed in a neat pile away from their reach. He told everyone on board to stick both of their hands out through the opening in plain sight.

"One at a time! Marines hold your fire!" Jackson responded succinctly through the speaker. One by one, the disc's occupants emerged. Each person that walked by was a reality check for the marines, who respectively did not know what to expect each time. It was like pulling surprises out of a stocking. The motley crew of recognizably normal-looking civilians, somehow thrown together in this situation, was baffling to everyone.

Paul was the last one to emerge, purposefully slow, hands raised. His garments alone, he knew, could turn a nervous finger into a pulled trigger.

"Up to the bridge, now!" Jackson commanded. Marines responded in kind by grabbing Their arms and leading them to peripheral staircases leading up in to the belly of the bridge structure. Once inside, Paul had no intention of wasting any time.

"Time to explain yourse-" Jackson began, but was unceremoniously interrupted.

"Captain Jackson. Captain Edmund Jackson. I know who you are." Paul said, removing his helmet, revealing for the first time his cleanly shaven, tattooed skull. Jackson held his hands to his sides, and the marines waited for him to issue an 'I'm the boss around here' command, but it never came.

"My name Is Paul. I am a member of the Special 38 covert tactical operations unit. I have fought for the military industrial complex my entire life. I have . . . *no life*. I have seen and done things common men would never believe possible. Everything I have seen and done has led me to this point." Paul spoke, walking toward Jackson. The tension rose, and a few marines thought about raising their rifles. They couldn't help but notice Paul still had a rather large bowie knife strapped to his chest. Jackson, with a discernable gesture of respect, inspected Paul up and down as he got closer. Given all of his years in the service, it didn't take long for him to decide, based on the many scratches, bruises and damaged sections of Paul's armor, that he was going to allow the man to speak freely.

"In all my battles, I have had to be absolutely sure about the situation I was in, in order to survive." He continued, removing his gauntlets and allowing them to thud onto the floor.

"And I can tell you, Captain Jackson, that I have never been so sure in my life, that this moment, right now, is a moment in which you need to listen to what this young woman has to say." He finished, turning slightly and pointing his hand unmistakably at Stacey. All eyes now on her, she momentarily became flustered, but pushed it down with a deep breath.

Everyone sat in silence listening to Stacey tell Jackson everything. Once in a while, the marines would give each other a look that entailed utter disbelief. Whenever she said something absolutely absurd (knowing full well it sounded that way coming out), Jackson would look at Paul to see if his facial expression gave anything away but it was firm, unchanging. The flat seriousness of his eyes portrayed nothing but truth.

"Aliens huh?" Jackson remarked after having said nothing for at least ten minutes. A brief silence made it tense for everyone. They were relying on Jackson believing their story. Pete padded his chest, looking for the cigarettes he threw away. His thoughts raced about what would happen to him if Captain Jackson found it what list he was on. Paul and Jasper relinquished the grace of their license to kill, would the Navy be so understanding?

"Well, always knew the bastards would show up some day, didn't we?"Jackson exclaimed, slapping his knees. "So this Lester Desjardins. Where is he?"

"Boston. He is in Boston." Stacey blurted.

"Sir do you really believe all of this?" Haverstock asked.

"I don't know yet Haverstock, but I'm – *we* are going to find out, got it?" Jackson responded. "Get word out. We're turning around." He ordered. He took the time to look at each passenger of the UFO, and was completely baffled as to how they all came to be in this situation. Their faces were worn and revealed visible exhaustion. None of them, except Paul, could look him directly in the eyes.

"And Haverstock. Get some food up here."

"Yes sir."

"Now it's time to tell me a bit about yourselves. You-" He pointed at the young woman, there only because she happened to work as the lab technician in the hangar. "What is your name?"

"Alexis."

"And where are you from Alexis?"

"West Virginia. But I-"

Before she could utter the words, Jackson snapped his fingers, and two marines took them by the arms. They became immediately alarmed, but Jackson reassured them they were in no trouble. His mind quickly told him Alexis and her similarly dressed male cohort didn't belong there.

"You." He said, pointing at Terrence. "Who are you and why are you here?"

"I-I'm Terrence. I-I b-build things and uhhh . . . fix computers." Terrence responded, jittering like a caught thief. Each second of Jackson's gaze tortured Terrence.

"You." Jackson pointed once again, this time directly at Mark.

"My name is Mark Brathurst. I work at a facility called S4 in Nevada. This is Eugene." Mark explained, noticing how nervous Eugene was. Luckily for Pete, he was the last on Jackson's list.

The sound of boots thudding heavily against metal grate interrupted the interrogation. The ovoid door creaked open again, revealing a marine panting heavily. "Sir! We've made contact! It's terrible! The whole world – everywhere, it's all –"

"PRIVATE!" Jackson growled, standing to his feet quicker than a man his age should have been able to. "Catch your breath. *Who* did you make contact with?" The kid took a deep breath and recollected the name.

"Someone named Jones with the FBI. Said he was in Boston and the city is under attack." The words gave relevance to everything Stacy had explained, solidifying their objective. Jackson's tone changed. His eyes flattened, his voice did as well.

"Alright. You've got my attention now. I hope you ain't pullin' my fleet into a shitstorm, 'Paul'."

Paul was already re-strapping his gauntlets and reaching for his helmet, readying himself for another bout.

"I can almost certainly guarantee that I am, Captain."

Chapter 18

INFILTRATION

Each step led them deeper into darkness. The further they got from the group of cyborg soldiers and the entrance to their refuge, the more cautious they became. There could be more soldiers, or more Reticulans waiting for them in the darkness. The Commander trudged robotically, without any flaws in his gait. Even the swing of his arms was uniform down the millimeter. He led them to a point he claimed would allow them to teleport back from whence he came; a feat that by design of the method that brought him there, should be impossible. The glow of their suits was luminous enough to allow them to see where their feet would land, but also enough to give their position away. After twenty minutes that seemed like days, the specifically raised portion of the cavern bearing the out-of-place train tracks came into view. As the unlikely trio approached it, they cautiously slowed their pace. The smoldering ruin of the train spread messily over the tracks provided an unwanted flashback for Sagittarius. It had been barely more than a day since he was here, but it seemed like an eternity. The silence compounded his thoughts and left a dauntingly dark feeling in his soul. It felt like the epitome of doubt, of uncertainty, and foreshadowed a near definite realization that his new life was going to challenge him both mentally and physically in much greater ways than he had already endured.

Somewhere in the concoction of despair and angst, was the spark that kept his feet moving, and his focus laser-like. He knew it was the fabric of his soul pulling at him; reminding him that he was meant to be here, at this time, doing what he was doing. It reminded him that he was meant for great things, and that all of his training, skills and accomplishments were about to culminate into his purpose for existing. Once again, Sagittarius consciously thanked his uncle for providing him with tools he needed, as a human man, to cope with the trials of his life as a Darmerian. A bittersweet moment came and passed. He even broke a mental smile that helped him cope with his fate. He hoped Tarliss could sense what he was feeling, although he knew his new mentor would never show it.

A thousand questions that needed answers would enter his mind and leave, all in an attempt to define his *purpose*. In retrospect, looking at the completely destroyed train; the vessel that brought him to this fated position, he realized and accepted that those questions were as frail and vulnerable as the train was. It served as a metaphor for his own situation – the train served its purpose to get him to safety, and was destroyed in doing so. If his fate was to be destroyed in order to serve his purpose then he was ready to accept it.

"Now what?" Tarliss asked the Commander, who replied only by pointing an index finger straight up.

"Illuminate our path." He said, then lowered his finger. Tarliss responded by detaching a small orb from his suit, which quickly grew very bright. He flung his hand toward the ceiling, and so followed the glowing orb. On it's way up it grew brighter and brighter until it reached the ceiling which was covered in twelve meter-wide circular holes from the digging vessels that created them, now embedded in the floor, covered almost entirely in subterranean dust.

The commander stepped over the tracks and scanned the ceiling, using his built in enhanced binocular vision to zoom into each individual hole.

"That one." He said, pointing. "That one will bring us the closest."

"Are you sure?" Tarliss asked.

"Yes. When we get to the top, there may be a few guards. The housing port is largely abandoned and quarantined after operations."

"Curious you would wait until now to tell us that, Commander?"

The Commander looked at Tarliss, and to both of the Darmerians' surprise, his lip raised slightly on one side. It could have been perceived as an odd twitch, but to them was undoubdtedly a smile.

"Did you think it was going to be a walk in the park?" He asked, in quite a human way. The trio huddled close together directly underneath the hole with the Commander in the middle, whom Tarliss ordered to hold his breath and cross his hands over his chest.

"Do not flinch a muscle, Commander." Tarliss demanded.

"Or else?"

"Or else you may not transition in one piece."

The Commander locked all of his joints up, and even the fluttering green code stopped running across his eyeballs. He essentially 'turned off'. The two Darmerians postured on either side of his huge frame, and reached their hands in a circle around him.

This is going to require a lot f energy. Are you ready? Sagittarius heard in his head, to which he replied *Born that way.*

Their hands locked, and they began to glow burning white. The illumination swirled around them in a three meter wide circle. The electric vibrating hum signified their quickly heightening psionic power.

See the destination in your head . . .

Their polymorphous suits both elongated into third arms extending from their chests and connected to the Commander's motionless body, trickling over every inch of it until it was entirely covered in the shiny material. A second later, the connected unit of living beings shot up at break neck speed, leaving a vitrified circle in their wake. Their line was not completely straight, they had to angle themselves in mid-hypertime to bend around the once bustling troop capsule jutting into their path. The orb light from Tarliss' suit accompanied them during the 'leap', travelling about a hundred feet above them to light the way. The ribbed glass tube extended three miles straight up with only moderate deviation, nothing to warrant worry about crashing. They made it to the top in just under seven seconds, and slowed down just in time to avoid slamming into the stalactite covered ceiling.

At the last available moment they slowed themselves down, and altered their course just enough to carry them up and over the lip of the hole and onto the ground. They landed rougher than expected, mostly because they had to compensate for the Commander's body, which weighed nearly half a ton.

Sagittarius detached and tumbled end over end a few times in the sand, which was littered with diamonds ranging from the size of a baseball to a grain of sand. The whole chamber had an entirely different look and feel to it than the one a few miles beneath it. Tarliss landed hard on his back, only discarding the commander's body feet before they hit. He was fine, but the Commander's joints locked up awkwardly and he bounced awkwardly a few times off the dusty floor.

Neither of the Darmerians had time to check his status, as the jump temporarily weakened them – for the next few seconds a well placed bullet could have pierced their all-but -invincible second skin.

Like the Commander had warned them, a few guards were in the vicinity and would have had to be blind and deaf to miss their arrival. Four streams of fire rained down on them. Sagittarius quickly identified one of the vectors, and leapt directly toward it – some two hundred feet on a raised metal platform overlooking the chamber floor. He didn't need to get close or be fancy about it – he flung a spear from his hand that connected directly between the eyes of his attacker and burned a hole into the ground. The piece slithered back along the floor and reintegrated with his suit as he landed.

Tarliss tried to block hollow point bullets coming from one angle but it wasn't easy – the force of multiple impacts knocked him down to his knees, forcing him to shape the liquid metal of his suit into a body-covering shield. Even then, he was having trouble.

A much larger caliber bullet struck him in the shoulder from the other direction. This time, there was nothing he could do to stop the next attack. Sagittarius spotted the second attacker in the distance but even with all of his psionic might, could do nothing to stop the next shot from coming. The soldier re-cocked his rifle and steadied his aim. Tarliss raised his hand as if to try and deflect the spike, while simultaneously using his other arm, shaped in an umbrella covering his body to stave off the initial attacker's pummeling rounds.

The soldier's finger began to squeeze down on the trigger, but two well-placed shots hit him in the neck and torso, in the sweet spot between his breast plate and shoulder, bringing him down. Sagittarius looked down to see the smoking barrel of the Commander's obligatorily large rifle.The first attacked shifted his focus toward the new threat, but hesitated to shoot. His tracking system identified the Commander as a friendly and sent his techno-brain into a fritz. The delay gave Sagittarius the time he needed to dispatch the soldier by removing his head. He pointed his hand like a gun and unleashed a thin beam of energy that left survival impossible. Tarliss let his head hit the floor, and his suit retook its common form around his body. It sparked and fizzled. He breathed heavily.

The Commander walked over to him, and looked him in the eyes. Neither of them spoke, and a telepathic conversation was nearly impossible with the half-organic soldier. He extended his large hand to help Tarliss to his feet. Despite the lack of communication, Tarliss was grateful. He knew the Commander had just saved his life.

"We should move swiftly. The track will lead us back to the main facility." The Commander said, then turned and began walking. The 'track' He was referring to was a long, thick conveyer belt entrenched in the floor adjacent to the many holes spread along the linear path of the cavern. Huge mechanized clamps hung from the ceiling above them on a similar track system.

They had a fair bit of walking ahead, and neither of the aliens believed it was a good idea to perform another 'jump'. After fifteen minutes of following the track from a healthy distance, they came up on the entrance. A set of doors that looked comically small against the expansive backdrop of the cavern walls. There was no one there to resist them from entering, so they took their time to elaborate a plan.

"Now what?" Tarliss asked. It was peculiar to Sagittarius that Tarliss was allowing the Commander to call the shots – to *lead.*

"We go in. You have refractive tech, don't you?"

"Yes"

"It will work well in here. They are far too trusting of their own power. They have not installed the proper detection in this facility."

"How do you know?" Tarliss asked. Sagittarius was witnessing Tarliss beginning to fully trust the cyborg. He would always need verification – to know the *why* of the situation – but was willing to allow the Commander to make decisions that could risk their lives. He couldn't help to wonder if Tarliss was more desperate, and if the Darmerians as a whole were more desperate than they let on.

"I have blueprints of the entire facility in my brain. I can also override the existing security system."

"What are you suggesting?"

"I will enter the Doppler wing. That is where they construct those like myself. I believe I will be able to override the neural interface systems of the SubTerra troopers in this facility."

"Are you sure you can do that?"

"82% certain." The Commander responded coldly. "Follow me, but keep a distance. Should anything go wrong, we will be forced to engage in combat."

Tarliss mulled over the plan in his head for a moment, then handed Sagittarius a capsule removed from his waist. The two of them vanished before the Commander's eyes.

Once inside the complex, the Commander seemed to know exactly where to go. There were many tunnels, stairs, doors leading to other rooms and tunnels, enough to make navigating a nightmare for one without previous knowledge of the facility. Unlike Starset, this place had largely abandoned areas; catacombs whose electric components had either run out or been purposely dismantled. The Commander felt comfortable enough to speak out loud in certain areas, knowing his invisible followers could hear him. Just before a thin set of very steep wooden stairs, some of which had eroded and splintered, he said, out loud, "My estimation was correct. I am now 98% certain my plan will succeed." It sounded both odd and reassuring at the same time.

The top of the stairs led him to a sealed vault-like door that required all three of them to force it open. It slammed into the floor quite loudly, revealing a room that was anything but barren. Stainless steel floors and bright lights adorned the new chamber. Fans in the ceiling kept the air fresh and the walls lacked the dusty covering from the previous areas. After a left, two rights and one more pristinely maintained set of steel steps, they encountered the first human being since they had entered the facility. The nearly eight foot ST soldier engulfed the entire doorway, making him impossible to miss.

The man was visibly startled, and dropped a see-through holograph-projecting tablet on the floor.

"Can-Can I h-help you?" He managed, trembling with deathly fear. His cheeks were eerily pasty evidently from a severe lack of sunlight. His blush could be seen from a hundred feet distant. The Darmerians calmly observed what the cyborg would do next, as there ensued a moment of silence that elevated the pressure on their nerves. The Commander's head twitched noticeably once to the left, and again to the right although his body remained awkwardly stiff. It worked well by portraying vulnerability; weakness, to the scared human man.

"I have malfunctioned." He explained, in a much less menacing tone than the one he used to communicate with the aliens. "Take me to the Doppler Exchange." The human's shoulders dipped with relief.

"W-Well why didn't you say so? F-Follow me. What unit are you with?" The man asked while spastically bending his knees to pick up his tablet, making sure not to lose eye contact.

"I am ST-101C. You programmed some of my subroutines, Dr."

"You are – ST101! How is that possible? You were deploy-"

"I SAID I *malfunctioned* Dr., along with the rest of my unit." The Commander interrupted, beginning his trek toward the Dr. His gainful, clattering gait, the mechanized pulse of his body movements, was an intimidating gesture for any human being; even for a man supposedly in control of the thing's brain.

"Bring me to the Doppler facility so I can continue my mission."

The human had no choice but to oblige the trudging giant.

"Very well. Commander!" He responded, and turned down the hallway, turning his back to the cyborg. He wasn't a complete fool – he could tell something wasn't right – but was his *malfunction* causing the awkward discourse? Or was the Commander lying to him? The Darmerians watched in silence, thoroughly impressed with the Commander's manipulation: he had the man too scared to disagree, and curious enough to play along in the banter. He noticed, but didn't bother to address, the fact that the cyborg walked past him and was in fact on his *own* way to the Doppler room.

"What happened to your regiment, Commander?" The man asked, scurrying along with the determined soldier.

"Our Enemies attacked us and disabled the entire unit. I managed to escape."

"So you didn't malfunction after all? How did you make it *back* up here?"

"We failed in combat and failed our mission. That *was* our malfunction, Doctor. I stole a device from the Aliens. I was able to integrate it into my suit and use it to return safely."

Coming from the monotonous, deep voice of the robot, it sounded believable. The human was more in awe; his scientifically inquisitive mind sparked, to question the statement's validity.

"That is fascinating! But . . . but the entire regiment . . . gone you said? Wh-wh-what-where are they? Are we in danger!?"

"I believe we are safe, for now."

"For now!?"

"Yes. I managed to detonate our vessels. The explosion was sufficient enough to deny them access to our location." Explained the Commander, then took a sharp right toward a cylindrical elevator embedded in jagged rock. The man, encapsulated and mystified by what he was hearing, walked a few steps before adjusting his path in the same direction.

As he stood and waited for the crank-and-cogwheel platform to lift his mass into the air, he looked directly at the Darmerians, whom upon the robot's gaze, were convinced he could actually *see* them. His right hand, hidden from the Doctor's view, fluttered a series of symbols he could have otherwise dismissed as a 'twitch' had the Doctor been keen enough to pick upon. Both of the camouflaged aliens instantly committed the signals to memory.

Along with the hand signals came a sense of something else – the Commander was being unnecessarily coy with the human, and lying when he didn't need to. Attempting to understand why he would do such a thing, it dawned on Tarliss that the Commander's motives may not be entirely what he portrayed. He tried to peer into the robot's mind, but was unable to see his thoughts clearly. There was something there though – something he had become all too familiar with – a resentful, brooding anger.

"What is it?" Sagittarius asked, picking up on Tarliss' thoughts.

"He wanted revenge. I think all other objectives are secondary to him."

"You can't tell what he's thinking?"

"I can't."

A moment of silence, denoting an unwelcome feeling of uncertainty ensued as they watched the slow-moving lift ascend, the Commander's gaze still resting firmly upon them.

"Be prepared for anything Sagittarius. I don't think our new ally is going to wait to get his revenge."

The elevator ground to a halt at a ledge a hundred meters high on the rock face. The Commander wasted no time in trudging onto the platform. His human counterpart was becoming visibly more aware of the robot's strange disposition; walking faster and ahead as if to lead the way.

"Are you nervous, Doctor?"

"W-why do you ask?"

"It is a logical response. My entire regiment is missing."

"B-but we have more, much more!" The man exclaimed, excited, "We have enough to replace you!"

The commander remained silent as the duo approached the only door available.

"So what will you do with me, if I am *replaceable?*" The commander asked.

"Decommissioning, I suppose, you are now obsolete." The Doctor responded, continuing his cheerful tone. The large metal doors hissed, a cylindrical bar in the middle compressed and twisted. They slid open.

"If that is what is necessary. I should debrief the battle coordinators before I am destroyed."

"That won't be required of you. Please proc-"

"I will tell them *exactly* what happened." The Commander interrupted, twisting his head down at the human, whose face was sucked of joy and filled with doubt. "But first I must tell you something. My regiment is safe, outside the enemy's refuge. I found it and made a deal with our enemies."

"You're malfunctioning!" The Doctor yelled, trying to assert himself as a last ditch effort over the cyborg he *thought* was programmed to obey him. The shriek alerted seven other humans in the room, all wearing similar labcoats, monitoring and tweaking half-built versions of himself; propped vertically on slabs of fluorescent metal, with machines and needles surrounding their bodies.

"That may be true," The Commander responded calmly, "But I am *irreplaceable*." The robot snapped his arm like a cobra onto the doctor's shoulder and squeezed, snapping bone instantly. The frail man shrieked in pain, and then was tossed like a frisbee a dozen meters into the circular chamber. Pieces of his ripped clavicle and flesh remained in the Commander's hand.

The Darmerians, following just close enough, both stood and flexed a battle-ready posture.

"Wait!" Tarliss telepathed, "Do not interfere. Let him have what he wants."

The robot mercilessly murdered each and every man and woman in the room, with the kind of ruthless precision that impressed even them. Some of the worker bees tried to flee but the exits slam closed. As the lights above each doorway flickered, so did a red light built into a shoulder plate on ST101C's back. A double barreled pulse-pistol attached to his hip was enough to dispatch most of the helpless targets, his speed, power and bare hands did the rest. Sagittarius and Tarliss crept into the room, their path lit by a green hue in the floor. It led to a hip-level pedestal housing a holographic screen with buttons.

After the massacre had finished, and every human in the room dead, the Commander removed his helmet and dropped it to the ground. His gun fell as well. He walked at a seemingly relaxed pace to a slightly raised, circular pad in the middle of the chamber with a number of larger holopads encircling it.

"You saw my message, Darmerian?" He said, aware of their presence.

"Of course, Commander." Tarliss responded, but his reply lacked confidence. By now, the aliens knew the cyborg Commando could read, calculate and interpret every action, every word they said to a point where he had a psychological upper hand. After Tarliss nodded his head to Sagittarius, who was visibly reluctant to so easily be compliant with the Cyborg's *methods*, punched the five digit code into the pad.

'54545'

"Thank you for not interfering, Tarliss." The Commander uttered, rapidly slamming his huge fingers into sequences on the screens in front of him.

"What does the code do?"

"You will see soon." He responded, after entering the last lines of necessary codes and commands.

Both of the aliens couldn't help but think they had just been lead into a trap – he was being purposefully coy with them, just as he did with the now dead Doctor. Like the door that allowed them entrance, a vibration made the loose dust on the floor dance, then a loud, decompressing hiss whistled loudly inside the chamber. Ringed, stair-like circular sections of the floor began descending, while parallel concentric rings in the ceiling began to raise. As the cracks formed in between the concrete slab implements, indigo blue shone brightly into the room. As they grew wider, they realized they were actually inside a much bigger room.

A hexagonal tunnel, each panel spanning ten meters or more and brimming with suddenly awakened lights, housed row upon row of ST shock troops. They slept steadily and received injections from a series of metal arms suspended from conveyor tracks in between rows. Some, like the ones being worked on by humans, were missing body parts. Floating robotic drones carried legs, arms, chest plates and helmets along with the tools to install them. They carried out their work oblivious of everything around them.

The Commander made use of a silver metal stairway that extended from his platform down to another pedestal stuck in one of the hexagon's panels. It was obvious by their back and forth flimsiness they weren't designed to harness his weight.

He removed the thick armor plate covering the left side of his chest, and reached into the area where his heart would be and detached what looked like an oversized silicon chip, followed by wires.

He stuck the chip into a slot in the pedestal like an ancient video game cartridge. The indigo light switched to red, the track system came to life. The entire honeycomb contraption vibrated.

"Don't worry, Tarliss, They are all under my control." The Commander said. "Now, as promised, we will disable the grid and allow your escape."

Even though the Commander seemed to be honoring his word, the Darmerians were still weary of deception. He now had complete control of the facility, every soldier inside of it, and the situation as a whole. He trudged back up the staircase and approached them. "There." He said, pointing at a barren section of rock wall behind them. As they walked toward it, the faux rock slab slid away, revealing a motherboard of circuitry.

"I can override the entire system. But it won't be long before it resets itself."

"How long?" Tarliss asked. The Commander's eyes flickered for a few seconds, calculating.

"29 minutes and 48 seconds."

The Darmerians looked at each other, then back at the Commander.

"Do it."

The Commander plugged himself into the motherboard. It lit up like a Christmas tree; blue green, red and white lights flickering. He removed his chip.

"Your clock has begun, Darmerians." The Commander proclaimed, then strode toward an area of the room housing a chair, and sitting in it a lifeless, half-built ST trooper.

"What will you do?" Tarliss asked, truly curious of the Commander's intentions, now that he had achieved virtual omnipotence. The Commander swept the unfinished soldier onto the floor, adding to the lifeless corpses around him, and sat firmly in the chair.

"There have been upgrades to my design since I was created. I will become a more efficient soldier." He said, as the metal implements surrounding the chair came to life.

"And then what?"

"Do not worry, Darmerian. My enemy is your enemy. I will use all of my resources to destroy those who oppose my objective."

"Objective?" Tarliss continued, to which the Commander, after careful consideration, responded: "Revenge."

The two Darmerians looked at each other, realizing there was not a moment to spare. The Commander had stayed true to his word, helping them to achieve their goal. They had no choice but to leave him to his own devices. Before they turned to leave, The Commander had some advice for them.

"You do not have time to make it back, Tarliss. The system will reboot before you and your ilk can leave the planet." He said, as a series of mechanical arms went to work on his oversized body. One removed his chest plate, another unhinged the gauntlets drilled into his arms. Tiny bits of blood trickled out, but the wounds quickly cauterized.

"What do you suggest we do then?" Tarliss asked, this time with a modicum of annoyance. More red lights flickered above a seemingly bare section of rock meters from the 'upgrade' chamber. The five meter slab rumbled open, revealing a long chasm.

"Follow the path. There will be a vessel waiting for you — I can order one of my soldiers outside your refuge to fall into the portal, and deliver the message to your leaders to leave the planet."

Staring down the long tunnel, a microcosmic representation of the risk they were about to take, the Darmerians felt an overwhelming sense of vulnerability. Sagittarius mentally pestered Tarliss, reminding him that following through with the cyborg's plan would yield what little leverage they had left.

It is our only option . . . .

"Very well Commander. Although you may not understand, or care to hear it, we are thankful."

"I understand your sentiment, Darmerian, but your thankfulness is not necessary. We are bound by a common enemy."

Tarliss absorbed the reality for a moment, then began moving toward the seemingly endless cavern that would bring them to their destination. Just before they disappeared from the Commander's view, he said one last thing to them, which seemed very odd considering the unlikelihood of them ever meeting again.

"I am not just a machine, Darmerian. I am . . ." The Commander stuttered, his head twitched, "I am a man. My name . . .My name is Adam." He said, more for himself than the aliens.

The Darmerians glowed bright, enough to illuminate the entire room, then all at once, shot into the cavern, leaving the Commander alone with his thoughts, and the mindless minions now exiting the honeycomb structure beneath.

"I-. . ." he whispered to himself, "I am Adam."

The mechanical arms continued their work on his body, breaking down sections and reconstructing them with brand new armor plates. He closed his eyes, and tapped into the network controlling the facility. An overwhelming displacement of information – even for his augmented brain – flooded his synapses. He learned at a rate even *he* didn't know was possible, exponentially increasing his intelligence and knowledge. It did nothing to deter him from how he felt about his enemies – only exacerbated the hatred still brewing fiercely inside of him.

As promised, he sent the order to one of his soldiers to enter the Darmerian facility via the portal he discovered, with the proper message, simultaneously viewing the events through the eyes of another nearby minion.

It took only seconds for him to search every nook and cranny of every underground facility connected to the network. No secret could be hidden, no technology existed without his knowledge. His eyes opened abruptly, after his mind stumbled upon something that made his calculative superbrain slow down. In the deepest sublevel of this facility was a room that housed, among other things, a treasure he could not resist. Some of the material comprising the suits worn by the Darmerians was being held inside of an all but inaccessible chamber, lightly protected. Evidently the ones who created this place were occupied with the destruction of the world he once knew, and hadn't the resources to protect the gift from his grasp. ST101C stood up from the chair, fully reassembled and upgraded with the best advancements available to him. A dozen fresh ST troopers, the next *batch*, stood before him, motionless, awaiting his command. One of them looked nearly identical to him, safe for a slightly thicker gauntlet wrapping his right arm and a less cumbersome helmet. Underneath the triangular Dynatech insignia etched above his heart, 'ST401C'.

:://VERY MINIMAL THREAT LEVEL . . . ADVISE TECHNO-MENTAL COERCION . . . TO BE SAFE

He relayed the information to the brains of his minions, which were surprisingly unhindered by the transfer – something that would have definitely caused problems for the now *obsolete* regiment he was assigned to originally. What little free thought his upgraded version was gifted with was instantly smothered and locked into subroutines. ST104C was as much a threat to him as an ant underneath his boot.

:://WHAT WILL YOU DO?

The Darmerians' question resonated in his mind, over and over, and after some literal and spiritual searching, the answer presented itself. He came across video recording of the battle at Starset, where ten Darmerians destroyed ten full regiments of ST troopers, seventy three Reticulans, and four cloned warriors for which there was very little available information, at least not that he could find, as to their creation or existence.

They left in haste, after successfully disabling the HEAR relay. Had they the time or the presence of mind, they would have searched the facility in depth, and found a deep chamber only accessible by a cleverly hidden door on the first sublevel. Inside the steel trap, a series of frozen capsules housing frozen genetic material - enough left over to possibly replicate one of the creatures.

* * * *

"Get me something to plug this hole, I need to stop the bleeding!" Yelled the nurse, who'soccupation made her the only one in the building Lester trusted to manage Jim's injuries. Her cashmere sweater dripped blood, soaking her skin. Lester took a moment to admire her resolve, she couldn't have been older than twenty-five. No one in the room moved to acquire a plug for her, so without hesitation she ripped the sweater off, tore it into strips and fashioned a very crude tourniquet around Jim's leg.

"That's all I can do for him. We have no drugs." She said, hands on her hips. Silence ensued, alluding to the fact they all knew. Jim was going to die.

"Lester!" boomed a voice from the hallway, "My men are in position. Mild resistance on the 16th and 18th, but Gary is telling me their numbers are still gaining. We can't hold them forever" It was Jasper, who for the first time since Lester commandeered him, relayed a genuine aura of panic as he spoke.

"Give me some better news, Jasper." Lester responded, leaving the room with him.

"Gary is on the line with the Atlantic main battle group. They say they are with Paul. I think he convinced them to come and help us."

"How long?"

"Their systems are in bad shape, no satellite coverage. It will be half a day before they are within weapons range."

"That's better than I thought." Lester murmured. He stopped, looked Jasper directly in the eyes, with a stare sharp enough to cut diamonds.

"What is the endgame, soldier?"

"I don't know Captain. I don't know. This may very well be our last stand. It's only a matter of time before we're overwhelmed. If those things can't take the building by force, I suspect they'll just level it."

Lester was surprised it hadn't happened already. He peered out the window at the far end of the hallway, now lit bright orange by the setting sun. Two large, bird-shaped silhouettes hung in front of it.

"Fuck. . ." He muttered, looking at Jasper, who's eyes were devoid of the hope he had come to rely on. Boots thudded around the corner. It was

Mike. Carrying a weapon that looked too heavy for one man to carry, let alone run with.

"We can lase the targets, Jasper."

"They're too far away it's imposs-"

"I KNOW it's far-fetched, but do you have a better idea?" Mike interrupted, slowing his pace. "Those ships pack a wallop, and you know it."

Looking at the matte green tube decorated with buttons and levers, and with a large reticule housed in plastic, it became obvious that hey at least had to try. Lester remembered bits of footage he had seen in years past, detailing the full destructive power of modern US warships. No aircraft, no matter how large and menacing, could withstand their onslaught.

"Alright." Lester exclaimed. "You two head to the roof with that thing. Make it happen boys." The way it came out sounded fatherly and subtly deafened their doubts. Lester turned and jogged as briskly as a man of his stature, age, and level of fatigue could.

"Gary. Tell them we are lasing."

"But sir the chances of that working are nearly impossible. We have no telemetric imaging available to us-"

"JONES!" Lester growled, and slammed both his hands onto Gary's chair, squeezing it with bear-like ferocity.

"*Tell* them, we are lasing. I don't care what you have to do, just *make* it happen, got it soldier?"

"Are they fucking crazy? We can't lase, not even close!" Haverstock yelled.

"I believe I can be of some assistance." Said Terrence above a whisper, although everyone on the bridge focused on him.

"You should bring me to your communications room."

"What for?" Jackson asked him angrily. "Captain, For all intents and purposes, I have the most skilled technological mind in the world. There is not a vehicle, computer or mobile phone on this planet I cannot hack within minutes."

"What are you saying?" Paul asked him, intrigued. Terrence took a few seconds to collect his thoughts, made evident by the way he grasped an invisible object with his hands.

"If . . . If there are any satellites left up there, I believe I can hack into one of them and trick into believing it is under our control. We won't be able to use it's guidance systems, but with the computer inside of it, I can calculate a trajectory that will allow your missiles to go where you want them to, even at long distances."

The room was silent for an awkwardly long moment, Terrence waiting for a response, his hands still formed into an invisible basketball.

"So you're telling me," said Haverstock, "That you want us to just pick a spot in the sky and *shoot?*" He finished, looking around the room to quantify opinions. The feat sounded more like a fairy tale then part of a strategic attack plan. Jackson stepped closer to Terrence as if to examine him like a wounded animal. His eyes squinted, his lips raised inquisitively.

"I thought you just *built stuff*, Terrence. You sure you can pull off something like that?"

"I was given a life sentence for hacking into US military satellites, Captain. You might say I was born to do it."

"You're *sure?*" Asked the Captain, realizing he had no other option.

Smiling, Terrence couldn't resist.

"I guarantee it!" He cheerfully exclaimed, even pointing his finger skyward.

The silence of the sixteenth floor, and of the fourteen warriors occupying it, was broken only by the mechanical jostling of another squad of Dynatech monstrosities on their way to kill them. They lent no regard to stealth, and their plan didn't seem to extend further than overwhelming by sheer number and force. They had already managed to remove tons of demolished concrete and twisted railing in order to continue. The sixteenth had a much different layout than the twenty second – once out of the stairwell, a ten-foot hallway spanned twenty meters straight ahead, with doorways leading to a sprawl of cubicles on each side. A perpendicular hallway connecting to it at the entrance reached the full diameter of the building, nearly sixty meters.

"Thirty seconds." Vinh whispered over his closed-link comms, relaying the message only to the men on the floor. They sat deathly silent and waited for their enemies to enter the killbox.

"Fifteen seconds."

Erfan, Jack and Peter slid onto the floor at the very edge of the long hallway and set up their rifles in a mounted position behind the cover of a desk. Jack set up in the middle with the higher caliber STOP rifle.

"Five seconds."

Eric, Marcus and Ramy took a similar position at the end of the other hall, with a straight view of the entrance, also covered from sight. On cue, the lumbering Dynatech soldiers began to pour in and disperse, weapons raised, scanning the angles. When twenty-five or so of them were inside, Vinh whispered into his radio: "Grenades."

A half dozen of the bombs bounced into the hallway, heaved accurately from behind cubicles. The troops' numbers were cut in half immediately. The rest fired at anything and everything, hoping to get lucky. The two three man firing teams popped up from their respective enclaves and began picking off the disoriented robots with pinpoint accurate fire. When the smoke cleared, one of the troopers, cut in half at the waist, continued crawling down the hallway towards its rifle. Vinh popped around the corner and fired a shot through its helmet.

"Ammo Check." He whispered. The entire floor resumed the eerie silence, as more troops were on their way. A few clicks and clacks meant the group was ready for more. The next wave had learned their lesson — the first soldiers in carried body-engulfing metal walls with bullet proof windows at eye level. They once again began to push down the hallways, most taking cover from the shields. Still, the accurately placed shots of the spec38 thwarted them before they could achieve an advantageous firing position. The lifeless bodies were beginning to pile up high enough to take cover behind.

"Ammo check." Vinh whispered again, although he was waiting for the first of his brothers to tell him they were low on ammunition. Three different voices made the acknowledgement. No level of efficiency would suffice for the sheer numbers being thrown at them.

"I'm hit. Need field dressing." Said Eric, to which Vinh fluttered a series of hand signals at Yasser, who sat behind a desk in the most well-protected area of the cubicle sprawl. He rushed over to Eric, who had three pieces of shrapnel sticking blatantly into his side. He coughed up blood and breathed with a heavy wheeze, but otherwise showed no signs of impairment.

They followed this routine four times, until the whole group was running low on ammunition. A few had elected to pick up the rifles dropped by the brainless soldiers and scavenged magazines from their bodies. They found the rifles to be incredibly heavy, too heavy to carry normally, even for their densely muscled arms. They did however, prove to be extremely powerful and effective when propped on top of something and used as a stationary turret. After dozens of bodies lay dismembered and destroyed, and enough of the Spec38 injured and bloodied to the point where Yasser could not tend to them all effectively, Vinh decided it was time to leave.

"Eric, time for the HLEV."

"But sir, that'll leave us he-"

"I've got that covered, we can't let them get past the 17th."

"Roger that sir!"

Eric raised the huge cylinder to his shoulder, aiming it directly at the hole. He left himself exposed to a robot soldier stepping over one of his dead comrades, as Marcus stuffed a rocket into the back of the tube.

"Fire in the hole!" He yelled, then squeezed the double-trigger.

The rocket obliterated the entrance, along with what little remained of the staircase. The explosion sent concrete and glass in every direction. Vinh popped his head into the hallway, and switched on his IR scope to bypass the thick dust. The entrance was completely destroyed, along with a few enemies. A twitching gauntlet protruded from between two slabs of concrete.

"Jasper this is Vinh. We have to abandon the 18th, we are being overrun." Vinh yelled into his headset, waiting for a reply, which after a more than five seconds, took too long for comfort.

"Roger that Vinh, there's a clear spot on the adjacent building. West side. Can you make it?"

Vinh sped to the end of the hallway to get a clear look out of the window on the far west side. The building was significantly lower than their current position. They would have just enough time to safely deploy their parachutes.

"Another jump, Vinh?" Eric asked, with a playful smirk etched to his face.

"You bet, soldier. Gear up!"

"Jasper, the Obama says they have fired eight warheads, they'll be here in under five minutes! They've got additional salvos ready if we need them!"

"Roger that Gary, keep them on the line."

Jasper and Mike laid at the very edge of the building, facing the two incoming ships, which were now hovering above a part of the city covered in three and four story buildings, roughly a half mile from the site of the explosion at the G8 summit. It wasn't until they had finally come so close that they both realized the sheer scale of the vessels. Each one rose twenty five stories, and spanned more than ten city blocks. They both slowly lowered to the structures beneath, easily crushing everything under their immense weight. They were essentially flying buildings, designed solely for the purpose of destruction and chaos.

"You seeing his?" Mike asked, after Jasper had finished communicating through his headset.

"Pretty hard to miss. Anything happening on the ground?"

"One second." Mike responded, then carefully aimed the scope of his oversized rifle at ground level. A considerable amount of dust and debris blocked his vision.

"Can't see a thing. Switching to IR."

"Anything?"

"Lots of movement down there. Hard to be clear exactly what . . ." Mike's voice trailed off abruptly as if he had fallen asleep mid sentence.

"What is it Mike?"

"My . . . god . . . either I'm crazy or . . . See for yourself."

Jasper stood up, Mike rolled over to his position holding the lasing gun. Jasper looked through the powerful scope, which provided a clear picture up out to five miles. The IR showed dozens of man-shaped silhouettes pouring out of the vessel, growing more numerous by the second. A quick glance at the opposite end showed a line of heavily armored assault vehicles leaving the ship and filling the streets.

"In the middle, two stories up." Mike told him. Jasper quickly shifted his focus, and turned off the IR scope – giant vents from the vessel itself were quickly clearing away all of the dust and debris, giving him a clear line of sight. Standing almost twice as tall as the legions of soldiers in it's thrall, was the most ghastly, unsightly creature Jasper had ever laid eyes upon. Its skin was repulsively green and scaly, it's chest covered sparsely in thick sections of dirtied feathers. Drool hung off the end of it's elongated snout, and it's eyes burned as red as blood. The thing lifted one of its arms and pointed down the corridor of a street, to which every soldier in front of it began marching. In its other hand, it held a two-pronged blade big enough to dispatch two of the soldiers with a single swipe.

"Now we've seen some pretty fucked up stuff together, Jasper, but you wanna' venture a guess as to what the hell *that* thing is?"

Jasper hadn't the intent to waste any time. His killer instinct took over naturally. He began adjusting the rifle's reticule to prepare for a shot. The creature did not move quickly. It was obvious to him that it was there to give orders to the brainless warriors surrounding it. An opening in the buildings would allow him the opportunity.

"You're not actually going to . . . " Mike asked in disbelief, trailing off.

"Keep your focus on that laser, Mike."

Jasper sucked his breath in deep, and began to slowly squeeze the trigger. The bullet erupted from the barrel, jolting him slightly. Two full seconds later, the spike hit it's mark, and did what he had hoped it would – the projectile hit the creature directly in the chest, splattering it's red guts onto the concrete.

"Wow. Nice shot, that was over a mile and a half." Mike said.

"I had to know."

"Know what?"

"If we can kill them. At least, by conventional means."

"I think you've answered that question."

"Jasper, missiles inbound in two minutes! You got that laser on target?" It was Lester booming over the headset from the hub, presumably with Gary.

"Yes Captain. We're waiting patiently. I should probably tell you, there are giant reptiles with them."

Lester did not respond, although Jasper knew he heard the words. In a different scenario it would have been a stretch to believe, but considering what they had already been through it seemed completely appropriate.

"Good news though, I put a bullet in one. They *are* mortal."

"That is good news Jasper. I'm going to check on Jim."

Lester threw down his headset and patted Gary on the shoulder, who returned an 'I've got it under control' sort of head nod. He rushed to the room where Jim's life hung in the balance. The nurse was doing everything she could to stop the bleeding, but to no avail. To his surprise, Jim was conscious. He slid onto his knees and clutched Jim's bloodied hand. It was cold and lacked the strength to return a full squeeze.

"Lester . . " He murmured, eyes barely open.

"I'm here Jim, I'm here. You're gonna' make it, the nurse has stopped the bleeding."

"Don't bullshit me Lester. You know I can always tell." Jim said, spitting up blood as the words came out. Lester bowed his head to the floor, fighting back the tears that he had been staving off for quite some time.

"I'm sorry Lester. I shouldn't have lied to you. I – I . . . "

"It's okay Jim. You did what you had to do to keep Anthony safe. We made contact with the navy – they say Anthony is alive!" Lester exclaimed.

"Thank God," Jim said, with considerable pain, although he managed a smile. "He is meant for great things, that kid. Always knew it."

"Me too Jim, me too." Jim's head rolled back, his eyes drew nearly shut. The entire room flashed bright orange as the missiles from the Atlantic fleet hammered into the huge vessels sent to destroy them.

"Look, Jim! We've been saved!" Lester yelled. He turned the makeshift gurney around, (a trolley meant for transporting documents around the building) so that Jim could see the fire show for himself. Seconds later, the building rumbled from the shockwave.

"Direct hit! Direct hit!" Jasper's voice screeched over Lester's headset. He removed the earpiece and dropped it to the floor.

"It's . . . beautiful . . ." Jim exhaled, "So . . . beautiful." It was his last breath. Lester felt the life leave his body as Jim's already weakened clutch dissipated to nothing. His hand fell to the wayside. The nurse walked over and held Lester by the shoulder. He tried to fight it, to stay strong, but could not help it. He broke down and cried in a way he hadn't in years – not years – *ever*.

His headset buzzed on the floor. Jasper waited for an update. The nurse picked up the device and handed it to Lester.

"Good work Jasper." He managed, "What's going on below us?"

"The rest of my soldiers made it off the seventeenth. The attackers seem to have stopped altogether. I have a few men on the 16th doing a sweep of the building. Mike and I are en route to your position now."

"See you soon." Lester said, once again peeling the sweat-and-blood drenched earpiece from his cranium, and wiping the tears from his eyes.

"I know this is a hard time for you, Mr. Desjardins." Said the nurse, who couldn't help but share his sentiment, shedding tears of her own. "But it was you who saved *us*. without you, we'd all be dead." She finished. Lester looked around the room to see the worn, dusty faces of half a dozen civilians. They looked at him in awe, with tired eyes. Some were crying, some remained straight-faced, but all unanimously agreed with the nurse's words, as was evident by their body language.

"I guess what I'm trying to say is . . . thank you, Lester."

"Yeah, thanks Lester. Forreal." Said the dark-skinned civilian who had bravely helped them when the elevator full of warriors was coming to kill them.

Lester stood to his feet, staring down at his fallen comrade, realizing that Jim was not the first, nor would he be the last. He truly would have traded places with the man if he could.

"Thanks, everyone. I wish I had some words of reassurance for you." Lester said, as Jasper and Mike bustled into the room.

"But I have to be honest when I tell you, that our fight has just begun."

* * * *

Tarliss motioned for Sagittarius to enter the expansive hangar bay, after visually scanning every nook and cranny. Although the Commander showed no signs of treachery, they couldn't help but err on the side of caution. They knew all too well how easy it would be for the Commander to trap them, and to lead them into that trap by coercion. Despite their weariness, there was a boomerang shaped plane waiting there for them, just like he told them there would be. Sagittarius cautiously entered the quiet hangar, waiting for their thoughts of mistrust to become reality. The path that brought them there slid shut and disappeared entirely seconds after Sagittarius moved away from it. They weren't sure to be nervous, or reassured, in knowing that the Commander (or at least part of him) was still carefully watching their movements. A hissing release of steam pierced their eardrums – a hatch on the underbelly of the wing-shaped craft peeled open as lights all over the thing came alive. The Darmerians entered it carefully.

"So far so good." Tarliss said. Sagittarius sensed the hesitation in his tone.

"If he's trying to kill us, I doubt he'd go so far to gain our trust."

"That's exactly how he wants you to think, Tarliss."

Tarliss brushed off the comment and shifted his focus toward the cockpit, where an array of holopads, buttons and levers awaited their input. Sagittarius would need a few minutes to decipher it's method of operation, but to Tarliss it might as well be Egyptian hieroglyphics.

"This one is all you." He said, acknowledging his lack of understanding of the apparatus. Sagittarius sat down in the pilot's chair and began to scan the devices, wondering where to start. Before he could push a button or type in a command, a large screen in front of him bristled with energy and popped up. An impossible to confuse message glared in green writing:

```
://AUTOPILOT ENGAGED.  COORDINATES CONFIRMED//:
```

The hatch to the aircraft shut on its own, sealing them inside. Another message flashed beneath the first.

```
://IT WILL TAKE YOU TO YOUR SHIP.  GOODBYE
DARMERIANS.//:
```

On cue, the dual turbines housed underneath the broad wings of the craft began to vibrate And spin. A beam of light illuminated the cockpit; caused by an opening in the distant roof. For Sagittarius it was very welcoming – he had almost forgotten how daylight felt. In fact, it made him feel so good he knew it was more than just a thought.

"The sun on this planet offers a multitude of benefits for our suits. You will get used to the feeling." Tarliss told him.

"What kind of benefits?"

"An increase in psionic capacity of up to forty percent."

The craft lifted off slowly like a space-bound rocket, but quickly and exponentially gained speed. A sudden jolt pinned them to their seats, and within seconds the only thing visible was deep, uniform bright blue.

The craft reached ten thousand feet and tilted horizontally, leveling out perfectly even. They both expected to see a bit of green, perhaps blue or even the expansive tan of desert, but most of the terrain was blistered red. Fissures of lava criss-crossed the terrain for miles, stopped only by the steaming, churning ocean.

"My god . . ." Sagittarius muttered, wide-eyed. On the edge of their vision, a violent storm raged. A hundred tornadoes swirled among thousands of lightning blasts. Spurts of hard-hitting rain pummelled the glass.

"Not God, Sagittarius. Humans." Tarliss reminded him why all of this was happening. He wondered if the entire planet was suffering a similar fate. Another jolt accelerated the craft toward a point in the sky. Within seconds, a massive, egg-shaped outline came into view on the very border of the atmosphere. Although far away, the vessel's immense size was near impossible to miss.

"There." Tarliss pointed. "It appears the Commander's message got through." As they began to absorb a sense of relief, the cockpit's sensors went haywire. Red lights flashed on the holopad:

!INCOMING ATTACK CRAFT. TWO ON APPROACH. 11 MILES SOUTH ENCLOSING FAST. READYING COUNTERMEASURES!

"That can't be good!" Sagittarius yelled. "I don't think this plane's got weapons." He searched the control panel, but found nothing alluding to armament. Had the Commander tricked them after all?

"How far are we to the target?" Sagittarius asked firmly. That was one thing Sagittarius *could* find out. After some careful button mashing, "Eighteen and half miles AKA 2 minutes. They'll be on top of us in half that!"

!INBOUND PROJECTILE!

The missile closed the gap in just five seconds, but the countermeasures did their job. The hot flares connected with it causing it to explode only a half-dozen meters beneath the right side of the craft. It shook the cabin violently but the Darmerians held their composure. Sagittarius, refuting the autopilot, grabbed the dual handlebars, yanked hard to his left and carried the momentum of the blast into a barrel roll. Another missile whizzed by, lost its bearing and sputtered downwards.

"Pure luck, we won't last long." Sagittarius said, belittling Tarliss' impression of the move. "I'm taking it straight up."

"Why?"

"Their engines may stall. It's our only shot."

"Do it!" Tarliss yelled.

With that, Anthony slammed his foot down into a pedal at his feet. His gauntlets wrapped around the handles. He pulled back on them as hard as he could. The shift in G-force pressed down on his chest. A meter on the dash flickered, recording the amount of Gs – it sat at 9.5 for nearly a full second. Normal men would have passed out, maybe even suffocated, but they were not normal men.

!INBOUND PROJECTILE! The screen read again, but the sudden change of direction was just enough to throw it off. They watched the missile speed past the cockpit and into the blue, but this time it didn't sputter. It slowed, turned and continued following them.

"They're still on us! We're not gonna' make it!" Sagittarius yelled, gripping the handlebars; the very life of the craft. The base of them was thick and connected just above the pedals. It shook violently. If not for Sagittarius' grip, the craft would have spun out of control. It was not meant to handle the kind of stress being put on it. Tarliss had to make a difficult decision.

!INBOUND PROJECTILE! The screen read again. Sagittarius suddenly felt his wrists being squeezed tightly; confined to the chair. He immediately clued into what was happening, and tried to stop Tarliss, but he could not move. Two more silver bands detached from his suit and wrapped themselves around Sagittarius' ankles.

"Don't do it Tarliss! WE CAN BOTH MAKE IT-"

"NO, we cannot." Tarliss interrupted, walking toward a yellow and black painted section of the cabin that had a large latch above it, and a parachute on the wall beside it. He bypassed the contraption and stepped onto a section of floor enclosed by a bright yellow band.

"I'm sorry Sagittarius, but this is the only way." Tarliss said, with pure conviction in his eyes. Sagittarius wanted to scream at the top of his lungs, but couldn't. He simply stared at an angle his twisted neck could manage, and watched Tarliss pull the latch. Logically knowing he had no choice in the matter stuffed down any thought of resisting.

A metal box enclosed around Tarliss' body. A five second timer above the escape pod counted down, and the thing dropped into the blue. A metal sheath quickly slammed the holed section shut. Tarliss was gone.

Sagittarius finally let out a lung busting scream that physically shook the whole vessel. A raw bolt of energy surged into the control pad and throughout every available piece of metal in the cavern. The plane held intact. He quickly regained his senses – he wasn't about to make Tarliss' sacrifice for nothing. Gripping the controls, and focusing his energy into them, he righted the ship and eyed the massive vessel hanging on the very top of the world.

Even for a considerably powerful Darmerian, catching a missile travelling at supersonic speed while in a freefall would be difficult. His escape pod broke open, as it was designed to. The attacker was coming at him so fast he had less than two earth seconds to adjust. He concentrated and began to glow. Everything slowed down for him. The two earth seconds, by his perception, became ten. He locked on to it visually, stuck his hand out and shot a thin strand of his suit from the tip of his fingers. It connected with the missile and enveloped it entirely.

"WHAT THE HELL IS THA-" Yelled the foremost pilot. To him and his wingman, the event simply looked like the missile disappeared instantly; snatched from existence by a ball of light. He tried to yank at the single joystick controlling the F22A raptor fighter jet, but it was too late for him.

Tarliss corkscrewed and hurled the missile back from whence it came. The polymorphous metal whip snapped the bomb into the belly of the jet, vaporizing it in a bright fireball of blue and red.

Chunks of synthetic radar-absorbing plastic, glass and bone flew in all directions. Tarliss managed to attach his leg to a piece of the fuselage. It slithered like a floating island along his suit down to his head.

The second pilot decided to avoid the situation altogether. He veered hard to his right and continued climbing. Tarliss adjusted his trajectory by natural means as much as he could. The angle was narrow, he would have to hit it perfectly . . .

He shot across the open sky more horizontally then downwards. He nearly overshot the target, but was able to slow down just enough. On impact, the piece of the other plane acted as the spearhead of the battering ram that was his body. This time, however, he wasn't at all unscathed. The expenditure of raw power left him momentarily vulnerable, and the effects of the impact and explosion left his body crippled.

"AAAAAAHHHHH!!!!" Tarliss screeched in pain. Every bone in his right shoulder was broken or fractured, and his left leg was impaled. The suit had failed him. Accepting his fate, he relaxed, spread out his limbs and obeyed gravity. Past the debris field and smoke, at the very edge of his enhanced vision, the plane carrying Sagittarius pierced the threshold of space and entered the massive vessel through an opening in it's belly. He breathed a sigh of relief. He had completed his mission.

Until we meet again, Sagittarius . . .

But that meeting was never going to happen. The moment ended, and the pain returned. Beckoning beneath him, the scorched Earth that would bring his death. Patches of green, untouched by the destruction, dotted the landscape. He contorted his body and directed himself toward one straight beneath him, doing his best to ignore the seething pain. It wasn't enough. His consciousness faded, his body went limp.

Before impact, the last resonance of raw power the psionic creature possessed focused into a circle on his chest. The majority of the suit shot a hundred feet down in a split second, leaving his bare skin exposed. It smashed into the ground and embedded itself in the soil. Tarliss slowed down considerably but still met the ground with bone-crushing force, breaking more of his ribs and worsening the impalement in his leg. He breathed in as much air as his damaged body could withstand, preparing to get back on his feet. There was no yield in the mighty psionic warrior; he'd die on his feet before he allowed himself to succumb to the pain.

A blast of energy emerged from the tree line, engulfing and paralyzing him. He hollered loud, and with ferocity, shaking and vibrating the very essence of the Earth around him. The blast burned hot and powerful enough to completely melt the metal jackknifed in his calf. The suit sparked and fizzled. He had nothing left. Four silhouettes drew nearer, peeling out of the forest. The craft that brought them hovered above, with more like them on the distant horizon.

"Finally, great Tarliss, you are mine." Said the middle silhouette, revealed as a tall, muscular man wearing a suit, with peculiar tattoos etched on his fingers. The man plunged his cumbersome boot into Tarliss' chest, and looked him in the eyes.

"Finally, *I have defeated you.*"

He leaned in closer and squeezed the alien tightly by the neck, with an evil, delighted smile.

"*Tarlisssssss. . . . Darmerusssssss . . . . .*

Sagittariusssss will be next."

The whisper sparked what life Tarliss had left in his soul. Rage filled his broken bones. He tried to toss the man off of him, but was slammed even harder into the Earth. Before consciousness slipped away, he locked eyes with the man. They lacked the unmistakable concentric circles of a human eye; instead housing vertical slits inside multiple overlapping diamonds.

* * * *

"TARLISS! WE HAVE TO GO *BACK!* We . . ." Sagittarius yelled, but it was futile.

"We cannot. He sacrificed himself for you."

A dozen or more Darmerians, some with long gowns on, watched as Sagittarius fell to the floor.

"The pain will pass. You will soon be free of your emotional weakness, Sagittarius, you will soon be a true Darmerian." Said the elder Rikthinius, who had personally dethroned and traversed the lengthy vessel to meet him as he entered.

"What if . . ." Anthony stuttered, "What if I don't want to?"

The question took Rikthinius by surprise. His eyebrows squeezed. Anthony was sure his comment angered the withered, hunched alien, even though their race was supposed to be devoid of sentiment.

"What if I don't want any of this!?" He asked, voice raising in amplitude as the words emerged, "WHAT IF I WANT TO STAY HERE!" He boomed, to which Rikthinius and his band of subordinates grew more unnerved. He stood there, truly not knowing what to say to calm Anthony down. He was aware – Of Anthony's *human* mind – that it was corrupted with anger, stress and fear.

Anthony began to glow white hot. If not for Aremis' timely entrance into the room, he may have lashed out in a way that he would have regretted soon after. The sight of her had an instant calming effect on him, and the whole room was aware of it. They moved out of her way and allowed her to approach Anthony, who felt to his knees and began sobbing like a child.

"It's not over Anthony." She assured him, "You are safe now."

He looked up, wiping the fluorescent tears from his face, indulging in her spirited embrace. He looked deep into her large, beautiful eyes . . .searching for the love that was supposed to be non-existent. Whether he imagined it, or it was real, he felt it – as purely as he felt the pain of accepting Tarliss' death. Aremis was the only one keeping him from delving deeper into his loneliness and despair. Were she not there for him, his thoughts would have consumed him.

"I'm alright." He uttered, much to the relief of his onlookers. His glow diminished, the vibrant hum of psionic rage dissipated.

"I'll be fine. I . . . I need rest."

"Bring him to the regeneration chamber." Rikthinius ordered.

"No." Anthony said, in a much calmer tone. "Real rest. I need to lay down."

Rikthinius and Aremis looked at each other, acknowledging what they knew. No matter how mentally or physically strong, a few days was not enough for any creature to cope with what he was going through, and that they were foolish to believe such a thing was possible.

"Come with me Anthony. We've got a long journey ahead."

EPILOGUE

The whispering winds of the inner-earth carried a dull and lonely tone. Nothing was alive in this place. It had never felt the glorious illumination of the sun, and it never would. Traversing through the cavern's relentless ominousness were the trudging boots of half-mechanized warriors. Dust collected and encrusted their armour and gritted their dried skin. They hadn't the mind to care. The powerful lights adorned by their armor allowed them the vision to make out the legs of the soldier in front of them. Only one thing was evident in their brains - the objective.

The Commander had chosen this route specifically for it's lack of proximity to . . . anything. He wanted to remain hidden, to not exist even. It would give him the time he needed to learn. To plan his re-emergence onto the surface. His mind had already transcended every ability his creators had intended. He would continue to sharpen it, to see how powerful his sentience could become. To acheive this would require isolation from the inhibiting influences of the now warring factions scattered on the planet above.

There was, however, one major threat on this route, one that was made apparent every few hours by the subtle rumblings beneath his feet. Some were earthquakes, others came from the mighty Rhakthfer. He had built-in seismic sensors that could distinguish between the two. They were far away, and to his knowledge unaware of his presence, and if they were they didn't seem to care. Even so, everything he had become and all of his power still feigned when pondering would what happen should they encounter one of the massive beasts.

He marveled at the creatures. What files and documents the humans had compiled on the beasts were now floating around in his nano-cortex. After calculated analysis, he could make better assumptions about their origin then the humans could. As best as he could tell, they were not native to Earth. They had been left there sometime ago, used by a race of extra-terrestrials called the Induguutk for cultivation and terraforming purposes. Although he couldn't be certain, he suspected the Rhakthfer had broken free of their confinements and escaped deep into the Earth. The Induguutk, known to the humans as 'Tall Whites', even with their advanced technological and spiritual knowledge, could not contain the mighty Rhakthfers.

The information he possessed, stolen from the research archives pertaining to the Induguutk and at least eighty-seven other known extra-terrestrial races, was fragmented at best. The humans had documented only three physical encounters with the species, the rest was from information passed on to them by the Draconians and Reticulans.

The Commander's thirst for revenge and lust for power was made into a child, on it's knees listening to their parents tell them the rules as a metaphorical, intelligent respect for the sheer capacity for destruction the creatures possessed. He calculated a thousand different scenarios in his mind of how he would go about conquering one, and each one failed. He truely did not know how he would kill one of the creatures should they decide to attack.

After prying through the many yottabytes of documents and information about the myriad extra-terrestrial species known to humanity, one thing became painfully clear - there was a much wider and more terrifying world than even *he* could account for. For the first time since he could remember becoming fully sentient, he decided to literally 'turn off' the inquisitive part of his mind that wanted to know more. He had more immediate concerns, and needed the full power of his processing core to stay focused on the primary objective.

Three weeks of silent marching left his numbers slightly thinned out. Every so often one or more of his minions would seize up, glitch, malfunction or simply stop moving. They fell unapologetically into the dust; statues to be buried forever as a testament to the failures of their creators. In total, seven percent of his troupe succumbed to their flaws, and were left behind without the slightest inkling of retreival or repair. He wanted it that way. There was no room for weakness in his thrall, and weeding out those unfit to adhere his command was seen as a necessary sacrifice. He was pleasantly surprised by the number that had made it - by his calculations at least eleven percent of the now two-thousand plus soldiers should have perished.

With recognition of his humanity came inherent weaknesses. The soles of his feet were calloused and sore. They *hurt*. He could choose to engage an electronic subroutine that would essentially block out the feeling, but he chose not to. He wanted to feel it. It was a constant reminder of why he was still alive - his *purpose* - a taste of what had been stolen from him, and what he was trying to regain.

His boots came to a halt. He raised his hand, and the bucking joints of his soldiers came to a full mechanized stop as well. A glittering section of wall lay before them, unusually flat and angled against the jagged, non-uniform outcropping of the cavernous rock surrounding it. This was his destination.

A series of telepathic orders fluttered out of his cerebral cortex, ordering three minions to approach the section with a series of powerful explosives. They arranged what looked like conference-room telephones in a triangle formation, one as high as could be reached and the other two closer to the ground. He moved back at least a hundred feet, without relaying the order to the three soldiers. If they were too innate to realize what would happen to them, without having to be told, they did not deserve to survive the blast. Two of them instinctively turned and ran for cover, while the last remained stiff until it was too late.

A ferocious shape-charged explosion illuminated the cavern and sent a shockwave into the dunes of dust. The plasma filaments bored a hole clean through the rock, large enough for them to walk through. The bright lights from the other side flooded the black cavern. One by one, the troupe of robotic Commandos entered the Starset facility. Like the one before, the facility was barren. He revelled in the short-sightedness of his creators. Did they not realize, or revere the importance of what they had in their possession? The Commander would not make that mistake.

As he entered, he took a moment to look at the obliterated soldier who hadn't the self-sufficient knowledge to avoid the blast, revealing a sadistic grin. He brought twelve escorts into the facility with him. The glittering dust swirled onto the clean, stainless steel floor of the facility, creating a noticeable drop in pressure within. The air inside smelled different. The ventilation system made sure the air inside was clean and crisp, but now it was under *his* control. Like a kid in a candy store, the Commander nonchalantly made his way to the room outlined in his databanks. Simply by thinking it, the huge metal door hissed as steam vents depressurized the room. It peeled open, revealing an indigo capsule. Inside of the capsule, the very essence of a Darmerian.

Two of his minions, who had been carrying a large metal chest the entire journey, brought the thing into the room and pushed a series of numeric buttons on a holographic pad on its outer shell. Cryogenic gas leaked into the room, some of it touching the soldiers in it's proximity. The cold gas froze their joints almost instantly. Once again with a simple thought, the Commander sent a message to the facility's ventilation system to inhale the gas before it could touch him. The affected soldiers, now useless, locked up and fell to the floor under his whim. They had served their task and were discarded accordingly.

He carefully removed the indigo capsule from its constraints, marvelling at the pure power he held in his hand. It was a surreal moment, even for him. The shiny fluid metal shot out of the metal trunk and wrapped itself around the capsule and over his large hand, itching to get inside.

Just as he predicted, the wondrous alloy was instantly and irrefutably attracted to the Darmerian genetic code. Speaking aloud, and with a general, most-human tingle of excitement, he ordered his escorts to their next objective.

"To the infusion room."

On the way there his eyes remained fixated on the suffocating alloy enveloping his arm. He could feel it's raw energy. Twenty percent of his processing power was devoted to constantly monitoring every camera in the facility. It was plenty. A few mindless drones carried on in the sublevels, tending to massive crops of corn and wheat, but for the most part it had been abandoned. After the loss to the Darmerians, he suspected his creators were more afraid than they had been during his creation.

After his final upgrade, the one that would grant him the same power held by the magnificent alien warriors he helped to escape the planet, there would be nothing and no one on the planet to stop him from exacting his revenge upon the tyrants that sought to control the Earth.

<:// NOTHING WILL STAND IN YOUR WAY //:>

www.ingramcontent.com/pod-product-compliance
Lightning Source LLC
Chambersburg PA
CBHW060301100726
47907CB00002B/229